PEGGY'S WAR

KARL RHODES

Dale Enterprise Literary Society
Richmond, Virginia
2023

Copyright © 2023 by Karl Wayne Rhodes

All rights reserved. No part of this book may be used or reproduced or transmitted in any manner whatsoever without written permission from the publisher except in the case of brief quotations appearing in critical articles and reviews. For more information, contact:

Dale Enterprise Literary Society
11223 Byfield Court
Richmond, VA 23233

www.PeggysWar.com

Library of Congress Cataloging-in-Publication Data Pending
Peggy's War | Karl Wayne Rhodes | 1962–
Fact-Based Novel with Bibliographic References
LCCN 2023911369
First Edition

Subjects
United States—History—Civil War, 1861–1865—Fiction
Mennonites | Dunkers | Brethren | Nonresistance
Shenandoah Valley | Virginia
ISBN 9798988495208 (paperback)
ISBN 9798988495215 (ebook)

Cover Information
Portrait Photography: Mark Rhodes
Background Photography: Scott Hotaling
Cover Model: Jessica Chandler
Costume Design: Louise DiGennaro

Printed in Harrisonburg, Virginia, USA

To Kim

My Wonderful Wife

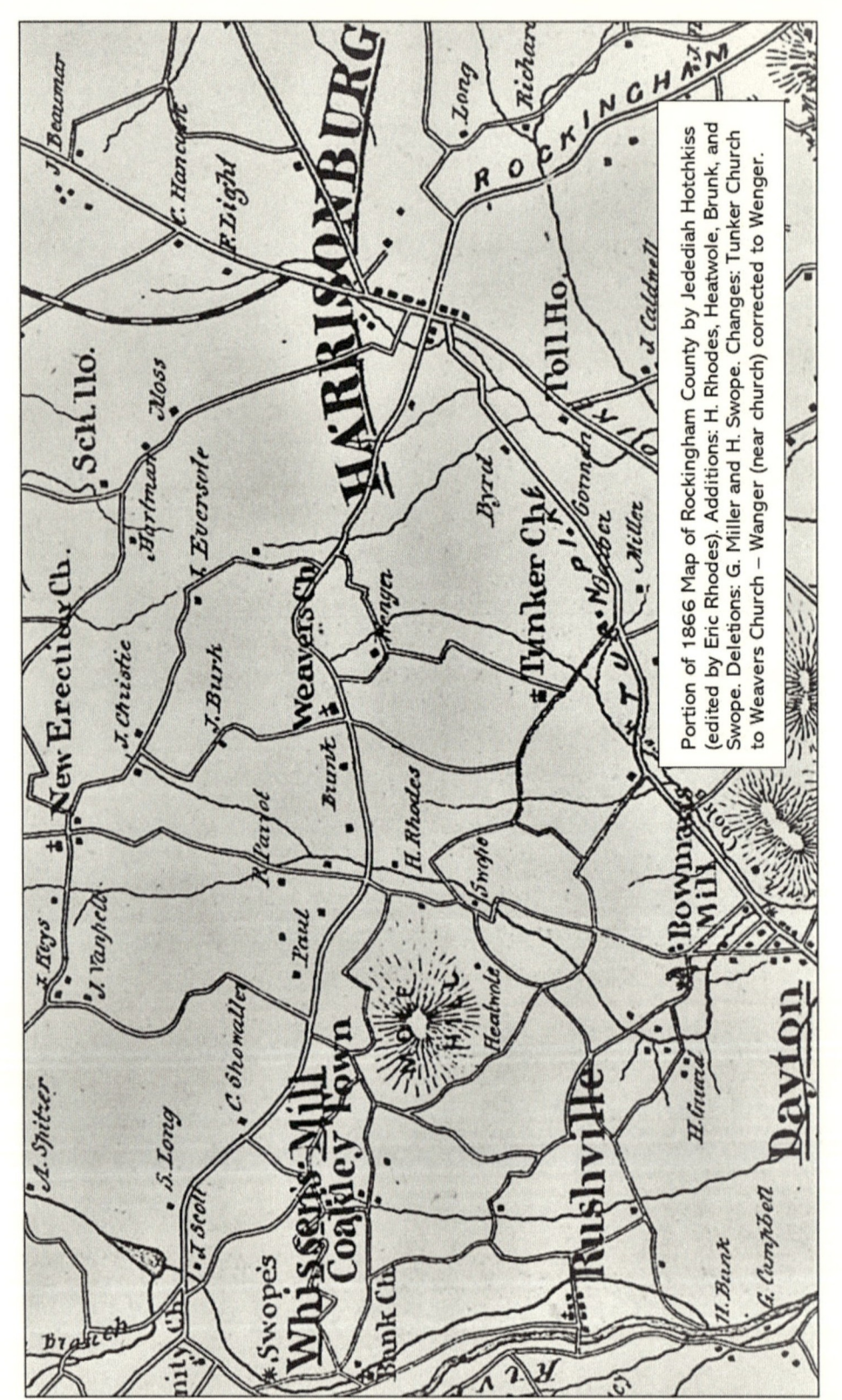

Portion of 1866 Map of Rockingham County by Jedediah Hotchkiss (edited by Eric Rhodes). Additions: H. Rhodes, Heatwole, Brunk, and Swope. Deletions: G. Miller and H. Swope. Changes: Tunker Church to Weavers Church – Wanger (near church) corrected to Wenger.

Author's Introduction

When you are four years old and the youngest of three brothers, you will do anything—almost anything—to play some small role in their grand adventures. So when my older siblings, Gene and Elvin, said they needed my help to recover some Civil War guns from a cave, I was all in.

They had discovered a glorified groundhog hole on the hill behind Weavers Mennonite Church. And maybe, just maybe, this was an entrance to the cave where our great-great-grandfather, Peter S. Hartman, had hidden guns during the Civil War.

By age four, I already had heard this legend many times. Hartman took guns from Confederate soldiers and hid them in a cave on the hill behind Weavers Church. That was the whole story—perhaps the most succinct legend of all time—no details whatsoever, no wiggle room for exaggeration or embellishment.

I wanted to find those old guns more than anything, so I followed my brothers up through the cow pasture behind our home on the Rawley Pike three miles west of Harrisonburg, Virginia. We dodged dozens of fresh cow pies and climbed three wobbly fences topped with barbed wire before entering the woods near the top of the hill. Within a minute or two, I was down on my knees shining a flashlight (they let me hold the flashlight) into a snug little tunnel about two or three feet in diameter.

"It's easy to crawl down there about fifteen feet," Elvin informed me. "Then you'll come to a tight spot. It looks like the tunnel opens up into a big room after that, but I can't get past the pinch. Maybe you can squeeze through."

Say no more! Here was my chance to find those Civil War guns. Flashlight in hand, I plunged headfirst into that hole like a fox in foul weather. The tunnel sloped down at a 30-degree angle, leveling out a bit as I approached the rocky pinch point. Sure enough, the flashlight revealed a sizable limestone cavity just beyond a vertical crevice that was about fifteen inches high and ten inches wide. My initial impulse was to poke my head in there.

"If my noggin goes through, my shoulders will surely follow."

I don't know if I said that out loud or not, but the next voice I heard—I think it was the proverbial voice of reason—clearly came from deep within my being.

"Karl! Don't be stupid!"

Suddenly, the thought of getting my head stuck in that ten-inch slot made me frantic for fresh air, and I backed out of that hole faster than you can say Punxsutawney Phil.

Safely above ground, I gladly gave up my turn with the flashlight, but I never abandoned my search for the Civil War guns. For the next ten years, I imagined they were hiding just around the corner from that limestone pinch point, but then I learned something about Weavers Church that changed my thinking. At the time of the Civil War, the church was on the *other* side of the Rawley Pike. My brothers and I had been looking for the guns on the wrong hill.

Later in life, I explored the rocky hill on the proper side of the pike, but I never found the cave. I also began to question the old family legend. How does a teenage boy go about taking guns away from Confederate soldiers? Did Hartman think that hiding a few guns would stop the war? If not, then what was his purpose?

The answers came from a remarkable series of books called *Unionists and the Civil War Experience in the Shenandoah Valley*, researched and compiled by David Rodes and Norman Wenger and edited by Emmert Bittinger. Their six-volume set, published from

PEGGY'S WAR

2003 to 2012, highlights the stories of Mennonites and Dunkers (German Baptist Brethren) who remained loyal to the United States during the war. Many of them operated an underground railroad to help draft dodgers and deserters escape the Confederacy, and volume three made it clear that members of Weavers Church, including my great-great-grandparents, were deeply embedded in this underground.

For the first time, the legend of the guns in the cave on the hill behind the church made sense to me. Confederate deserters—out of uniform and carrying guns—could easily be mistaken for bushwhackers and shot on sight by soldiers from either army. So when they entered the underground railroad, they had to give up their guns, and the cave on the hill behind Weavers Church was an ideal disposal site. The testimony compiled by Rodes and Wenger does not mention hiding guns, but several first-hand accounts emphasize that deserters who traveled west and north via the underground railroad almost never carried weapons.

With the mystery of the muskets solved to my satisfaction, I turned my attention to the bigger story revealed by Rodes and Wenger and expressed dramatically in the testimony of Margaret "Peggy" Rhodes, my great-great-grandmother. Peggy ran one of the busiest depots on the underground railroad. She also served as a postmaster for the underground, delivering and picking up letters between refugees and their friends and families.

"Mrs. Rhodes was in many ways a remarkable woman," Rodes and Wenger wrote. "Not only highly intelligent, she was courageous enough to stand with her husband for their religious and political principles. Also, she did not hesitate to take what risks were necessary to obtain what was her due. As a loyal Unionist, she decided to petition for a claim (with the Southern Claims Commission) and seek payment for her losses."

Peggy sought federal reimbursement twice, failing in 1871 and succeeding in 1875. Filing those claims was dangerous because many people in the Shenandoah Valley still harbored strong resentment against Union sympathizers, and Peggy's declarations of loyalty were particularly bold.

"From the beginning of the rebellion to the end thereof, I was willing and ready to do all a woman could for the Union cause and its supporters," she said.

Peggy's courage and tenacity motivated me to write this book. She was indeed a remarkable woman, and I wanted to tell her story in a way that is perhaps more reader friendly than the testimony that Rodes and Wenger transcribed in their 5,000-plus pages.

Some people might pigeonhole this book as "historical fiction," but I think that label is misleading. *Peggy's War* merely uses the devices of fiction to make historical facts more accessible to a wider range of readers. In other words, I based the plot on every historical fact I could find about Peggy, her family, and the refugees who hid in her secret cellar. Then I connected those dots with fictional dialogue and day-to-day happenings that seem plausible and reasonable based on my research. Extensive notes in the back of this book invite readers to discover what is substantiated, what is highly probable, and what is merely supposition. All the people named in the book are real except one: Amos Shiflett, the peter monkey, is fictional, but his occupation—looking for saltpeter in crawl spaces under houses—is well-documented in Rockingham County during the Civil War. Peter monkeys would have been a constant concern to Peggy and to anyone who happened to be hiding in her secret cellar.

As for the cave on the hill behind Weavers Church, I have learned that this cave was partially explored by a class of schoolboys in 1901. They used rope ladders to climb down vertical shafts into limestone cavities big enough to conceal dozens of deserters *and* their guns.

PEGGY'S WAR

After those boys "discovered" the cave in 1901, I suspect that the owner of the property sealed the entrances with some rather large boulders. Even so, I have not given up on finding the guns. I have contacted one of the current landowners, and—if my brothers will let me hold the flashlight—I'll squeeze through this time.

—Karl Rhodes
July 2023

Prologue

On June 24, 1875, Peggy Rhodes walked briskly north along Cooks Creek toward Dale Enterprise, a rural crossroads west of Harrisonburg, Virginia. Peggy never walked for idle exercise. There was always a distinct purpose to her gait, and on this fine summer day, she advanced on her objective with great resolve. Dale Enterprise was only half a mile from Peggy's farm, so she didn't bother saddling a horse or hitching up the spring wagon. She simply cut across Hugh Swope's pasture to the Rawley Pike, a dirt road that bridged the creek and ran past the post office and general store.

The postmaster and proprietor, J. W. Minnich, was sweeping the six-pillared porch of his two-story establishment as Peggy approached. He was a thin man in his mid-thirties with slumping shoulders, an uncompromising face, and a billy goat beard.

Many of the Mennonites who lived near Dale Enterprise didn't care much for Minnich. They complained that he was "brickety and overbearing," but their main objection to the ambitious storekeeper was the fact that he had served *voluntarily* as a quartermaster in the Confederate army. After the war, Minnich educated their children, married their bishop's daughter, and literally put their community on the map with his substantial whitewashed mercantile. But in the Shenandoah Valley of 1875, men were still judged mostly by what they had done during the war. Through that lens, the Mennonites of Dale Enterprise viewed Minnich as a facilitator of the failed rebellion against the legitimate government of the United States, while the general population of Rockingham County saw him as a hero of the glorious struggle for Southern independence.

Peggy was also a hero of sorts, but no one dared speak of her in that way. The bishop at nearby Weavers Mennonite Church preached against hero worship, which was just as well, because it was still dangerous to reveal what Peggy had done during the war. She had sided with the Union from start to finish—even after the Yankees took her wheat, sheep, horses, hogs, and hay. Peggy rarely spoke of such things, but today she would tell the whole story.

"Hello, Peggy," Minnich said, without looking up from his busy broom. "Your attorney and the special commissioner are here already. Perhaps the commissioner will see things your way this time."

Peggy chose to ignore Minnich's rather rude reference to her previous—unsuccessful—attempt to obtain satisfaction from the federal government.

"Thank you for your good wishes, Mr. Minnich," Peggy said, with her tongue sarcastically placed in the cheek she pretended to turn. "If I receive some compensation from the commission, the first thing I shall do is settle my account with you."

Peggy stepped inside the store, where she was greeted more pleasantly by Minnich's wife, Lizzie, a vivacious woman in her mid-twenties. She was plump and pretty and every bit as gregarious as her husband was gruff.

"Good mornin', Aunt Peggy," Lizzie said, with an engaging smile. "Mr. Baker and Mr. Baldwin are waiting for you in the office. They asked to borrow my Bible. I think that's a good sign."

Both men stood as Peggy entered the small back room. Her lawyer, John Baker, introduced her to Isaac Baldwin, a special commissioner for the federal agency charged with settling claims against the government for property taken by Union forces during the war.

"I am pleased to make your acquaintance," Baldwin said, as he shook hands with Peggy. "Mr. Baker has told me a great deal about you. Please sit down and make yourself easy. Have your witnesses arrived?"

"No sir, not yet, but I'm sure they will be here soon. There are five of them. My bishop and my brother will attest to my loyalty to the Union. As to the property taken, my daughter, my foster son, and my near neighbor will support my claim."

"In the meantime, I am prepared to take your testimony," Baldwin announced, as he slid the borrowed Bible across the small desk that separated them. "Just place your left hand on this Bible and raise your right hand to God almighty."

Peggy did as she was told.

"Do you swear to tell the truth, the whole truth, and nothing but the truth concerning the matters under examination?"

"The Bible bids me *not* to swear," Peggy replied, as she retracted her hand and glanced anxiously at her attorney. "It bids me to tell the truth in all matters at all times."

"Oh … my apologies," the commissioner said. "I forgot about your quaint Mennonite customs. I will put the question to you in a different way: Do you *affirm* that the testimony you are about to give is the truth, the whole truth, and nothing but the truth?"

"Yessir. I do."

"What is your name, your age, your residence, and how long has it been such, and your occupation?"

"My name is Margaret Rhodes, but most persons call me Peggy. I am forty-four years old, a housekeeper. I live at Dale Enterprise three miles west of Harrisonburg, Rockingham County, Virginia, where I have resided for twenty-six years."

"If you are not the claimant, in what manner, if any, are you related to the claimant or interested in the success of the claim?"

"I am the widow of Henry H. Rhodes."

"Where were you born?"

"I was born and raised in this county."

"Where were you residing and what was your business for six months before the outbreak of the rebellion, and where did you reside and what was your business from the beginning to the end of the war?"

"I lived where I now do on our own place when the war began."

"On which side were your sympathies during the war, and were they on the same side from beginning to end?"

"I sympathized all along with the Union, the same as my husband did. We were both members of the Mennonite Church and did not believe in slavery and had no sympathy with the war."

"Did you ever do anything or say anything against the Union cause?"

"No sir. I never did."

"Were you at all times during the war willing and ready to do whatever you could in aid of the Union cause?"

"Yessir. I was not only willing but I did aid persons to escape from the Confederacy. Many times they came and stayed at our place, five or six together at a time, and would stay sometimes several days waiting for the guides to take them through the mountains. Then I would prepare their rations, and they would start off for the mountains at night. This was done many times. Our house is in a secluded place and very favorably situated for concealing persons. We had a place under the floor, under the house, where we would conceal persons when necessary. It was entered by a trap door in my bedroom and covered with a carpet so no one would suspect anything."

"Were you in the service or employment of the United States government at any time during the war?"

"No sir."

"Did you ever voluntarily contribute money, property, or services to the Union cause?"

"What I did for the refugees and deserters was done to aid the Union cause. Many of those I harbored and fed I never saw before nor since, and I know only a few of them by name."

"Which side did you take while the insurgent states were seceding from the Union in 1860 and 1861, and what did you do to show on which side you stood?"

"I took the side of the Union, of course. I did not believe in secession nor did my husband either. I am very certain he did not vote for it, for he used to talk a great deal about it and against it altogether."

"Did you adhere to the Union cause after the states had passed into rebellion, or did you go with your state?"

"I adhered to the Union all the time."

Baldwin asked Peggy many more questions that day. Then he interviewed the five additional witnesses who testified in support of Peggy's claim. After the last witness left the office, the commissioner jotted a note to himself: "No question as to the loyalty of claimant and of her husband, too. Both witnesses as to loyalty are Mennonite preachers. They are all highly respected conscientious people."

The Southern Claims Commission ultimately paid Peggy $569.25, which covered slightly more than half her property losses, but no amount of money could compensate for all she lost during America's worst war.

CHAPTER 1

Mole Hill
"Johnny was right. Mole Hill is evil."

Peggy Rhodes never saw a more delightful day than April 17, 1858. The air was so crisp and clear that the mountains surrounding the Shenandoah Valley appeared green, instead of their usual blue, as bright sun and soft shadow revealed the contours of each ridge and ravine. A cool breeze flowed freely through Peggy's tidy two-story farmhouse, swishing curtains inward and outward, conveying the unmistakable stench of fine manure mist.

Looking west from the front porch of her white weatherboard home, Peggy studied the smooth, symmetrical shape of Mole Hill. Rising 500 feet above the valley, this densely wooded knoll wasn't big enough to be called a mountain, but its proximity to the farm made it seem like one.

Peggy watched her husband, Henry, shovel manure onto a wagon on the other side of Cooks Creek, the gentle stream that bisected their farm. Henry's father had built the house and barn on opposite sides of the creek, connecting them with a bridge that was strong enough to withstand most floods and wide enough to accommodate most wagons. When Henry crossed the creek in the morning, he was going to work. When he crossed the creek in the evening, he was coming home.

"I leave all my troubles on the other side," he liked to say, with a big smile and a carefree flourish of his hands above his head.

Henry was named after his father, Big Henry, who never stood more than five feet tall. The younger Henry was about the same height but much leaner. His broad-brimmed hat shaded deep-set eyes and a receding crop of brown hair that was thin for a man of only thirty-three years. Peggy was five years younger and a good four inches taller than Henry, but she looked up to him nonetheless. He was a devout Christian and a devoted husband, who provided well for their growing family. Unlike most of the Mennonite men around Mole Hill, he smiled and laughed easily. He sometimes winked at Peggy during fourth-Sunday preaching at nearby Weavers Mennonite Church, a subtle flirtation that pleased and embarrassed her in the same moment.

On this fine spring day, Peggy laughed as she watched Henry's helper, eleven-year-old Johnny Bell, splatter a fresh cow pie on her husband's boots as he tried to keep up with the furious shoveling.

Peggy also kept an eye on the younger children. Seven-year-old Mary was learning how to churn butter beside her mother on the porch. She was an obedient child with a round face, fair skin, small features, and long brown pigtails. Henry sometimes called her Little Peggy because she so strongly favored her mother.

Five-year-old Davy was less obedient and more mischievous. He was darkly tanned, like his papa, but his hair was a much lighter shade of brown because his straw hat refused to stay on his head as he scampered barefoot from one adventure to the next. The hat tumbled to the ground again as Davy chased a stray chicken across the bridge toward Henry and Johnny. Two-year-old Suzy was not nearly that ambitious; she leaned comfortably back into the front folds of her mother's long black dress, while Peggy rocked baby Becky in her arms.

Suddenly, this peaceful scene was shattered by the loudest clap of thunder Peggy had ever heard. Looking up toward the source of the sound, she saw a giant ball of fire rolling down the slope of Mole Hill toward the farm. Flames surged through the barn and leaped across the creek setting the house ablaze. Peggy saw Johnny crawl into the creek, but she could not see Henry or Davy on the other side.

Peggy tried to shout their names, but intense fear rendered her speechless. With extreme effort, she finally regained control of her tongue, but her exclamations sounded like they were coming from someone else.

"Henry! Ach du lieber! Davy! Ach du lieber Gott!"

Peggy also heard a more distant voice that gradually grew louder and more insistent: "Du sollst den Namen des Herrn, deines Gottes, nicht missbrauchen! Sogar nicht im schlaf!"

These urgent German words were coming from Henry. Peggy opened her eyes and saw his face pressed close to hers.

"Do not take the Lord's name in vain!" he repeated in English. "Not even in your sleep!"

Peggy gasped and sat up in bed, propping herself on one elbow. She looked around the room as though she were seeing it for the first time. She turned to Henry, sucked in a long breath, and said, "We must save the children. Johnny was right. Mole Hill is evil."

"Ach du lieber ... Johnny Bell!"

Henry spit out Johnny's surname like a pesky strand of tobacco wedged between his teeth.

"I oughta tan that boy's hide. You were *dreaming*, Peggy. Go back to sleep. The children are fine. Everything is fine. Mole Hill is not evil, and I will deal with Johnny Bell in the morning."

Peggy stared at Henry for a few seconds, still half asleep. Then she said, "Yes, Henry. I'll just say a prayer first." She stood up cautiously and crept to the parlor window. When her eyes adjusted to the light, she could see the dim outline of Mole Hill protruding above the barn's roof. It was a reassuring sight—no fire, no smoke, no sign of evil.

Peggy returned to the bed, took another deep breath, and placed her prayer covering on her head. She closed her eyes and whispered. "Dear Lord, please forgive me for taking thy name in vain. Amen." She started to remove her prayer cap but then decided to keep it on for another moment. "And, dear Lord," she continued, "please keep us safe from the evils of Mole Hill."

Peggy awoke earlier than usual on the following morning. Still lying between the sheets—before she could think of anything else—her nightmare revisited her in vivid detail. It seemed so dreadful, so disturbing, so *real*. Once again, Peggy was drawn to the parlor window and its view of Mole Hill. It looked the same as it always did in the predawn light, a symmetrical silhouette against a clear sky that was beginning to transition from black to blue.

Baby Becky was sleeping soundly in her crib, so Peggy pinned her long brown hair up into a tight bun and carefully capped it with her prayer covering. She dressed quickly, stirred fire in the stove, and climbed the split-log stairs to check on the older children.

She looked in on the boys first because in her nightmare she could not see Davy on the other side of the creek, and she always worried about Johnny, who had suffered so much for a boy his age. Henry and Peggy had taken him in after his father died. It was supposed to be a temporary arrangement, but Johnny's mother could not take care of herself, much less a child, so the Rhodes farm was the only home he had ever known.

After making sure that Johnny and Davy were alright, Peggy checked on Mary and Suzy. Then she went downstairs to fix Henry's breakfast. She scrambled three eggs and fried three slices of panhaus in her big iron skillet. Panhaus was easy to cook and good to eat, but Peggy tried not to think about what it was—pig innards and scraps pressed into a loaf with cornmeal and broth from boiling down a pig's head or some less-desirable part. Sizzling in the skillet, it smelled better than bacon, good enough to lure Henry to the table while the children were still sleeping.

"Mmmm-Mmm-Mm," he flattered, as Peggy set the food on the table. "Poultry and pork ... scramble and scrapple ... fried up together ... just the way I like it."

Henry bowed his head, closed his eyes, and prayed quickly and silently before sliding the eggs and panhaus onto his plate. "You really scared me last night," he said, as he slathered dark brown apple butter on a piece of yesterday's bread. "That musta been some nightmare."

"It was terrible," Peggy said. "A giant ball of fire rolled right down Mole Hill, just like Johnny said. The barn and the house were burning down, and the smoke was so thick I couldn't see you or Davy. It's an omen, Henry, I can just feel it. There's evil in the air."

"It's not an omen," Henry insisted, as he finished his breakfast and headed out the door. "It was just a bad dream, a bunch of wild stories Johnny put in your head. You tell him I wanna see him—if he ever gets out of bed. His night schoolin' with your brother is startin' to cost me on both sides of the ledger."

Peggy's brother, David Heatwole, taught night classes for some of the neighborhood boys at Walnut Grove, a tiny schoolhouse on the other side of Hugh Swope's pasture. Henry and Peggy had never been to school, but their parents taught them to read and write in German and English. They studied nothing beyond the Bible and the *Mennonite Confession of Faith*—plenty of fire and brimstone but no revelations regarding the evils of Mole Hill.

At the first glimmer of dawn, Peggy called up the stairs to make sure Johnny was awake.

"Johnny Bell! It's past time for breakfast! Let me hear those feet hit the floor!"

Johnny, who was already on his way down the stairs, tried to strike up another conversation about Mole Hill, but Peggy was in no mood for idle talk.

"Eat your breakfast and go find Henry," she instructed. "The last time I saw him, he was hitchin' up the wagon to haul manure. If you hurry, you might catch up to him without havin' to walk through that stuff."

Johnny spotted Henry pulling a load of manure through the upper field with a two-horse team. The boy was out of breath by the time he caught up to the old farm wagon.

"Ain't you done spreadin' manure yet?" Johnny asked, as he climbed onto the seat beside Henry.

This was Johnny's best joke because he knew that spreading manure was an endless task for any good farmer. And he knew that mentioning "manure" would prompt Henry to recite his favorite rhyme, which always restored him to good spirits.

"Manure! Is *that* what you call it?" Henry asked, with feigned surprise. "The Germans call it dünger. The English call it sh--. But even in your fancy French, it schtinks a little bit."

They laughed at this barnyard humor as they always did.

"I suppose manure smells bad in any language," Johnny agreed.

"My father used to say that manure smells like money," Henry recalled. "More manure makes better crops, and better crops make more money."

Johnny laughed even harder at this new twist to the old joke, but when he stopped laughing, Johnny noticed a forlorn look on Henry's face.

PEGGY'S WAR

"You sometimes miss Big Henry, don't you?"

"I miss him all the time," Henry said, "but more than usual today 'cause he married my mother on this exact day fifty years ago."

"I didn't know that," Johnny responded. "Is there anything I can do to make you feel some better?"

"Oh ... I feel fine," Henry said, with a little grin, "but there is something you could do, or better still, there's something you could *quit* doin'. You could stop fillin' your Aunt Peggy's head with wild ideas about fireballs. You gave her a bad dream last night. And what's all this nonsense about Mole Hill being evil?"

"Mr. Heatwole says he saw a big ball of fire roll right down the side of Mole Hill, and some of the boys say that proves Mole Hill is evil."

Henry thought for a moment before he spoke.

"You listen here. David Heatwole's a smart man and a good teacher, and we best not forget he's your Aunt Peggy's brother, but he don't know everything about everything. Ain't no such thing as balls of fire, and Mole Hill ain't evil."

"Yessir," the boy chirped, as he grabbed a shovel and stepped into the bed of the wagon. "I'll tell Mr. Heatwole what you said about Mole Hill."

"No you won't!" Henry hollered. "I said that for your benefit, not for Mr. Heatwole's sake. At school you mind him, but around here, you mind me."

CHAPTER 2

Consumption

"The body becomes divided against itself."

Johnny attended Mr. Heatwole's classes three nights a week until June, when Henry needed more help in the fields. Summer was the busiest time for farmers in the Shenandoah Valley—cutting wheat, hauling wheat, cutting corn, hauling corn, spreading manure, plowing the fields, and planting the fall crops.

Peggy thought Johnny was too young for twelve-hour days in the field, but as the weather turned hotter, it was Henry's strength that waned. Working hard all day under a sweltering sun always made him tired, but the summer of 1858 seemed different. He was exhausted at the end of each day, and his strength didn't fully return in the morning, not even with a belly full of pork and poultry.

On a hot, humid Saturday in August, Henry crossed the creek a good five hours before the sun disappeared behind Mole Hill, but he failed to leave his troubles on the other side. He sat on the porch steps with his forearms propped on his knees, sweat dripping from his chin, as he leaned forward and coughed. His ribs ached from coughing and hacking all day, and he felt like he was suffocating.

Peggy stood in the front doorway watching Henry for a while. She usually didn't question her husband's judgment. He was a wise man, but not when it came to medical matters.

"When are you going to go see Doc?" she finally asked.

"Doctors do more harm than good, and that includes your Uncle Gabe," Henry managed to say, as he continued to cough. Finally, Henry was able to draw a deeper breath and recite the rest of his familiar objections. "Doc's not even a real doctor. He just bought some mail-order book about weeds and roots and bark."

"I suppose you'd rather go see a town doctor who bleeds people with leeches and poisons them with calomel," Peggy countered.

"Maybe so," Henry replied. "Doc thinks puke weed cures everything, and throwin' up is just about as bad as being poisoned and bled at the same time, iffen you ask me."

"Oh … pshaw! What do you know about Uncle Gabe and puke weed? You've never once been to see him—not for doctoring anyhow."

Peggy and Henry rehashed this argument with greater frequency throughout August and September. Henry insisted that his cough would get better with the weather, but the crisp October air brought no sign of relief.

Overwhelmed with fatigue, Henry was particularly slow getting out of bed one morning in early November. Peggy was trying to keep his breakfast from burning, but the eggs were beginning to singe, and the smell suddenly turned her stomach inside out. She spun away from the stove just in time to vomit on the floor.

"Better there than on the hot plates," she reasoned.

Henry dashed into the kitchen half-dressed and fully flustered. The combination of burned eggs and fresh vomit almost made him puke, too.

"What happened?" he asked, as he rescued the heavy iron skillet from Peggy's trembling hand.

"I've been feelin' sick every morning this week," she confessed. "I wasn't going to say anything until I was sure, but I think we're gonna have another baby."

"That's wonderful news!" Henry exclaimed. "You go on outside and get some fresh air, and I'll clean up this mess."

Henry used the dustpan to scoop up as much vomit as he could. He slid it into the slop jar and carried the caustic container down to the creek. He returned to the house with the empty jar and a bucket of water, but before he went inside, he sat down beside Peggy on the porch steps.

"You might not wanna go back in there for a spell," he said. "I'll check on the children. I imagine all the commotion woke them up. We can all eat breakfast out here on the porch. Is there anything else I can do?"

"There is one thing," Peggy said softly.

"What is it? You just name it, and I'll do it."

"Would you please go see Doc?"

After a long pause, Henry said, "Well ... I ain't makin' no firm promises ... but I'll study hard on it."

Three days later, after shucking the last of the corn, Henry saddled the gray mare and used the edge of the watering trough to boost himself onto the horse. He figured he could get to Doc's and back before Peggy knew he was gone, but as soon as he started down the lane toward Mole Hill, Peggy called to him from the other side of the creek.

"Henry! Where you goin' in such a hurry?"

Henry tugged on the reins and turned his mount just enough to give Peggy a sideways look. "I'm ... uh ... gonna go see Doc."

"What for?"

"To get some puke weed, I reckon."

❖ ❖ ❖

The Rhodes farm was less than a mile from Doc Heatwole's home on the southeastern edge of Mole Hill, just below the timberline, where steep woods gave way to gently sloping pasture. Doc's red brick house stood two stories tall with thick walls, a spacious front porch and large fireplaces on each side, a substantial home that reflected Doc's prominent position in the Mennonite community and far beyond.

Despite Henry's skepticism of all things medical, he greatly respected Doc's other accomplishments. Forty years ago, the ambitious old settler had purchased a small patch of woods on the side of Mole Hill. He worked as a cooper to support his growing family while acquiring and clearing more land. He and his wife, Polly, raised twelve children, and each of their sons and daughters spawned sizable families of their own. Together they worked 3,000 acres of farmland, a thriving sawmill, and a busy cooper's shop. Now in his seventieth year, Doc delegated those exhausting enterprises to his offspring and in-laws and devoted most of his time to practicing botanical medicine.

At the end of each week, patients gathered in his front yard—women on Fridays, men on Saturdays—and when the weather was good, these gatherings were as much social as they were medical. Such was the scene that Henry encountered as he tethered his horse beside a dozen others on the long rail beside Doc's house. He immediately recognized everyone in the yard as kith and kin.

The Heatwole and Rhodes families were tightly bound by blood, marriage, and the church. This was true for most of the Mennonites who lived near Mole Hill, but the Heatwole-Rhodes connections were especially close. Five of Henry's sisters had married four of Doc's sons. (After one of Henry's sisters died, Joseph Heatwole waited the requisite six months and married another one.)

Henry greeted his relatives and in-laws with all the relish he could muster in his sickly state. They were surprised to see Henry, who never had anything good to say about doctors. Even in recent years, he was known to boast—between fits of coughing—about never being sick a day in his life.

After the obligatory exchange of howdy-dos and how're-yous, Henry cornered his brother-in-law, David Heatwole, to ask some more pointed questions.

"How do I go about gettin' a turn with Doc?"

"Just take a number," David replied, pointing to a small pile of papers on the top porch step. "Doc does everything by the number; even his medicines are labeled one through six."

Henry grabbed a slip of paper and returned to interrogating David.

"What's this nonsense I'm hearin' from Johnny about Mole Hill bein' evil?"

"Oh … you heard about that. Well, I told the boys about fireball lightning rolling down the slope of Mole Hill. I saw it myself when I was about their age. And the next thing I knew, they were going on and on about how Mole Hill is haunted."

"Now you know how I feel about superstition," Henry scolded. "I'll grant you that Mole Hill is different from all the other hills around here. There are some mighty strange rocks up there, but I wish you would put a stop to all this idle talk about Mole Hill being evil. It's nothin' but nonsense."

Before David could reply, Doc called Henry's number.

"Can't be my turn yet!" Henry hollered at Doc. "I just got here!"

"I moved you to the front of the line," Doc yelled back. "You've had that cough for more than a year, and I think it's time you did something about it. Now get on up here before I change my mind."

The men in the yard laughed as Henry climbed the seven steps to Doc's front porch. He glanced back at the amused Mennonites, shrugged his shoulders, and sat down at the doctoring window.

❖ ❖ ❖

When Gabe Heatwole's doctoring business was brisk, as it was on this day, he saw patients through a window that opened onto the porch. This efficient approach afforded no privacy, but there were few secrets among the Mennonites who lived around Mole Hill. Everyone in the yard was familiar with Henry's cough, and most of them already suspected the cause of it.

Doc was an affable old man with large puffy jowls and a big Adam's apple that bounced up and down as he spoke. He had bushy white eyebrows and dark brown eyes.

"I've been hearing that terrible cough of yours in church," Doc said. "I believe it got worse last fall when the weather turned cold."

"I think that's right," Henry replied. "Or it mighta been the fall before that. Are you gonna give me some puke weed? Cause I just hate to puke."

"I reckon I will! The emetic herb you call puke weed is my No. 1 medicine, the most important one I use in my practice. But you are going to need more than No. 1. I don't like your color at all. Roll up your sleeves and let me see your arms."

Henry did as he was told, and Doc reached through the window to mash the muscles in Henry's arms with both hands.

"Other than that cough, how have you been?"

"Tolerable bad, Doc. I'm tired all the time, even in the morning, and I'm not nearly as strong as I used to be."

"Arm wrestle me," Doc challenged, planting his right elbow on the wide windowsill between them.

Doc was much bigger than Henry, but he was thirty-six years older, so Henry expected to whip the old coot like an Irish potato, but he could not budge Doc's surprisingly sturdy arm.

"That's enough," Doc said, after three or four seconds of straining. "I won't make you say 'uncle' since I'm already your uncle by marriage."

"So what's wrong with me, Doc?"

"Well ... I'd say you have consumption. Your flesh is wasting away because you are not digesting your food properly. This allows canker to become seated in your stomach and bowels, and then it takes hold of your lungs. That's what makes you cough all the time."

"Consumption! People die from that, don't they?"

"Deed they do! More grown men die from consumption than anything else, unless you count poor judgment."

"What causes it?"

"Poor judgment? I wish I knew."

"No. I mean what causes consumption?"

"Well, Dr. Thomson's guide says that consumption can come from any number of disorders that are allowed to fester. Patients get run down because they haven't been treated properly by the fashionable practice of the *learned* doctors. At some point, nature makes a compromise with the disease, and the body becomes divided against itself."

"That sounds more like a war than a disease."

"It *is* a war, Henry. Consumption, like any disease, is a life-and-death struggle between the outer cold and the inner heat. The outer cold ultimately causes paralysis and death, but the inner heat sustains rigor and life. And, in your case, I'm afraid the outer cold is winning the war."

"Does that mean you can't cure me?"

"Well, most of the *learned* doctors would say that consumption cannot be cured once it becomes seated in the lungs. Fortunately for you, I am not a learned doctor. I think there's a good chance we can restore your inner heat by promoting perspiration and clearing the canker from your stomach and bowels. Then you will be able to digest your food properly, and your whole body will become nourished and reinvigorated."

"How much puke weed would I have to take?"

"My No. 1 medicine will cleanse your stomach and raise your inner heat, but it won't last long enough to cure you. We'll use cayenne—my No. 2 tonic—to hold the heat in your stomach until your system can be cleared of obstructions, such as canker and putrefaction."

"Pew … tree … what?"

"Putrefaction is the undigested food that rots in your stomach and bowels, doing more harm than good."

"How do I get shut of it?"

"Well … my No. 3 remedy usually does the trick. It's a strong tea from the bark of bayberry roots and the roots of white pond lily. Drinking this tea will cleanse your stomach, but it might not completely clear your bowels, so I want Peggy to give you some extra No. 3 by injection."

"Injection! What's that?"

"Injection just means cleansing the putrefaction from the other end. Do you have a syringe?"

"I don't even know what that is."

"That's alright. You can make one with a bladder and a pipe. Do you have a pipe?"

"None that Peggy knows about, but there *might* be a corncob pipe in the barn somewheres."

"Well … you can keep that pipe hid. I want you to buy a new one for this purpose—a brand new clay pipe. Then I want you to wash out a bladder as best you can. Tie off one end, pour a half cup of warm No. 3 tea into it, and stretch the open end over the bowl of your pipe. Then bend over and get Peggy to insert the pipe stem into your rectum and squeeze the bladder gently to push some No. 3 into your bowels."

"Uh … you say … put the pipe stem *where?*"

"Rectum, Henry, Rectum. It's the same word in English as it is in German, so don't act like you don't hear me. And make sure you have a chamber pot close by. The No. 3 injection will cause a rigorous bowel movement just pretty quick."

"I'm afraid to ask what else, or is that it?"

"There's one more thing you must do, Henry, and it's very important. I want you to take a steam bath after the No. 3 does its dirty work."

"Steam! Won't that scald me?"

"Not if you do it right. I want you to place several stones in the fire till they're red hot. Take off your clothes and put a clean blanket over your head and around your entire body. Stand directly over a kettle of water and put the hot stones into the kettle one at a time. If you start to feel like you're going to faint, get Peggy to splash a little cool water on your face and belly."

"How long must I do this?"

"At least twenty minutes and as long as you can tolerate it after that. When you can't stand it anymore, take a bath with cold water. Then put on clean bedclothes and get between clean sheets with plenty of blankets.

"In the morning, you should take some of my No. 4 medicine—a tea from stinking poplar bark—to increase your appetite and restore your digestive powers. When you start to feel hungry, eat whatever you crave, but the best thing is to take a slice of boiled salt pork and eat it with a pepper sauce of cayenne, vinegar, and salt."

When Doc finally finished his long litany of instructions, Henry struggled to process the mental picture of his proposed treatment. He knew what to expect from the puke weed, but he worried about the manifestations of the other medications. The steam bath didn't sound too bad, but the pipe-and-bladder injection seemed completely devoid of dignity.

"I don't think I can remember to do all that," Henry hedged.

"Just take the medicine by the numbers. Peggy knows how to brew the teas and how much of each one to give you."

Doc handed Henry four small bottles of powder with handwritten numbers on homemade labels.

"Does … uh … Peggy know about injections?" Henry inquired sheepishly.

"Deed she does! She's birthed four children, and I gave her an injection after each one to get her bowels going again."

"Can I just drink some extra No. 3 and skip the injection?"

"That might work, Henry, but it's better to administer ten injections that are not needed than to skip one that is necessary."

Much to Henry's surprise, Peggy was quite familiar with Doc's medical methods. She had grown up with injections and steam baths and teas made from all six of his botanical powders. She also kept small-mammal bladders on hand for a variety of purposes that Henry knew nothing about. She turned one inside out and scrubbed it clean, while Henry procured a clay pipe from Potter John.

After supper, Peggy put the children to bed early and placed several stones in the fire. She set out clean bedclothes for Henry and started brewing the medicinal teas. When all was ready, Henry carried a swig of No. 1 outside so he would not wake the children with the loud guttural sounds he expected to make. He planned to drink the tea while standing on the bridge over the creek, hoping that the babbling brook would drown out the puking noise and float the vomit away from the house.

His plan worked to near perfection. He swallowed the tea in one gulp, and his stomach rebelled in a matter of seconds. He dropped to his hands and knees and spewed his supper into the creek with three violent heaves. His stomach was empty now, but the involuntary contractions persisted one, two, three more times. Henry could feel his inner heat boiling through his skin in the form of perspiration. As blood rushed to his stomach, and away from his brain, he became extremely light-headed, so he laid down on the bridge to keep from passing out and falling into the creek.

Henry remained motionless on the bridge for a minute or two. He could hear a swishing sound in his ears as the blood returned to his brain. When he had regained some of his senses, he struggled to his feet and trudged toward the house. Peggy met him on the front porch with the No. 2 tea, which he drank without saying a word. He could feel his inner heat continuing to rise as the tea burned his throat on the way down.

"I hate to puke," he grumbled, as he entered the house, pulled off his boots, and peeled off his pants. "I don't 'zactly know what dyin' feels like, but it can't be much worse than pukin'."

Peggy pursed her lips to keep from laughing as she draped her best blanket over Henry and instructed him to straddle the steaming kettle in front of the chamber pot stool. Beads of sweat and snot began running down Henry's face as he drank a double dose of No. 3 tea and eased himself down onto the three-legged convenience. He leaned forward and waited, but nothing happened.

After a minute or two, Peggy said: "We need to hurry up and increase the steam to keep the sweat flowing. C'mon, Henry. Injections ain't so bad."

"Alright then," Henry conceded, as he stood up and stooped down. "Let's get this over with."

CHAPTER 3

Dropsy in the Head

"There's no disease in the head that doesn't come from the stomach."

Henry tolerated the steam for nearly an hour. Then Peggy wiped down her hard-boiled husband with cold water and tucked him between her best linen sheets. He slept all night and well into the following morning, longer than he had slept since he was a child. He awoke with a powerful thirst, and Peggy gave him the No. 4 tea and plenty of well water. After another productive session on the stool, Henry's stomach loudly proclaimed his hunger, and the salt pork with pepper sauce that Doc recommended was just the thing.

"I think I'm cured," Henry told Doc, who stopped by the house on Sunday noon on his way home from Weavers Church.

"I'm glad you feel better," Doc replied, "but you'll need to repeat the whole process one or two times before we know whether you're cured or not."

Henry endured the full treatment one more time. After that, Peggy continued giving him weekly steam baths followed by No. 4 tea before bed and plenty of salt pork in the morning. The steam seemed to help, but the cold, wet winter soon made it abundantly clear that Henry was not cured.

By the time the ground thawed in March, Johnny had to do most of the plowing. He handed down his garden work to Mary, who delegated some of her household chores to Davy. Henry's widowed mother, Mottie, who lived nearby in the tenant house, often watched Suzy and Becky so Peggy could attend to whatever else needed doing.

Gradually, Henry's health improved with warmer weather, and on May 21, he felt good enough to make the three-mile trip to Harrisonburg. He and Johnny hitched up the spring wagon and enjoyed the clear sky and cool breeze as they rode into town to see about buying a horse.

It was spring court day, the most important time of the year for many residents of Rockingham County. Farmers flocked to town to buy, sell, and swap everything from eggs and vegetables to wagons and horses. There were other court days on other third Mondays, but spring court day coincided with the annual muster of militia companies from across the county.

Johnny loved to watch the citizen soldiers march in rows and columns up German Street and down Main Street with guns resting on their shoulders, swords dangling from their belts, and bayonets glistening in the sun. Some of the men sported the same uniforms that their fathers or grandfathers had worn during the War of 1812. They stood at attention, while Colonel S. B. Gibbons and General Gilbert S. Meem reviewed the troops with great fanfare and gave the order to fire the town's rusty old cannon.

Johnny was enthralled with these proceedings, but Henry abhorred such spectacles.

"War is sin, and enthusiasm for war is just about as bad," he always said.

According to the law, all able-bodied men of Rockingham were members of the militia, but the Mennonite men paid fines to avoid the periodic musters. They did not believe in taking up arms against any man, and the cost of their nonresistant convictions was minimal, a fine of 75 cents for each missed muster. Henry's militia company

PEGGY'S WAR

normally drilled in the large field beside New Erection Presbyterian Church, but he always refused to participate, and he forbade Johnny to watch.

"Don't be deceived by parades and charades," Henry warned. "There is no glory in war."

Peggy wished she could have gone with Henry and Johnny to town, but she was nearly nine months pregnant, and she didn't want to give birth in the bed of a wagon. She also was worried about Davy. He had not been his mischievous self for nearly two days, and he had begun to cough and complain that his head hurt. At first, Peggy thought he was merely imitating his father, but when Davy didn't beg to ride into town with Henry and Johnny, she knew he was seriously sick.

Peggy put Davy to bed early that evening, and he slept all night, but even after the sun came up, he remained lethargic. At the breakfast table, he propped up his head with his left hand and picked at his oatmeal with his right. This posture made his neck stiff and sore, so Peggy put him back to bed, and he slept all day. Davy tried to come to the table for his supper, but his legs were too weak to support his weight, so Peggy sent Johnny after Doc, who arrived as the sun was going down.

"I'm glad to see you," said Peggy, who was waiting anxiously on the porch. "It's Davy. I'm afraid he's got dropsy in the head."

Doc followed Peggy into the house and up the stairs.

"I'm sure he'll be fine," Doc said, "but where did you get this notion about dropsy in the head?"

"From my sister, Susan. Seven years ago, her little boy—you remember Jacob—he had a terrible headache and died within a week. The town doctor said he had dropsy in the head."

"I *do* remember Jacob," Doc said, as he sat down on Davy's bed and examined him. "But this business about dropsy in the head is pure nonsense. There's no disease in the head that doesn't come from the stomach. If the town doctors understood this, they would prescribe natural medicine to cleanse the stomach. But when a child is sick, they give him calomel, or some other poison, which makes the stomach worse. And when the child dies, they blame everything on dropsy in the head."

"But Davy's *head* hurts, not his stomach."

"The effect is *felt* in the head, which is the seat of all the senses, but the problem comes from bile that has lost its digestive powers, leaving food to rot in the stomach. After Davy vomits, his head will begin to feel better, and then you will see that the stomach was the problem. Just give him a dose of No. 1 in a tea of No. 3 and some bitters to correct the bile. Oh … and give him some No. 2 to warm his stomach."

As Peggy began to brew the medicinal teas, Doc reminded her to give Davy less than half the amounts she had given Henry for consumption.

"It may take three courses of treatment before he feels better," Doc said, as he headed out the door. "Let him rest one day between each course, but the tea and the bitters should restore his inner heat by the end of the week."

Davy vomited that night but felt no better on the following day. He threw up again during the second course of treatment and became delirious during his second day of rest. The third round of treatment elicited no response at all. Peggy sent Johnny after Doc again, but Davy died before he arrived.

Henry was stunned. Peggy was devastated. She cried hysterically for nearly an hour. Then she realized there was grim work to be done, and she did not trust it to anyone else. She knew from sad experience that Davy's lifeless body would become stiff, so she removed his night clothes and cleaned his final discharges.

"Warm some well water on the stove," she instructed Mary. "Make sure it's just right—not too hot, not too cold."

While Mary did as she was told, Doc sat down next to Peggy and gently said what Henry was thinking.

"Cold creek water would be better, Peggy. There will be a funeral tomorrow, so we must do what we can to preserve the body."

"But warm water might restore his inner heat," Peggy pleaded.

"I'm afraid not," Doc said. "We've done all we can. The outer cold was too strong this time, and the embers of life have turned to ash. The outer cold always defeats the inner heat in the end. For me, the war has been long, but for Davy the battle was brief. Who's to say which is better?"

Sobbing and crying, Peggy carefully cleansed Davy's lifeless body, as she had done when he was a baby. As she set out his best clothes, she remembered how difficult it had once been to dress such a rambunctious child.

"Why can't you just lay still?" she had scolded.

Now she prayed for miraculous animation—any small sign of a quickening spark. But Davy's legs were limp as she guided them into his best pair of pants. His arms remained motionless as she slid them into the sleeves of a clean white shirt.

Davy was fully dressed by the time Abram Swartz came to the house to take the boy's measurements and carry them to the undertaker in Dayton, a small town about two miles south of the Rhodes place. That was all Henry asked of him, but Swartz—a lover of hammer and nails—returned in just a few hours with a beautiful burial box he had quickly made as an expression of sympathy.

PEGGY'S WAR

Peggy padded the finely crafted coffin with her best wool blanket and gently laid Davy's cold body down for the last time. Then she placed wet handkerchiefs over his face and hands to keep the exposed skin from turning dark during the wake and funeral.

That evening, Henry told everyone who came to the house that he would dig Davy's grave in the morning. Friends, nephews, and cousins offered to help, but Henry told them all the same thing: "It's much easier for a small man to dig a child's grave."

After the clock struck ten, Peggy put the children to bed and asked everyone to go home, but her sister, Susan, insisted on staying. She knew what it was like to lose a young child. Doc lingered for a little while, too. Then he gave Peggy some nerve powder, and she finally drifted off to sleep.

At the first hint of morning light, Henry hitched up the spring wagon, but before he could gather his digging tools from the barn, Peggy jerked awake and shouted, "Davy! We have to keep Davy warm! He must not lose his inner heat!"

Henry bolted back into the house and found Susan hugging Peggy on the edge of the bed.

"Davy died yesterday," Susan said softly. "He's now in the care of his Heavenly Father. The Good Lord is holding Davy in his arms right now, just as tight as I'm holding you."

Henry was glad that Susan was there to comfort Peggy. "Sisters are better than husbands at this sort of thing," he thought to himself.

Peggy's outburst woke Johnny, who was quickly downstairs and ready to go.

"I'm going with you," he informed Henry. "You can't dig that grave all by yourself. Peter Hartman is going to help, too. He's meeting us at the graveyard. It's decided."

Henry looked at Johnny in disbelief. He was not used to anyone—much less a twelve-year-old boy—telling him how things are going to be. Henry was tempted to admonish Johnny for his insolence, but he stopped himself.

"You're a good boy, Johnny Bell, a little too big for your britches, I'd say, but a good boy. I accept your kind offer, and I'll be glad for Peter's help, too."

Henry tossed one more pick and one more shovel in the bed of the spring wagon, and they started up the Rawley Road toward Weavers Church. It was nearly one mile from the creek to the church, which stood in front of several tall oaks near the top of Fairview Hill, the highest point on the road between Harrisonburg and Rawley Springs. The church was forty feet long and thirty feet wide, made of logs that had been covered with whitewashed weatherboard in recent years.

Henry and Johnny passed the church, crested the hill, and turned right onto a narrow road that took them the last half mile to the graveyard. Distracted by grief, they failed to notice the stunning sunrise that illuminated the clouds along Massanutten Mountain to the east.

Peter was waiting for them at the cemetery. Henry pulled the wagon up to the split-rail fence that protected the fifty-plus graves from Jacob Shank's grazing sheep. And without saying much more than "good morning," Henry and the boys unloaded the tools and carried them through the gate. Henry thought about burying Davy next to Big Henry, but he decided to save that spot for Mottie, so he started a new row at the top of the cemetery, where he and Peggy could both be laid to rest beside Davy someday.

The boys struggled not to cry as Henry began to dig. He made no sobbing sounds, but tears streamed down his cheeks, mixing with the sweat that soon started dripping from his chin. As the soft brown topsoil gave way to hard orange clay, Peter took the first turn swinging the pick, while Johnny shoveled out the dirt he loosened.

Then the boys alternated between pick and shovel, while Henry coughed and wheezed and rested. He did not speak for fear that his voice would waver and betray the depth of his sorrow.

It took four hours to dig the grave deep enough to accommodate three feet of dirt on top of the coffin. Finally, Henry lowered a measuring stick into each corner of the rectangular hole and pronounced the sad undertaking complete.

Back at the farm, as the hour of the funeral approached, Henry hitched two horses to the spring wagon to pull the extra weight up the hill to the church. Peggy sat up front with Henry and Mottie, while Johnny and Mary rode in the back. Sitting on top of Davy's occupied coffin made them queasy, but this arrangement was better than taking the larger wagon because Johnny had been using it to haul manure.

No one spoke on the way up Fairview Hill, not even when Henry pulled the wagon alongside the church to allow the ladies to climb down onto the stile. The men's entrance was in front, the side facing the road, but for funerals, everyone used the women's door in the back corner of the building. It was almost at ground level, while the men's door was eight steps up. This was not a major consideration for such a small corpse and coffin, but adhering to tradition allowed the family to go through the motions of a funeral without thinking about such details.

Peggy and Mary hung their black bonnets in the women's ante-room before taking their place on the first bench of the women's side of the simple sanctuary.

There were seven rows of backless benches on each side of the church. Facing the pulpit, men sat on the left, and women sat on the right, where the benches were slightly lower. This segregated seating kept sexual distractions down to a minimum, which helped the men pay attention to the sermon instead of their wives or, worse yet, the wives of their Christian brothers.

The bishop and preacher occupied the bench behind the pulpit, which was centered precisely between two amen corners, each with three short pews perpendicular to the rows of longer benches.

As senior deaconess of the church, Mottie anchored the front row of the women's amen corner. She sat next to Peter's mother, Lizzie Hartman, who was the junior deaconess. As always, they were joined by Betsy Weaver, the widow of the church's namesake sexton. In the men's amen corner on the other side of the pulpit, Peggy's brother, David Heatwole, waited on the front bench with Deacon Frederick Rhodes.

After everyone settled into their customary seats, Johnny and Peter carried the little coffin into the sanctuary. Henry held the door for them before taking his place on the front row of the men's side with his brother, David Rhodes, and Peggy's father, Abraham Heatwole. They sat directly across from Peggy, Mary, and Susan.

Johnny and Peter placed the coffin on a small bench in front of the pulpit and opened the lid. Then Johnny sat down on the row behind Henry, and Peter joined his father on the back bench of the men's side.

The funeral began precisely at 3 p.m. David Heatwole led the congregation in several mournful hymns, then Samuel Coffman preached from behind the pulpit. Coffman was a modest man of thirty-six years with a worried face and a thick crop of unruly brown hair that almost covered his ears. He opened his Bible and read methodically from Psalm 103, beginning at verse thirteen and continuing to the end of the chapter.

"Bless the Lord, O my soul: and all that is within me, bless his holy name. Bless the Lord, O my soul, and forget not all his benefits."

Peggy had heard these words dozens of times at dozens of funerals, and Coffman's monotonous voice quickly faded from her consciousness as she dwelt on the loss of her only son. After a few more verses, she again became vaguely aware of what the preacher was saying. The words were more than familiar; they were standard fare for any Mennonite funeral.

"Like as a father pitieth his children, so the Lord pitieth them that fear him. For he knoweth our frame; he remembereth that we are dust. As for man, his days are as grass: as a flower of the fields, so he flourisheth. For the wind passeth over it, and it is gone; and the place thereof shall know it no more. But the mercy of the Lord is from everlasting to everlasting upon them that fear him, and his righteousness unto children's children; to such as keep his covenant, and to those that remember his commandments to do them. The Lord hath prepared his throne in the heavens; and his kingdom ruleth over all."

Coffman preached for an hour on this scripture and concluded his sermon by repeating the last verse of the psalm: "Bless the Lord, all his work in all places of his dominion: bless the Lord, O my soul."

After Coffman said amen, Bishop Martin Burkholder took his turn at the pulpit. He preached a second sermon and repeated his message in German for the benefit of the older congregants. Then he led the faithful in an English prayer and instructed them to reconvene at the graveyard.

Everyone sat still while Johnny and Peter closed the coffin, carried it out the women's door, and slid it back into the bed of the spring wagon. The congregation filed silently from the church, and Henry led a slow procession to the cemetery, where Bishop Burkholder read more scripture and said another English prayer.

Abram Swartz nailed the coffin shut, and Peggy winced with each blow of his hammer. When the pounding finally stopped, her labor contractions started, but Peggy ignored the spasms in her back as the men carefully lowered the beautiful little box into the ground with ropes. Henry put in the first shovelful of dirt, and the men who had managed the ropes finished the job as the congregation sang another hymn. The mourners mingled among the tombstones until a mound of fresh orange clay was packed down tightly across Davy's sad little grave.

On the wagon ride home, the anguish of death and the pain of birth intertwined and became indistinguishable to Peggy. Her water broke before she reached the house, and she delivered a healthy baby girl in the early morning hours of the following day.

Mottie served as the midwife, as she often did, and Doc came to the house at noon to give Peggy an injection of No. 3 and another dose of nerve powder.

For the next three days, Peggy took care of the baby, but she did not speak. Finally, Henry asked her what name they should give their daughter. Her blank stare became more focused as she considered the possibilities.

"If we name her Priscilla, would you please not call her Prissy?"

"What makes you think I'd do such a thing?"

"Well … you changed my name from Margaret to Peggy. David became Davy. Susanna turned into Suzy, and Rebecca became Becky."

"Alright then, just Priscilla," Henry promised.

Getting Peggy to talk was a significant breakthrough, but she remained severely depressed for several months. She dutifully nursed Priscilla and fed the rest of the family, but Davy's death seemed to drain the joy from her life. Henry didn't know how to help her, but Peggy never murmured nor complained. When well-wishing neighbors asked how she was feeling, her dreary reply was always the same: "tolerable ... just tolerable."

It was a long sad summer, and autumn brought only more misery. David Rhodes—Henry's only brother and one of Davy's two namesake uncles—died on October 6. After the funeral, Peggy rocked Priscilla on the front porch with her eyes fixed on the top of Mole Hill. Her nightmares of fire and destruction had persisted. She had no way of knowing how long her trials and tribulations would last, but she feared the deaths of Davy and David were just the beginning.

CHAPTER 4

Rumors of War

"Late News by Telegraph: An Insurrection in Virginia!"

"It's true! It's true!"

Six-year-old L. J. Heatwole could not contain his excitement as he ran toward the house carrying the latest issue of the *Rockingham Register*. He often brought the weekly newspaper to Henry on Sunday afternoon after L. J.'s father had finished reading it, but this news could not wait.

L. J. was David Heatwole's eldest son and Peggy's favorite nephew. He reminded her so much of Davy, especially when he sported a straw hat that was identical to the one Davy had worn. Sure enough, L. J. outran his hat—just like Davy used to—as he scurried up onto the porch, where Henry and Doc were visiting on the afternoon of October 21.

Henry had heard rumors of a slave rebellion in the northernmost reaches of Virginia, but he assumed the rumors were false and said nothing about them to Peggy. He knew exactly what L. J. meant by "It's true!"

Henry disappeared into the house and returned with two nickels. "One's for you," he told L. J., "and one's for your daddy. If he don't want his nickel, tell him to put it toward some sensible books for the Fairview School House."

This is what Henry always said to his paper boy, and it would take more than a bloody insurrection to prompt one iota of deviation from this customary exchange.

L. J. pocketed the coins and put the *Register* into Henry's hands. "Page 2. Read it! It's true!"

Henry opened the four-page, broadsheet newspaper as Peggy and Johnny came out on the porch to see what all the excitement was about.

"Read it!" L. J. repeated, as Doc got up from his rocking chair to look over Henry's shoulder.

"Late news by telegraph: An insurrection in Virginia!" Henry began, trying hard to filter the fear from his voice. "United States troops sent to the spot. Citizens of Harper's Ferry shot."

Henry skimmed silently down the page for a few seconds then summarized the first few paragraphs of the story.

"It says there was a slave rebellion at Harper's Ferry. Armed abolitionists took over the United States arsenal there. The mob was composed of 250 whites and a band of negroes."

"How many negroes?" Doc asked.

"Wait a minute ... it says there were 500 to 700 whites *and* blacks engaged in the insurrection. Troops arrived in Harper's Ferry from Virginia and Maryland, but the battle for the town was fought mainly by railroad and tonnage men from Martinsburg. A conductor on the railroad got killed, and two other conductors was wounded. The rioters also killed some people from the town."

"Who was the leader?" Doc asked.

"He has a strange name, Osa-wa-to-mie John Brown. It says, 'His feats in Kansas are notorious.'"

"Deed they are!" Doc exclaimed. "John Brown is a deranged abolitionist. He killed many people out in Kansas and Missouri. I wonder what he's doing in Virginia?"

PEGGY'S WAR

"Well … it sounds like he was tryin' to free the slaves."

"And he got hundreds of them to follow him?"

"Well … it sounds like there was 500, maybe more. It says, 'A scouting party has just come in, having captured tents, blankets, spades and about 1,500 Sharpe's rifles with ammunition. … A train is now getting ready to convey horses and men from here to pursue the rioters into any state or locality where they may have fled.'"

"This is dreadful news," Doc said. "A gang of violent abolitionists roaming around Virginia could start a war between North and South over slavery."

"Which side would we fight for?" Johnny asked. "We live in the South, but we ain't got no slaves."

"We would refuse to fight in *any* war," Doc replied, with great conviction. "We are opposed to taking up arms against our enemies because war is inconsistent with the peaceful Kingdom of God. We obey the government in all things that do not oppose the teachings of Christ, but when the government demands that we wield the sword, we must obey God rather than man. We must follow the words of our Lord and Master, who said, 'Love your enemies, bless them who curse you, do good to them who hate you.'"

"If Christians in the South and Christians in the North keep this one commandment, there will be no bloodshed, but if they disregard the love of God and heed the passions of men, I'm afraid there could be a terrible war, and it would be fought right here in Virginia. The suffering would be unimaginable."

"I can imagine it," Peggy volunteered. "It couldn't be any worse than losing Davy."

"You musn't say such a thing," Doc admonished. "You have no idea what war is like. Davy died a natural death, and a natural death is hard on a grieving mother, but natural death is a necessary part of God's plan. War is *never* part of God's plan."

"But, if we stay out of it, won't we be alright?" Johnny asked.

"We do need to stay out of it, but I'm afraid that the young men of the church are not sufficiently prepared to resist an urgent call to arms. There has been peace in this valley for nearly fifty years. The War of 1812 was fought long before the young men of our church were born."

"Were you in the militia in 1812?" Johnny asked.

"Deed I was! Virginia has always required able-bodied men to join the militia."

"What was it like back then?"

"I really don't know. I made it a point to miss every single muster, and I refused to march off to war when the governor called out the militia, and that caused me a lot of trouble. But I'll tell you the one good thing I remember about that war. When it was over, all the people around here rejoiced by roasting an ox on top of Mole Hill."

"What about the Mexican War?" Henry asked. "I was in the militia then, and I don't remember it causin' me no trouble."

"The Mexican War wasn't fought anywhere near Virginia, and it didn't last long enough to test our nonresistant principles," Doc explained. "But there would be no way for us to escape a war between North and South. Virginia would be the battlefield and the burying ground."

As a movement to free slaves, John Brown's insurrection failed miserably, but as a catalyst for fear, it succeeded beyond Osawatomie's wildest dreams. Panic-stricken towns near Harper's Ferry frantically prepared to defend against further violence. Even in Rockingham County—100 miles up the valley from Harper's Ferry—children were afraid to go outside, and no one knew how many renegades might still be lurking in the mountains.

Rumors and false alarms kept the Shenandoah Valley on edge even after it became clear that the number of insurrectionists at large was closer to five than 500. But there was another nagging question that perpetuated and magnified the fear. Who financed the substantial stores of guns and ammunition that Brown had amassed *before* his men stormed the arsenal? The *Register*, like many newspapers in the South, was quick to suggest a provocative answer.

"Listen to this, Peggy," Henry said, as he anxiously scanned the next issue of the newspaper. "The *Register* now says there were only twenty-five insurrectionists at Harper's Ferry. It says, 'A large majority of the villains were killed on the ground—five of them taken to the Charlestown jail, and will, no doubt, have full justice meted out to them. So far as the attack on Harper's Ferry is concerned, this will be the end of it.' But here's the catch. It goes on to say that 'Brown and his followers at Harper's Ferry were not alone in this movement. The large quantity of ammunition, found in possession of the insurgents, shows that they had at their command a large amount of money. The conclusion is irresistible that men of means in the North are sympathizing with the cruel attempts to incite the slaves of the South.'"

Brown was quickly tried, convicted, and condemned to hang on December 2—as soon as possible by Virginia law but long enough to foster more fear in Rockingham. Peggy grew tired of hearing about the insurrection, but Henry was hooked, and every week the *Register* provided more details of Brown's ill-conceived plot. He had planned to travel south—in the general direction of Rockingham—killing slaveholders along the way and sweeping the liberated slaves into his abolitionist army. The *Register* also continued to note that many people in the North were sympathizing with Brown.

"Here's a letter to Governor Wise from a woman in Massachusetts, who wants to come to Virginia and nurse John Brown's wounds," Henry marveled. "She says, 'I, and thousands of others, feel a natural impulse of sympathy for the brave and suffering man. ... He needs a mother or sister to dress his wounds and speak soothingly to him. Will you allow me to perform that mission of humanity?'"

"I can't imagine the governor would even consider such a thing," Peggy scoffed.

"Then you'd be wrong," Henry said. "Governor Wise replied to her letter. He said that as governor of Virginia he is sworn to protect any citizen of any state coming to Virginia for any lawful and peaceful purpose. He said, 'You have the right to visit Charlestown, Va., Madam, and your mission, being merciful and humane, will not only be allowed, but be respected if not welcomed.'"

Peggy shook her head and made sucking sounds of disapproval between her tongue and the roof of her mouth.

"That woman wouldn't be safe in Virginia no matter what the governor says."

"Well ... he does warn her about that. He says, 'A few unenlightened and inconsiderate persons, fanatical in their modes of thought and action to maintain justice and right, might molest you, ... and this might suggest the imprudence of risking any experiment upon the peace of a society very much excited by the crimes with whose chief author you seem to sympathize.'"

One week later, Henry saw the first hint that Doc might have been right when he said that Brown's raid could ignite a civil war.

"We are liable to be attacked at any moment by the hordes of abolitionists who live in the North," the *Register* warned. "For such a struggle we must prepare ourselves. ... Soldiery should be armed, and our people taught the use of the gun and the sword."

Amid rampant rumors that abolitionist groups might try to rescue Brown, Governor Wise called out several volunteer militia companies to provide security for the execution. The Valley Guard, a company from Rockingham under the command of Colonel Gibbons, arrived in Charlestown on November 28, bringing the total military presence to 2,000 men.

Henry wasn't going to mention that story to Peggy, but he could not resist an out-loud reading of a letter titled "Our Country—Our Soldiery—Our Townswomen."

"Here's something from the 'old ladies' of Harrisonburg," he began. "That's what they call themselves. They're scolding the younger women who want to 'control their husbands and prevent them from obeying the call of duty and of their country in the present struggle with fanaticism.'"

Peggy rolled her eyes and retreated to the kitchen.

"I won't read the whole thing," Henry called after her, "just enough to give you the general idea. The old ladies say, 'We love our boys, who are bone of our bone and flesh of our flesh, yet we had rather follow them to their graves than to see them shirk in this hour of their country's calamity and call to arms. ... We are ready to prove, by our actions, that the spirit of '76 animates us, and that our country can have our boys and the blood of our boys, if necessary, to defend our institutions from outrage.'"

"And I suppose," Peggy responded, "that the precious institutions they want to defend are slave trading and slave owning."

"That's the whole beef in one bite," Henry agreed. "They are prepared to sacrifice their sons to defend slavery."

On December 2, 1859, the civil authorities of Jefferson County executed John Brown without incident, but Southern fears of violent abolition did not die with him on the gallows of Charlestown. Northern newspapers continued to inflame those fears by printing expressions of sympathy and admiration, while Southern newspapers exploited such stories for provocative purposes. Citing the *New*

York Herald, the editor of the *Register* said: "The Republican Party is declared to be completely abolitionized, and its intention to hurry a remorseless and bloody revolution is openly proclaimed: 'Slavery must be throttled.'"

❖   ❖   ❖

Mottie moved to the main house on the Rhodes place in the spring of 1860. At age seventy-seven, she was not afraid to live alone in the tenant house, but as Henry's health declined, Peggy was doing more farm work, and she needed help taking care of the children.

Mottie's real name was Elizabeth, but "Mottie" was Henry's way of saying "Mommy" when he was a child, and the name endured, along with Henry's habit of adding an "ie" or "y" to the names of his loved ones. This term of endearment extended to Henry's nephew, Sammy Rhodes, who moved into the tenant house in June to help with the summer harvest. His mother was Henry's sister, Anna, one of two Rhodes daughters who did *not* marry into Doc's family. Anna's husband died before Sammy was born, so Sammy had always looked up to his Uncle Henry as a father figure.

At age eighteen, Sammy was nearly a grown man by chronology, but he remained an excitable boy by temperament. He never missed a chance to tell Peggy that if Abraham Lincoln were elected president, it would almost certainly lead to war. Henry tried to dampen his nephew's dire predictions, but the newspaper quite often echoed the same sentiment.

In June, the *Register* endorsed Stephen A. Douglas for president, noting "the distracted and divided condition" of the Democratic Party. The Black Republicans (those who advocate abolition) would "trample the Constitution in the dust," which would lead to war, the newspaper insisted. "We go, then, for any man that can defeat Lincoln and Hamlin. The election of these men, the embodiment of

PEGGY'S WAR

the Black Republican party, would do more to facilitate the dissolution of the Union than anything that has ever occurred."

In August, Virginia's new governor, John Letcher, also endorsed Douglas, and Henry became nearly obsessed with reading whatever the *Register* reported about the upcoming election.

"Here's what the governor says," he hollered to Peggy, who had once again retreated to the kitchen. "'I have purposely avoided committing myself to the support of either Breckinridge or Douglas in the hope that a compromise would be agreed upon by the two conventions recently held in our state. ... All hope of an adjustment having now failed, I have no hesitation in declaring that my support will be given to Douglas.'"

"Hey! Here's some more election news!" Henry teased.

"I believe I've had all the politics I can stomach," Peggy groused.

"Now wait a minute," Henry said. "I think you'll like this story. The headline asks, 'IS THE UNION TO BE DISSOLVED?' And the story says, 'It is believed by some persons that a dissolution of the Union will occur in the event of the election of Abraham Lincoln to the Presidency. But whilst we do not believe the foregoing to be true, yet we do believe it to be the duty of everybody to go to D. M. SWITZER'S MERCHANT TAILORING ESTABLISHMENT and supply themselves with some of the most elegant goods it has ever been his pleasure to offer.'

"I'd say that's pretty funny," Henry laughed. "Don't you think that's funny?"

"Not particularly. It's bad enough that everybody talks about nothing but war. It seems to me that making fun of war is just that much worse. I don't understand why you keep reading that old rebel-rousing rag."

"Well ... even if I disagree with the *Register*, it still helps me fix my mind on who I'm gonna vote for."

"Who *are* you gonna vote for?"

"Why ... I'll vote for John Bell, of course," Henry said, with a wink at Johnny. "He's the standard bearer of the Constitutional Union Party. He supports the constitution of the country, the Union of the states, and the enforcement of the law."

"What about voting for Douglas?" Johnny asked. "Don't he have the best chance of beatin' Lincoln?"

"Nawsir. I ain't gonna vote *against* anyone," Henry insisted. "I'm gonna vote *for* Bell."

Many Unionists in the upper South did vote for Bell, but to no avail. On the afternoon of the following day, a close neighbor trotted his horse down through the white pine field. Seeing Henry in the barnyard on the other side of the creek, the rider reined his mount just long enough to shout, "It's Lincoln!"

CHAPTER 5

Secession

*"Virginia ain't hitched to North nor South,
and I wanna keep her that way."*

On November 16, the *Register* heralded "REVOLUTION IN THE SOUTH … a perfect fever of excitement" caused by Lincoln's election. The South Carolina legislature called for a state convention to consider secession, but by the end of the month, Henry and Peggy were more concerned about succession than secession.

Bishop Burkholder, who had long suffered from acute rheumatism, died unexpectedly at age forty-three. The sudden loss stunned the Mennonite Church throughout the valley. The people loved and respected the bishop for his benevolence, intelligence, and wisdom. Peggy especially admired Burkholder for promoting a greater acceptance of English among the Virginia Mennonites. Martin Burkholder had succeeded his father, Peter Burkholder—who had preached only in German—but Martin preached in English *and* German, as he had done at Davy's funeral.

Above all else, Burkholder was steady with the reins of the church at a time when unflinching leadership was in short supply. His death, it seemed, could not have come at a worse time. Three days after the bishop died, South Carolina seceded, and lame duck President James Buchanan designated January 4 as a day of fasting and prayer.

On that day, there were many earnest prayers in the churches of Rockingham County, but there was more bad news on the pages of the *Rockingham Register*. Federal troops had fled to Fort Sumter in Charleston Harbor.

Two weeks later, the newspaper reported that South Carolina legislators had unanimously proclaimed that any attempt to reinforce Fort Sumter would be considered an act of war. Henry also noticed a story that brought the secession question closer to home.

"Peggy, it says here that the Virginia General Assembly is callin' a state convention to consider secession. Each county will elect representatives to the convention, including three from Rockingham."

The next issue of the *Register* carried letters from several convention candidates summarizing their views on preserving the Union or seceding from it. The newspaper also announced that Georgia had severed its ties to the North, joining South Carolina, Mississippi, Florida, and Alabama.

"Hey! Here's some good news under the heading of HOPE," Henry marveled. "It says, 'We are most happy to announce that our decided conviction now is that our distracted and bleeding country is soon to have peace—peace without the intervention and arbitrament of the sword!'"

"Sounds like the *Register* is changing its tune," Peggy said.

"Maybe so. The editor says, 'We have been charged with being disunionists. If those who made such silly and groundless charges had known a tithe of the anguish we have felt for the fate of our country … such unkind and untrue insinuations never would have been made. Whatever else we may have lacked, we have never been wanting in the fondest and truest affection for that glorious country which is claimed by American citizens as the land of the free.'"

Apart from the annual musters, February 4 was the most animated Monday Henry had ever seen in Harrisonburg. Secesh and Unionist alike crowded around the courthouse, promoting their opposing views to any undecided citizens waiting in line to vote for convention delegates. Henry tethered his horse on the western edge of court square and made his way toward the ballot box, ignoring all the canvassers who begged to bend his ear.

By the end of the day, almost everyone in Rockingham knew the outcome of the election, but Henry waited patiently to read the results in the *Register*.

"So who won?" Peggy inquired, as Henry opened the newspaper to page two.

"Let's see ... Sam Coffman got 2,588 votes. That was the most. John Lewis was next with 2,081, and Algernon Gray came in third with 1,999."

"Are all three of them for the Union?"

"Well ... I know that Lewis and Gray are solid Union men. I felt good about votin' for them, but I ain't so sure about Coffman. He says he wants Virginia to stay in the Union, but only if the federal government guarantees that states can go their own way on slavery. That seems like a mighty big if to me."

"I can't believe that Sam Coffman would say such a thing."

"Oh ... I'm not talking about *preacher* Sam Coffman. I'm talking about *doctor* Sam Coffman."

"Well ... that still gives us two out of three," Peggy said. "Maybe Virginia can stay out of this mess."

"I sure hope so. It says here there's a peace conference with seven delegates from free states and seven delegates from slave states, but former President John Tyler fears that the conference will not adopt any measure that will satisfy the border slave states."

"Most folks around here don't own slaves," Peggy noted.

"That's true, but the people who oppose slavery—people like us—are quiet, while the people who support slavery are loud."

The *Register* made that point abundantly clear with a letter that distorted the peace churches' position on slavery.

"The Tunkers and Mennonites do not hold slaves themselves, yet they have not a word to say as to what other folks should do on the subject," the letter said. "They carefully and promptly pay their taxes to support the government which protects the slaveholders as well as themselves."

"What's a Tunker?" Mary asked.

"Tunker is just the way some people say Dunker," Peggy explained.

"What's a Dunker?" asked five-year-old Suzy.

"Dunkers are much like Mennonites," Peggy explained. "They speak both English and German, like we do, and they don't believe in fighting wars and killing people. They are good Christians. Most folks around here don't see much difference between Mennonites and Dunkers, so they just call us all Dunkers or Tunkers."

"So what *is* the difference?"

"Well … the biggest difference is that Dunkers take people's heads all the way under the water when they baptize them. That's why folks call them Dunkers."

"I saw people get baptized like that in Muddy Creek one time."

"Well … some Mennonites do get baptized that way. Others just kneel in the creek, and the preacher pours water over their heads. We leave that up to the person who's getting baptized, but the Dunkers say you have to get dunked."

"I don't want no preacher pushin' my head under the water," Suzy said. "I think I'll be a Mennonite."

"That's fine, Suzy, you have plenty of time to decide."

❖ ❖ ❖

As the war crept closer, penalties for avoiding militia musters increased dramatically, a fact that Henry shared with Peggy while reading the March 8 issue of the *Register*. A letter from George Chrisman noted that the 145th Regimental Court had raised the fines to two dollars for each missed muster, which would amount to six dollars for the year.

"Six dollars!" Peggy exclaimed. "That's more than twice what you've been paying."

"He has an answer for that. He says, 'This may have been an error in the court martial, but all who have conscientious scruples about mustering may relieve themselves from the burden which these fines impose upon them by the payment of three dollars in advance to a volunteer company.'"

"That sounds some better. I reckon you'll do that."

"I don't think so," Henry hedged. "It might be some kinda trick. If I was to pay $3 to a volunteer company instead of $6 to my regular militia, that'd make me a *volunteer*, and I don't much like the sound of that. Once you volunteer, you can't un-volunteer. Musters begin in April, so I guess I'll just pay my fines $2 at a time."

April of 1861 turned out to be a momentous month. Peggy realized that she was pregnant again, and the state convention voted ninety to forty-five *against* secession. But since the standoff at Fort Sumter was unresolved, the delegates remained in Richmond, and it didn't take them long to reverse the vote. On the morning of April 17, Secesh celebrants rang church bells in Harrisonburg when the news arrived by telegraph that the convention had voted eighty-eight to fifty-five *for* secession. The delegates also called for a state-wide referendum that would allow voters to accept or reject their momentous decision.

On April 19, the *Register* announced the "OPENING OF CIVIL WAR!" The South Carolina militia had attacked Fort Sumter.

"I guess that's why the Virginia Convention changed its mind," Peggy said.

"Well, that's part of it, but here's the bigger piece," Henry said. "President Lincoln issued a proclamation calling out the militias of all the states that remain in the Union—including Virginia. Here, I'll read it to you. It says, 'I, Abraham Lincoln, President of the United States, by virtue of the power in me vested by the Constitution and the laws, have thought fit to call forth, and hereby do call forth, the militia of the several States of the Union, to the aggregate number of 75,000, in order to suppress said combinations, and to cause the law to be duly executed.'"

"So that's it?" Peggy interrupted. "No more prayers for peace?"

"I just hate Abraham Lincoln," Johnny fumed. "That old Black Republican is declaring war on the South pure and simple."

"That's no way to talk!" Henry shot back. "You're startin' to sound like the Secesh agitators. We musn't give in to such temptation. We must love our neighbors as much as we love our own selves. The Carolina rebels are our southerly neighbors, and the Black Republicans are our northerly neighbors."

"Well ... Abraham Lincoln's no neighbor of mine!" Johnny declared.

"Now you listen here, Johnny Bell!" Henry countered. "My granddaddy and Abraham Lincoln's great-granddaddy lived pert near side by side on Linville Creek in the old days. Now, I only say that for your benefit; the Bible says that *every* man is my neighbor. If you're gonna live in my house, you'll remember that!"

The Virginia Mennonites held their annual conference at Weavers Church on the fourth Friday and fourth Saturday of April. Henry was surprised that the leaders of the church made no official statement regarding secession, but they at least clarified the church's position on hiring slaves for day labor. This practice was forbidden unless the slave's owner agreed that the slave would receive all the pay, but church members could still accept slave labor as payback for their own work. The conference also called for the selection of a new bishop to serve the Middle District of Virginia in place of the dearly departed Martin Burkholder.

In the following two weeks, the Middle District congregations—members of Weavers Church, the Bank Church, and the Pike Church—nominated two young preachers to enter the lot, Sam Coffman and Peggy's brother, Daniel Heatwole. At a special service on May 11, each candidate selected a hymn book. Daniel's book was empty, while Sam's contained a piece of paper that said, "Dear Brother, the Lord has chosen you to serve as bishop." Daniel did not say if he was disappointed or relieved, but he pledged to do everything he could to assist and support Coffman.

The lot settled the succession question, but unfortunately, the secession decision would not be left to divine providence. The headline in the May 17 *Rockingham Register* said: "TO THE POLLS! TO THE POLLS!" But this democratic exhortation was accompanied by a thinly veiled threat.

"There are a few disaffected and disappointed demagogues and their sympathizers who will show their disregard of the popular will by voting against the vast mass of their fellow citizens," the editor wrote. "They have a right to do this, of course, and we hope they will do it. ... We want to see and to know the men who would, by their votes against secession, encourage, if not assist, Lincoln to subdue and subjugate the yet free people of the proud old commonwealth."

Mary interrupted Henry's out-loud reading of the newspaper to ask, "What's a demagogue?"

Henry thought for a moment and said: "Someone like me, I reckon."

"Here's what it says about Dunkers and Mennonites," Henry continued. "'We have heard that some of our peaceful, orderly, law-loving fellow citizens, the Germans, will vote against it, or not vote at all. We cannot believe this. ... They have intelligence enough to see that division on this subject amongst ourselves invites Lincoln to come into our state with his vagabond soldiery to quarter upon us and to compel our people to join his standard.'"

Henry scanned the rest of the newspaper, but he found nothing but discouraging words.

"It says here that Algernon Gray, one of our delegates to the state convention who voted for the Union, has changed his mind and now 'advocates a united sentiment of the whole county in sustaining the ordinance of secession.'"

Henry looked up at Peggy and said: "The Secesh hotheads are in charge. Reasonable men who were totally against secession last week are now completely for it."

Three days before the May 23 referendum, John Lineweaver, a fellow farmer who lived near Weavers Church, came looking for Henry. Peggy directed him to the barn, where Henry was greasing harnesses. Lineweaver was neither Mennonite nor Dunker, but Henry had exchanged labor with him during the past two harvests. He was a reasonable man who worked hard and fostered goodwill among his neighbors, and Henry was always glad to see him.

"Henry Rhodes!" Lineweaver called out, as he entered the barn. "Are you gettin' smaller, or am I gettin' taller? Tell you what," he offered, as he shook Henry's hand, "I'll grease that harness for you if you'll spread the rest of my manure."

"Manure! Is *that* what you call it?" Henry replied, lapsing into his favorite rhyme. "We Germans call it dünger. The English call it sh--. But even in your fancy French, it schtinks a little bit."

Lineweaver had heard Henry's joke more than a dozen times over the years, but he laughed at the never-ending amusement Henry derived from repeating it.

"Actually, I'd rather talk about your harness than my manure," Lineweaver said, steering the conversation into politics. "It sounds like Lincoln wants Virginia's militia to pull his war wagon down South. Don't you reckon it's time we cut that harness loose?"

"Oh ... pshaw!" Henry replied. "Seems to me like you're lookin' to spread a different kinda manure in here. Virginia ain't hitched to North nor South, and I wanna keep her that way. Governor Letcher turned Lincoln down flat. He said the Virginia militia ain't fightin' Lincoln's war, and that's good enough for me."

"But what if I told you there don't need to be no war?"

"Well ... I reckon I'd agree with you on that."

"Alright then. Maybe you'll also agree that a unified vote for secession would mean that the North might let the South go without *any* bloodshed," he proposed.

"That ain't gonna happen," Henry countered, "not after South Carolina attacked Fort Sumter. Lincoln shouldna called out the Virginia militia. I'll give you that much, but South Carolina shoulda stayed in the Union, and so shoulda those other rebel states. All they care about is keepin' their slaves, and I'm against slavery."

"I agree with you on that," Lineweaver said. "I don't own no slaves, and I don't want no slaves, but it's a waste of time to argue about who brought these troubles upon us. It's enough to know that Lincoln intends to invade Virginia. We need to send a message to him. He needs to know that former Unionists, like you and me, will not betray our home state."

"I hear what you say, John, but I just don't agree," Henry finally said. "You're not gonna change my mind, and I'm not gonna change yours, so I reckon I oughta get back to greasin' this here harness, and you can go spread your manure somewheres else."

Henry wasn't about to budge, but two days later—the day before the referendum—two more visitors arrived on the Rhodes place. Henry did not know these men, and their approach was more menacing than neighborly.

"We're looking for Henry Rhodes," the smaller man said, as he walked up to Henry in the pasture just south of the house.

"Well … I reckon you found him," Henry replied.

"We hear you had quite a philosophical discussion with John Lineweaver the other day. We thought you might like to tell us what you told him—somethin' about votin' against secession."

"I don't remember sayin' that," Henry replied, "but that's what I'm gonna do."

"Then you better change your mind before tomorrow," the bigger man said. "That's just a little neighborly advice. We're your friends, Henry, but we know people—a lotta people—who ain't gonna tolerate men in our midst who side with our enemies. Armed men will be watching the polls tomorrow, and if you vote against secession, they will hunt you down like a wild beast. And if you stay away from the polls and don't vote, they will take away everything you own and run you outta the country."

"How would anybody *know* how I vote?" Henry asked.

"Tomorrow's ballot won't be no secret, Henry. You will proclaim yer vote as you place yer ballot in the box. That's so everyone will know where everyone stands."

"Then I'll just stay home," Henry countered. "You can take my property. And you can run me off my land, but I ain't agonna vote for secession."

"Suit yourself, Henry. You're a damn Black Republican, and after tomorrow, everyone in the county will know it."

Henry stayed away from the polls on May 23, and the *Register* reported that only twenty-two people in the county dared vote against secession. More than 3,000 voted for it.

"MAKE WAY FOR ROCKINGHAM!" the headline shouted. "The election was the most orderly, quiet and peaceable one we have ever had in the county, no scent of disorder, no interference with the rights and privileges of any citizens occurred at any of the places of voting."

But Sammy told Henry and Peggy a different story. His older brother, H. L., voted at Mount Crawford, a small town seven miles south of Harrisonburg. He had intended to vote against secession, but he changed his mind when he saw that the Mount Crawford Cavalry had turned out in force—ostensibly to ensure order but more obviously to dissuade anyone who might side with the Union. And, sure enough, the ballot was not secret. Each voter had to orally declare his decision. William Jordan, captain of the cavalry, made a big show of voting for secession. Then each member of his militia group voted for secession in order of their rank.

"There was more than thirty of 'em," Sammy said. "They stood around the ballot box defying anyone to vote otherwise. There was one man who was a stranger. When he voted, I don't think he said for or against, he just shouted, 'Secession!' and everyone cheered. But when they opened the box to count up the ballots, they found one vote against, and everyone said it musta come from that stranger who left in a hurry."

"But Sammy, according to the newspaper, *no one* voted against secession at Mount Crawford," Henry said.

"That's just it! Some of Captain Jordan's boys rode out after the stranger and brought him back. I thought they was gonna hang him fer sure, but Reverend Perry preached 'em outta it. He asked the man his name and where he was from, and the stranger said he was John Harrison from Sparta. Reverend Perry told him that he was at the wrong poll, but Mount Crawford would still count his vote if he changed it to secession. So he switched his vote right quick, but they still arrested him and carried him off to the magistrate."

CHAPTER 6

Conscription

*"I will not go to war.
They'll have to bring the war to me."*

Even before the secession vote, volunteer militia companies from Rockingham were already heading north to Winchester to join the Confederate training camps there.

Only a few members of Weavers Church volunteered. The others stayed home, partly because they were opposed to war and partly because Bishop Coffman made it clear that if they volunteered, the church would excommunicate them. And if they were not already members of the church, they would never be allowed to join.

This was how things stood on the fourth Sunday of June when Henry hitched up the spring wagon and made the one-mile trip up Fairview Hill to Weavers Church with Peggy, Johnny, and Mottie. They left the younger children at home with Mary.

"I sure do miss Bishop Burkholder," Henry said, as he guided the wagon around the potholes on the Rawley Road. "He was such a fine fellow—a wise man and a strong leader. I'm not as sure about Sam Coffman yet."

"Well … I was hoping the lot would fall on Daniel," Peggy said. "He knows everybody around here much better than Sam does, but we must bow to the will of the Lord. The lot fell on Sam, not on Daniel, and I'm sure Sam will make a fine bishop."

"I like Sam," Henry mused, "but his sermons put me to sleep, and that worried look is just frozen on his face, even when he smiles. I believe I could plant potatoes between his eyebrows iffen he went two weeks without washin'."

"I wish you wouldn't always have to poke fun at people," Peggy chided. "Do you think Sam talks about *you* on his way to church?"

"Why ... I reckon he does," Henry said, tilting his head skyward, squinting his eyes, and furrowing his brow as if he were trying to look and think like the bishop. "Let's see now. What would Sam say about me? Oh ... I got it! 'Old Henry Rhodes is shorter than short. He sleeps through my sermons and wakes with a snort.' That's what Sam would say about me."

"Well, you're not all that old," Peggy said, "but otherwise ... it fits you."

"I'm older than my years, Peggy. Bishop Burkholder was only forty-three when he died, and he was gettin' along a lot better'n me. I 'spect I'll be lucky to see forty."

"You musn't say such things, Henry. I think you will live to a ripe old age," Peggy lied.

"I reckon you're right. Maybe I just need s'more of Doc's No. 1 medicine and maybe s'more 2, 3, 4, 5, and 6. And iffen Doc ever comes up with a lucky No. 7 medicine, I'm *sure* gonna get me some of that."

❖ ❖ ❖

Fourth-Sunday preaching at Weavers always began promptly at 10 a.m., and Mottie liked to take her place in the women's amen corner no later than quarter till.

The worship service always started with singing, and the music at Weavers had improved dramatically. At Davy's funeral, the mourners sang the melody of each hymn as best they could, but in the two years since then, many of the faithful had taken singing lessons from Timothy Funk. He and his brothers were teaching many Mennonites how to read music and sing in three- and four-part harmonies. These precise harmonies—not to mention the correctly rendered melodies—elevated the Weavers congregants from joyful noisemakers to accomplished singers. And in good weather, such as it was on June 23, latecomers gathered around the open windows of the church to enjoy the sweet sounds of praise.

The preaching, however, had not improved, so some of the outdoor audience may have wandered away from the windows on that Sunday as Bishop Coffman droned on with his message. Henry caught Peggy's eye from across the sanctuary and pretended to nod off and jerk awake. She was not amused.

Halfway through the sermon, Henry and Peggy heard horses galloping into the churchyard followed by boots stomping up the steps to the men's entrance. Many of the worshipers gasped as they turned and watched two soldiers in gray uniforms stride down the aisle between the benches. They took seats in the men's amen corner on the bench behind the deacon and waited for Coffman to finish his message. When the bishop said amen and announced the last hymn, one of the soldiers stood up and stepped into the space between the pulpit and pews. He unfolded a single sheet of paper and read its contents aloud with the most official-sounding voice he could summon.

"To the citizens of Rockingham County, Commonwealth of Virginia, Confederate States of America: On the 21st of June, in obedience to the requisition of His Excellency Jefferson Davis, President of the Confederate States, General Joseph E. Johnston has ordered General Gilbert S. Meem to form two regiments from the Third Division of the Virginia Militia. Pursuant to this order, all men of Rockingham County between the ages of eighteen and forty-five are hereby required to report to the medical boards and enrolling officers of the regimental courts at Harrisonburg on July 1."

Without saying another word, the soldiers walked briskly between the rows of benches and out the men's door.

Nearly all the women and a fair number of the men burst into tears. Coffman returned to the pulpit, shaking noticeably as he stood at the front of the church with his hand raised, waiting for the sobbing to subside. It never did, but he took some time to regain his own composure and to think carefully about what he would say.

"Brothers and sisters," he began, "the time of conflict for our people has arrived, a conflict of spiritual forces involving right and wrong. Each man of military age will have to make a choice, and I am afraid you will have to make it very soon."

After another long pause, he continued. "I pray that each man will make the *right* choice. You all know the church's position on peace and nonresistance, and I encourage you to remember that we are children of God and subject to a higher law than that of man."

The congregation was too choked up to sing the final hymn. As they filed out of the sanctuary, the bishop asked members of the church council to stay behind for a few minutes. Johnny brought the wagon around to the men's door and waited for Henry. After a good half hour, Henry came through the door and down the steps, using the last runner to boost himself into the driver's seat.

"What did the council decide?" Peggy asked.

"Well ... for now ... we have agreed that men who are members of the church or expect to join the church in the future may report to the regimental court, but they must first pledge to the bishop and to God almighty that they will not intentionally kill or harm anyone, no matter what may come to pass."

They rode home in silence. Peggy had never seen Henry so agitated. The thought of her sickly husband marching off to war terrified her, but she did not want to burden Henry with any admission of fear. Finally, as they rode down through the white pine field, Peggy ventured one question.

"What are you going to do come July 1?"

"I haven't figured that out yet, but I'll tell you one thing I won't do. I ain't agonna report to no regimental court. I will not go to war. They'll have to bring the war to me."

Even as many of his Mennonite neighbors reported for duty, Henry still clung to the hope that a compromise might be reached at a peace conference rumored to be taking place on July 4.

On that day, he and Johnny were hauling wheat to the barn and keeping an eye on the peculiar weather. The sky was so hazy they could hardly see the sun. The southern horizon was extremely dark and foreboding, as though a tremendous thunderstorm were brewing, yet there were no distinguishable clouds to indicate rain. The northern horizon was perfectly clear with a straight line running east to west that separated the clear sky from the haze.

On the hazy edge of this celestial divide, there was a comet. It was barely visible in the twilight, but Henry and Johnny were watching it as they brought the day's last load of wheat down through the white pine field. Halfway to the barn, the horses became jittery for no apparent reason. Then Henry and Johnny heard a strange noise that seemed to come from the sky.

As the sound progressed from a low shush to a high shriek, they saw a bright light descending from the tail of the comet. The light moved quickly from west to east, accelerating and growing until it became a ball of fire the size of a bushel basket. It exploded in midair with the sound of a point-blank cannon report and shattered into a dozen pieces that exploded and re-exploded in rapid succession.

All this happened in less than two seconds, but it took longer than that for Henry and Johnny to calm themselves and settle the horses. Then they stared at each other in wide-eyed amazement.

"You said there's no such thing as balls of fire," Johnny gasped.

"That's what I said, sure enough, but I stand corrected. ... I just hope Peggy didn't see that. She'll have fireball night fits for the rest of her days."

❖ ❖ ❖

On Sunday evening, Henry was more eager than ever to read the *Register*. He was hoping to find a sensible explanation for the explosions in the sky, but instead he found nothing but enthusiasm for war. As was his custom, Henry shared the highlights with Peggy.

"Here's a letter addressed 'To the Tunkers, Mennonites, and others opposed to war.' The writer asks if it's right to preach peace, 'when such preaching only weakens the hands of the government in maintaining the position into which, by your votes, you have helped to bring it?'"

"I'm glad you didn't vote for secession," Peggy said. "I don't see how anyone who reads the Bible can turn around and vote for war."

"Well ... this man reads the Bible, but you won't like his interpretation. He says, 'If the government under which you live calls for your services in this war, then by your principles of nonresistance, you cannot refuse—but ought to (as Christ bids you) go for twice the length of time demanded. Second, if the government drafts one of your sons into the militia, you ought to send another as a volunteer.'

"He's talking about going the second mile," Henry explained. "Back in Jesus' day, a Roman soldier could force someone to carry his haversack for one mile, and Jesus said that when that happens, the put-upon person should carry the pack for two miles."

PEGGY'S WAR

"I *know* what he's talking about," Peggy replied, "but there's a world of difference between carrying haversacks and killin' people."

"Well … the man who wrote this letter has an answer for that, too. He says, 'There is no compulsion for you to kill anybody when you go to war, but you can take your own choice of making yourself a target at which the enemy may shoot—and thus carry out your nonresistant principles fully—or you may defend yourself. The battlefield would be one of the very best stages on which to exhibit your deep conviction that all resistance is wrong. Yours kindly, Ne Qui Nimis."

"What a funny name," Peggy remarked.

"Ain't nothin' funny about this man," Henry scoffed. "He knows his Bible, but he twists its edicts to fit his politics."

Some of the Mennonite men did exactly what Ne Qui Nimis suggested—they went to war and became defenseless targets—but Henry and some of his neighbors stayed home. And in the middle of July, the conscription scouts came looking for them.

Sammy told Henry and Peggy that Michael Shank, who lived near the Pike Church, was carried away by eight Confederate soldiers.

"I got the whole story from his near neighbor," Sammy said. "The scouts carried him off in his shirt sleeves and dirty clothes in a wagon. I sure don't want anyone doin' me that way."

Sammy had come to the Rhodes place to tell Henry that the regimental court had granted him a medical exemption because he suffered from consumption. He showed Henry his exemption papers and volunteered to help with the summer harvest.

"I get coughin' spells jus' like you do," Sammy said, "but I can still work on most days."

"I will take whatever help you can give," Henry replied. "You can stay in the tenant house again, and I will pay you one dollar for every day you are able to work."

❖ ❖ ❖

On Sammy's first full day on the farm, two conscription scouts came looking for Henry, who had retreated to the parlor to escape the afternoon heat. Henry immediately recognized one of the scouts as a Secesh neighbor that he tried to love but failed to like.

"Good afternoon, Mr. Rhodes. We're so sorry to disturb you," the scout said sarcastically, "but we're having a little war here in Virginia, and we want you to know that you are cordially invited."

"I ain't goin' to any war any where," Henry replied. "You can drag me to Winchester iffen you please, but I ain't agoin' voluntary."

"Maybe it won't come to that. The enrolling officer might say you're too short, or the medical board might decide you're too sick. Our job is to take you to Harrisonburg. That don't necessarily mean you're goin' to Winchester."

"I *am* short, and I *am* sick," Henry replied. "So why don't you boys jus' leave me alone?"

"You don't seem too sick to come with us to Harrisonburg, and that's all we're askin' of you. Now are you gonna saddle your horse and ride to town like a man? Or are we gonna have to tie you to your horse and carry you to town like a dead doe?"

"It's been nearly six months since I set foot in Harrisonburg for anything," Henry said. "And I doubt that I will ever go there again. I'm too sick to travel."

"If you're so damn sick, how come yer farm looks like it's doin' just fine?"

"I have a boy who lives with us and takes care of things for me."

"Oh, yeah ... well ... I saw a whole heap 'a kids runnin' around outside," said the sarcastic scout, as he leaned down and pressed his face close to Henry's. "So I guess you're not too sick to make babies; or does your hired boy take care of that, too?"

Henry choked on this insult and coughed violently before he could cover his mouth. Bright red droplets of blood spritzed across the scout's face.

The angry rebel jumped back, wiped the blood on his sleeve, and cursed Henry black and blue. "You ain't nothin' but a runt, a galvanized Yankee runt!" he fumed. "I'll tell the regimental court that you're not fit to fight, but you'll regret this day. Mark my words, Henry Rhodes: You *will* regret this day."

As soon as the scouts stormed out of the house, Peggy rushed to Henry and said, "You never had a hemorrhage before. I'm going to go get Doc."

"Please don't do that," Henry said. "Just sit with me for a minute. I have something to confess."

Peggy sat down and waited for Henry to speak. After a long pause, he said, "I was getting very angry at my neighbor. I was beginning to think hateful thoughts about him, and I was tempted to say things to him that shouldn't be said to anyone, so I didn't say anything. I just bit the inside of my bottom lip and coughed."

CHAPTER 7

The Perfect Place
*"The roof leaks, the floor creaks,
and the walls ain't got no plaster."*

Panic gripped the residents of Rockingham on July 21. Word spread quickly that gangs of escaped slaves were roaming the countryside killing white men, raping their wives, and snatching their children. Henry and Peggy did not believe it, but Sammy did.

"We'll all be dead by morning," he insisted. "And then … I'll jus' say, 'I told you so.'"

Sammy was not alone in his unfounded fear. Many people in the valley were terrified, but they soon discovered that the story was nothing more than rumors run amok.

Unfortunately, the dreadful news that arrived by telegraph on the following day turned out to be true. The Confederate rebels had routed the Union regulars at Manassas, a small Virginia town about thirty miles west of Washington. There were heavy casualties on both sides, but the federal forces had retreated in disarray, dashing Henry's hopes for a quick war.

The August 2 *Register* reveled in the gory details of the battle, including the abortive attempts by Confederate troops to bury the remains of Union soldiers: "They were compelled, because of the horrid stench of the rotten Yankees, to retreat from the field they had so gloriously won, and abandon the humane undertaking."

Henry was shocked that the rebels had won the first battle of the war, and he was deeply concerned that Secesh Southerners would begin to believe that God was on their side, but he thought it best to keep such worries to himself.

"That's only once," he said to Peggy. "Next time will be different; the North are sure to overcome because they are in the right."

Peggy desperately wanted to believe her husband, but her persistent nightmares of fire and destruction were far more convincing than Henry's undaunted declarations of right and wrong.

Johnny did most of the field work that summer, with help from Peggy's father and brother, because no other neighbors were available for hire. Sammy worked as much as he was able, but he had become nearly as weak with consumption as Henry.

All the farms in the valley were shorthanded, but help was on the way. General Thomas "Stonewall" Jackson knew that the soldiers of his Valley District would starve if the farms did not remain productive, so he granted furloughs that allowed many Mennonites and Dunkers to tend their farms in the fall. They rode the railroad cars from Winchester to Mount Jackson and walked home from there. Many of them cheered loudly when they caught sight of Mole Hill on the horizon.

Most of the Mennonite men were reluctant to talk about their experiences in the war, but Christian Good, on leave from the 146th Virginia Militia, told his story after Sunday worship at Weavers Church. Henry and Johnny and Doc were among the men and boys who gathered around Good in the oak grove behind the church to hear what he had to say.

"I got caught up in a battle, but I stuck to my pledge," Good insisted. "Some of the soldiers told the captain that I did not shoot, and he asked me if this was true. I admitted that it was, and he asked me *why* I didn't shoot. I told him that I didn't see anything to shoot at, and he said, 'Didn't you see all those Yankees?' And I said, 'Yes. I saw them, but Yankees are people, and I don't shoot people.' The captain threatened to court-martial me and have me shot, but I told him that I would not kill anyone no matter what he did to me."

"What did he say to that?" Doc asked.

"Well … if it had been jus' me, I think he woulda rode me on a rail till I had no chance at children, but all the Mennonite and Dunker boys stuck to their pledges, so I reckon he figured he'd try something diff'rent to keep his company together. Most of us eventually got detailed as teamsters or cooks."

"Did the other soldiers hate you for not holding up your end of the fight?" Johnny asked.

"I reckon some of 'em did," Good replied, "but I'll tell you one thing that helped with that. At night, some of us Mennonite and Dunker boys would get together and sing hymns. At first, we just sang the hymns we knew best by heart, and then we took a notion to sing some songs that the other fellas might know. When we sang 'Am I a Soldier of the Cross,' I thought those boys was gonna cry."

While Good continued telling his story, Doc pulled Henry aside.

"I would like to invite myself and some friends to your house this evening for a private meeting," Doc said, in a confidential tone.

"Fine with me," Henry said, "who all's gonna be there?"

"It'll be me and you and maybe eight or nine other men."

"Do I know these people? Cause my house ain't hardly fixed for proper company."

"Don't worry about that," Doc replied. "I think your house will be fine. In fact, I'd say it's the perfect place."

"Ain't nothin' perfect about my place. It's right big, but the roof leaks, the floor creaks, and the walls ain't got no plaster."

PEGGY'S WAR

"It's the perfect place for what I have in mind," Doc assured him. "But you musn't tell anyone about this meeting. It's very important to keep it secret. Do you understand?"

"I won't tell a soul 'cept Peggy. I kinda have to tell Peggy."

"That's fine. Tell Peggy we'll be there around 10 o'clock and not to go to any trouble."

"Alright, Doc, we'll look for considerable company late tonight."

The puzzled look on Henry's face was still there as he climbed up onto the wagon seat beside Peggy.

"What did Uncle Gabe want?" Peggy asked.

"I'm not entirely sure, but he's invitin' eight or nine men to our house tonight at 10 o'clock for some sorta secret meeting. He said not to say anything about this to anyone 'cept you. He said our house is 'the perfect place.' What do you s'pose he meant by that?"

At the appointed hour, six men arrived at the Rhodes place—Doc, John Brunk, David Hartman, Daniel Good, Jacob Shank, and John Wenger. Brunk and Hartman brought their teenage sons, Chris Brunk and Peter Hartman, who were Johnny's close friends from Weavers Church.

Henry was surprised that Doc had invited Wenger to this clandestine meeting. Wenger was a fine upstanding man, a prosperous farmer who lived just south of the church, but he had recently left the Mennonite church to join with the Dunkers.

Peggy welcomed the men and boys and brought them two pots of coffee and three plates of freshly baked apple butter pigs.

Doc turned to Johnny, Peter, and Chris and said, "You boys take your pigs outside. I want you to keep careful watch and tell me right away if you see anyone approaching the house. Johnny, you watch out front. Chris, you watch out back. And, Peter, you make sure no one sneaks up behind the barn. Watch and listen just as closely as you know how, and don't make any noise."

"Yessir," the boys said in unison, as they claimed their apple butter pigs and slipped outside.

"Well ... if you gentlemen will excuse me, I will tend to my sewing in the other room," Peggy said. "Give me a holler if you run outta coffee, and I'll fix you another pot."

Soon after Peggy shut the bedroom door, Johnny burst into the house and said he could see a light moving along the lane between the house and the Dayton Road.

"Looks like two riders," Johnny said. "One of 'em is carryin' a lantern that don't seem to be workin' right."

"That's the sign I'm looking for," Doc said, as he got up from the table and followed Johnny onto the porch. A few minutes later, Doc ushered two men into the house. They were both Dunkers: Daniel Bowman, who owned a large grist mill near Dayton, and Elder John Kline, a preacher who lived in Broadway, a small town about ten miles north of Harrisonburg.

Henry considered Bowman to be honest and trustworthy. He always paid top dollar for wheat and charged a fair price for flour. Henry had never met Kline, but he knew his reputation as one of the most respected Dunker elders in Virginia. Kline was in his sixty-fifth year, but he had the bearing and constitution of a much younger man. He was somewhat short and stocky with a large round symmetrical face and long white hair parted precisely across the middle of his crown. He maintained a bushy beard on his chin and cheeks but no stubble whatsoever between his nose and upper lip.

"You all know Daniel Bowman," Doc began, "but you may not know John Kline. He has been an elder for many years among the Dunkers and a botanical doctor among all the people of the valley and beyond. Elder Kline has traveled extensively through the mountains west of the Shenandoah and befriended more people there than the rest of us put together."

"Doc exaggerates my importance," Kline said modestly. "But it is true that I have enjoyed more than my share of hospitality among the mountain people. And those longstanding bonds of fellowship have put me in a unique position to make a simple suggestion to you regarding our mutual conviction against war.

"It has become my considered opinion that Dunkers and Mennonites must work together to keep our members and our young men out of the rebellion. Many of the brethren have already expressed to me their determination to flee from their homes rather than disobey God. What I propose is an underground railroad like the one that conducts runaway slaves to the North. The escape routes would run through the homes of loyal Union men, mostly Dunkers and Mennonites, who would give our refugees safe places to assemble until a pilot can take them through the mountains."

Doc explained that he had been discussing this idea with Kline and Bowman ever since the Battle of Manassas. Now, with many of the reluctant soldiers home on furlough, the time seemed right to set such a plan in motion.

"Like everyone in this room, I thought the war would be short, but the rebel victories at Manassas and in Missouri have changed my thinking," Doc said. "We're telling our young men they must not go to war, yet it's impossible for all of them to hide here in the valley, so we must give them a way out, a reasonable means of escape."

"What we need, more than anything, is safe gathering places," Kline said. "We need depots within a few miles of the Shenandoah Mountain, where four or five men can hide for several days without fear of being discovered. We also need pilots—men who know the mountains beyond the Shenandoah—to conduct large groups to New Creek, where they can catch the cars of the B&O Railroad."

Doc pointed to Henry and said: "This morning after preaching, I told Henry that this house right here is the perfect place. Do you know now what I meant by that?"

"I believe I do," Henry answered. "This house is close to the Rawley Road and the Dayton Road, but it ain't visible from either one. The farm is rimmed by woods, yet there's open fields between the woods and house on all four sides, so no one can come close without bein' seen. This here's the perfect place for hidin' draft dodgers and deserters."

"You're also close to the church, where I'm already hidin' some men," Brunk added. "A refugee leavin' the church could slip across the Rawley Road, duck into the trees on the other side, and stick to the woods till he arrives on this farm."

"It's the same way comin' and goin' from my place," Wenger said. "They could cut through the woods on Fairview Hill and make it to your farm without being seen."

"My home is not as well-situated," Hartman said. "I am surrounded by Secesh neighbors who watch me closely, but I will gladly do my part."

"I'll help any way I can, but I wanna hear what Peggy says first," Henry hedged. "I suffer from consumption, and I'm gettin' weaker by the week. My wife has her hands full takin' care of me and the children and the house and the farm. On top of all that, what you're talkin' about sounds downright dangerous to me."

"It *will* be dangerous," Doc conceded, "but your failing health is another reason why this is the perfect place. Eventually, the conscription scouts will give up on you, if they haven't already, and since Johnny's a long way from eighteen, they might leave this place entirely untouched."

After the men left, Peggy emerged from the downstairs bedroom with a puzzled look on her face.

"I reckon you heard most of that," Henry said, with a grin.

"I did hear some of it but not everything. What did Uncle Gabe mean about our house being the perfect place?"

"Doc wants me to dig a cellar under the house."

"I don't understand. We already have a fine root cellar."

"Not like this one. This cellar's not for storing turnips and taters; it's for hiding turncoats and traitors. Doc wants me to dig a secret cellar for hiding deserters and draft dodgers."

"The young men of the church are not turncoats or traitors," Peggy said. "They are loyal to the church; they are true to their faith. They are trying to obey the Word of God."

"I agree," Henry said, "but the men who come lookin' for 'em—and they *will* come lookin'—won't see it that way. If they find men hidin' under our house, they'll treat 'em like turncoats, and they'll punish us like traitors."

"So what did you tell Uncle Gabe?"

"I told him that I would leave it up to you."

"Me? Since when do you need my permission? You've never asked my blessing for anything, and I trust you to do what's best for the family."

"This might *not* be what's best for the family," Henry replied. "That's what I'm tryin' to tell you. This cellar will be dangerous for all of us, even the children, and you'll be the one to bear the burden. I will do what little I can, but before long, I will not be much use to you, and before this war is over, I will be dead."

"Please don't say such things," Peggy pleaded.

"I'll keep sayin' it till you hear it. You are about to give birth to our sixth child, and Mary is the only one old enough to give you much help. This is all gonna fall on you."

"What did Uncle Gabe say?" Peggy deflected.

"Well ... this is mostly his idea, him and Elder Kline, so he's all for it. He says he'll help us, but Doc might be too old to make good on that promise."

"And what did you say?"

"I agreed with them, but I worry about you hidin' draft dodgers and—worse yet—deserters under the house."

"Henry, you're starting to sound like Bishop Coffman with all your worrying. It seems to me like it's already decided."

"No it ain't. Nothin's decided. I told 'em I'd leave it up to you."

"You really told them that?"

"I surely did."

"Well then ... if it's up to me ... I'd say we need another cellar."

In the morning, Johnny ran a message to Doc, who said he would send a carpenter to help Henry fashion a trap door. Two of Doc's sons were good coopers, but Doc trusted the job to Abram Swartz, the young craftsman who had built little Davy's coffin. Swartz had become an excellent carpenter, but more importantly, he was raccoon clever.

Swartz arrived on the following day, lugging a large toolbox that he perched on the porch. Then he asked Henry where he should put the trap door.

"I want you to put it where the conscription scouts won't find it," Henry replied.

"I vas hoping dat's vat you vould say," Swartz jested, with an exaggerated German accent.

He motioned for Henry to follow him around the north side of the house to the root cellar entrance beside the chimney. He opened the door, descended the steps, and explored the small storehouse for a minute or two. Then he climbed out and paced off the distance between the cellar door and the back corner of the house.

"What's in this corner?" he asked.

"That's our bedroom."

"Is there much space under there?"

"It's too tight for you, but I could crawl up in there if you tell me what you're lookin' for."

"I'm lookin' for rocks."

"Rocks? What kinda rocks?"

"Big rocks that would make it impossible to dig. I don't wanna cut a hole in your bedroom floor and then find out you can't dig there."

"You want me to crawl under there and scratch around with a knife or what?"

"You'd do better with an ice pick. You can use the space between the floor joists to swing the hammer enough to tap the ice pick into the ground. I want you to do this every two feet in every direction between the root cellar wall and the back corner of the house. Can you do that?"

"I 'spect I can. I ain't as spry as I used to be, but I'm thinner than I ever was."

Henry put a hammer and ice pick in a small bag with two tallow candles and a box of matches. He tied the bag onto his belt and crawled through a small opening in the limestone foundation. There was plenty of space to maneuver under the front rooms, but then Henry had to squeeze under a beam that ran the length of the house. It was a tight fit, even for a thin man, but Henry made it through and started working his way toward the back corner."

"Are you there yet?" Swartz hollered.

"Not yet. Hold on while I light a candle. ... Alright. I see one big rock, but that's about it. Let's see what the ice pick turns up."

The ice pick easily penetrated the soil, and Henry found evidence of only one more sizable rock near the far corner of the house.

"I think it'll be alright," Henry announced, as he emerged from the crawl space. I don't know what we'll find after we dig down a foot or two, but we should be able to hide at least two or three men down there."

Henry washed up in the creek and took Swartz inside to look at the bedroom floor. The carpenter pushed aside a rag rug and picked his spot beside the bed.

"Can I borrow yer ax?" he asked.

Johnny fetched the tool from behind the front door and handed it to Swartz.

"Stand back!" the carpenter warned, as he swung the ax high over his head and slammed it down into the floorboards, sending splinters in every direction.

"Hey! Stop that!" Henry objected. You're bustin' up good wood."

"That I am," Swartz said with a grin. "But this way, if anyone asks why these floorboards don't match, you can honestly say that the old ones were damaged and had to be replaced."

Henry stared at Swartz for two full seconds, trying to process this preconceived deception. He squinted at the floor, nodding his head in guarded approval. Then he smiled in sheer admiration.

"Alright then! That's good thinkin', Swartzy. I'm sorry I yelled at you. I see now that you're the right man for this job—in more ways than one, I'd say."

Next Swartz marked several floorboards for cutting, outlining a rather large, irregular shape.

"Looks bigger'n need be," Henry observed.

"Tis bigger'n need be," Swartz agreed, with a grin. "If I was making a trap door, I'd make it small and square between the joists, but I'm replacing damaged floorboards. Right?"

"I get it," Henry said. "It won't look like a trap door at all. It'll look like a jackleg repair job."

"Jackleg Swartz at yer service, sir," the carpenter said, as he began drilling small holes along the lines he had marked on the floor. Then he used a chisel to cut the boards at various splicing points on the floor joists and carefully cut new boards to fill the opening. He put them in place and tacked two thin laths across the deceptive door to hold the wood together temporarily. Then he flipped the entire assembly over and nailed two permanent crosspieces to the underside. He flipped it again and pried the temporary laths off the top.

"There she be. What say you?"

"It looks pretty good," Henry replied. "But I kinda wisht you hadn't used that board in the middle with the knot hole."

"Looks like somethin' a jackleg would overlook," Swartz said with a wink. "But I don't see a knot hole at all. I see a trap door *handle*." He reached down, stuck his middle finger through the hole, and lifted the door easily with one hand.

"Mighty handy hole," Henry said, "but what's to keep some conscription scout from doin' the same thing?"

"Well ... I ain't done yet. What this jackleg job needs now is some special nails."

Swartz used short cut nails to tack the trap door lightly down to the floor joists. Then he pried the door up to show Henry how easily the nubby little nails vacated their holes.

"I still say it comes up too easy," Henry said.

"Well ... these nails is jus' for looks and to line up the door. Now I'll show you how to fool the scouts. Johnny says you have some old bridles. Can I have 'em?"

"Sure you can. Johnny, go fetch 'em from the barn."

Swartz used the worn-out bridles to fashion a leather sling that he attached to the underside of the trap door.

"We'll find a big rock that someone in the cellar can put in this here sling to hold the door down tight if anyone takes a notion to pry it open," Swartz explained.

As soon as Abram finished the job and packed up his tools, Henry and Johnny started digging. They quickly discovered that the width between the floor joists was barely big enough for Johnny to maneuver. Henry was a better fit, but he had lost a lot of strength since the day when he dug Davy's grave, and his endurance faltered every few minutes.

They had to work around a few boulders that protruded into the new cellar, but after several days of persistent digging, they had hollowed out a hiding place about four feet deep, six feet wide, and ten feet long. Then Johnny dug a trench behind the house to channel any rainwater away from the big hole.

One month after Henry and Johnny completed the secret cellar, Peggy gave birth to a healthy baby boy. He was born on November 7, 1861, the day after Jefferson Davis was elected president of the Confederate States.

"Let's name him William," Henry suggested.

"That's fine with me," Peggy said, "but where did you come up with that name?"

"Well … Doc keeps tellin' me I oughta make a will," he joked. "Maybe now he'll leave me alone about that."

So they named the baby William Henry Rhodes, and Henry, of course, called him Willy.

While the Rhodes family made room for its sixth child, the Rhodes depot welcomed its first deserter, a straggler from the Thirty-Seventh Virginia Infantry. He had abandoned his regiment as it approached Harrisonburg on its way from Monterey to Manassas.

PEGGY'S WAR

After his regiment and three others passed through town, large-scale troop movements came to a halt in Rockingham as armies on both sides settled into their winter camps.

Almost every day in January brought at least some rain, sleet, or snow, but the secret cellar and its lone occupant stayed tolerably dry and reasonably warm. Then, in late February, the weather turned nice enough for Johnny and Peggy to re-employ the plow. This early onset of spring also reminded the Dunker and Mennonite men that their farming furloughs were about to expire, and their militia captains would soon expect them to return to Winchester.

By the first week of March, the Rhodes depot was concealing three deserters and three draft dodgers, and Peggy remembered what Henry had said about everything falling on her.

CHAPTER 8

Sword of the Spirit
"Why do you Dunkers keep tryin' to give us yer Bibles?"

On the second Monday of March, Mary burst through the front door and breathlessly reported that a man was walking north along Cooks Creek toward the house.

"Dinner's over. Get in the cellar!" Peggy commanded, as she scrambled to clear the extra forks from the table.

The six refugees had been hiding at the Rhodes depot long enough to know the drill. They dashed into the downstairs bedroom and closed the door behind them. One by one, they slipped through the opening in the floor, with the last man pulling the trap door snugly into place.

Peggy listened at the bedroom door until all was quiet. Then she went inside and stomped on the trap door to seat the nail stubs and let the refugees know to put the rock in the harness and keep quiet. Peggy slid the rug over the trap door and returned to the kitchen.

Mary poked her head back inside the front door, and said, "It's alright, Mama. It's just Sammy."

Peggy went out onto the porch and greeted Sammy, as Henry crossed the creek from the barn to see what his nephew needed.

Sammy, it turned out, was mostly seeking advice. Governor Letcher was calling for another 40,000 soldiers, so all men of militia age who were previously exempt had to report to the courthouse on March 14.

"My consumption is doin' some better," Sammy said, "so I might not get another medical exemption. It also struck my mind that maybe this was some trap they are plotting to get the men together and take them right into the army."

"You can hide here," Henry offered, "but you'll have to stay in the cellar all night every night, and you'll have to get in the cellar whenever someone comes to the house during the day. Do you think you could abide by that?"

"Nawsir. I don't reckon I could. I don't think my health would tolerate it."

"Well … if you don't wanna hide, your other choice is to go through the mountains with a refugee train, and that would be even harder on your health. March can be cold and windy and wet, and it's a long walk from here to Yankeedom."

Sammy thought for a minute and said, "I think I can tolerate the walkin' better than the hidin'."

Henry stared silently at Sammy for a long time before he spoke.

"You musn't tell this to anyone," he finally said. "Do you understand me? Not *anyone*, not even your mother."

"Not even my mother," Sammy echoed. "I understand."

"A refugee train will leave on Thursday night at 10 p.m. from Whissen's Mill near the Bank Church. About fifty men are meeting there. Don't be late, but don't be more than fifteen minutes early. Bring enough provisions for one week. Do you understand?"

"I understand."

Henry thought for a moment, then decided to amend his instructions: "Now that I study on it, there is one person I want you to tell. See if your brother, H. L., will go with you. Tell him that I'd feel better if you and him was together on this train."

"I'll tell him you said that. He's been drivin' teams for the rebels for more than a month now, and I think he's had about enough of that. I'll see what he says."

❖   ❖   ❖

It rained nearly all day on Thursday, March 13. Cooks Creek was starting to rise, and the Rhodes depot was overflowing with refugees waiting for a guide to take them to the hideout at the foot of the mountains.

Among the fugitives was twenty-nine-year-old Peter Blosser, a deacon of the church, who was married to one of Sammy's sisters. While Peggy helped the other men pack their provisions into haversacks, Henry pulled Blosser aside and asked him to look after Sammy.

"I think H. L. will be on this train, too, and I'm sure he'll keep an eye on Sammy, but it might take both of you to keep that boy outta trouble. Sammy will say he don't need help, but I'd appreciate it if you would let him ride your horse every now 'n' agin."

"Of course," Blosser replied. "I'll do anything I can for Sam. You know that. Are Sam and H. L. meeting us here?"

"No. Sammy went home to fetch H. L. and gather some supplies, but you should see 'em at the mountain depot."

Before the clock struck nine, Mary rushed into the house with another warning: "There's one rider and two walkers coming down through the white pine field with a flickering light."

"That should be the guide," Henry said. "I'll go see for sure. Keep an eye on me from the bedroom window, Peggy. If all's well, I'll bring 'em straight here, but if it ain't the guide, I'll stall 'em long enough for you to squeeze everyone into the cellar."

Henry left by the back door and greeted the visitors about 100 yards from the house. Peggy witnessed only a brief exchange before the men hurried down the hill, so she went out on the porch to welcome them. The two walkers were thirty-six-year-old Henry Brunk and twenty-seven-year-old Charles Rodgers. They had become nearly inseparable after marrying two of Peggy's first cousins, both daughters of Uncle John Heatwole, who was also a near neighbor. Brunk and Rodgers had been dodging the draft for nine months, so Peggy was not surprised to see them. She was shocked, however, to discover that the rider was fifteen-year-old Peter Hartman. She could not imagine why Peter's father would involve him in the underground at such a young age.

"How many refugees do you have?" Peter inquired.

"Eight men and one horse, and that's more than I can handle," Peggy replied, "so I sure hope this train goes north tonight. Are you the guide?"

"I am."

"Aren't you mighty young for such doins?"

"I'm old enough to take cattle to the mountain for summer pasture," Peter boasted, "and I reckon that mindful men drive easier than senseless steers. Either way, I'm the only one here who knows where the mountain hideout is, so you're stuck with me. We've got less than three hours to get there. Is everyone ready?"

"None of these boys are in a hurry to leave their families," Peggy replied, "but they're all past ready to stop hiding under my house."

Blosser emerged from the barn with his horse, and the men followed Peter north along Cooks Creek toward the Rawley Road. Peter led them seven miles farther north, cutting across fields and through patches of woods to avoid the roads as much as possible. They arrived at Sam Beery's place at the foot of Little North Mountain just before midnight. About sixty-five men were waiting in the woods behind the house, including five of Doc's sons, two sons-in-law, and two grandsons.

"This looks more like a Heatwole get-together than a refugee train," Brunk observed.

Blosser counted about as many Dunkers as Mennonites among the men, and a few of them were not associated with either church. He searched for Sammy and H. L., but they weren't there yet, so he asked Beery for a favor.

"If you see Sam Rhodes or H. L. Rhodes in the next few minutes, tell them which way we went. I'll hang back for a while at the rear of the train."

❖   ❖   ❖

The leader of the group was fifty-three-year-old Daniel Suter. He was well above militia age, but he was the only one in the group who knew the way to New Creek, where they planned to take the cars of the B&O.

It took Suter only a few minutes to get the men and horses organized and moving west. They began by crossing the southern end of Little North Mountain instead of going directly through Hopkins Gap because Beery had warned Suter that conscription scouts were patrolling the pass. Little North Mountain was in fact a small mountain, but crossing even a small mountain without the benefit of a trail was tricky at night, especially in the rain, so the men and horses moved slowly and deliberately.

"This ain't so bad except for the rain," Rodgers said.

"Actually, I'm glad for it," Brunk responded. "Just think how much noise our horses would make if these woods was dry."

Brunk was right. The thirty-plus horses and seventy-plus men were crushing thousands of sticks and compressing countless leaves under hoof and foot. But the soggy ground softened the sounds of their escape, which were further obscured by billions of raindrops cascading through the trees, peppering the forest floor, and sustaining the constant reassuring sound of shhhhhhhhh.

There was little chance that conscription scouts down in the gap could hear them, but Brunk was a cautious man; he and Rodgers stopped talking and followed the men and horses in front of them as quietly as they could. It took them two hours to go up the small mountain and down the other side, where they spilled out onto a wagon road that took them north by northeast.

After another two hours of walking and riding, the entourage branched off onto a smaller path that went straight north behind Third Mountain. As the sky became lighter, the path connected with Brock's Gap Road, and the fugitives followed this better route north for six miles along the North Fork of the Shenandoah River. Then they turned left and headed west-by-northwest on a smaller wagon road that ran beside one of the river's tributaries.

Right before noon, they passed through the small settlement of Dovesville. Despite the town's innocuous name, there were no nonresistant allies waiting for them there. The younger men of Dovesville, many of them proud members of Brock's Gap Rifles, had dutifully returned to the war, and their wives, sisters, and parents resented the sight of able-bodied men running scared through the mountains.

"You're goin' the wrong way, you damn cowards!" a haggard old woman shouted from the front porch of a simple farmhouse. "The war's back down there in the valley!"

About two miles past the tiny town, Brunk caught his first glimpse of a large mountain looming ahead of them as they began to slowly ascend the Shenandoah. The group had been walking slightly uphill for several hours, but now the incline was becoming much steeper. Brunk's leg muscles were starting to burn with exertion as the road wound toward a gap that was surprisingly flat at the apex of the pass. The men rested there, at the westernmost reaches of Rockingham, while the horses grazed in a grassy clearing.

"I sure do wish the girls and the children could go with us," Rodgers said sadly. "It might be a long time till we see them again."

Rodgers was married to Magdalene Heatwole, and they had three children, the oldest not quite five and the youngest not yet one. Brunk was married to Magdalene's younger sister, Susanna, and their only child, John Albert, was between one and two.

"I feel so guilty for leaving them," Brunk said. "Two years before I married Susanna, I promised to take care of her and her brother, R. J. They had no one, and now I'm afraid they'll have no one again."

"The girls have each other," Rodgers reminded him, "and they have plenty of aunts and uncles and cousins. We will send for them when we get settled in Maryland."

"I hope so, but it might be a long wait. There ain't hardly any letters going back and forth between North and South right now, so they won't even know if we made it or not."

The road on the other side of the Shenandoah sloped down gently at first, and it felt good to be walking downhill for a change. As it became steeper, Brunk's tired knees and feet started to ache, but after another hour, the downhill grade became more forgiving as the road descended into Peru Hollow.

At twilight, the men and horses splashed through Rohrbaugh Run and arrived on the farm of Nimrod and Mary Ann Judy. They waited until the sky was completely dark, then Suter approached the house, while everyone else stayed in the woods. After a few minutes, he came back and told the refugees to turn their horses out into the pasture with Judy's cows and enter the house by the back door.

As Brunk and Rodgers emerged from the woods, they were surprised to see such a large house and barn in such a remote mountain valley. They followed the other men through the back door as the group crowded into the kitchen, dining room, and parlor, with some of them spilling into two downstairs bedrooms.

Nimrod waited until everyone had squeezed into the house. Then he invited them to sit if they could find a spot. He was a stern-looking man of fifty-two years with deep-set eyes, a hawkish nose, a long bushy beard, and a full head of hair that was going gray.

"Welcome to Judy's on the South Fork," he said. "My name's Nimrod Judy and this here's my wife, Mary Ann. We wasn't expecting near this much company, but we're glad to see all of you. Mary Ann is fixin' supper, and while she's doin' that, I'll help you tend yer horses and find places to bed down either here in the house or out in the barn."

At the Judy place, Brunk began to feel somewhat safer. He and Rodgers ate plenty of creamed corn and smoked ham, and they slept soundly on piles of straw in the barn. In the morning, their host told Suter that the way to Petersburg was clear at last report, but he was not sure what they would find there. (Later in the war, this town became Petersburg, West Virginia.)

"There are Union pickets camped to the north," Judy said. "They ain't likely to bother you, but the Confederate irregulars might run 'em out at any time, and those home guard boys would be mighty resentful of a big gang of Dunkers headin' north. But … you gotta cross the South Branch of the Potomac somewheres, and with all this rain, the ford at Petersburg is yer best bet."

As the men prepared to leave, Mary Ann served up a huge pot of maple oatmeal, enough for each man to fill his belly for breakfast. Then the refugees thanked the Judys for their hospitality and started making their way toward Petersburg. Following Nimrod's directions, Suter led them north along the South Fork for about four miles before turning left onto a wagon road that crossed South Fork Mountain via Ketterman's Gap. Near the top of the mountain, Elder Kline's trusted friend, Adam Ketterman, told them that Petersburg was not currently occupied by either army.

Encouraged by this news, the refugees confidently crossed another sizable ridge and arrived at the ford across the South Branch of the Potomac, with the buildings of the town clearly visible on the other side. A teenage boy offered to take them across two or three at a time on his ferry, but Suter decided that would cost too much and take too long.

"You best be careful," the boy warned. "You don't know this ford, and with the river running high and fast, it's a heap more dangerous than it looks."

The river was about fifty yards wide, and it would indeed prove difficult to ford. Brunk and Rodgers waded into the ice-cold water, but less than halfway across, the strong current swept them to a spot where they could no longer touch bottom. Brunk did not know how to swim, and his flailing arms became entangled in the straps of his floating haversack. As he struggled frantically to free himself from his provisions, his head dipped under the water for a few seconds, and he experienced a surge of fear that was more intense than any he had ever known. He wanted to scream for help, but he instinctively closed his mouth and held his breath. When his head bobbed back above the surface, he saw Rodgers clinging to the branch of a large tree that had fallen into the river. Rodgers grabbed Brunk by the haversack and pulled him to the relative safety of the tree. Then they started working their way back to the shallows by moving from branch to branch.

When Brunk was finally able to stand on the bottom of the river, he felt a great sense of relief and no small amount of gratitude.

"Thank you for saving me," Brunk said. "I thought I was gonna drown."

"You're welcome," Rodgers replied, "and we best thank God for felling that tree right where he did."

As Brunk and Rodgers waded back to the ford, they saw that several of the other men were having similar problems. A few made it across without the help of horses, but most of them retreated to the south side of the river.

The young ferry operator, who was busy fishing fugitives from the water, called out to the two dozen men who had made it across with their horses.

"You gotta take yer horses back over to get everyone across," he shouted. "You'll need at least one horse for every two men."

Convinced now that the boy knew his business, Suter advised the refugees to follow the teenager's instructions. It took two more trips to get everyone across the river, a clamorous undertaking that entertained the townsfolk who had gathered on the other shore to watch. The soaking-wet entourage trudged up the embankment and through the village without further difficulty, but the silent citizens of Petersburg showed no signs of sympathy.

With the raging river behind them, Brunk was starting to feel safe again, but about one mile north of town—thirty miles shy of New Creek—two men wearing mismatched Confederate uniforms came up quickly from behind on horseback. They galloped past the group and stopped at a narrow bend in the road. One soldier leveled his rifle at Joseph Heatwole, who was riding in front, and ordered him to halt.

Heatwole turned in his saddle and exclaimed, "Oh, brethren! Pray mightily unto God, and he will deliver us!"

"Shut up!" shouted the man with the rifle. "You needn't pray for deliverance. God done delivered you to *me*."

PEGGY'S WAR

❖   ❖   ❖

Within a few minutes, three more irregular rebels caught up with the group, and the five captors herded the seventy-plus refugees back toward Petersburg. As they approached the town, Brunk and Rodgers struck up a conversation with one of the guards at the rear of the train. He spoke kindly to them and apologized for his role in detaining the group.

"I'm sorry to be part of this," he admitted.

"Are you boys Virginia volunteers?" Brunk asked.

"We used to be, but now we're parolees. We was captured by Union patrols, and they let us go after we took the oath of allegiance to the Union. By my own word of honor, I have no right to bother you."

One of the other parolees overheard the repentant rebel and cursed him brutally.

"Don't you dare feel sorry for these deserters. They are traitors to Virginia and a disgrace to the South. The damn Union rascals ought to be shot, and if you don't see it that way, then maybe you ought to be shot right along with 'em."

With no further discussion, the parolees took the prisoners to a room on the second floor of a large building in Petersburg. At the top of the stairs, the guards ordered each man to surrender his weapons before entering the room, and the captives produced two small pistols, a few penknives, and dozens of pocket Testaments.

"Why do you Dunkers keep tryin' to give us yer Bibles?" asked the man at the door.

"You said to surrender our weapons," one Dunker replied, "and the New Testament is the Sword of the Spirit."

"Ah ... that is very good, you can keep that kind of sword."

After the prisoners got something to eat, eight guards marched them fourteen miles south along the Franklin Road to John Bond's place near the confluence of Brushy Run and North Mill Creek. The guards impressed Bond's house and barn for the night, and thanks to his generosity, the entire group fared well for supper.

Before the war, Bond had been a justice of the peace in Pendleton County, and he was opposed to the rebellion. He volunteered to help the refugees with their horses and took the opportunity to confer privately with Suter.

"These rag-tag rebels are bound and determined to take you to Staunton and put you on the cars to Richmond," he revealed. "They are Secesh to the core, but many people in this part of the county remain loyal to the Union. I am organizing a new company of home guard to take up for the loyal people around here. I would like to help you escape, but it's too soon to show my hand."

"That's alright," Suter replied. "We would not ask you to take such a risk."

"Well ... I appreciate that, but why not just do it yourselves? There are more than seventy of you and only eight of them. You could easily overpower them and take their guns."

"We could do as you say, but if we did, someone might get hurt, and we don't want to hurt anyone. I understand your desire to set us free, but Jesus is the only savior we need."

"If that's how you feel, then why are you running away?"

"If we stayed in Virginia, many of these boys would be forced into battles where they must kill or be killed, and I don't want that to happen—not any more than it already has. Our faith prohibits violence against our fellow man."

"You sound like Elder John Kline, the Dunker preacher who travels through here in the spring and summer. Do you know him?"

"I've never met him, but many of these Dunker boys would know him quite well."

"What if one of your boys was to slip away and deliver a message to Elder Kline?"

"That might be alright. He could tell our people what has become of us. What message do you suggest?"

"Tell Elder Kline that John Bond has promised safe passage to New Creek for peaceful Dunkers and Mennonites. Tell him to wait two months and then send seventeen at a time instead of seventy at a time."

Suter entrusted the message to Blosser, who had a sturdy horse and a good sense of direction. At first, Blosser was reluctant to abandon the group, but he agreed that someone should try to make it back to the valley, and he figured he had a better chance than most of the other men.

On the following morning, while the refugees were washing up in the creek, Blosser slipped through the corral fence and saddled his horse. He walked his mount for the first quarter mile, then paced the mare at a fast trot back to the ford of the South Branch, where the ferry operator was eager to talk about the excitement of the previous day.

"It was the funniest thing I ever saw," the boy said. "Those Dunkers got dunked alright. I thought some of 'em would drown for sure. They finally made it across, but they was captured by some parolees on the other side of town. I don't know what they did with 'em, but I'm gonna go find out after I eat my breakfast."

The boy did not recognize Blosser, who quickly headed southeast into the mountains. He backtracked through the gap at Ketterman's place and returned to Judy's on the South Fork, where Mary Ann gave him a good supper and enough provisions for two days. He thanked her and Nimrod for their help and left in the morning before first light. It turned into a warm, dry day as Blosser crossed the Shenandoah. He spent the next night in the gap behind Little North Mountain and made it back to the Rhodes depot on the following afternoon.

Henry and Peggy were shocked to see Blosser and gravely concerned when he told them that the refugees had been captured. He repeated what Bond had said about sending seventeen instead of seventy, and Henry immediately told Johnny to relay the message to Doc, who would know how to contact Kline.

"What about Sammy?" Henry asked. "Is Sammy alright?"

"We never did see Sam. He wasn't at the mountain depot."

"What about H. L.? Was he on the train?"

"Nope. I never saw hide ner hair of those Rhodes boys."

CHAPTER 9

Which Way Is West?

"Looky here, we don't need no pilot."

On the night when Sammy and H. L. missed the train, they started from their home on Pleasant Run near Jacob Byerly's Mill about six miles south of Harrisonburg. They walked several miles northwest to Whissen's Mill, where they expected to rendezvous with fifty men, as Henry had indicated, but they found only a few other latecomers. The disappointed men concluded that the refugee train had left already, and they decided to go home and reconvene at the same spot on the following night. They hoped that the extra day would allow them to secure horses and hire a pilot.

Sammy and H. L. spent the night at their sister's home on Muddy Creek, where they picked up some additional supplies and another refugee, cousin Peter S. Heatwole. At 10 p.m., they returned to Whissen's Mill and found five of the men from the previous night. None of them had been able to find a pilot, and H. L. was reluctant to set out for New Creek without a guide, but one of the fugitives insisted that he knew the way.

"Looky here, we don't need no pilot," he said. "I can get us there. We'll just go west across the Shenandoah Mountain and then north along the South Fork of the South Branch. It's simple."

After quite a bit of discussion, the men took their self-appointed leader at his word and headed northwest, traveling five miles over fields and through woods before reaching Rawley Springs. From there they followed Dry River Road until 2 a.m, when they arrived at the home of Henry May, a young man they knew they could trust.

H. L. approached the house alone, while Sammy and the others waited in the woods. After a minute or two, May invited everyone inside and built up a roaring fire that tempted them to linger longer than they should. While they rested, May quickly rounded up four more refugees from among his neighbors. Then he directed the twelve travelers onto a rugged path north to the Pendleton Road.

The men thanked May and started walking again at 4 a.m., following the trail over Tomahawk Mountain before descending to a creek as the sun came up. They ate breakfast there in the morning fog and started up the next ridge in the pouring rain.

"I'd give anything for an oilcloth cape," Sammy said.

"What good would that do when we're already wet to the bone?" H. L. replied. "I'd rather come across a nice cozy cave with a good supply of dry firewood."

What the Rhodes brothers really needed was a compass. The rain finally subsided as they approached the crest of the Shenandoah, but a thick fog covered the top of the mountain, making it nearly impossible to discern east from west. Most of the men were tired and disoriented, and they wanted to rest and wait for the fog to lift, but the leader insisted that he could see the tracks of the larger group they were trying to follow. H. L. was not so sure. He saw no tracks, and he had a hard time believing that any sign of tracks would remain after so much rain.

Just when Sammy was certain he could walk no farther, they arrived at the Pendleton Road, which was right where May had said it would be. Reaching the road and cresting the top of the Shenandoah lifted the men's spirits and propelled them forward with renewed energy. They walked briskly down the mountain for several miles until Sammy was completely exhausted. He was coughing and hacking, and his overtaxed legs were knotted with cramps and spasms.

"I jus' hafta stop," he finally insisted.

"Well … we can't camp here," the leader said. "We gotta get off the road, or we're bound to get caught."

He was right about this, so H. L. and Peter coaxed Sammy along as the men traversed a small ridge and settled into a deep hollow. There they worked together to start a fire. Wet wood made the task extremely difficult, but some of the men used their pocketknives to peel the wet bark from a large collection of small sticks. Another man coaxed a few sparks from flint and steel to ignite some tender shavings he had miraculously managed to keep dry. He nursed his fledgling fire along, while the others whittled more kindling and gathered some bigger sticks.

For several hours, the refugees alternated between maintaining their smoldering fire and attempting to sleep. They had little in the way of bedding, but H. L. gave Sammy his blanket, and Sammy used a stone for a pillow. He was too uncomfortable and too worried to get much rest, but at least the muscles in his cramped legs were beginning to relax. Most of the other men stayed awake as well—some reclining, some sitting—until a late-night downpour doused their fire and forced them back onto their feet.

They returned to the Pendleton Road and followed it across more ridges and streams, including one with water running knee-high. The rain finally stopped at 4 a.m., but as the horizon ahead of them started to show the first signs of light, H. L. began to suspect they were going east instead of west. While the others trudged past a crude cabin near the road, he knocked on the door and made some inquiries.

The occupant of the place was not pleased to be rousted from his warm bed. He offered no hospitality but grudgingly confirmed that the refugees were going the wrong way. Instead of walking west toward Pendleton County, they were traveling east toward Brock's Gap. In fact, the gap was straight ahead of them and closely guarded by Confederate pickets, according to the half-woke man. He also informed H. L. that the large group they were trying to follow had been captured on the previous day near Petersburg.

All twelve travelers were stunned, but H. L. took the news particularly hard, and he focused his anger on the group's leader.

"You said we was following the tracks of the fifty men ahead of us!" he shouted. "But there *were* no tracks. It was all in your otherwise empty head!"

H. L.'s outrage was contagious, and several others in the group took turns tongue-lashing their deposed leader.

"Back at Whissen's Mill, you said we didn't need no pilot. In the middle of all that rain and fog, you said you *knew* which way was west, and now we find out we've been walkin' east all night long."

Back at John Bond's place on North Mill Creek, Blosser's escape from the larger group created quite a stir. The parolees decided not to pursue him, but they guarded the rest of the refugees more closely as they again headed south.

Blue sky began to emerge, the muddy road started to dry, and the March breeze became much warmer, but the refugees continued to struggle against fear and fatigue. They took turns riding the horses as they traveled fifteen miles to the Pendleton County Courthouse in Franklin, where the rebels stopped for the night and took charge of some additional deserters that the local home guard had rounded up.

After a skimpy supper of hard crackers and cold coffee, the guards crowded the men into the courthouse. As they were bedding down on the floor, the officer in charge came to the front door and said: "It's time for you boys to answer some questions. I'll choose six men to interrogate, one at a time, and I expect to get the truth. If your stories don't match, I'll stop asking questions, and we'll just hang the lot of you."

The officer scanned the group, and his eyes settled on Brunk.

"You there. Come with me."

Brunk stood up hesitantly and followed the officer outside.

"I meant what I said in there about getting the truth," the officer asserted. "If you lie to me, you better hope that the other five boys tell me the exact same story."

"I will speak only the truth," Brunk promised, "and I feel sure the others will do the same."

"Well … I hope you're right about that. I'll start by askin' where you thought you was goin'."

"We was tryin' to get to New Creek. From there, me and my friend was gonna go east to Hagerstown.

"Are you boys all from the valley?"

"I believe so. Most of us are from Rockingham, and I think the others are from Augusta."

"And why do you wanna leave Virginia?"

"Only to keep from fighting," Brunk said. "It's against our faith and contrary to the Gospel to fight and kill our fellow man … entirely wrong to do so."

"If you had made it to Maryland, would you have fought for the Yankees?"

"No sir! Up North there's a law that allows men who object to war on account of their religion to stay out of it."

The stories that the five other men told matched Brunk's close enough to avoid violence, but before the sun came up, two of the guards could not resist taunting the refugees with a rude awakening.

"Who wants to hang first?" one of the bullies shouted at 5 a.m., as he stomped through the courthouse brandishing a noose. "You boys told your lies last night, and now you're gonna face the truth! I say you're nothin' but a bunch of horse thieves! And we don't tolerate horse thievin' on this side of the Shenandoah."

The men were terrified at first, but after they recovered from the initial shock of waking up to death threats, they remained calm and quiet and ignored the noose.

After eating only a few bites of breakfast, the group traveled twenty-four miles south and spent the night in the Highland County Courthouse at Monterey, where the guards turned their prisoners over to the Churchville Cavalry. By morning, their rations had dwindled to half a barrel of crackers and a few scraps of bacon, so hunger became their constant companion as they headed east on the road to Staunton. Their endurance started to wane as they moved slowly through narrow valleys, over steep ridges, and across rocky mountain passes. As they traipsed down one ridge and started up another, the group became quite scattered. And when they stopped to rest atop the Shenandoah, one of the Dunkers just kept going, and none of the road-weary soldiers seemed to notice.

It was getting dark when the exhausted entourage came upon an abandoned house beside the road. The shack was not large enough to accommodate all the men—not even if they slept shoulder to shoulder—so the Churchville Cavalry impressed another nearby house as well. As the sun was going down, the officer in charge said, "Gentlemen, I will trust to your honor tonight. If you will promise to remain here until I return in the morning, we can all rest easier. Will you give me your word on it?"

The prisoners readily agreed to remain in the abandoned house, but after the soldiers left, some of the men started making plans to escape. Brunk and Rodgers were tempted to join them, but they knew it would be wrong to break their promise. One of the Dunkers, who must have felt the same way, left the house abruptly and returned with some of the soldiers, who stood constant watch for the rest of the night.

The next day was warm and pleasant as the men trudged down through the eastern foothills of the Shenandoah. Once again, they became scattered, and there were several opportunities to escape, but Brunk and Rodgers continued to stay the course. When they reached Staunton on the afternoon of March 19, the cavalry confined them to the courthouse and posted guards at every door and window. They confiscated the men's horses but gave them generous portions of food.

With his supper plate piled high, Brunk sat down on the floor next to Rodgers and said, "Well … we lost our horses, but at least we have plenty to eat."

"I was just about ready to eat the horses," Rodgers joked. "So I figure it comes out pert near even."

Later that evening, Brunk overheard two of the guards talking. "Don't tell them that they have to go to Richmond tomorrow," one said. "They will not sleep well."

The next morning dawned cloudy and cold with drizzling rain. The Churchville Cavalry provided another nourishing meal and allowed the prisoners to divvy up the remainder of the crackers from the bottom of the barrel. Then they paraded the seventy-plus men from the courthouse to the train station.

The Virginia Central Railroad did not extend into Rockingham, so Brunk had never seen a train. He marveled at the steam locomotive and wished he could watch it run, but that would be impossible from inside the boxcars, which smelled suspiciously like cow manure. The guards forced the men to sit on the muddy floor, packed tightly together with their knees drawn up to their chests. There was no way to change positions after the door slammed shut.

As Brunk's eyes began to adjust to the lack of light, the train lurched forward, and he heard the strange sound of steam escaping from the pistons that powered the rods that turned the locomotive's wheels. There was a slow "chug" followed by another and another. At first there was more than a second between these novel noises, but as the train gradually gained momentum, the sounds came closer and closer together until "chug … chug …chug" became one continuous strain of "juggajuggajuggajuggajugga."

Brunk peeked out through a knothole in the side of the boxcar and was mesmerized by the visual sensation of super-equine speed.

"We're going twice as fast as the best horse I ever rode," he marveled. "Jus' wait till I tell Susanna about this!" Then it occurred to him—for the first time—that he might not see his wife and son again. He tried not to dwell on this very real possibility, but the guard's words from the previous night echoed in his memory: "Don't tell them that they have to go to Richmond tomorrow, they will not sleep well."

In fact, many of the boxcar brethren expected to die in Richmond. They imagined that execution was the final Secesh solution to men who refused to fight.

As the train began chugging up Afton Mountain, the boxcar rocked from side to side. Brunk's stomach was on the brink of rebellion when the train leveled out for a few seconds before plunging into total darkness.

The men gasped and fell silent as the noise of the train became much louder, reverberating into their ears from every direction. Their terror lasted for several seconds until one of the more educated men shouted: "It's a tunnel!"

Brunk exhaled and sucked in a new supply of air and manure mist. "A tunnel," he mused, trying to process the concept of going faster than a horse … in the dark … on a train … through a mountain.

After emerging from the tunnel and rolling down the other side of Rockfish Gap, the train made stops at Mechum's River and Ivy before taking on water at Charlottesville. The guards did not allow the men to leave the train at any of the depots because it would have taken too long to pack them back into the boxcars. As night fell, their cramped quarters gradually became totally dark again. The prisoners prayed and sang hymns, including this one.

> Broad is the road that leads to death,
> And thousands walk together there;
> But wisdom shows a narrow path,
> With here and there a traveler.
>
> Deny thy self and take the cross,
> Is the Redeemer's great command;
> Nature would count her gold but dross,
> If she should reach the heavenly land.
>
> The fearful soul that tires and faints,
> And walks the ways of God no more,
> Is but esteemed almost a saint,
> And makes his own destruction sure.
>
> Lord, let not all my hopes be vain,
> Create my heart entirely new,
> Which hypocrites could ne'er attain,
> Which false apostates never knew.

Their singing became more somber and their prayers more pronounced as the train made stops at Louisa Courthouse, Beaver Dam, Hanover Courthouse, Atlee Station, and finally Richmond—the Capital of the Confederacy.

By the time the first rays of morning sun touched the top of the Shenandoah, Sammy's hapless group had reversed course and was hurrying west along the Pendleton Road, retracing the thousands of steps they had taken during the night. The road that had been mostly downhill in the dark was mostly uphill in the light, and the men were nearly exhausted, but they knew they had to get away from Brock's Gap as quickly as possible.

Sammy's legs and lungs begged him to stop, but fear pushed him onward and upward, and by midmorning, the men had regained the top of the mountain, the exact spot where they had taken the wrong turn on the previous day. They walked a short distance into the woods and sat down on some logs to discuss their next steps. After much deliberation, which devolved into arguing, they agreed it would be best to go home and gather more supplies before making another attempt to reach New Creek. With this new plan in place, they took the path back toward Dry River, instead of the road to Pendleton, backtracking over more ridges and hollows.

The weather improved dramatically in the afternoon, and they found a nice level clearing where they could camp for the night. They made a big fire and pulled leaves from bushes to feather their beds. Sammy slept soundly in this comfortable camp until 3 a.m., when some of the men said it was time to continue walking down the mountain.

"This makes no sense!" H. L. objected. "For the first time in three days, we're warm and dry and safe—all at the same time! We know where we are, and we know where we're going, but if we try to follow this path in the dark, we're just gonna get lost again."

Despite H. L.'s protests, the majority ruled, and the group resumed their retrograde march. H. L. and Peter were tempted to stay behind, so Sammy could get more rest, but they decided it would be best for everyone to stick together. The men pressed on for an hour or so in the dark, but they eventually realized that they were hopelessly off the trail. Now they had little choice but to hunker down in the briers and brush and wait for daylight.

When the sun finally came up, the men found the trail and continued to backtrack. Later that day, as they approached the headwaters of Dry River, they made another fire and rekindled their heated debate about what to do next. Should they gather more supplies and strike out again for New Creek? Or should they find a good place to hide in the mountains closer to home? They argued all afternoon and well into the evening until they finally agreed that they were much too tired to think straight.

In the morning, hunger cast the deciding vote, and the men readily resolved to return to their homes, gather more supplies, and reconvene at a new time and place. Their compromise plan was to establish a comfortable camp deep in the mountains, where they would wait for a more prudent time to venture north.

Sammy, H. L., and Peter walked back to Muddy Creek and spent the night with their relatives west of Mole Hill. Then they gathered more provisions and carried them back to the rendezvous point on the following night. The boys from Henry May's neck of the woods did not show up, but Sammy, H. L., and Peter reunited with four of the other fugitives, including two who were dragging a canvas wagon cover piled high with supplies. They headed west again and soon came to Dry River which, contrary to its name, was running near its high-water mark.

One of the men had the mumps and was reluctant to wade into water that was ice cold and waist high. After some consulting, his companions decided to take their boots and provisions across and then attempt to carry their feverish friend on their shoulders. But the water was colder than they expected, and it was all they could do to cross the river once before their feet became too numb to feel the uneven footing on the rocky river bottom.

"Fever or not, you must trust in providence and brave the cold on your own!" Sammy shouted, over the rush of the river.

"And if providence don't keep you warm," one of the other men hollered, "I got some whisky over here with yer name on it."

After the sickly man stumbled through the river, all the refugees took a shot of whisky. Then they dragged their provisions over several ridges to a remote mountain hollow, where they rigged up the canvas wagon cover as a tent.

On the next day, a stiff wind started to blow, and a thunderstorm rolled in from the south. The temperature plunged that night, and the raindrops turned into giant flakes of heavy snow, enough to cover the ground and cause their makeshift shelter to sag badly. In the morning, the refugees sloshed the wet snow off the tent and stretched it across some sturdier branches. They were terribly cold, but at least they were safe and dry and away from the war.

CHAPTER 10

Castle Thunder

"The war department must have good reasons to hold people in prison."

The larger group of refugees arrived in Richmond around midnight on March 20. They waited anxiously inside the pitch-black boxcar for what seemed like an hour before a Confederate officer slid the door open and ordered them out.

Brunk, who was closest to the passenger platform, fell to his knees when he attempted to walk. He was barely able to crawl, and his cramped muscles rebelled in spasm after spasm as he eventually struggled to his feet.

"Walk it off, but don't get any ideas about running," the officer laughed. "I'll give you boys five minutes to get your legs under you, and then we're marchin' down to the river."

Five minutes was not nearly enough. Brunk endured intense pain as he staggered through the depot and down five steps to the dark street, where the guards were organizing the men into six columns and twelve rows. Brunk's knees, hips, and ankles complained bitterly as he limped four blocks downhill to a one-story brick building near the river.

"Gentlemen, this is the best we can do for you tonight," the officer said, as the guards ushered them into some sort of machine house. "Make yourselves easy."

"What an odd thing to say at a time like this," Brunk thought to himself. "Make yourselves easy?"

Indeed, this would not be an easy night. There was no bedding on the stone floor, no fire in the stove, and barely enough room for everyone to lie down at the same time. The prisoners rested as best they could, but they were too cold and too uncomfortable to sleep. The younger men stumbled about the room for most of the night, while the older men flopped from one side to the other on the stone floor, unable to tolerate any single position for more than a few minutes at a time.

At 9 a.m., breakfast arrived in buckets. The food was an indistinguishable mixture of greasy gravy and animal entrails, but there was plenty of it, and the men ate as much as they could stomach. Then the guards marched them two blocks east to Castle Thunder, an old tobacco warehouse that the rebels had converted into a prison. The large brick building was four stories tall with thick walls and evenly spaced windows that were securely barred. The guards took the prisoners to a third-floor room that was larger than the machine house but still tight quarters for seventy-plus men to share with two slop jars. Looking down from a south-facing window, Brunk could see a narrow street that ran between Castle Thunder and a canal. Beyond these man-made conveyances, there was a spit of land with the James River flowing rapidly on the other side.

The prisoners were still cold, but another meal and tolerable bedding warmed them considerably. Brunk was so exhausted that he slept soundly that night even though one of the guards had told the men they would face firing squads on the following day.

Sure enough, two of the guards returned in the morning and abruptly removed Doc's youngest son, Gabriel Heatwole Jr., from the group. He thought his life would soon be over as they led him out the door and down the stairs.

"Where are we going?" he asked.

"We're goin' down to the courtyard," one of the guards said with a smirk. "After that, since you're a damned traitor to the God-blessed Confederacy, I'd say you're goin' straight to hell."

The idea of death did not disturb Gabriel at this point because, as he walked down the steps, he surrendered himself completely to the will of God. He felt a strange sense of serenity with each step toward martyrdom, a blessed assurance that he would be with Jesus in a matter of moments.

When they reached Castle Thunder's courtyard, Gabriel was almost disappointed to discover that the guards had no intention of shooting him. Instead, they forced him to shoulder an old musket and march back and forth between the buildings. This was particularly painful for him because the tip of a knife blade was lodged in his hip, a souvenir from his militia training at Winchester.

After two excruciating hours, Gabriel was no longer able to keep the gun on his shoulder. He dragged it behind him in the dirt as he plodded painfully forward, preaching peace to the soldiers with all his remaining might.

On the following day, two guards came to the third floor and selected twelve men for interrogation. They escorted them downstairs to a small office, where a man wearing a nicely tailored civilian suit greeted them politely. He asked the sentinels to squeeze some additional chairs into the room so that no one would have to remain standing. Brunk had forgotten how wonderful it felt to simply sit in a chair.

"My name is Sydney Baxter," said the well-dressed man. "I am a habeas corpus commissioner for the war department. Do you know what habeas corpus means?"

Each man shook his head sideways.

"Habeas corpus is a Latin phrase that literally means 'you should have the body.' Simply put, it means that the war department must have good reasons to hold people in prison. It is my job to determine whether there is a good reason in your case."

The men were somewhat puzzled by this explanation, but Baxter didn't seem to notice.

"Now I am going to ask you a number of questions," he continued, "and if I ask any that you cannot answer, you need not say anything. It would be more efficient for one man to speak for the entire group," he said, as he surveyed the room. "Would that be possible?"

Brunk and the other Mennonites looked at Frederick Rhodes, who at age forty-three was easily the oldest refugee in the room. Rhodes stood up and said, "I am a deacon in the Mennonite church, so I suppose I can speak for the Mennonites, but I will ask my Dunker friends to correct me if I say anything that differs from their principles."

"Alright then, Deacon Rhodes. I'll start with something simple: Do you know why you are being detained at Castle Thunder?"

"Yessir, I believe I do," Rhodes said, as he reclaimed his comfortable seat. "We got caught tryin' to make our way through the mountains to New Creek."

"And why did you want to leave Virginia?"

"We didn't *want* to leave Virginia, but we couldn't stay if it meant going to war. We believe that it is wrong to take up arms against our fellow man. My church—the Mennonite churches in Rockingham County—has decided that if any man goes to war voluntarily, he can no longer commune with the church. Those of us who are members would be excommunicated without a trial, and these younger boys, who are not yet members, would not be allowed to join the church."

"For how long?"

"Forever, I 'spect."

"Doesn't that seem rather harsh?" Baxter asked.

"It is right strict, but not as harsh as killin' people on purpose."

"Is this absolute prohibition against war true for the Dunkers as well?" Baxter asked, as he looked around the room at the other men.

"Our convictions regarding war are the same," Joseph Miller agreed. "We believe that fighting and killing, even in a war, goes against the Gospel. The Bible bids us to be peacemakers, not warmongers."

"I'll try not to take that personally," Baxter responded wryly. "Let me ask you this, Deacon Rhodes. Before the war, did you drill with your local militia company?"

"I don't believe any of us did. We paid a small fine for each muster we missed—never more than $3 per year until after Lincoln got elected."

"When General Johnston called out the Virginia militia last year, did you report to your regimental court?"

"Most of us did, but some went into hiding, and others escaped through the mountains."

"What did *you* do?"

"I reported to the courthouse at Harrisonburg," Rhodes said, "and they mustered me into the 146th Virginia Militia."

"Isn't that going to war? I thought you said your church would not permit you to take up arms."

"The church takes that position now, but at the beginning of the war, the bishop only asked that we take a solemn pledge not to kill or hurt anyone."

"And did you honor that pledge."

"Yessir, I did."

"Did you not fight in any battles?"

"My company was in some skirmishes, but I did not fight."

"Did you carry a gun?"

"Yessir. I obeyed the order to carry a gun, but I did not obey the order to fire the gun at the Union soldiers."

"When did you leave the 146th Virginia?"

"On the last day of the year, I was furloughed for five months to look after my farm."

"So you are not a deserter then."

"No sir. Not yet anyhow, but I never intended to go back."

"But some of the others in your group *are* deserters. Isn't that right?

"Yessir. I'd say so."

"While you were on leave from the 146th, did you do anything to help the families of soldiers who were killed or injured or the families of those who were unable to obtain furloughs?"

"Yessir. I did, and I think many of these boys did, too."

"Let me ask you this," Baxter proposed. "If Confederate soldiers came to your home? Would you feed them? Would you give them shelter?"

"Yessir. Many of us have done so, and I believe all of us would do so tomorrow if we had the chance."

"Would you feed the *enemy* if he came to your home?"

Before Rhodes could answer, Baxter said, "As Christians, we are commanded to feed our enemies. Are we not?"

"Yessir. That's Gospel."

Again, Baxter looked around the room at the other men. "Are you all satisfied with what Deacon Rhodes has said on your behalf?"

The men nodded their approval.

"Is there anything you would like to add?"

After a brief pause, Rhodes gave Baxter a copy of the *Mennonite Confession of Faith*.

"This book explains our beliefs better than I can," Rhodes said. "Beginning on page 295, there's a good section on peacemaking."

Baxter opened the pocket-size book to the proper page and read for ten minutes while the men waited anxiously. Then he closed the book, leaned back in his chair, and stared out the window. Finally, he said: "I cannot say for certain how long you must remain at Castle Thunder, but for now, I have decided that there is reason enough to keep you here. It is my *opinion* that peaceful men, such as yourselves, would be more useful to the Confederacy as farmers, but I'm sure that the war department will not allow every farmer who objects to the war to stay out of it entirely. Before I make my final recommendations, however, I must question each man in your group individually, and that will take some time."

Later that day, the Richmond prisoners were visited by Algernon Gray and John Hopkins, men who represented Rockingham County in the Virginia House of Delegates. The politicians assured the men that they planned to introduce legislation that would establish an exemption for members of churches that have steadfastly practiced nonresistance.

"If we are to succeed," Gray explained, "we must demonstrate that Mennonites and Dunkers are opposed to all war as a matter of longstanding religious scruples."

"Would you like to borrow my copy of the *Mennonite Confession of Faith*?" Rhodes offered. "Peter Burkholder's reflection on nonresistance explains our objections to war better than anything we can tell you, and I believe the Dunkers also agree with the gist of it."

Gray took the book from Rhodes and read pages 295 through 313, while Hopkins explained the General Assembly's procedures for passing a new law.

"It won't be easy," Gray added, as he looked up from his reading, "but this little book will help. In the meantime, we'll see to it that you are allowed to send and receive letters. Tell your families that you are safe, for now, and that your representatives in Richmond are doing everything they can to secure your release, but I would advise against giving them false hope. We don't yet know how this will end."

On Sunday, Benjamin Byerly, an influential Dunker from Rockingham, visited the prisoners and preached a sermon, and on Monday he returned to Castle Thunder with as much good food as he could carry. Before he left, he promised to return in a few days with more food.

In the meantime, John Baldwin, who represented residents of Augusta County in the Confederate Congress, also visited the men.

"Elder John Kline has been writing letters to me and to several other Confederate officials pleading for your release," Baldwin reported. "I'm going to ask some of my congressional colleagues to come speak with you. I'm sure they will ask many questions about why you refuse to participate in war. Just answer them honestly and plainly, and you will be alright."

Several members of the Confederate Congress did visit the men, and they posed many of the same questions that Baxter had asked. Some of the legislators suggested that the men could work as teamsters, but the captives told the politicians that they would not support the war in any way.

On the following day, all the prisoners who were not members of Mennonite or Dunker churches were taken—one by one—to see Baxter. By the time it was Brunk's turn, he knew what to expect. A guard took him down the steps to the little office, where another prisoner was coming out as Brunk was going in. When their eyes met, Brunk saw no sign of serious trouble.

"Please sit down," Baxter invited. "I have some good news and some bad news. I imagine you already know that the General Assembly is considering a measure that would provide exemptions to members of the Mennonite and Dunker faiths. If this proposal passes, many of your fellow prisoners will be set free as soon as they pay a fine. But it's my understanding that you are not a member of either church, and you are also not a Quaker. Is that correct?"

"Yessir. That's true. I generally attend a Mennonite church, but I have yet to be baptized into the faith."

"In that case, I'm afraid you will not qualify for the exemption. The war department, however, has decided to offer you noncombatant status if you would be willing to serve voluntarily in the Stonewall Brigade. I am compiling a list of such volunteers, and with your permission, I would like to add your name to my report."

"What does noncombatant status mean?" Brunk asked.

"Noncombatant means you would not be required to fight. You would not have to carry a gun, and you would not have to wear a uniform, but you would support the brigade by working as a teamster or perhaps as a cook or an orderly in the relief corps. How does that sound?"

"What other choice do I have?"

"Well … if you do not volunteer, you likely would remain here at Castle Thunder as a political prisoner until the war is over. After that, I cannot say what would become of you."

"Alright," Brunk conceded. "If it'll get me outta this jail, you can put my name on your list."

❖   ❖   ❖

On March 28, Baxter issued a report to the war department listing twenty-seven prisoners who were willing to volunteer for noncombatant duty in the Stonewall Brigade.

On the afternoon of the following day, delegates Gray and Hopkins returned to Castle Thunder to tell the prisoners that the General Assembly had indeed created an exemption for members of peace churches who pay a fine of $500 and a two percent property tax.

"The bill passed on a vote of seventy-nine to eighteen, and the governor has already signed it into law," Gray said proudly, as he handed the *Mennonite Confession of Faith* back to Deacon Rhodes.

"Did this little book help explain things?" Rhodes asked.

"I believe it did," Gray replied. "But the fact that two parolees captured all of you boys without a fight did more to impress the General Assembly than all other influences put together."

Responding to the new law, Baxter sent another report to the war department on March 31 listing forty-five "persons whose religion forbids shedding blood." These church members remained in prison, waiting for their fines to be paid, while the war department sent Brunk, Rodgers, and the twenty-five other nonmembers back to Staunton in the converted cattle cars.

On that same day, Stonewall Jackson—probably unaware of the new Virginia law—ordered Colonel John R. Jones to offer an amnesty of sorts to the wayward militia men of Rockingham.

"All militia men will promptly report themselves, and avoid the mortification of arrest," Jones declared. "I am authorized to say to the Tunkers and Mennonites that Gen. Jackson believes them to be sincere in their opposition to engaging in war, and will detail them as teamsters etc."

But few Dunkers or Mennonites—if any—took Jackson up on his offer.

CHAPTER 11

The Jury Room

"We, the accused, find ourselves impaneled in the jury room."

Soon after Jackson proposed his noncombatant compromise, Doc noticed that conscription scouts were watching him from just above the timberline of Mole Hill. There was no one hiding under his house at the time, so Doc was happy to be the center of attention.

He made frequent trips across the backyard, glancing nervously left and cautiously right, before walking briskly to the barn with a sack of anything that Polly wanted out of the house. After a few minutes, he would emerge from the barn with an empty sack and a face full of guilt.

Polly enjoyed watching Doc stage his comical sideshows, but she worried about how his antagonistic audience might react.

"Maybe you shouldn't make these men more suspicious than they already are," she suggested.

"I don't know if that's possible," Doc replied. "Half of the prisoners in Richmond are related to us one way or another, so the scouts figure I know where the rest of them are hiding."

"Do you really think they're that smart?"

"Some of them don't seem too bright; I'll give you that, but it would be a mistake to underestimate any of them."

On April 5, two days after Jackson's amnesty offer expired, a midday thunderstorm chased the scouts out of the woods and onto

PEGGY'S WAR

Doc's front porch. They pounded on the door, and Doc pretended to be surprised to see them.

"Come in out the rain," he invited. "Are you here for doctoring? Saturday's my regular day for men, but I don't see hardly anyone in weather this bad. I reckon people would rather stay tolerable sick than get soaking wet."

The scouts ignored Doc's gregarious greeting, but they accepted his invitation to step inside the house.

"You're drenched!" Polly observed. "Give me your coats, and I'll dry them by the fire. Sit down and rest while I fix you some coffee."

"We won't be staying," said the older of the two scouts. "We're here on behalf of the provost marshal to arrest your husband."

"Arrest me? Whatever for?"

"Treason against the Confederacy. To be exact, we are arresting you on suspicion of assisting deserters and helping able-bodied men shirk their duty to defend Virginia."

By the time he reached the courthouse in Harrisonburg, Doc was every bit as wet as his captors, who escorted him up the steps to the jury room, ushered him inside, and locked the door.

The large room was crowded with eighteen young men, mostly Dunkers but a few Mennonites, and Doc was surprised to see his son-in-law, Hugh Brunk, among them. At age twenty-nine, Hugh was the oldest man in the room other than Doc.

"Father Heatwole! What are you doing here?" Hugh asked, with great astonishment.

"Apparently, I stand accused of treason," Doc replied. "What are *you* doing here?"

"We were on our way to New Creek when some pickets from Turner Ashby's cavalry stopped us on this side of Moorefield," Hugh said. "They took our gold and silver and marched us back over the mountains to Woodstock, where they impressed our horses. We spent a day or two at Mount Jackson, and we figured they was gonna put us on the cars to Winchester, but then they brought us here."

"They probably didn't know what else to do with you," Doc explained. "The General Assembly has passed an exemption for members of peace churches, and most of you boys qualify for it, but they must have caught you several days before that law passed."

Doc tried to conceal his concern as he spoke with Hugh and the rest of the boys. He had hoped that reports of their capture were nothing more than rumors, but now he was beginning to worry that the entire underground railroad was collapsing. His rising fears approached panic when the door opened again, and the guards pushed Elder Kline into the room.

Doc shook Kline's hand and said, "This is the first time in my life when I have *not* been glad to see such a fine old friend."

"The sentiment is mutual," Kline responded.

Within the hour, the guards deposited another political prisoner in the jury room, fifty-two-year-old Joseph Beery, a Mennonite whom Doc knew well. Doc introduced him to everyone in the room then pulled him aside, to the extent possible, and lowered his voice to nearly a whisper.

"I have a pretty good idea why they arrested Elder Kline," Doc confided, "but what do they want with *you*?"

"I voted against secession and made no apologies for it," Beery explained. "My farm is surrounded by Secesh neighbors who have persecuted me ever since. I expect they'll hang me on Monday."

Doc shook his head and said, "They told me that there would be a fair trial and *then* they would hang me."

"These are troublous times," Kline added, as he joined their quiet conversation. "Men's hearts are failing them for fear."

"Not Brother Beery," Doc said, with great admiration. "He just might be the bravest man I know. He's one of the few who voted against secession and has been staunch to the backbone all along."

The second-floor jury room occupied the northeast corner of Rockingham's stately brick courthouse. The room had a ten-foot ceiling and three double-hung windows with twenty panes in the upper sash and fifteen panes in the lower sash. It was not uncommon on court days for impaneled jurors to appoint one of their number to lean out the window and lower his hat on a rope to swap cash for ginger cakes and hard cider.

"Send up a dozen cakes and a jug of o-be-joy-ful!" the juror would shout. "And keep the change fer yer trouble!"

But on that first Saturday of April, the mood in the jury room was entirely sober. The space was big enough to accommodate twelve jurors seated around a table for an hour or two, but it was insufficient to house twenty-one men for any longer length of time. The guards had removed all the chairs to make room for the prisoners to sleep on the floor, but there was little space for them to move around. A stove stood between the two windows that faced east, but there was not enough wood to maintain more than a few embers of fire. The most dramatic discomfort, however, involved the necessities of clean water and dirty discharge. The guards had placed two porcelain pots in opposite corners of the room; one jar contained drinking water while the other held urine and excrement. By the time Doc arrived, the odor from the slop jar was overpowering, and the morale of the men was as low as the stench was high.

On Sunday morning, Kline did what he could to lift the men's spirits.

"Today is the Lord's Day!" he observed. "Let us worship the Prince of Peace. Perhaps some singing would warm our hearts—if not our hands and feet."

One of the younger Dunker boys with a clear baritone voice sang the first line of "The Lord into His Garden Comes," and the others echoed the words and melody back to him in the lined-out style of singing. The last two lines of the third stanza seemed particularly apropos: "Our troubles and our trials here will only make us richer there, when we arrive at home."

The younger men also volunteered to sing a song they had written while cooling their heels at Mount Jackson.

> We are in prison close confined,
> But this not one of us should mind,
> For Christ has told us in His word
> That we should always trust the Lord.
>
> We know it is God's holy will
> Our fellow man we shall not kill
> That we should lead a Christian life,
> And not engage in war and strife.
>
> But there is One who reigns on high,
> He always will to us be nigh,
> He will from prison us redeem,
> If we put our trust in him.
>
> Then let us all the Lord obey,
> And from the truth we'll never stray,
> So that we all may stand the test,
> And when we die go home to rest.

After they sang a few more hymns, Kline turned to Doc. "Would you care to bring us the sermon?"

"I'm not much of a preacher," Doc confessed.

"Mr. Beery," Kline inquired, "are you moved to speak?"

"I'm no preacher either," Beery replied. "I believe the lot falls on you, Elder Kline, but should we not say a prayer first?"

"I have not stopped praying since they arrested me," Kline said, with a slim smile.

"Tell you what," Doc offered. "I'll say an out-loud prayer if you'll preach the sermon. Do we have a deal?"

Kline nodded his approval, and Doc placed his right hand on Kline's shoulder. Everyone bowed their heads and fell silent.

"Dear Lord, we thank thee for sending thy humble servant to minister to our spiritual side. We ask that thou might give him the right words to soothe our troubled souls and calm our trembling hearts. Grant us now thy blessings of wisdom, courage, and strength so that all our deeds might be acceptable in thy sight, O Lord. And ... uh ... may the communion and fellowship of the Holy Spirit rest with us all forever more, for we ask these things in the name of our Lord and Savior, Jesus Christ. Amen."

"Amen," the young men echoed, as they sat down cross-legged on the jury room floor.

Kline made his way slowly to the front of the group with his head bowed in deep thought. He glanced at Doc and said, "I was hoping for a longer prayer to give me more time to think."

"Take all the time you need," Doc obliged. "We're not going anywhere."

"As a matter of fact, your prayer changed my notion of what sermon to preach. I believe you asked God to 'calm our trembling hearts,' did you not?"

"Deed I did. That's *exactly* what I prayed."

Kline nodded and scanned the room. He intertwined his fingers and thumbs, striking a prayerful pose and waiting just long enough for anticipation to rise among his captive audience.

"My subject," he began, in a strong, clear voice, "is righteousness, temperance, and the judgment to come. We, the accused, find ourselves impaneled in the jury room. The irony of our circumstances reminds me of the Apostle Paul's trial before Felix, the governor of Judea, a story you may recall from the 24th chapter of Acts."

Kline paused as several of the young men opened their pocket Testaments and quickly thumbed to the proper page.

"As a rule, prisoners are nervous and sometimes tremble when taken into court, but judges are proverbially calm and self-composed. Hence the old adage 'as sober as a judge.' Brethren and friends, I say unto you that in this time and place, we have no cause to tremble. Those who should tremble are those who seek to lay obstacles in the way of men who aim to do only good. This is what we find when Paul appears before Felix. The apostle is calm, collected, and self-possessed, while Felix is the one who trembles from fear. It appears that the judge is convicted of guilt by the prisoner, and the prisoner shows himself clear of all charges."

Kline paused for a moment and lowered his voice to a more confidential tone.

"Paul's trial before Felix is not the *only* case in which an innocent prisoner has stood before a guilty judge."

Kline glared at the door separating the twenty-one peaceful men from their families and farms. Then he spoke with great conviction.

"Felix *knew* that Paul was innocent, but I don't think Felix expected him to confess falsely. I believe he was detaining Paul for some other purpose. Perhaps he was waiting for the apostle to offer a bribe or some other form of face-saving flattery, but Paul chose instead to preach, and Felix had never before heard such a sermon.

"The Bible does not reveal what course of reasoning Paul used to cause Felix to tremble, but we may justly conclude that his first point was the righteousness of civil authority—contrasting corrupt and perverted government with what it ought to be."

Kline paused again, staring at the jury room door.

"The Bible tells us that the only true basis of civil authority is love—or good will toward men at the least. Government based on anything else is tyranny. Roman rulers, for example, sought no righteousness in the administration of their laws. They employed no temperance in their demands for obedience, and they feared no judgment to come."

Reverting to his more confidential tone, Kline said: "Brethren and friends, I do not believe Felix was made to tremble by anything Paul may have said concerning civil authority. The Roman governor was too firmly fixed on his own concept of government to be deeply moved by anything a prisoner might say about civil authority. No, we must look elsewhere for the cause of his conviction.

"Felix was a *pagan!*" Kline asserted, switching back to his louder voice. "His religion, if he had any belief at all in the supernatural, was idolatry, but Paul told Felix that God had appointed a day in which he would judge the world by that man whom he hath ordained and raised from the dead. That man ... is none other than Jesus Christ.

"It was the fear of God's judgment—the fear of Jesus Christ himself—that made Felix tremble!

"All moral and religious truth depends on the fear of judgment to come. If we take away from man all fear of accountability, his bestial appetites will devour him. He will eat, drink, and be merry, but then he will burn in the fire."

Slowing down and adopting a more advisory voice, Kline came to his conclusion.

"For our instruction here today—captives like Paul in this cold jury room—we must consider that righteousness is obedience to the law. But when the laws of man depart from the laws of God, obedience to man's law is disobedience to God's law. Here arises a conflict in which each man must decide for himself which he will do, the will of men or the will of God. The decision of the apostles was to obey God rather than men. To be sinners in the eyes of men gave them no distress—no cause to tremble—as long as they knew they were righteous in the sight of God."

Rain and sleet continued on Monday as the jury room prisoners loaded wagons with provisions bound for Jackson's army, which was camped near Rude's Hill about twenty-five miles north of Harrisonburg. The men were glad to be doing something physical to calm their nerves and warm their extremities, but their cold incarceration was beginning to wear them down.

When the guards allowed some Dunker men to visit the prisoners in the afternoon, Kline asked them to bring food and blankets as soon as possible.

"These men are becoming sick," he said. "They are beginning to lose their inner heat, and the guards are not providing enough wood to maintain sufficient fire in the stove."

On Tuesday and Wednesday, the weather turned even more severe, making it nearly impossible to load wagons, so one of the friendlier guards brought newspapers to the jury room for the prisoners to read. The rebel rags, however, were filled with nothing but enthusiasm for war.

"Confinement in these conditions is physically difficult for you and me," Kline confided to Doc, "but I am more concerned about the mental state of the younger brethren. I am trying to encourage them, but they are so broken down by the sad state of the country and the dim prospects for the future that I can't seem to engage them in constructive conversation."

Just when some of the younger men were beginning to lose all hope, the friendly guard allowed them to have visitors again. The Dunker men returned with the blankets that Kline had requested, and Catherine Showalter brought a large basket of provisions.

"Your dear wife carries sunshine with her wherever she goes," Kline said to Jackson Showalter, as they sampled her delectable ginger cakes.

When it came time for Catherine to leave, she asked her husband if he wanted her to bring their little girl, Sallie, to the courthouse on her next visit. Overcome with emotion, it was all Jackson could do to articulate one word: "no."

After their visitors left, the prisoners heard a distant commotion that gradually became more pronounced. They looked out the window and saw endless columns of Confederate soldiers marching north past the courthouse, a somber parade that extended late into the night.

The rain came down hard again on Friday, and one of the more hostile guards delivered several copies of the *Rockingham Register*, which carried an article that branded the prisoners as traitors to the Confederacy.

"When people around here read this story, they'll see what a worthless bunch of galvanized Yankees you are," said the belligerent guard. "Wouldn't surprise me at all if some right-thinking citizens was to come down here and hang every single one of you."

The prisoners did not react to the guard's threats and insults, but the newspaper story greatly disturbed them—especially Kline.

"Have you seen this article?" Kline asked, when the friendly guard returned to the room.

"That's why I'm here," the guard replied. "I think you would be wise to keep your boys away from the windows. This story has turned all of you into targets."

Kline and Doc instructed the men to follow the guard's advice, but one of the younger prisoners did not take the threat seriously. He was looking out the window that night when a gunshot shattered several panes of glass and dropped him to his knees. Kline moved quickly across the room and knelt beside the bleeding boy.

"What happened?" the prisoner stammered, as Kline eased the young man's trembling hands away from his bloody face.

"Someone tried to bushwhack you, but I'm glad to report that he missed," Doc said. "I can see the bullet hole in the ceiling. It appears we are not the only ones who read that story in the *Register*."

The boy was bleeding from several small cuts caused by the shattering glass, and he refused to open his eyes. Kline called for the sympathetic guard and asked him to bring his saddlebags, which contained his medical kit. Doc told the guard to also bring plenty of clean water and all the lamps and candles he could spare. The guard promptly complied, while two of the captives helped the wounded boy lie down on the table.

"The first thing we need to do is get that glass out of his eyes," Kline said to Doc, as he rummaged through his medical kit looking for a needle. "Do you have any experience as a surgeon?"

"None whatsoever," Doc replied. "How 'bout you?"

"I'm no surgeon, but I have removed plenty of splinters in my time. Here! This needle might just do the trick, but I'll need you to hold his head perfectly still."

Doc placed his left hand under the man's chin and his right hand over the top of the man's bloody head. Then he tightened his grip.

"I got his head; now some of you boys hold down his arms and legs," Doc instructed.

When everyone was ready, Doc used his thumbs to pry open the young man's right eye.

"I see only one small sliver of glass," Kline announced. "I think I can remove it without too much trouble." The boy flinched and stiffened when the needle first touched his eyeball, but Doc maintained his grip. Kline gently teased the glass from the boy's eye, and he relaxed a little bit.

"Alright, son, you can close that eye."

"It still feels like something's in there," the boy said.

"That doesn't surprise me," Kline replied. "It probably will feel like that for a few days, but I think that eye will be fine. Now let's have a look at your other eye."

Doc and Kline switched places around the table, and Doc took the same approach to force open the boy's left eye, which was oozing a little bit of blood.

"I see three small shards of glass in this eye," Kline announced, with a bit more concern in his voice. "This might hurt a little bit, but they have to come out, and the sooner the better."

The boy shrieked as Kline nudged the largest piece of glass with his needle.

"Hold him down as tightly as you can," Kline instructed his helpers. "I think I can get it now with my tweezers."

The glass slid neatly from the eye with just a little bit of blood lubricating the extraction.

"That worked tolerable well," Kline said, with a big grin that reflected his relief. "Now that I know what I'm doing, the other two pieces of glass should come out easily."

Then Kline removed six or seven more slivers of glass from the young man's nose, cheeks, and forehead. He gently washed the blood from the boy's face and dabbed some herbal ointment on each of his wounds.

"Keep your eyes closed for now," Kline advised, "but tell me something. When Doc pried them open, could you see anything?"

"I can see," the man reported. "Thank the Lord, I can see."

CHAPTER 12

Oath of Allegiance
"Ein Versprechen zu brechen."

The broken window invited more cold air into the jury room as the miserable mix of rain and snow persisted on Saturday and Sunday.

Kline preached another sermon, taking Matthew 11:28–30 as his text: "Come unto me, all ye that labor and are heavy laden, and I will give you rest; take my yoke upon you, and learn of me; for I am meek and lowly in heart; and ye shall find rest unto your souls: for my yoke is easy, and my burden is light."

Indeed, the prisoners' prospects seemed to improve as they entered their second week of captivity. More food arrived from Catherine Showalter, Sarah Bowman, and several other Dunker ladies. And on Monday evening, the guards released John and Joseph Cline after their father paid their exemption fines.

On the following day, however, it was Kline's turn to be sick. He woke with a bad cough and a hoarse voice, but he would not be silenced by his temporary loss of oration. He requested pen and paper and wrote a scathing response to the editor of the *Register*, a letter he shared with Doc and Beery.

Mr. Editor of the Register:
 In your issue of the 11th inst. I see an article headed Union Men Taken. In the article several names are mentioned who

are known to have strong Union proclivities. Otherwise, the article made no nominal charge against us, which of course, it was out of your power to do, but the article carries with it a strong insinuation as though we had used our influence against the Confederacy. If this has been so, why not come out and point to the ... act, or deed, and if this cannot be done, which I know it can not, then why shut us up in the guardhouse? Why make such false insinuations against good and honest citizens, and publish them to the world? Why contrary to the constitution take up men without their accusers making affidavit that the thing charged was to their knowledge true? But all that is now necessary, is for some vague fiend to raise a falsehood and tell it to some of his captains who have no better principle than themselves, and law and constitution is at end. If this is the kind of laws that we are contending for, then may the Lord save us from it. ...

On Wednesday, the weather improved considerably, and the men returned to loading wagons. While they were working, Daniel Bowman brought Doc some clean clothes and took the opportunity to convey a quick message to him in German.

"Speak only in English or I will arrest you," the belligerent guard shouted at Bowman. "If I had my way, I would cut out your German tongues and feed them to the pigs, but General Jackson will deal with you soon enough. I only wish I could be there to watch you old goats hang."

The thought crossed Doc's mind when a sergeant from the Stonewall Brigade arrived at noon, took charge of the prisoners, and marched them north along Main Street toward Jackson's headquarters at Rude's Hill. Two of the courthouse guards went with them as far as Judge Smith's house, where the sergeant consulted with someone inside the white-columned mansion and released all the prisoners except Doc, Beery, and Kline. Then the sergeant sent the other guards back to the courthouse, and the four men continued their trek toward Rude's Hill.

"Are we bound for some sort of military trial?" Doc asked.

"I have no idea what General Jackson wants with you," the sergeant replied. "I just do what I'm told."

The foursome walked ten more miles along the Valley Pike to Bethlehem Church, where they spent the night. In the morning, the weather continued to improve as the men started walking north again, but after going about two miles, they heard heavy artillery fire coming from the general direction of New Market.

The sergeant consulted briefly with two cavalry scouts, who were riding south along the pike, before turning his attention back to his prisoners.

"We're going right back to Harrisonburg," he announced. "Union forces are advancing on Rude's Hill, and I'm afraid there might be a battle brewing."

The men hurried back to the courthouse, and the guards once again locked the three old patriots in the jury room. After walking sixteen miles that day, Doc was glad for any chance to lay down and rest his elderly bones.

The next day was Good Friday, and there was great excitement and confusion in Harrisonburg as Jackson's troops retreated rapidly south through the town. General Nathaniel Banks' Union army was expected at any moment, so the provost marshal authorized the guards to release the prisoners on one condition.

"They must take the oath of allegiance to the Confederacy," he insisted. "Otherwise, they will have to fall back with the army as prisoners of war.

The friendly guard first approached Beery, who hesitated as long as he dared.

"I am an old man, and I do not want to die in prison," he mumbled to himself, as he signed the oath. Then he looked up at Doc and said, "Perhaps I am not as brave as you imagine."

"Courage must be tempered by wisdom," Doc replied, as he read the document the guards placed before him. "I consider General Jackson to be a man of great courage, yet his army marches past us in temporary retreat. Is our situation so different than his?"

With great reluctance, Doc took the oath as well. Then he turned to Kline and whispered: "Ein Versprechen zu brechen."

"My German is rusty," Beery confessed, as he left the courthouse with Doc. "What did you say to Elder Kline?"

"I said, 'Ein Versprechen zu brechen'—a promise to be broken."

The Mennonites and Dunkers of the valley had feared that the larger group of prisoners in Richmond were going to be executed. But with the new exemption law in place, they quickly redirected their efforts from pleading with legislators to raising money to pay the exemption fines. During the second week of April, David Hartman visited the Rhodes depot and asked Henry and Peggy to contribute.

"A good many of the prisoners don't have enough money to pay their fines," he explained, "so the church has decided to take up a collection and loan them the money so all the men can come home at the same time. The good news is the war department is obliged to accept Confederate currency," he added, with a grin.

"We don't have much of that," Henry laughed. "Peggy accepts it sometimes when she sells eggs and vegetables but only from poor people who have nothing better to barter. You are welcome to what little we have, and I will give you some silver coins to exchange."

"I have never seen people rise so generously to any cause," Hartman marveled. "We soon will have enough money to ransom the men. Emanuel Suter will carry the funds to Richmond next week, and we feel certain that the prisoners who are members of the church will be home by Easter."

"What about the others?" Peggy asked.

"They had to choose between staying in prison or volunteering for noncombatant duty in Jackson's army. So most of them are probably back in the valley by now, somewhere between New Market and Mount Jackson from what I hear."

"Then I 'spect we'll be seeing some of 'em soon," Henry said, with a wink.

Henry's suspicions were confirmed on the night of April 18. He heard someone tapping on the bedroom window, so he carried a grease lamp onto the porch and whistled a tune until he heard a hushed voice beside the house.

"Henry ... it's me."

"Me who?"

"Henry Brunk, and I got Charles Rodgers with me," Brunk said, as the two men stepped into the light of the lamp. "Pap says you're still running a depot. Got room for a couple of hungry deserters?"

"Well ... supper done came and went," Henry teased, as he shook their hands, "but come on in the house, Brunky, and we'll see what we can find. You, too, Charlie."

Henry turned them over to Peggy while he rousted Johnny and Mary from their beds and posted them as lookouts.

"I'm so happy you boys are safe," Peggy said. "Have you seen your wives and children yet?"

"Pap said to come here first," Brunk replied. "He's gonna let the girls know we're alright, and we'll try to see them tomorrow night if the way is clear. That is ... if we can stay here tonight."

"Of course you can," Peggy assured. "You are always welcome here, but how did you *get* here?"

"They gave us a choice," Brunk began. "We could stay in Castle Thunder or volunteer for the Stonewall Brigade. They told us that we wouldn't have to wear uniforms or carry guns and that we could be teamsters, so we agreed to it."

"They railroaded us back to Staunton, and then we drove teams with supplies from there to Jackson's army," Rodgers said. "We made two more trips between Staunton and Rude's Hill, but it just didn't seem right to be part of the war machine, so we started looking to desert."

"We saw our chance today," Brunk said. "We was waiting in line to pick up loads of hay at a barn north of Harrisonburg when Jackson's whole army started marching right past us. There was a lot of confusion, and no one was watching us, so we abandoned our teams and hid in the woods until dark."

On the day before Easter, three earnest men arrived in Richmond with three large bundles of Confederate cash. Suter was ready to ransom all the Mennonites; Byerly was prepared to pay the fines for the Dunkers of Rockingham County, and Christian Cline was ready to pay the fines for the Dunkers of Augusta County. They presented the money and the affidavits to Baxter, who stared at the piles of paper on his desk and took a long, deep breath.

"I sent letters," he began, in an embarrassed voice, "but obviously they did not reach your hands. Two days ago, the Confederate Congress passed a conscription act, and—unlike the Virginia law—it provides no exemption for members of your churches."

The three men were stunned.

"Does that mean our brethren must remain in prison until the end of the war?" Byerly asked.

"I frankly don't know what it means at this point," Baxter said. "Conscription has been a thorny states' rights issue from the very beginning of the war, when General Johnston called out Virginia militia regiments before consulting with Governor Letcher. Now the Confederate Congress has passed a national law that would seem to supersede the Virginia exemption that promised to set your friends free."

"So what are we supposed to do?"

"You'll have to wait and hope that the politicians make some sort of adjustment. If it were simply a matter of releasing forty-five harmless Mennonites and Dunkers from prison, I'm certain that no one would object, but their release could set a precedent that might apply to every man in the Virginia militia. Under state law, they are required to provide one year of service, and for many of them, that year has come and gone. Do you see the problem?"

"Thousands of soldiers could just walk away from the war," Byerly marveled.

"Some of them *already* have walked away, and General Jackson has dealt with them as deserters," Baxter said. "In Rockingham County—your county—dozens of men barricaded themselves in the Blue Ridge until General Jackson sent troops and artillery to dislodge them."

"How much longer would the new Confederate law keep the militia men in the army?" Byerly asked.

"Three more years ... if the war lasts that long. All I can tell you today is to come back tomorrow or, better yet, come back on Monday. I doubt that President Davis and Governor Letcher will settle their differences over Easter, but perhaps the war department can divine a solution to the immediate problem."

Suter and Cline waited outside, while a guard escorted Byerly to the third floor, where he tried to explain the situation to the disappointed prisoners. They did not grasp all the legal ramifications, neither did Byerly, but they fully understood that their chance to go home might be slipping away.

On the Monday after Easter, the three emissaries returned to Castle Thunder and found Baxter waiting for them on the front steps of the fortified warehouse.

"I have good news," he said. "The war department has decided that its agreement to release your friends under Virginia law remains legally binding because it was reached before congress passed the new conscription act."

"What exactly does that mean?" Byerly asked.

"It means that in the Commonwealth of Virginia, a promise is still a promise."

"Does that mean our brethren can go home today?"

"Each prisoner must take an oath not to engage in war against the Confederate States," Baxter said, "but after that, they will be free to go."

Byerly made one last trip to the third floor of Castle Thunder. As soon as the guard unlocked the door, the preacher flung it open and said: "Now you can all go home."

After taking the oath, the forty-five men walked up the hill to the Richmond train station and rode the cattle cars to Waynesboro. Then they walked home in a steady rain, arriving on April 23. They had lost a lot of weight, and their clothes were tattered and torn, but they were free, and walking in the rain had rinsed the edge off their odor.

The Mennonites and Dunkers of the valley rejoiced, but the new Confederate conscription law remained an ominous threat, and the Virginia exemption did nothing to help the young men who were not members of the church when the General Assembly passed the law. While Peggy's neighbors celebrated the return of their husbands and sons, her fiery nightmares persisted. She could not look at Mole Hill without fearing the evil to come.

CHAPTER 13

Sammy's Escape
"I can't keep livin' under the ground like a mole."

By the time the prisoners returned from Richmond, Banks' army had taken control of Harrisonburg, and Jackson's troops had retreated twenty miles to the east. For the first time since the war began, roles were reversed in Rockingham: the conscription scouts hid from the federal forces, while the deserters and draft dodgers came and went as they pleased. Brunk and Rodgers took this opportunity to leave the Rhodes depot and return to their families.

With no one hiding in the secret cellar, there was no need for lookouts on April 24 as Peggy set the table for supper. Rain was pounding on the windows, hard enough to obscure the sound of footsteps on the front porch, so the unannounced knock at the door startled Peggy. Henry peeked out the parlor window and saw an emaciated young man slouching on the steps.

"Sammy!" Henry exclaimed, as he opened the door. "Where you been? We was worried sick! What happened to you?"

The ragged refugee smiled and responded to Henry's questions with one of his own: "Would it be alright if I stayed fer supper and spent the night?"

"Of course you can! C'mon in the house and sit by the fire while Peggy sets another place at the table."

Sammy mindlessly tracked mud into the parlor and plopped down on Mottie's wicker rocker—the chair closest to the fire. Peggy cringed, but she was more worried about the state of Sammy's health than the appearance of her parlor. He looked extremely pale and frail, and he was coughing and hacking more than Henry ever did.

Before supper, Henry said an out-loud prayer of thanksgiving for Sammy's safe return, and as soon as he said, "Amen," Peggy repeated the questions that Sammy had left unanswered.

"Where have you been, Sammy? What happened to you? And where's H. L.? Is he alright?"

Very slowly—between massive mouthfuls of sausage and sauerkraut—Sammy told the story of missing the refugee train, getting lost in the rain, shivering through the snowstorm, and running out of supplies. Sammy and his cousin, Peter Heatwole, obtained more provisions from their relatives along Muddy Creek, but when the food ran out again, Sammy returned to Pleasant Run and hid for two more weeks at Abram Heatwole's depot. H. L. came home as well, but he no longer needed to hide.

"H. L.'s gonna claim the religious exemption, but that don't help me none 'cause I ain't a member of no church yet," Sammy said. "But today, H. L. told me that the rebels are gone and the Yankees are in charge, so I jus' took a notion to visit some of my family."

"Well, we are glad you did," Peggy said, "and you are welcome to stay with us as long as need be."

"That's right," Henry agreed. "Johnny ain't done spreadin' manure yet, and it sure would go faster with an extra pair of hands."

Sammy spent the next day with Peggy and Henry, but he did not spread manure. It snowed for most of the morning, and then the giant snowflakes turned into heavy raindrops that beat against the windows as they had done on the previous day. When the rain eased off, Sammy went to Bishop Coffman's house, where he spent the next night. It rained again on the following day, and Sammy hurried to his Aunt Betsy Weaver's house near the church. He spent the night there and returned to the Rhodes depot for dinner.

Three days later, Sammy was strolling around the southern side of Mole Hill when it started to rain again. He took shelter at Doc's home, where he spent the night and gave Doc and Polly a full account of his travels. While Polly fed Sammy his breakfast, Doc rushed to the Rhodes depot to fetch Henry.

"You need to come talk some sense into Sammy," Doc said.

"What's he done now?" Henry asked.

"He says he's been to your house two times in the past ten days, and he was on his way to your place again yesterday. Even with Banks' army in charge of Harrisonburg, the conscription scouts are still watching, and if they follow Sammy, he'll lead them right to your door."

"I don't know if I have the strength to make it to yer house and back," Henry confessed. "I haven't left the farm in pert near a year. Maybe I could send Johnny."

"Sammy won't listen to Johnny," Doc said, "and it might do you some good to stir your blood a little bit."

"Alright. I'll get Johnny to hitch up the spring wagon, and we'll see what I can do."

Henry struggled mightily to climb onto the wagon seat. He felt terribly weak at first, but the cool rain invigorated him, and he was able to take the reins for the first time in several months. He arrived at Doc's house at noon and told Sammy that they must return to the Rhodes depot immediately.

"Can't we at least wait till the rain stops?" Sammy pleaded.

"No. The more rain the better 'cause I don't want anybody stoppin' us along the way," Henry explained. "I don't expect to meet anybody on the Dayton Road in this weather, but jus' to be safe, I brought a tarp you can hide under in the bed of the wagon."

Sammy spent the night of May 1 at the Rhodes depot, and when the rain stopped on the following day, Henry forbade Sammy to resume his Mole Hill meanderings.

"You're always welcome to stay with us, Sammy, but you can't just come and go as you please from one depot to the next. It's downright dangerous. You'll have to stay in the house during the day and in the cellar at night. Do you understand?"

"Nawsir, I don't reckon I do, but I know I'm done hidin', and I suppose I'm done visitin' my kin. I'm agoin' home."

Sammy returned to Pleasant Run on Friday and slept in his own bed, and on Saturday, he helped his friend, A. J. Bowers, dig a child's grave. While they were working, they made plans to visit Harrisonburg on Monday to see about going north with Banks' army.

At first light, they started toward town but soon discovered that the federal troops had left and several companies of Colonel Ashby's Confederate cavalry had taken their place.

"It looks like we missed our chance," A. J. said. "Maybe we should just go back to Abram's house. No one will ever find us there."

"Nosiree!" Sammy replied. "I can't keep livin' under the ground like a mole. My health won't tolerate it. If we leave tonight, I'm sure we can flank Ashby's cavalry and catch up with the Yankees. I am well-acquainted with the back roads from here to Muddy Creek and as far north as Broadway. That oughta be enough to get us around Ashby."

"I'm not so sure," A. J. hedged. "You said yourself that the last time you ran away, you got completely turned around."

"That was different. We was in the mountains in the fog and rain, and we was followin' the wrong leader. This time'll be diff'rent. We'll travel at night, just long enough to get around the rebels, but we'll stay outta the mountains. I got some money, and I'll pay our way as far as it takes us."

"I wish I had a better idea, but I can't say that I do," A. J. admitted. "Alright ... let's go north, but we have to leave tonight, or we'll never catch up to Banks' army."

It rained that afternoon, but the weather became clear and cool in the evening. Under cover of darkness, Sammy and A. J. headed northwest across the Valley Pike and around Shaver's Hill to Dayton. After midnight, they reached Daniel Bowman's Mill on Silver Lake just north of the village. The smooth water was reflecting a crescent moon that made it easy to see everything around them, including the symmetrical outline of Mole Hill to the north.

"I don't like being out in the open in the moonlight," A. J. said. "Let's get around this lake as fast as we can."

Using Mole Hill as their landmark, they hurried on to Muddy Creek, where they knocked on the front door of Peter Heatwole's house at 4 a.m.

"Is this the fellow you got lost with in the mountains?" A. J. whispered, as they waited on the porch.

"Naw, that was Peter S. Heatwole," Sammy replied. "This here place belongs to Peter O. Heatwole. He's an uncle to Peter S., and he's married to my sister."

Sammy knocked one more time, but no one answered, and the door was locked.

"Maybe they went north with Banks' army," A. J. speculated.

"Nawsir ... not with five little kids and another'n on the way."

The boys walked around to the back door, which was also locked, so A. J. boosted Sammy up to one of the windows. He pushed up the sash, squeezed through the opening, and let A. J. in the front door. They searched the house, but no one was home, so they went upstairs, crawled into bed, and slept till nearly noon. By the time they awoke, the sun was shining brightly and the air was crisp and cool. They foraged in the kitchen for a cold breakfast and walked out to the barn, where they found Sammy's sister hiding in the loft with the children.

"Elizabeth! What are you doing up there?" Sammy asked.

"Trying to keep away from Ashby's cavalry," she said. "They were all around here yesterday."

"Where's Peter?"

"He took the horses up on Mole Hill so the soldiers wouldn't get 'em. He told us to stay quiet in the loft till he gets back."

Within a few minutes, Peter arrived with the horses, and they all returned to the house for dinner. Then Sammy and A. J. went upstairs to get more sleep, but it wasn't long before Elizabeth tapped on the bedroom door.

"Sammy," she hissed. "Look out the window."

Sammy crawled out of bed and carefully nudged the curtains aside, catching a glimpse of fourteen mounted soldiers about 100 yards from the house."

"Let's get out of here!" Sammy said.

"I don't think that's such a good idea right now," A. J. countered. "They don't know we're here, and I bet you they wouldn't care if they did know. They're probably looking for Union troops, not for you and me."

The cavalry squad moved quickly north along Muddy Creek toward the Rawley Road, but Sammy remained anxious, even after the soldiers were out of sight.

"Maybe we ought to go west and hide in the mountains," he suggested. "I know a good spot near Flat Rock."

"I'm not much interested in roughing it," A. J. said. "Let's stick to our plan. The best thing we can do now is get some more sleep."

❖   ❖   ❖

Sammy and A. J. started walking north again at 10 p.m. with Sammy's brother-in-law leading the way. Peter guided them as far as Daniel Showalter's depot on Linville Creek about two miles south of Broadway. Peter gave the signal on Showalter's rear window at 2 a.m., and the sixty-year-old preacher came outside and invited them into his home. They slept in his hiding place until sunrise, and then Peter said farewell and headed back to his home.

Showalter had seen no sign of Ashby's men, but another refugee at the depot reported that they were following close behind Banks' army, which might indicate that General Richard Ewell's Confederate forces were pursuing Banks as well.

"You need to talk to Jacob Fifer," Showalter said. "If anyone around here knows the whereabouts of the armies, it's Jacob. If he's not home, he'll be at the church."

Sure enough, they found Fifer at Trissels Mennonite Church, where he served as the sexton. His wife, Frances, gave Sammy and A. J. their dinners, while Fifer offered his interpretation of the troop movements.

"I think Ashby's pursuit of Banks was just a bluff," Fifer said. "Banks' troops are still camped somewhere near New Market, and Ewell's army don't seem too keen on following them. If I was you, I'd go to Broadway and talk to Abraham Funk. Maybe he can tell you where Ashby is now."

Funk was not at home, but one of his neighbors directed the refugees to Elder Kline, who met them in the road near his house.

"I don't think you need to worry about Ashby," Kline reassured them. "He has returned to Harrisonburg."

"That's wonderful news," A. J. said. "Now all we need is a place to get our suppers and spend the night."

"I would gladly invite you to my home," Kline said, "but the conscription scouts are still watching me. Your best bet is Emanuel Hoover's farm about two miles east of Timberville on the North Fork of the Shenandoah.

Hoover was an affable man in his mid-30s, who warmly welcomed the boys and referred them to Captain Green, a Union commander who was bivouacked with his men near the Valley Pike. Green told them that if they returned at 7 a.m., they could ride with his mule team to New Market.

Sammy and A. J. spent an anxious night in Hoover's barn and returned to Captain Green's camp soon after sunup. Then they rode in the back of a wagon to New Market, where they secured passes that gave them three days to travel to Winchester.

With official travel papers in hand and Banks' army between them and the Confederates, Sammy and A. J. felt safe for the first time since they had left Pleasant Run. On the crowded streets of New Market, Sammy was glad to see many of his Mennonite and Dunker friends, who were also preparing to go north with Banks' army. One of them was Bishop Coffman.

"What are you doing here?" Sammy asked. "I thought you was exempt 'cause you're a preacher."

"Well ... I am exempt from the military, but I am not immune to the noose," Coffman quipped. "The threats against me have become more serious since I started preaching directly against conscription. Colonel Jones said he would come to Weavers Church on Sunday, hang me in the oak grove, and arrest every man there."

Sammy's chance encounter with Coffman gave A. J. an idea about where they could find their next meal and a comfortable place to spend the night.

"One of the ministers in my church lives about twelve miles north of here," A. J. said, as the boys left New Market. "He's the most Secesh man I know, but he's a good Christian, so he won't turn anyone away hungry."

It took the boys about five hours to reach the home of Henry Saint John Rinker, a reverend in the German Reformed Church. Rinker and his wife had three sons in the Confederate army, nine children living with them, and one more on the way. They welcomed the boys kindly, but as they ate supper, Rinker challenged their reasons for going north.

"Why would you want to abandon Virginia in her time of greatest distress?" he asked.

A. J. was quick to answer: "I was enrolled in Franklin and Marshall College in Lancaster when the trouble started in South Carolina," he explained. "I returned to the valley because my home is here, but I have refused to fight for either side in this war. So now I am going back to school … if the college still wants me."

"You can finish your schooling when the war is over," Rinker insisted. "Right now, we need all the able-bodied men we can get to defend Virginia from Lincoln's hirelings."

"I just don't see it that way," A. J. countered. "Among the first things I learned at Franklin and Marshall were the college's founding principles, and one of them was to preserve our republican system of government. I don't think either Benjamin Franklin or John Marshall would approve of this rebellion."

"Your education is lacking!" Rinker shouted, his face turning red with rage. "American patriots, such as Franklin and Marshall, took action when British governance devolved into tyranny, and that is the *same* thing that Southern patriots are doing now. The Black Republicans say they want to free the slaves, but what they really want is to subjugate the South!"

"What about you?" Rinker asked, turning his attention to Sammy. "Are you also going North to attend Franklin and Marshall?"

"I don't know nothin' about no college," Sammy said. "I jus' don't wanna kill nobody. I jus' wanna work in the harvest field and live in peace, and I figure I can do that easier in Ohio than in Virginia."

"Do not deceive yourself," Rinker retorted. "If you make it to Ohio—and I doubt that you will—the Union will just draft you into Lincoln's army, and you'll be right back where you started. Wouldn't you rather defend Virginia than fight with the North against the South?"

Sammy could not come up with a good answer, and Rinker didn't give him much time to mull it over.

"I advise both of you boys to turn around while you still can. Go back to Harrisonburg; turn yourselves over to the provost marshal, and volunteer for the Stonewall Brigade."

After supper and another Secesh lecture for dessert, Sammy and A. J. thanked the Rinkers for their hospitality and retreated to the barn, where they did not sleep well.

"You reckon he's gonna report us to General Jackson?" Sammy asked.

"I don't think he can right now," A. J. replied, "but I believe he would if he could."

Sammy and A. J. left the Rinker farm at first light without saying goodbye or inquiring about breakfast. A heavy frost covered the ground, reflecting the bright morning sun into their eyes as they angled east toward the Valley Pike. A cold wind quickened their pace, but before long, May 9 turned into a fine spring day.

The two refugees begged for their dinners at several Secesh farms and were rudely repulsed, but they finally found hospitality at a Unionist home near Bowmans Crossing. They got nothing more to eat until 8 p.m. the next day, when they supped with another Unionist family at Strasburg. They were still eighteen miles short of Winchester, so they walked for two more hours before slipping into a barn without announcing their presence. They slept soundly until the owner of the barn surprised them in the morning.

"What are you vagabonds doing in my barn?" he demanded.

"We was just takin' a rest," Sammy replied, as he struggled to his feet. "We was on our way to Winchester, and it was nearly midnight, so we thought we could jus' borrow a little sleep here in yer barn without troublin' you."

Whenever Sammy spoke without thinking, which was most of the time, there was a disarming innocence to his voice that made strangers want to shake his hand, slap his back, and make his acquaintance. And that's just what the farmer did.

"C'mon in the house, my friends," he invited. "My wife and daughters will wanna meet you boys. You look hungry. Will you join us for breakfast?"

Sammy and A. J. washed up in the kitchen, ate a splendid breakfast, and thoroughly enjoyed the company of their newfound friends. The farmer's daughters were attractive young ladies who spoke kindly to their eligible guests. Sammy wanted to stick around for dinner, but A. J. insisted that it was time to go.

"C'mon, Sammy. The provost marshal gave us three days to get to Winchester, and that was three days ago."

Sammy and A. J. enthusiastically thanked the farmer and his wife and reluctantly bid farewell to their endearing daughters. Then they hurried to the provost marshal's office in Winchester, where they obtained passes to Martinsburg. They also exchanged their paper money—three Confederate dollars for each Union greenback—and bought some cheese and crackers.

After spending another unannounced night in somebody's barn, the fugitives hitched a ride on a big wagon headed north along the Valley Pike. The man driving the team told them they could easily find harvest work in Maryland, so Sammy decided he would stay there instead of moving on to Ohio. The road-weary refugees crossed the Potomac River together on a ferry, and then it was time to take the parting hand.

"I don't know if we will be permitted to ever see each other again in this world," Sammy said sadly.

"You must visit me at the college in Lancaster," A. J. replied. "It's the garden spot of Pennsylvania. We'll go up in the steeple. You can see the whole city from there."

"That sounds like a jolly time. I will try to find you there," Sammy promised, with tears welling up in his eyes.

"This goodbye won't be forever," A. J. assured. "We'll only say farewell till we meet again—in this world or the next."

CHAPTER 14

War Arrives

*"If they try to cross this creek,
there's gonna be a fight."*

As soon as Banks' army left Harrisonburg, Brunk and Rodgers returned to Peggy's secret cellar, and the cavalry squad that Sammy had seen near Muddy Creek put down roots in the oak grove behind the church. The rebels used the meetinghouse as a commissary and barracks, with soldiers sleeping on the floor, on the benches, even on the pulpit.

A few days later, Peggy heard that Jackson's army had won a battle at McDowell, a tiny town about forty miles to the west. And by May 19, the entire 52nd Virginia Infantry was camped just east of the church.

On the following morning, Jackson's forces marched through Harrisonburg and started north along the Valley Pike, joined by General Ewell's men, who had been waiting near Swift Run Gap. The Confederates won a battle at lightly defended Front Royal and a much larger confrontation at Winchester on May 25. They drove the Yankees all the way to the Potomac River, but with three Union armies closing in on them from three different directions, they retreated rapidly back toward Harrisonburg. The war was headed straight toward Peggy, Henry, and the children.

❖ ❖ ❖

Rain arrived at the Rhodes depot on June 2 and quickly progressed from a refreshing shower to a destructive downpour. Deluge after deluge drenched the valley for the next two days. The torrential rain finally relented on June 5, but by then, Cooks Creek had flooded the foundation of the barn and was creeping close to the front steps of the house. On the following day, as Peggy was putting the noon meal on the table, Mary spotted four soldiers in blue uniforms sloshing along the east bank of the swollen creek. While Brunk and Rodgers climbed down into the soggy cellar, Henry peeked through the curtains of the side window on the second floor.

"Well, I'll be John Brown!" he exclaimed. "Looks like we are havin' *Union* soldiers for dinner today."

Within a minute or two, the men were on the front porch, and their sergeant was pounding on the door. Henry armed himself with as much kindness as he could conjure and invited them inside.

"What can I do for you gentlemen?" he asked politely.

Seeing food on the table, the sergeant said, "You can step aside while we eat our dinners."

Henry calmly turned to Johnny and the children, who were already seated at the table.

"I believe these men are hungrier than us, so we'll do what they ask. Johnny, take their coats and spread 'em out in the parlor. Mary, take Willy and your sisters upstairs and stay there till I say it's alright to come down. Me and your mother will take care of these men."

The soaking soldiers tracked massive amounts of mud into the house as they claimed the children's seats at the table and tore into their food like stray cats. The men didn't bother to remove their caps, which were decorated with thin strips of deer hide that resembled bucktails.

"Could I interest you in some fresh-baked bread?" Peggy offered, taking her cues from Henry's polite approach.

"I think these boys would be *very* interested in that," the sergeant replied in a more conciliatory tone. "Got any butter to put on it?"

"Churned it myself," Peggy replied, as she placed a basket of warm bread and a dish of cool butter on the table.

Henry pulled up a chair and attempted to engage the sergeant in friendly conversation.

"You're the first Union soldiers we ever had for dinner. Do you mind if I ask you some questions?"

"It's your house and your food. Ask all the questions you like."

"Well … uh … what's your name?"

"Hunt."

"Just Hunt?"

"You can call me Sergeant Hunt if that'll suit you better."

"Alright … where you from, Sergeant Hunt?"

"Up north," the officer said, with a derisive laugh and a little snort that greatly amused his charges.

"I figured that much, but what state?"

"Pennsylvania! We belong to Colonel Thomas Kane's Bucktails, the sharpest shooters and finest woodsmen in the entire Quaker State."

Henry was quick to claim this common ground.

"My mother and father was both born in Pennsylvania. I reckon I got more cousins up there than you can shake a stick at."

"Is that so? What part of Pennsylvania?"

"Lancaster County."

"Ever been there?" Hunt asked.

"Nawsir. I ain't never been past Mount Jackson to the north. I 'spect you boys marched right through there on your way here."

The sergeant abruptly stopped chewing his dinner and looked Henry straight in the eye for the first time.

"It ain't none of your business where we've been or where we're goin'," he growled. "Do you take me for some kinda fool?"

"The Bible says to call no man a fool," Henry replied.

"Hmm ... you claim to live by the good book do ya?"

"I do the best I can."

"Don't it say something in there about feeding your enemy?"

"Deed it does."

"And by feeding me, you think you're heaping hot coals on my head. Am I right?"

"Wellsir ... I wouldn't heap hot coals on anybody's head, and I don't rightly know that you *are* my enemy. The fact that you hail from Pennsylvania don't offend me one bit. Does the fact that I was born in Virginia bother you?"

"Hmm ... let me study on that one," the sergeant said, as he buttered another hunk of bread. "I'll tell you one thing: I ain't offended by your wife's good cooking."

When the conversation was over and the food was gone, the soldiers thanked Peggy properly for their dinners, retrieved their coats, and stepped out onto the front porch with Henry.

"I better not ask where you plan to camp tonight," Henry said, "but you best be careful which side of the creek you favor. If it rains again tonight, you won't be able to cross it tomorrow. I ain't never seen it this high before."

"We'll keep to the high ground, you can count on that, and here's some advice for you: there's a company of rebels camped on the north slope of that big round hill beyond your barn. If they try to cross this creek, there's gonna be a fight. So if you hear gunshots, you get your wife and kids in the cellar and you keep 'em there till all's quiet. You hear me?"

"I hear you plainly, and I'll do as you say," Henry promised. "Thanky for the warnin', Sergeant Hunt."

Hunt smiled at Henry and extended his right hand. "My name's Jacob, by the way. People call me Jake fer short."

"Nice to meet you, Jake. My name's Henry. People call me short fer sport."

Jake laughed and snorted. The two men shook hands and parted friends—or at least not enemies.

❖   ❖   ❖

Around 4 p.m., Henry heard several sharp cracks that sounded like Peggy snapping the dust off a rag rug. The sporadic cracks and pops gradually increased in frequency like kernels of corn exploding in a kettle of hot oil. Then the thunderous sound of a cannon blast emanated from Iron Ore Hill. The refugees quickly returned to the cellar, taking the children with them. The rest of the Rhodes family hunkered down in front of the fireplace. They prayed earnestly for the soldiers on both sides of the fight, especially Sergeant Hunt and his men.

The shooting seemed to go on for hours, but it lasted only thirty minutes. After the gunfire and cannonading ceased, everyone remained in the house until Peggy's father, Abraham, called out to them from the other side of the creek. He reported that a group of rebels had made it through the high water, and the Bucktails were pursuing them down the Rawley Road toward Harrisonburg.

"Doc needs help tending to the wounded!" Abraham hollered. "Can you spare Johnny?"

"We'll send him right over," Peggy answered.

The water was too high to cross the bridge between the house and barn, so Johnny walked north along the swollen creek until he reached the road, where he was able to wade across the bridge with the water running waist high. On the other side, Peggy's brothers, David and Daniel, were loading wounded Confederate soldiers onto beds of straw in the backs of wagons.

"Where're we gonna take them?" Johnny asked.

"We're gonna try to make it to John Wenger's house," Doc replied. "Take my horse and ride over there to see if he can accommodate six or seven wounded men for two or three nights. If not, see if John Brunk will open up the church."

Johnny found Wenger at home, and he readily agreed to shelter the wounded men. He started moving bedding from his hiding place to his parlor, while Johnny rode back to the creek. By the time he got there, the wagons had crossed the bridge, but two of them were stuck in deep mud between the creek and the blacksmith shop.

"Go get John Brunk and his boys," Doc ordered. "We're gonna need more help to get these wagons up the hill."

Johnny quickly returned with the Brunks, and they were finally able to rock the wagons out of the mud holes and keep them rolling up the deeply rutted road. Johnny helped push the ambulances until they crested the ridge at Weavers Church and turned right onto the road toward Wenger's makeshift hospital.

The skirmish near Mole Hill was just the beginning of the fighting in Rockingham. On the same day, some of Kane's Bucktails shot and killed Turner Ashby in a firefight southeast of Harrisonburg. And in the days that followed, there were two full-blown battles between Jackson's Confederate forces and the Union armies of Frémont and Shields. The first was at Cross Keys and the second at Port Republic.

Jackson's men won both battles, and on June 11, Rodgers left the Rhodes depot to go north with Frémont's defeated forces. Brunk decided not to accompany Rodgers because his wife was suffering a difficult pregnancy.

Late that night, there was more tapping on the bedroom window. It was H. L., who was bringing a Confederate deserter to the depot. The young soldier was neither Mennonite nor Dunker, but he said he was done with the war and wanted to go west. Fresh from the Battle of Cross Keys, he was still carrying a gun.

While Mary stood watch from the second level of the barn, Peggy gave the soldier something to eat, and Henry asked him a few pointed questions. He did not want to offer sanctuary in the secret cellar until he was certain the man was not a conscription scout posing as a deserter.

"I might know someone who can help you go west," Henry volunteered, "but you'll have to take off your uniform and give up your gun."

"I'm more than happy to shed this uniform," the man said, between big bites of apple butter bread, "but I'm bound and determined to keep my rifle close."

"If you carry a gun without wearing a uniform, soldiers from either army might take you for a bushwhacker," Henry explained. "You have to give up your uniform *and* your gun if you want me to help you. Do we have a deal or not?"

"I tell you what," the young man responded. "If you keep feedin' me this apple butter bread, I'll give up my uniform, my gun, and what's left of my shoes!"

"Keep your shoes, you're gonna need 'em," Henry advised, as he took the rifle outside and motioned for Johnny to follow.

"Take this gun up to John Brunk's place and give the signal on his right rear window. He'll know what to do with it. Stick to the woods as much as you can between here and there, and don't take no chances. Don't let anyone catch you with this here military gun. They'd want to know where you got it, and that's a question you must not answer no matter what."

Johnny carried the gun up through the white pine field, trotting as quickly as he could without making much noise. He cut through the woods near the Fairview School, crossed the Rawley Road, and crept around behind the Brunk place. He tapped on the right rear window and crouched beside the house, waiting for John Brunk to appear on the porch.

As soon as Brunk stepped outside and whistled a tune, Johnny slipped around the corner and said, "It's me, Johnny Bell."

"What's wrong, Johnny? Do you need a place to hide?" Brunk responded, in a voice that was barely above a whisper.

"No … not yet anyhow … but I need to get shut of a military gun. Uncle Henry said you'll know what to do with it."

"Wait for me around back. I'll put on my boots and show you where the guns go."

After a minute or two, Brunk came out the back door and whispered, "Don't say another word until I tell you it's alright. Don't make *any* noise if you can help it."

Brunk led Johnny through his cornfield and up across his pasture to the road that ran beside Weavers Church. They quickly crossed the road and entered the rocky woods on the other side. After continuing uphill for about 200 feet, Brunk sat down on a boulder and motioned for Johnny to do the same.

"You can talk now," he said quietly, "but first I want you to listen carefully to every word I say."

"Yessir."

"Getting rid of guns is serious business. If you get caught doing this, you could get yourself and a lot of other folks killed. I will show you what to do, but you musn't speak of this to anyone, not even your Uncle Henry or your Aunt Peggy. It's better they not know where the guns go. Do you understand me?"

"I understand."

"Next time, you must do this by yourself. Don't bring anyone with you. Don't come to my house. Just cut across my farm and climb the hill to this spot. These big rocks are easy to find, even in the dark. From here you must walk fifty paces back toward the church. Don't angle down the hill or up the hill, just walk south along the ridge straight toward the church. You try it now, and I'll follow you."

Johnny stood up and started counting his steps as he walked slowly toward the church.

"Make your paces a little bit bigger," Brunk advised.

Fifty bigger steps brought Johnny to a depression in the side of the hill near the edge of the woods.

"This sinkhole marks the spot," Brunk said, pointing to a cleft between two stones below a rocky ledge.

"Do I just throw the gun down that hole?" Johnny asked.

"Not yet. You must always do this first."

Brunk got down on his hands and knees and picked up a stone about the size of an apple and smacked it against the ledge three or four times. Then he leaned forward into the abyss and yelled, "Stand clear!"

He waited about five seconds and sent the gun clattering down the hole.

"What was *that* all about?" Johnny asked.

"I did that," Brunk replied, "because half a dozen deserters are hiding down there. That's why you must take every precaution to keep the location of this cave secret. If a conscription scout was to follow you here and discover this hiding place, your carelessness could cost these men their lives."

CHAPTER 15

Invisible Brunk

*"Who around here knows
where I might find Henry Brunk?"*

Mary sounded the alarm on a bright sunny day in late June when she saw a commissary wagon coming up the lane between the bottom field and the upper field. Brunk and three other deserters quickly returned to the cellar, while Peggy went out on the porch to see how much this latest incursion would cost.

"Hello, Mrs. Rhodes," the forage master called out. "It's been more than a month. I imagine you're glad to see me again."

"I was hoping you forgot where we lived," Peggy replied. "The armies are gone. Why are you still out foraging?"

"We're holding 2,000 prisoners of war on court square, and the provost marshal says they haft'a eat, so I naturally thought of you. I know you wanna help feed them damn Yankees 'cause you're a galvanized Yankee yourself. Ain't that right?"

"I've been called worse," Peggy replied, "but no one's ever called me a thief. Are you buyin' or stealin' today?"

"The provost marshal has authorized me to appropriate whatever's necessary to feed them Yankees. Now, if it were up to me, I'd let 'em starve, but I hear you Germans sympathize with Lincoln's hirelings, so I'll jus' see what I can scrounge up in yer smokehouse."

The flippant forager took several slabs of Peggy's best bacon and returned to his wagon seat.

"Yer corn's lookin' *mighty* good!" he hollered, as he turned his wagon around. "I'll be back next week for a load of roastin' ears."

The forage master was true to his word. Even after the rebels transferred their prisoners of war to Richmond, the commissary wagons returned to the Rhodes farm with unpleasant frequency. They stole corn, wheat, and horses with no sign of remorse. When they occasionally offered Confederate currency as payment, Peggy always declined, but her stubbornness only confirmed that she was an easy target. And during the summer of 1862, the foragers increasingly took food and supplies from the Mennonites around Mole Hill. Peggy soon realized that if they didn't do something to stem the stealing, the farms would fail, and the underground railroad would collapse.

"Henry," she said, "I think it's time for another secret meeting in our perfect place."

Henry was no longer fit to travel, so Peggy sent Mary to fetch Doc, who agreed that they needed to call another meeting to discuss ways to hide their valuables. He helped Peggy make a list of trusted Mennonites who lived near Mole Hill, including Bishop Coffman, who had recently returned from Pennsylvania.

"We musn't deceive the forage masters without the bishop's consent," Doc said. "People will want to know where the church stands on such trickery."

Everyone arrived at the Rhodes depot on the night of August 12. Doc thanked them for coming and spoke briefly about the urgent need to retain sufficient resources to keep their farms productive.

"Before we talk about ways of doing that, I've asked Bishop Coffman to speak on whether hiding our valuables would violate the principles of the church."

Coffman stood up and said, "In the Sermon on the Mount, Jesus instructs us to 'resist not evil' and to 'give to him that asketh,' but these Confederate foragers are not asking, they are simply stealing. So the way I see it, hiding our valuables is not resisting evil, it is simply removing temptation from those who easily succumb to it."

"Are you already hidin' things from the foragers?" Peggy asked.

"I trust you," Coffman replied, "and I trust every man in this room, so I will tell you now that I hide my silver and gold beneath piles of stones in the pasture. When Ashby's cavalry took over the church, I concealed my horses on the wooded ridge to the northwest. When Frémont's men camped nearby, my wife hid loaves of bread in the base of our clock. And to this day, my sons keep the best roastin' ears in a large box surrounded by bundles of fodder."

Coffman's confession primed the pump for a long discussion on clever hiding places.

"These are all good ideas," Peggy said, "but what about wheat? That's what they want most right now. It's the new money. How do you hide good clean wheat?"

"Put it in the walls of your house," Henry Brunk suggested.

"In the walls?"

"Yep. This here wall needs plaster. Ain't that right, Aunt Peggy?"

"I reckon they all do."

"Well … what if I plastered this wall and left six or seven inches of space between the logs and the lathing? I imagine you could hide twenty bushels of wheat in there."

"That's fine, but how would I get it out?" Peggy asked.

"Just drill a hole in the floor, take out what you need, and plug the hole till you need more."

"Well … how would I fill it back up?"

"In yer case, I would cut a hole near the ceiling and cover it with a pie tin. It would look like you're coverin' an old stovepipe hole. You could do the same thing under yer steps. Just remove the closet door, plaster over the opening, and turn the top step into a lid."

PEGGY'S WAR

❖ ❖ ❖

Brunk was busy building a granary under Peggy's steps when a new type of Confederate forager arrived at the Rhodes place. This scavenger was looking for something that was hard to hide, something that threatened to blow the cover off the secret cellar.

Mary sounded the alarm as soon as she saw a wagon coming up the lane, and Brunk hurried down the hatch to his hiding place. Henry was sick in bed, so Peggy answered the gentle knock on the front door. She was surprised to see a dirty little man, who was remarkably thin and every bit as short as Henry. He was also impeccably polite.

"Good morning, ma'am. Please allow me to introduce myself. My name is Amos Shiflett, and I work for the Niter Corps. I need to look around under your house."

Peggy's heart skipped two beats as she struggled to process the likely consequences of allowing this dirty little man to poke around under her house.

"Why would you want to do such a thing?" she inquired. Peggy was mostly stalling for time, but she was also genuinely curious.

"I'm a peter monkey," Shiflett said. "I crawl around under houses looking for saltpeter."

"Salt ... what?"

"Saltpeter. I sell it to the government, and they use it to make gunpowder. They mostly get saltpeter from caves, but I'm pretty good at finding it under people's houses."

"Why do you think this ... uh ... salt ... is under my house?"

"Well ... your house is right close to the creek, and I'm guessing that the creek sometimes floods your foundation, and a damp crawl space is a hotbed for niter dirt."

"Dirt? I thought you was lookin' for some kinda salt."

"Yes, ma'am. That's right. I boil down the dirt to extract the saltpeter. I see you have a cellar entrance on the side of your house. Does that lead to a full basement or just a root cellar?"

"It's ... uh ... it's ... only a root cellar," Peggy stammered, "but you're welcome to look around down there if you like."

Peggy followed Shiflett outside and watched him light a grease lamp and carry it down into the root cellar. She prayed as hard as she knew how that Brunk would not cough or sneeze.

"Do you see any salt, Mr. Shiflett?" she hollered down the steps, trying to alert Brunk that someone was getting dangerously close to his hiding place.

"Not yet, but it takes a minute for my eyes to adjust."

After a short time, Shiflett emerged from the cellar shaking his head. "There's no peter dirt down there, but that don't surprise me. I'll check your crawl space. I'm more likely to find it there."

"There's an opening under the porch, but I'm worried about your lamp," Peggy said. "There's enough room under the front part of the house, but I don't want you taking that lamp past the beam. It's too tight back there to be crawling around with an open flame."

"Don't you worry," Shiflett said. "I've done this a hundred times, and I haven't burned anybody's house down yet."

Before Peggy could concoct another reasonable objection, Shiflett had ducked under the porch.

Peggy ran back into the house to tell Henry what was happening. She woke him gently and whispered in his ear: "There's a man under the house looking for salt ... something. What must I do?"

"We must pray that he don't see Brunk."

Peggy and Henry knelt together on the floor and prayed silently until there was another knock on the door.

"Ask him if he'll stay for supper," Henry said, as he struggled to put on his pants.

Peggy went to the door and invited Shiflett into the parlor. "Would you like to stay for supper?" she asked. "I'm cooking two or three chickens, so we'll have plenty, and I know my husband would like to hear about your salt. We have such a hard time getting salt these days."

"It's mighty nice of you to ask, but I won't be staying."

"Did you find any salt?"

"Yes, ma'am. I found large deposits of niter dirt ... and I saw something else, too."

Peggy's heart nearly stopped. "What else did you see?"

Shiflett stared at Peggy for a long time before he mumbled his reply: "I saw ... well ... uh ... I saw ... nothin' worth mentioning, I suppose."

Peggy followed the dirty little man onto the porch and helped him gather his tools.

"Will you be back tomorrow to get the dirt?" she asked.

"No ma'am ... some dirt is better left alone."

Brunk's daughter, Sarah, was born on September 17, 1862, and for the next three weeks, the weather was cool and dry, ideal for escaping through the mountains. But Sarah's birth had been difficult, and Brunk's wife, Susanna, remained dangerously ill, so Brunk stayed at the Rhodes depot.

In October, the Confederate Congress passed a new conscription act that included a religious exemption for Mennonites and members of other peace churches, but Brunk still failed to qualify because he had not been a member of the church at the beginning of the war. He knew that the autumn window for escaping was beginning to close, but Susanna continued to struggle with postpartum complications. She began to recover in late November, but by then their two-year-old son, John Albert, had become seriously sick with a fever and sore throat. Doc did what he could to save the boy, but the little tyke died of diphtheria on the morning of December 5, just an hour or two after Brunk had left John Albert's bedside to return to the Rhodes depot. Brunk was distraught beyond all reason when Peggy delivered the awful news.

"I have to go see Susanna right now," he said, when he was finally able to speak. "I can't wait till dark."

"You can't go over there at all," Peggy insisted, "certainly not now and not even after it gets dark. The conscription scouts will be watching your house, and I'm sure they'll be at the funeral as well."

"Oh … I am *going* to the funeral!" Brunk declared. "I don't care if the scouts do catch me. I am *going* to the funeral of my one and only son!"

"You musn't talk like that," Peggy pleaded. "If the scouts catch you, they'll send you back to Castle Thunder forever. They might even hang you, and what good would that do Susanna and Sarah?"

Peggy and Brunk argued back and forth for a good five minutes, while Henry stared out the parlor window, as though he wasn't listening to either of them. Finally, when Peggy became too exasperated to hold up her end of the argument, she turned to Henry and said, "Don't you have *anything* to say about this?"

"Tell me something," Henry mused, as he continued to gaze out the window. "How tall is John Wenger?"

"What's that got to do with anything?" Peggy nearly shouted.

"Maybe nothin' but maybe a lot. How *tall* is John Wenger?"

"He's about five foot eight or nine, about the same as me," Brunk volunteered.

"That's what I thought. Matter of fact, I think John Wenger's about your size all the way around. Ain't that right?"

"I reckon he is, but I don't follow you."

Henry finally turned away from the window and spoke directly to Brunk.

"The conscription scouts *will* be lookin' for you at your home and at the funeral. Peggy's right about that, but they'll be lookin' for a 'mangy Mennonite,' as they like to say. But what if you showed up lookin' like a proper Dunker?"

"Oh ... I get it. I could borrow a blue suit from John Wenger."

"You could trim your beard the way the Dunkers do," Peggy said.

"I'll shave my mustache, put on a black hat, and no one will know me from Adam Ketterman."

"I'll get Mary to spread the word to the other lookouts," Peggy said. "We'll tell everyone that we need as many people as possible to attend John Albert's funeral—Mennonites and Dunkers alike."

"That's good, Peggy, but don't tell Mary why we need such a big crowd," Henry instructed. "That way she can't let anything slip."

Henry helped Brunk trim his beard just right, while Peggy hitched up the spring wagon to make the trip to Wenger's house under the guise of bartering eggs and vegetables for some second-hand clothes.

Wenger's old blue suit fit Brunk just fine. The black felt hat was too big, so Peggy put some padding in the top.

"Not too much," Henry advised. "Let it sag down over his eyes."

A large crowd of good neighbors turned out for John Albert's funeral at the Bank Church, but during the graveside service, Susanna stood alone at the grave. The scouts searched in vain among the Mennonites, while Brunk and Wenger mingled with the Dunkers at the back of the crowd. As the mourners sang the last hymn, Brunk rode away with Wenger and returned to the Rhodes depot late that night.

❖ ❖ ❖

Brunk could not stand to sit idle, and the death of his son agitated him even more. He flailed away at the wheat on the floor of the Rhodes barn until the threshing was entirely done. Then he came up with the idea of making willow-whip baskets. Peggy purchased a good supply of seasoned willow whips, and Brunk showed Suzy and Becky how to weave them.

The fugitive's industrious nature and Henry's sickly state inspired Peggy to invoke a new division of labor on the Rhodes farm. She focused Johnny on field work and kept the refugees busy in the barn doing whatever jobs they could accomplish indoors—tending horses, greasing harnesses, sheering sheep, shucking corn, and threshing wheat. They also worked in the barnyard, staying close enough to the house to duck quickly into the cellar whenever one of the girls gave the signal. Mottie took care of Priscilla and Willy, and quite often Henry, while Mary tended the garden and Peggy concentrated on keeping everyone safe, fed, and productive. Because of the exemption act, there were more men available for field work now, but Johnny was too overwhelmed to reciprocate, so Peggy traded goods for labor. In addition to Brunk's baskets, she bartered ham, apples, vegetables, and wool.

In late January, eighteen inches of snow fell, but by the middle of February, the weather turned nice, and Johnny started to plow. The warmer weather gave Brunk another opportunity to escape through the mountains, but Susanna continued to struggle with the loss of John Albert, and Brunk couldn't stand the thought of leaving her alone with her grief. He visited Susanna and Sarah at night and did whatever he could to help them.

The arrangement worked tolerably well until the middle of March, when Brunk ventured onto the Rawley Road at twilight. He carelessly crested a rise in the road and encountered a conscription scout whom he knew perfectly well. His first instinct was to run, but he decided to stand his ground and take his chances. The scout was John Albert Ayray, an old friend who happened to have the same first and middle names as Brunk's deceased son. On strict orders from the provost marshal, Ayray had come to arrest Brunk, but the friendly scout didn't seem to recognize him.

Suffering from temporary blindness, or perhaps conflicting loyalties, Ayray walked his horse right up to his fugitive friend and said, "Pardon me, sir. Who around here would know where I might find Henry Brunk?"

Brunk didn't know what to say. Was Ayray just pretending not to recognize him, or had the war affected his mind? Brunk's first inclination was to say, "It's me! Henry Brunk! Don't you know me?" But, on second thought, he decided to play along.

"I believe Mr. Petry, who lives about a half mile to the west, can tell you as much as any of Brunk's neighbors about his comings and goings." This was not a lie because none of Brunk's neighbors, not even Mr. Petry, had any idea where he was hiding.

Ayray thanked Brunk for the advice and trotted his horse west to seek Mr. Petry. As soon as the blind scout was out of sight, Brunk dashed into the woods and hurried back to the Rhodes place. He gathered up his meager belongings, waited for the safety of darkness, and moved to a different depot.

CHAPTER 16

Postmaster Peggy

"I don't know if this is good news or bad news."

Operating the depot was becoming considerably more dangerous in 1863. In the previous year, Peggy was well-acquainted with most of the refugees—they were relatives, in-laws, and close neighbors—but now she was concealing and trusting men she did not know.

In addition to the risks of aiding and abetting fugitives, Peggy started distributing letters from refugees in the North and picking up replies from their friends and families. The first letter was addressed to Rodgers' wife, Magdalene, "care of Peggy Rhodes." Rodgers wrote that he had made it safely to Maryland and was working on Bishop Michael Horst's farm near Hagerstown.

Peggy was delighted to deliver such encouraging news. It was the ideal tonic for her chronic depression, and she desperately craved a second dose and a third dose, but Henry cautioned her that this job was particularly dangerous.

"If the scouts catch you, they'll accuse you of being a Union spy," he said. "I don't think the war department would hang a woman, but they might lock you up in Castle Thunder."

Peggy understood the risk, and she felt the fear, but unlike the paralyzing terror she always encountered in her fiery nightmares, this defiant fear was invigorating. It made her feel stronger, more alive, more optimistic that she and her family could survive the war.

"Maybe this is why Sammy wanted to run when it was clearly safer for him to hide," Peggy said to Henry, as she attempted to articulate the difference, but Henry did not understand.

"Fear is fear," he insisted. "It don't come in different varieties. It's the most common of all weeds. You can't get shut of it entirely, but you can pray for courage and take precautions."

Peggy did not entirely accept Henry's explanation, but she followed his advice about taking precautions. She sewed two secret pockets inside her petticoat, and she always traveled under the guise of bartering a nice assortment of Brunk's willow-whip baskets.

Peggy was eager to deliver more mail when one of the guides arrived in June with a letter addressed to Sammy's mother in his unmistakable scrawl. Peggy asked Mottie to watch the children while she quickly hitched up the spring wagon. The five miles to Anna's house on Pleasant Run seemed more like fifty miles to Peggy, but she eventually knocked on her sister-in-law's front door. The sickly widow was slow to answer, but she was quick to interpret the excitement on Peggy's face.

"I have a letter from Sammy," Peggy blurted. "Do you want me to read it to you now, or would you rather wait until H. L. can come by and read it to you?"

"I wanna hear it right now!" Anna replied. "H. L. can read it later for his own self. C'mon in the house and sit while you read."

Peggy hurried into the house and sat down in the parlor.

"I don't know if this is good news or bad news, but here's what Sammy says:

Dear Mother,
    I take my seat this evening again to write a few lines to let you know that I am still in the land of the living. I am now situated in Altoona, Pa., but am writing this letter from the yearly meeting of the Tunkers near Martinsburg.

Anna's eyes filled with tears of joy before Peggy got past the first paragraph. "He's alright," she gasped. "My baby boy's alright."

Peggy looked up and smiled at Anna, pausing long enough to relish her relief before continuing to read.

> I sent you a letter soon after I settled in Maryland, but I suspect you never received such as I have not received any letters from Virginia. Since this letter has a better chance of reaching your hand, I will repeat what I wrote last summer. While situated near Frederick, Md., I was harvesting for David Engels, where I made my home, and for Elder Jesse Roop and several others, but I got tired of field work. The rebels came to Frederick and all around where I was then working, so I took a notion to go West, but then when the rebels all left, I got out of the notion and concluded to stay until that fall when I had a spell of hemorrhages followed by a very bad cough and shortness of breath which almost disabled me of work.
>
> Feeling some better, I rode the cars to Pennsylvania where my health improved considerable. On my way to Altoona, I crossed the Susquehanna river one mile and a quarter wide. I staid all night in Lancaster city with my friend, A. J. Bowers, and we walked all over the city and got up in the steeple to behold its beauties. The next day I took the cars the rest of the way to Altoona and staid with my friend, John Simpson, till I found carpenter work at one dollar and 60 cents per day.
>
> On my present journey to the Tunkers meeting, I enjoyed myself quite well and saw a great many of my old Virginia friends, but I was the most happy to see Elder John Kline, who I trust will deliver this letter. I want you to write me if you possible can. This is my chance, now you must watch for your chance. I would be very glad to see my kind mother, brothers,

and sisters and converse with you all on some points with regard to our spiritual and eternal welfare, but we must content ourselves as we are. It was us all that fetched this war upon us for we have rebelled against God, but with all the dark clouds that are hovering over us, God has spared us. May the grace of God and the communion and fellowship of the holy spirit rest with us all for ever more is the prayer of your unworthy son.

    Samuel A. Rhodes

After Peggy finished reading the letter, she visited with Anna longer than she intended. They jabbered on and on about Sammy's health and his travels, and Peggy tried to absorb some of the sunshine that Anna was radiating.

"I was praying for good news from Sammy so I could share my good news with you," Peggy finally confessed. "I'm going to have another baby."

❖ ❖ ❖

Johnny was harvesting wheat in the upper field when Peggy first heard about the Grim Reaper's heyday at Gettysburg. The initial reports were little more than rumors, but the general impression was accurate: large armies of North and South had fought a deadly and decisive battle in the rolling hills of southern Pennsylvania.

On July 10, the *Rockingham Register* heralded a "great, glorious, and overwhelming victory" for the South. But the truth began to glimmer between the lines of the next issue, which lamented "the large number of wounded Confederate soldiers who have been passing up the valley and through Harrisonburg for the last seven or eight days, on their way from the bloody battlefield at Gettysburg."

PEGGY'S WAR

Late that night, Peggy heard the familiar tapping on her bedroom window. She lit a lamp, carried it onto the porch, and did her best to whistle a tune. She expected to encounter yet another anonymous soldier seeking food, shelter, and concealment, but this time she recognized the young man who emerged from the darkness. It was Manassas Heatwole, Henry's nephew and Peggy's first cousin.

"Nas! We thought you was dead! C'mon in the house. Henry! Wake up! It's Nas!"

Manassas spent only one night at the Rhodes depot before moving to a hiding place under Doc's closet floor, but it was long enough for him to tell Henry and Peggy what really happened at Gettysburg.

"If there is such a thing as hell on earth, that was it," he said. "I never seen nothin' like it, and I never hope to again. Thousands of men was killed or wounded, and we finally retreated after three days of fighting. I looked after some of the wounded men on General John Imboden's wagon train, and we barely escaped across the Potomac after another fight. I quit the army for good when we got close to Harrisonburg."

The massive loss of human life horrified Peggy, but the true story of Gettysburg and the news of another Union victory at Vicksburg, Mississippi, raised her hopes that the war would soon be over. There were other signs, too, that the Confederacy was beginning to unravel. West Virginia had seceded from Virginia and emerged as a full-fledged Union state. The buying power of Confederate currency had fallen to nearly nothing, and the war department's efforts to recruit soldiers were becoming increasingly desperate.

One week after General Imboden assumed command of the Valley District on July 28, a notice appeared in the *Register* calling for every man between the ages of eighteen and forty-five who had not previously enrolled to report to the courthouse for military duty. The notice excused men who had hired substitutes or obtained medical exemptions, but it failed to mention any provisions for members of peace churches.

The Dunkers and Mennonites ignored Imboden's apparent oversight, but his decree put them on notice that their religious exemption was becoming tenuous. At the same time, Imboden put more pressure on the suspected leaders of the underground. The military authorities arrested Elder Kline on August 18 and released him on the same day. Then they detained him on August 24 and, once again, cut him loose on the same day.

Sympathy for Mennonites and Dunkers was eroding in Richmond as well. On September 7, Governor Letcher asked a special session of the General Assembly to replenish Virginia's militia ranks by eliminating the religious exemption and pushing the age limits down to sixteen and up to sixty. The state legislature rejected both ideas, but the governor's drastic proposals sent another wave of refugees into the underground.

Two of these newcomers were working in Peggy's barn when Mary sounded the alarm on October 4. The intruder turned out to be Doc, who was angry about what he had witnessed as he approached the Rhodes place.

"I saw two men running desperately from the barn to the house as I was coming down your lane," he scolded. "What if I had been a conscription scout?"

"I suppose we need to be more careful," Peggy admitted.

"I reckon you do!" Doc replied.

"He glared at Peggy for a moment, allowing the awkward silence to emphasize his point. Then he softened his demeanor and changed the subject.

"How's Henry doing today?"

"Not so good. The disease consumes his body, and the war devours his mind."

"Well … I wish I had good news, but I don't," Doc said. "The provost marshal has arrested Joseph Beery again, along with his son, Solomon, and his nephew, Henry May."

"I'm sorry to hear that," Peggy said, "but I've come to ignore such Secesh scares. They've arrested Elder Kline three times now, and nothing's ever come of it."

"I'm not as worried about Kline," Doc said. "He always gets a proper pass before he goes north or west, but Beery is reckless. He went off to Ohio without a pass, and when he returned, he hired a substitute for his son and then told the substitute he would help him escape to New Creek."

"That does sound dangerous," Peggy agreed, "but I don't see how I can do anything about it."

"Listen here: there's nothing you can do for the Beerys, but there is something you can do for me. I want you to shut down the depot for one week. No refugees should go outside for any reason, and you should post lookouts whenever a refugee is outside the cellar. And before it gets dark, the men must return to the cellar and stay there until your lookouts are back at their posts in the morning."

Peggy thanked Doc for the warning and did as he instructed for one week. No one came or went from the Rhodes depot until L. J. arrived on Saturday with the latest issue of the *Register*. Peggy opened the newspaper and quickly spotted a one-word heading in all capital letters:

> "ARRESTED—Joseph and Solomon Beery, father and son, residing near the Cross Keys, and Henry May, living at the head of Dry River in Rockingham County, were arrested and committed to jail in Harrisonburg on Saturday afternoon inst. charged with aiding, advising and assisting deserters from the Confederate service to escape from our lines. The elder Mr.

Beery has been known as a very determined and uncompromising Union man, and was one of the very few men in Rockingham who voted against the Ordinance of Secession. He was arrested, we believe, once before; but was acquitted for want of proof to convict him. Since then, he has been on a visit to some of the Abolition States and has come back, it would seem, to persuade and advise poor, simple, ignorant, and foolish people to attempt to abandon their country and her cause and make their way to the lines of the enemy. These prisoners have been sent to Richmond for trial."

One month later, the war department released the Beerys from Castle Thunder on bail, but as the Confederacy continued to struggle, it was becoming increasingly difficult for any able-bodied man to stay out of prison and out of the war at the same time. On December 7, President Jefferson Davis proposed removing all conscription exemptions. By the end of the year, the Confederate Congress had abolished the practice of hiring substitutes, but it retained the religious exemption.

The first day of 1864 started out moderately disagreeable and became downright contrary. The ground froze hard that night, the coldest night the valley had endured for many years, and the following day was not much better. Peggy fixed a bed for Henry close to the fire in the parlor, and for the first time, she considered the possibility that he might not live to see the spring.

Henry's health remained precarious for most of the month. On a good day, he made it to the dinner table and tried to eat something. On a bad day, he stayed in bed and invited death. But it was not yet his time. The weather began to improve on January 20, and within five days, the snow had melted, and the bees were flying strong. This remarkable foretaste of spring lasted for several days, and Henry regained some strength. By the end of the month, he was sitting on the porch watching Johnny plow the upper field on the other side of the creek.

On his best day, Henry was still far too weak to help Johnny, but he was determined not to be a burden on Peggy as her pregnancy approached full term. The birth of Lydia Rhodes brightened Henry's final days, but the weather took an abrupt turn for the worse on February 17, the coldest snap Peggy could remember. On that miserable day, the Confederate Congress passed a new conscription law that retained the religious exemption but pushed the age limits down to seventeen and up to fifty. General Imboden, who remained in charge of the Valley District, made it clear that seventeen-year-old boys would be the next candidates for conscription.

The weather moderated again by the end of February, and Johnny started spreading manure on Leap Day. He laughed to himself as he recalled Big Henry's old saying about manure smelling like money.

"I wonder what Big Henry would say about the odor of Confederate currency?" Johnny thought to himself.

Since rebel money had become nearly worthless, Virginia farmers were forced to make in-kind contributions to the Confederate cause—10 percent of whatever crops or livestock they produced. On top of that tax, the forage masters continued to target Mennonite and Dunker farmers because of their Unionist leanings and because they remained exempt from military duty. Despite this ongoing grain drain, many Mennonite and Dunker families managed to prosper, and many of their less-fortunate Secesh neighbors were becoming envious.

On March 4, an otherwise pleasant day, the *Register* published a letter that boiled the animosity down to a few spiteful sentences:

"We have been informed that some of our German friends, who have been exempted from military duty, have declared their intention to raise no more bread and meat than ... necessary for their own use. ... Men who will not serve the great cause ... ought to be put in the front ranks of our armies and if possible made food for gun powder."

Peggy did not share this disturbing story with Henry, who was no longer capable of reading the newspaper for himself, but she discussed it with her brothers and with Bishop Coffman.

"Mennonites have been too quiet on the pages of the *Register*," she insisted. "The people who read this story might mistake our silence as an admission of guilt, and I don't know anyone who isn't producing as much wheat and meat as the weather will allow."

One week later, Peggy was pleased to see that the editor of the *Register* had published a response to the hateful letter. It said, "We have been assured by several of the leading members of the churches of Tunkers and Mennonites in this country that they will ... raise all they can. ... Both branches of these churches ... have resolved to 'lay by' a portion for the poor outside of their respective communions. It has always been a part of their policy to take care of their own poor, but now they go a step beyond."

Johnny was too busy spreading manure and plowing for corn to read the *Register*, but he was keenly aware that he soon would be turning seventeen and that Rockingham County was beginning to activate "boy companies" of reserves.

"What should I do?" he asked Peggy.

"It's entirely up to you," she responded. "This is something you must decide, but there might be a way to buy some more time. If you report to the regimental court, like you're supposed to, you could stay here until they activate your company. Then you could hide in the cellar or go through the mountains if need be."

Johnny agreed that it would be best to keep his options open, so he reported to the courthouse on his birthday. Peggy went with him to make sure that the enrolling officer understood that her husband was dying and that their only son was not yet three years old. Without Johnny, the summer harvest would rot in the fields, and the fall planting would go undone.

The officer immediately enrolled Johnny in a boy company of infantry, but he also agreed to detail him to the Rhodes farm for five months. Peggy's plan was working.

CHAPTER 17

Swamp Dragons

*"We figure you's agoin' west or north,
and either way be fine wid us."*

The April call for seventeen-year-old soldiers worried Brunk, who had been hiding for more than a year at depots run by David Hartman and Jacob Shank. Brunk wasn't as concerned for himself as he was for his brother-in-law, R. J. Heatwole, who had turned seventeen in February.

R. J. finally agreed to head for the mountains, but only if Brunk would go with him. Brunk's wife, Susanna, was doing much better now, and she urged him to go north while the weather was good and the troop movement was minimal. After much discussion, Brunk decided to follow her advice. He and R. J. made plans to go to Hagerstown, Maryland, where Charles Rodgers had been living for nearly two years. They would send for Susanna and Sarah as soon as the way was safe.

At midnight on May 1, Brunk and R. J. met at Weavers Church with fourteen other teenage boys and David Frank, a twenty-five-year-old deserter who was married to one of Doc's granddaughters. Frank's predicament was almost identical to Brunk's. He had been among the men who were captured near Petersburg, imprisoned in Castle Thunder, and pressured into the Stonewall Brigade. Frank and Brunk both had deserted when Jackson's army was retreating through Harrisonburg, and they both were at the top of the provost marshal's list of wanted men.

Earlier in the war, desertion had been somewhat tolerated, but by 1864, deserters were being executed or brutally punished. And with the Confederacy becoming increasingly desperate for manpower, Frank and Brunk knew that conscription scouts were constantly combing the mountains of western Rockingham.

With all this in mind, the two deserters and fifteen draft dodgers started walking west from the church. They spread out along the Rawley Road with Frank in the lead, scanning the way ahead, and Brunk in the rear, watching the road behind. At the bottom of the hill, Brunk delegated his rear-guard responsibilities to R. J. while he swung by the Rhodes depot to say goodbye to Peggy and see if she had any letters bound for refugees in the North. She gave him a bundle of mail and implored him to keep the letters safe no matter what.

"You are holding the lives of many people in your hands," she stressed. "If you think you're about to be captured, you must find a safe place to hide these letters or a sure-fire way to destroy them."

"I won't fail you," Brunk said, "and I wanna thank you for all you have done for me and my family. I will never forget the time I spent in your cellar. As soon as we make it to Maryland, I will send Susanna a letter addressed to your care."

Peggy bid Brunk a fast farewell and stood on the front porch watching him fade into the darkness as he walked north along Cooks Creek. She glanced up at the top of Mole Hill and shuddered against the overwhelming intuition that she would never see him again.

Brunk cut across Hugh Swope's pasture and returned to the Rawley Road, where he quickly caught up with Frank and the boys. They arrived at the mountain depot near Rawley Springs just before sunrise and slept as much as they could during the day.

Late in the evening, two pilots arrived to guide them through the mountains. Each refugee paid them $20, and the group headed west on Dry River Road. The guides instructed them to travel two abreast with one person looking ahead and one watching behind. The pilots walked in front; the next two boys stayed just close enough to keep them in sight, and so on. There was an odd number of fugitives, so Brunk, Frank, and R. J. walked together at the rear of the train.

This approach seemed to work well. Twice the pilots gave the signal for everyone to hide, and twice they waited in the woods for people to pass on the road. The third time this happened, they were resting in some bushes near the road when a stranger suddenly stumbled onto their hiding place. This chance encounter terrified Brunk until he realized that the stranger was more afraid of them than they were of him.

"I'm trying to stay ahead of the scouts," the frantic man blurted. "There's a whole passel of 'em just north of here. They're taking horses and arresting deserters. They got my horse, but I slipped away before they could get me."

"Well ... you don't have to worry about us," one of the pilots said, "but thanky for the warning."

The stranger wished them luck and ran off through the woods in the general direction of Rawley Springs. As soon as he was out of sight, the pilots moved the refugees farther from the road and ordered them to lie down flat and remain quiet.

Frank and the boys did as they were told, while Brunk looked around for a place to hide Peggy's letters. As he was tucking the bundle of mail into a rotten log, he heard the scouts coming down the road. He peeked through the bushes and saw a small group of mounted men leading a dozen horses. They crossed the road at the exact spot where the fugitives had been hiding.

Brunk eased himself down to the ground and waited for the pilots' signal. After fifteen or twenty minutes, they returned to the road and followed it around Feedstone Mountain to the headwaters of Dry River. From there they turned north onto the same narrow path that Sammy and H. L. had twice traversed two years earlier. It was 3 a.m. by the time they reached the top of the Shenandoah. From there they followed the Pendleton Road down to the South Fork of the South Branch of the Potomac River, where they stopped for breakfast.

"We should be safe now," one of the pilots said. "We're in Pendleton County, where the Swamp Dragons and the Union regulars are in control more often than not."

This overstatement of safety greatly reassured Brunk, who began to recognize his surroundings as the sun rose above the Shenandoah.

"How far would you say we've come?" he asked the pilot.

"Oh ... twenty miles at the most."

"And how far do we have to go yet?"

"Oh ... it's about sixty more miles to New Creek."

"If we was to go it alone from here, and you was to turn back to the valley, could we get three-fourths of our money back?" Brunk proposed.

"Naw, you just can't figure it that way," the pilot responded. "We already did the most dangerous part. You boys ain't payin' us by the mile, you're payin' us by the heartbeat, and my heart was beatin' mighty quick when we slipped past those scouts back there on Dry River Road."

"Alright, how about half our money?" Brunk haggled. "If we was to part company right here, right now, would you give us half our money back?"

The pilot glanced at his partner, who shrugged his indifference, and Brunk looked at Frank, who wasn't quite so quick to discount the pilots' expertise.

"Are you *sure* you can get us there, Brunk?"

"I know I can. I did some plastering for a rich widow on the other side of the mountain that stands directly before us, and she don't live far from the road to Petersburg. And from Petersburg, we'll just go straight north until we get to New Creek. I don't see how we could go too far wrong."

"Well … I reckon it's alright with me if it's alright with these boys," Frank said.

The younger fugitives eagerly nodded their approval, and the pilots promptly refunded half of their fees.

"Your plan is reasonable," one of the pilots said. "If you run into trouble, jus' go straight north, and you'll eventually come out onto the Petersburg Road. Then, like you said, jus' keep goin' north till you get to New Creek."

The pilots said farewell, and the refugees charged up the next mountain with great confidence. There was a large rock formation at the top, so Brunk crawled out onto the giant boulders to scout the valley below. He returned to the group looking somewhat less sure of himself.

"There's a company of Confederate cavalry camped beside the stream that runs past the widow's house," he reported. "We can't risk going down there."

With the rebels blocking the most direct route to the main road, Brunk abandoned his plan to seek help from the widow. It would be safer, he reasoned, to go straight north, as the pilots had suggested. He took out his pocket watch and lined the hands up with the sun to make sure they were going the right way. Then they angled down the mountain just enough to give the rebels a wide berth.

About halfway down the ridge, they came upon a small cabin, where two young women spotted them and ran screaming down the mountain toward the cavalry camp. The fugitives ran the opposite way—as far up the mountain as adrenaline would carry them. They finally stopped to rest beside a wagon road that ran along the ridge, but they barely had time to catch their breath before Brunk heard horses coming. He led the boys back into the woods and wedged Peggy's bundle of mail under some rocks.

When the sounds of the horses faded away, Brunk retrieved the letters, and the group bedded down for the night. It felt good to rest their weary legs, but they were hungry, and their supply of food had dwindled to one piece of moldy cheese for each of them.

"I used to say cheese weren't fit to eat after it turns blue," R. J. joked, "but this here blue cheese tastes better'n anything I ever put in my mouth."

Brunk also had some of Doc's No. 6 medicine, so they all took a few drops because they had been without water all day. Then they nestled down into a large sink hole, covered themselves with leaves, and attempted to sleep.

When all was quiet, R. J. whispered, "Hey, Brunk. Can I ask you a question?"

"I ain't got no more blue cheese if that's what you're after."

"Naw, taint that. I was just wonderin' if you was worried about snakes and lizards crawlin' around in this here hole?"

Brunk harbored no irrational fear of reptiles, but worrying about the Confederate cavalry in the narrow valley below made it difficult for him to sleep.

In the morning, he led the fugitives north, gradually descending to the foot of the mountain, where they heard the sweet sound of a fast-running stream. The thirsty refugees were tantalizingly close to refreshment when Brunk caught sight of a stumpy little man squatting beside the creek. The leader signaled for Frank and the boys to lie down and be quiet while he sized up the squatter.

R. J. wanted to see the man, too, so he crept forward and peered over Brunk's shoulder for a few seconds. Then R. J. stood up and started laughing. He walked confidently over to the stumpy little man and kicked him about shoulder high. The man groaned and creaked and leaned to his left but did not fall, so R. J. kicked him again, and the man landed stiffly on the ground with a thud.

"We're hidin' from nothin' more than a rotten old tree stump," R. J. reported. "Brunk, you're blind as a bat!"

"I reckon I could use some spectacles," Brunk replied sheepishly, as he emerged from the bushes.

Frank walked over to the manly little stump and stared at it for several seconds. Then he looked up at Brunk and said what all the boys were thinking: "Back there ... up on the mountain ... are you sure you saw a cavalry camp?"

"Well ... I know I saw a dozen or more soldiers with at least that many horses and several rows of tents."

"Tell me something else, Brunk—that rich widow you keep talking about, do you s'pose she would give us our dinners?"

"I was hopin' she would, but she lives too close to the Confederate camp to risk it."

"Well ... what if it's a *Union* camp or maybe some Swamp Dragons. I don't see how you could tell the difference from way up there on the mountain. What if me and R. J. followed this stream for a couple of miles to scout it out. If it seems tolerable safe, then maybe we could see about gettin' somethin' to eat."

"Those soldiers looked Confederate to me, but I suppose they could be Swamp Dragons," Brunk conceded. "It might be worth a closer look, but you boys be careful—I mean *real* careful. Don't let anyone see you."

"We won't," R. J. promised, as he started walking southwest along the stream with Frank close on his heels.

The scouts soon returned with encouraging news. The rows of tents that Brunk had seen were only peach trees in full bloom, and the horses belonged to some farmers who were working in the orchard. Relieved that the danger was only imaginary, the refugees quickly followed the stream to the widow's house. Frank hid in the woods with the boys, while Brunk knocked on her door. Within a few minutes, he returned with four loaves of bread.

"How much do we owe you?" Frank inquired.

"Nothing," Brunk responded. "This bread only cost me a promise. I agreed not to tell the widow's slaves where we're going. I figured that won't be a problem 'cause I don't plan on telling *anyone* where we're going. Ain't that right?"

"I don't know about that," Frank said, with a frown. "I kinda wisht you hadn't made any promises about slaves. If they want to go to Yankeedom with us, I say let 'em come."

Most of the boys agreed with Frank, but with empty bellies and many more miles to go, they weren't about to turn down food. They took their bread into the woods, settled down in the brush, and ate breakfast and dinner combined.

"All we need to do now," Brunk said, as he chewed his butterless bread, "is cross one more mountain, and we'll come right down to the main road. After that, we will be walking on roads instead of scrambling over rocks and ripping through patches of greenbrier."

As soon as the refugees finished the bread, they started up the next mountain with renewed hope, but when they stopped at the top to rest, Brunk thought he heard footsteps coming from the woods behind them.

"All the way up the mountain, I felt like someone was followin' us, and now I'm sure of it," Brunk whispered to Frank. "I may be blind as a bat, but I got ears like an elephant, and I hear people coming toward us right now."

"It's probably just squirrels," Frank said, as he removed a sharp little rock from one of his boots. "You worry too much, Brunk."

"What I hear's too loud for squirrels. Deer maybe, but deer don't follow you up a mountain."

Frank squinted into the woods, trying to focus his eyes past as many trees as he could. Then he detected some movement, a few flashes of dark brown.

"Could be a she-bear with cubs," he said, with a bit more concern in his voice.

"Taint no she-bear," R. J. chimed in, as he studied the movements through the trees. "I think maybe yer rich widow's slaves decided to follow us after all."

"Hey there!" R. J. shouted, before Brunk could shush him.

"Yo! Don't shoot!" hollered one of the slaves. "We's friendly."

"We ain't got no guns, and we wouldn't shoot if we did," R. J. yelled back at them.

Three black men with large sacks slung across their shoulders gradually came into full view along the crest of the mountain. Brunk wasn't sure what to do as he watched the runaways come closer. He didn't want to ask where they were going because he didn't want them to ask him the same thing.

Brunk finally settled on something safe to say.

"You boys lost?"

"Nawsir. We ain't lost iffen *you* ain't lost. We's followin' *you*."

"But ... you don't know where we're going," Brunk countered.

"We figure you's agoin' west or north, and either way be fine wid us. We ain't agonna stay with that wida no mo."

"Whatchu got in yer sacks?" R. J. asked.

"All da food we could tote. We figure you boys jus' might be gettin' hungry."

Coming down the other side of the mountain, the expanded band of fugitives found the road to Petersburg, right where Brunk said it would be. They rested in the woods until dark then walked the road all night, arriving at the ford south of Petersburg as the sun began to rise.

"This ford brings back bad memories," Brunk confessed, "but the river is much lower this time, and I remember how to cross it."

Sure enough, they easily negotiated the South Branch of the Potomac and passed through the town without incident. On the following day, however, they were surprised by two rag-tag pickets carrying swords and brandishing guns. The soldiers demanded that the refugees surrender their arms, and the boys complied by producing two penknives and three pocket Testaments.

The soldiers laughed at this impressive array of armaments and identified themselves as Swamp Dragons.

"What's the difference between Swamp Dragons and regular Union soldiers?" R. J. asked.

"We's part of Captain Bond's home guard," one of the soldiers said.

"I thought all the home guards was rebels," Brunk replied.

"Well, we ain't rebels! We protect the people of Pendleton County and Hardy County that remain loyal to the Union. Are you boys Dunkers?"

"Most of us are Mennonites, but we have a good many friends that are Dunkers," Brunk said.

"Where you headed?"

Brunk hesitated. He still did not know if he should trust these men, but before he could decide how to respond, R. J. blurted out the answer.

"New Creek! We're on our way to New Creek to catch the B&O Railroad."

"Well … you got a ways to go yet," the soldier said. "About two miles ahead, there's a trail to the right that will take you to some regular Union pickets about two days north of us. They probably won't bother you, but they can get a might skittish with their guns, so make yourselves known before you get too close. The B&O station is just beyond their camp.

Brunk thanked the Swamp Dragons for the information and led the group along the mountain path for the better part of two days. When they finally caught sight of the Union camp, Brunk decided it would be better to skirt the pickets rather than risk a confrontation with skittish gunmen of any political persuasion.

So they took to the woods again, seeking higher ground and traveling parallel to the path for a mile or so. As they descended a steep rockslide to return to the trail, they were overjoyed to see the town of New Creek in the distance. They wanted to scramble down the mountain and run to the trains, but their legs and lungs were in no shape for traveling fast. They slowly made their way back to the path and stopped as soon as they found a shady spot where they could rest, but they were not alone. A Union picket suddenly emerged from the underbrush and pointed his pistol at them.

"Throw down your arms, and put up your hands," he ordered.

"We ain't got no guns," R. J. replied, as he raised his hands.

The soldier looked them over for a second or two and finally lowered his gun.

"I thought you might be some of McNeill's Rangers, but when I saw your slaves, I didn't know what to think."

"These boys ain't anybody's slaves," Brunk declared. "They are our traveling companions."

"Well, lucky for you I saw 'em when I did 'cause I was gettin' ready to start pickin' you off one at a time. What in tarnation were you doing up there on those rocks when there's a perfectly good trail down here?"

"We was trying to steer clear of you," Brunk admitted. "The Swamp Dragons said you wouldn't bother us, but they also said you're a might skittish with your guns."

"Well … I suppose they got that about right. Are you boys headed for New Creek?"

"Yep. We quit the Confederacy, and we're tryin' to get away from the war. We plan to take the cars east to Williamsport and then walk to Hagerstown, where we know some people."

"Well … first you'll have to ride the cars west to Clarksburg and take the oath of allegiance. Then maybe you can get passes to go east to Williamsport, but if you really wanna get away from the war, you should just keep going west, at least as far as Indiana. And if I was you, I'd go all the way to Iowa."

CHAPTER 18

Valley of the Shadow
"He was shot in the groin and breast with four balls."

The valley was called the breadbasket of the Confederacy, and in the summer of 1864, it remained strategically important because young boys, old men, and women of all ages worked hard to overcome the absence of able-bodied men from the harvest field. The farms of Rockingham stayed particularly productive because they benefited from significant numbers of Dunkers and Mennonites who still qualified for the religious exemption.

This agricultural capacity—combined with the Valley Pike and other geographical advantages—made the valley an excellent conduit for Confederate forays into Maryland and Pennsylvania. Residents of those states remained on edge, while Northern voters in general were growing increasingly weary of the war. So, for reasons both political and tactical, Lincoln ordered General Ulysses S. Grant to do whatever was necessary to render the valley useless to rebel forces. Grant, in turn, delegated this terrible task to General Franz Sigel, who marched his army up the valley toward Harrisonburg in the middle of May.

It rained hard on the night of the 14th, and it continued to rain on the 15th as Confederate troops under General John Breckinridge clashed with a good portion of Sigel's army at New Market just north of Rockingham. Bolstered by young cadets from the Virginia

Military Institute, Breckinridge's army won a clear victory, and Sigel retreated to Strasburg, but the Battle of New Market marked the beginning of a vengeful escalation of the war.

Grant promptly replaced Sigel with a more aggressive commander, General David Hunter, who moved quickly up the valley with a much larger army, arriving unopposed in Harrisonburg on the second day of June. His forage masters ravaged several Mennonite farms near Weavers Church, but they did not disturb the secluded Rhodes place.

At Staunton, Hunter's army burned the train depot, the wool factory, and the steam mill in addition to wagon shops, government stables, and warehouses packed full of in-kind contributions to the Confederate cause.

At Lexington, Hunter's forces torched VMI in retaliation for the cadets' role in the Battle of New Market. While ransacking the school, the soldiers found a proclamation, issued by Letcher when he was governor, urging civilians to wage guerrilla warfare against the "vandal hordes of Yankee invaders." This discovery prompted Hunter to burn Letcher's home as well.

The cycle of retribution accelerated and intensified as it crept closer to the Rhodes depot. On June 15, just ten miles north of Mole Hill, unseen assailants bushwhacked and killed Elder Kline on Howdyshell Ridge. Because Kline had routinely crossed enemy lines to attend Dunker conferences and other church meetings, his Secesh neighbors suspected he was a Union spy. Their suspicions intensified when they noticed that Hunter's men had bypassed his house when they were ransacking the town of Broadway.

News of Kline's death quickly reached Peggy, but she had learned to ignore such outrageous rumors. She didn't believe it until she read it in the *Register*. Under the stark heading of "MURDER," she found the whole sordid story:

"He was shot in the groin and breast with four balls, and is supposed to have been instantly killed. He had some money and his watch on his person when he was killed,—these were not disturbed by the party by whom he was slain. He was known as an uncompromising union man, and during the early part of the war had been arrested by order of Gen. Jackson for disloyalty. He had, however, been honorably acquitted, and was pursuing 'the even tenor of his way,' passing frequently by permission of our authorities within the Yankee lines to preach and hold other religious services. ... The motives which induced some assassins to waylay and kill him will probably be never fully known and understood; but the cause of his death doubtless had some connection with the troubles that now afflict the country, occupying as he was believed to do, a position of antagonism in feeling to the Confederacy. Whilst our people differed with Mr. Kline in the erroneous views which he entertained, yet all good citizens must deplore such a lawless wreaking of vengeance upon the person of an unarmed and feeble old man. Such things show how rapidly we are drifting into scenes which must be full of terror to us all."

Indeed, the atrocities of war were encroaching upon Peggy and everyone else in the valley, but Hunter's diversion to Lexington on his way to Lynchburg would prove particularly costly to the Union cause. The delay allowed General Jubal Early's army to arrive in Lynchburg by train in time to defend the city. On June 18, Early preemptively attacked Hunter's superior forces and bluffed them west into the mountains of West Virginia. This ill-advised retreat allowed Early's army to march unopposed down the valley into Maryland and to the outer defenses of Washington by July 11.

PEGGY'S WAR

❖   ❖   ❖

The letters that Peggy delivered usually conveyed good news; another young Dunker or Mennonite man had arrived safely in Maryland, Pennsylvania, or Ohio. But in late June, Peggy received a package that caused her heart to throb and her hands to tremble. It was addressed to Sammy's mother, Anna, but this time the handwriting on the package clearly did not belong to Sammy. Peggy immediately asked Mottie to watch the children while she hitched up the spring wagon and made the familiar five-mile trip to Anna's home on Pleasant Run.

Anna tore the package open and found a letter from Sammy, a journal in his handwriting, and a letter from cousin Peter S. Rhodes. Anna began to sob as she handed Peter's letter to Peggy, who read it out loud with great regret.

> Dear Aunt,
>
> The foregoing pages were written by your son, Samuel A. Rhodes, while he was yet sojourning with us in this unfriendly world. He wrote them expecting no doubt to carry the book to you himself. But alas, his hopes and expectations were thwarted. Disease came and preyed upon his vitals, followed by death, which removed him from our midst.

Before Peggy could finish the first sentence, Anna was crying uncontrollably, and by the end of the first paragraph, she was shrieking like a mortally wounded animal. Peggy stopped reading and comforted her sister-in-law for nearly an hour before Anna asked to hear the rest of the letter.

> When he first came to see us in Iowa, which was on the fifth of July 1863, his health was tolerably good. He went to

work first in the harvest field and afterwards in the wagonmakers shop. He appeared to stand the work very well and also to enjoy himself reasonably well. Time rolled on, fall came and went, and his health was still about the same. Winter set in but with it commenced a kind of hacking cough which at first appeared to be dry as he did not spit up much. It gradually grew worse and worse; all along through the winter, he would frequently take spells of coughing when he would have to sit down and cough till it caused him to vomit. He took a spell or two every day toward the latter part of the winter. Spring began to draw near. His cough still appeared to grow worse. He now began to spit up something of a mattery form which increased very rapidly in quantity until it became very troublesome to him and soon weakened him so that he had to quit work.

At this point, Peggy was struggling to contain her own emotions because the letter precisely described the progression of Henry's consumption during the past six months. Peggy paused for a moment, cleared her throat, and wiped her eyes before continuing with the letter.

Physicians and in fact many other persons told him that if he would take a trip to California that it would help him and perhaps cure him. So he took a notion to go, and we intended to go with him and were going to start about the first of May. [But] he kept going down very fast, so much so that nearly every day he spent appeared to leave him weaker and weaker until about the middle of March when he concluded he would not be able to stand such a long trip. He had no sooner give up the idea of going to California than he began to talk about going home. …

The next week we started for Indiana and arrived here on the 10th of April, ... but when Monday morning came, he insisted on leaving us and trying if possible to get home and see you once more before he left the shores of mortality. ... For us to leave him now to take such a journey without any company was a hard trial, knowing too, as we did, that we would never see him again in this world. But nothing else would do but he must try and see his mother, brothers, and sisters yet if possible. So about 15 minutes before train time, he got ready, and I went with him down to the cars, and when we got up to the car door, we found it full of soldiers. Here I had to leave him on the platform with nothing but his knapsack to sit on. It was a hard struggle, but we had to take the parting hand. The car moved off, and that is the last I ever saw of Samuel.

In a few weeks afterwards, we received a letter from Cousin Peter S. Heatwole informing us that he [Sammy] came to Maryland and there died. ... We who were with him the few last months of his life have every reason to believe that he was fully prepared to go. ... He often said he wished he could get with some of his Brethren or go to Menist (Mennonite) meeting, although we felt just like brethren when we were together and spent many happy hours about the family alter when he would lift his voice in fervent prayer to our heavenly father to remember and protect his kind mother and friends and imploring the God of Mercy to so guide and protect us through this life that we might all meet in the better land.

Thus did he spend the latter part of his life. God grant that we may also spend our lives in such a manner that we may meet with him in the Promised Land.

P. S. R.

Peggy had tried to comfort grieving mothers in the past, and she regretted all the trite little things she had said to them: "We must not murmur against God. ... The bitter always goes with the sweet. ... Time heals all wounds."

Peggy especially agonized over the many times she had said, "I know how you feel," when she didn't know anything of the sort. She had not experienced the intensity of a mother's grief until Davy died, but now she really did know how Anna felt. She also knew better than to say so. She simply sat and cried with Anna.

On the following day, five-year-old Priscilla complained that her head hurt, but Peggy barely noticed. She was too saturated with sadness to deal with any additional pain. Peggy attempted to concentrate on the daily routine of running the farm and the depot, but she could think of little else than memories of Sammy and Davy and the full realization that she would soon lose Henry as well.

As Priscilla's headache grew progressively worse, Peggy attributed the child's discomfort to the unusually hot, dry weather that had persisted for several days. The little girl was suffering the same initial symptoms that had foreshadowed Davy's death, but Peggy was reluctant to send for Doc.

"This cannot be happening again," she told herself, as she hesitated in the depths of denial. "God would not do that to me."

It became intensely hot and dry on June 24, and Priscilla had become quite sick. Johnny finally had to say something.

"Won't you let me go fetch Doc?" he pleaded.

"No ... not Doc this time," Peggy said. "I want you to go to town and bring back the best physician you can find. Ask everyone you see, 'Who is the best doctor in Harrisonburg? And where can I find him?' Beg him to come here. Tell him that I will give him five bushels of clean wheat to doctor Priscilla and five more bushels when she gets better."

Johnny saddled the gray mare and was gone for nearly three hours, but it seemed like three days to Peggy. Soon after he left, Priscilla's symptoms became far more violent than Davy's ever did. She lapsed into a restless delirium, moaning and groaning with her eyes tightly shut. She rolled her head from side to side until her tiny body clenched and convulsed for several seconds at a time.

These frightful episodes were becoming more frequent when Johnny finally returned with the best doctor he could find, a young physician on furlough from General Imboden's hospital.

The town doctor examined Priscilla and shook his head sadly as he packed up his medical kit.

"It's a classic case of brain fever," he said.

"I've never heard of such a thing," Peggy replied.

"Well, that's the *new* name for it. Most people around here still call it 'dropsy in the head.' All we can do in such cases is administer heroic doses of calomel and pray."

The doctor gave Priscilla two pills and instructed Peggy to give her two more every four hours. Then he loaded five bushels of wheat onto his wagon and headed for Harrisonburg. Priscilla died late that night after swallowing two more pills, and the doctor never returned to inquire about his five-year-old patient or his five bushels of bonus wheat.

Priscilla's unexpected death did not seem real to Peggy. She went through the motions of preparing her precious little girl's body for burial, but she was numb to the pain this time. She knew that Henry would be next, and she wondered how many of her loved ones would have to die before it would mercifully be her turn. She began to think that none of them would live to see the end of the war.

She stared at Mole Hill and thought, "The evil will never cease."

❖   ❖   ❖

In happier times, the hot, dry weather would have been good for Henry, but Priscilla's death sapped his strength and extinguished his will to live. He took to his bed for the last time.

When Peter Hartman came to the house during Priscilla's wake, Henry called him and Johnny into the downstairs bedroom and asked them to dig his daughter's grave.

"I want you to do just the way we did for Davy," he instructed. "Bury Priscilla right beside her brother, and do me the favor of buryin' me next to both of 'em in a day or two."

"You must not talk about such things," Johnny said. "You don't need buryin' yet. You just need some fresh air. I'll take you out on the porch tomorrow, and you'll feel better. Fresh air always helps you rest easy."

"Not this time," Henry said. "There's only one thing left in this world that would make me feel better about leavin' it. I would like to see you boys confess your faith and make your election sure. But don't join the church for my sake; do it for your own good."

"Well ... I was gonna wait till after the funeral to tell you this," Johnny said, "but I *have* decided to join the church. Me and Peter and a few other boys are gettin' baptized on July 4."

"I'm glad to hear it," Henry said. "Are you joinin' the Mennonite Church or some other faith?"

"Well ... I have always admired New Erection Presbyterian Church," Peter said. "But I was there last Sunday, and the preacher prayed for the destruction of his enemies, and that just didn't sit right with me."

"I thought about becoming a Dunker," Johnny admitted, "but I'm like Suzy. I can't stand getting water in my ears."

Priscilla's funeral was attended only by women, a few old men, and the two teenage gravediggers. Henry was too sick to leave his bed. As soon as the grave was filled, Johnny took Peggy and Mottie home and changed back into his dirty clothes. He had to tend to the summer harvest. The sun was shining, the wheat was heavy in the head, and Johnny knew that the conscription scouts would soon come looking for him.

On July 1, there was another urgent call for men age seventeen to sixty to report to the courthouse regardless of their exemption status. This time Johnny refused to comply. He continued to work in the field and hope for the best.

The following day, Henry suffered a massive hemorrhage and asked Mary to fetch David Heatwole to help him write his will. David jotted notes as Henry revealed his final wishes in a feeble voice. All his property would go to Peggy as long as she did not remarry and as long as she continued to pay his debts, raise orderly children, and give them a reasonable education. David told Peggy that he would return tomorrow with a will ready for Henry to sign, but during the night, Henry slipped into a coma.

Three days later, he rallied briefly and was able to speak. Peggy told him that the children were doing fine. He asked about Johnny, and she told him that Johnny and Peter had been baptized on the Fourth of July in Muddy Creek along with John Coffman and Abram Weaver. Henry's last words were: "Saved on Independence Day … free from sin … free from the shackles of sin."

Henry died on July 9, and Johnny and Peter dug yet another grave. It had not rained much since Priscilla died, so the work was especially difficult this time.

After Henry's funeral, Peggy tapped into her secret supply of clean wheat to barter for a special stone to mark the final resting place of her long-suffering husband. It was an extravagance, to be sure, but she was determined to do it.

CHAPTER 19

Sheridan

*"Those who rest at home in peace and plenty
don't see the horrors of war."*

After Henry died, Peggy resolved not to waste another nickel on the *Rockingham Register*, but when she heard that Early's army had burned Chambersburg, she sent Suzy to David Heatwole's home to see if L. J. would deliver the newspaper again for his usual fee. Peggy told Johnny that the *Register* would give the girls a chance to practice their reading. She could not admit, not even to herself, how hungry she had become for news of the war.

When L. J. arrived with the newspaper, Peggy asked Mary to read the Chambersburg story out loud.

"I want to know why the rebels thought they had to burn an entire town of old men, innocent children, and wretched widows," Peggy said.

"Here it is," Mary announced, as she opened the newspaper to page two. "It says, 'We are sorry to know that a necessity has arisen for acts of retribution and retaliation of this kind. ... They (Union armies) have burned whole towns; they have burned private residences; they have burned mills; they have burned churches; and even now they are doing their utmost to shell and to burn some of our chief towns and cities. That we were fully justified in burning Chambersburg, that den of Abolitionism, that harbor of stolen and runaway negroes from the South, that hole in which old John Brown found aid and comfort whilst getting ready to do his devilment at Harper's Ferry, we think can be easily demonstrated. And yet, we are sorry that our enemies have left us no other alternative. Much as we abhor Yankees, yet we cannot help pitying helpless women and children who are always the chief sufferers by these acts of retribution and retaliation. We hope and pray that the burning of Chambersburg may put a stop to burning elsewhere. If it does not, however, we hope the Confederates will again apply the torch to other towns and cities in the North.'"

Peggy stared out the parlor window at Mole Hill, while Mary read the rest of the story. When she finished, Peggy had but one thing to say: "This will only make things worse."

Indeed, Early's forays into Maryland, on the heels of heavy Union casualties near Fredericksburg and Richmond had caused increasing numbers of Northern voters to question the wisdom of the war. To win reelection, Lincoln needed decisive military victories, and he needed them soon. On August 6, while the embers of Chambersburg were still smoldering, Grant put General Philip Sheridan in charge of a revitalized Army of the Shenandoah—40,000 soldiers tasked with eviscerating Early's army and reducing the valley to waste. Sheridan's orders were the same as those Grant had given Hunter on the previous day.

"In pushing up the Shenandoah Valley … it is desirable that nothing should be left to invite the enemy to return."

The Virginia Mennonites were blissfully ignorant of such ominous external forces; they were more concerned about internal threats to their spiritual well-being. During their annual conference at Weavers Church in late August, the bishops and deacons cautioned members to guard against pride, a "formidable evil" that had been "manifesting itself in so many ways." They also warned against "the so-called innocent amusements indulged in by the young at apple-cuttings and butter-boilings." They strongly suggested that the young people's parents should "suppress these things as much as possible."

On the following day, nearly 250 Mennonites—including a fair number of deserters and draft dodgers—came to the church to partake in the sacrament of holy communion. This was the first communion for Johnny and Peter, a somber celebration with prayers for peace mixed with expressions of praise and thanksgiving for the rain that finally arrived in July and August. Despite the prolonged dry spell in June, and in spite of the war, the harvest of 1864 was among the largest they had ever produced. The Mennonite farms around Mole Hill were overflowing with grain— in the barns, in the walls, and under the steps.

Peggy was encouraged to hear that Sheridan's army had defeated Early's much smaller forces near Winchester on September 19 and again near Strasburg on September 22. Word reached Harrisonburg by telegraph on the following day. Then the wire went silent, but the faces of the soldiers in Early's vanquished army told the rest of the story as they trudged south through Harrisonburg.

On Saturday, September 25, Sheridan's vanguard swept into town followed by a cavalry band playing national airs as it marched through the streets. Dogs barked all night, and few people slept, as the main body of Sheridan's army amassed just north of town.

The fourth Sunday of September dawned completely clear and moderately cool, but there would be no preaching at Weavers Church. Johnny rode the gray mare to the top of the hill behind the empty sanctuary, where he found Peter Hartman watching and waiting for Sheridan's army. Both boys were anxious to see what would happen next, and they did not have long to wait. Soon after

10 a.m., they saw Union troops streaming toward them along the Rawley Road, spreading out rapidly across the countryside on both sides of the thoroughfare.

The boys froze for a minute, but the sound of gunfire animated them as the Yankees started shooting livestock on farms between Harrisonburg and the church. Johnny galloped the gray mare home to sound the alarm.

Some of the soldiers marched past Weavers Church and continued west on the Rawley Road, as far as Bishop Coffman's home, but they did not notice Peggy's secluded farmhouse. To the south, one of Sheridan's quartermasters impressed Daniel Bowman's grist mill to grind wheat and corn to help feed the thousands of Union troops that had swarmed into the valley. Another company of soldiers commandeered the church.

On Monday, a pleasant day in terms of weather, squads of Union cavalry began combing the countryside for horses and food. A small detachment rode up to the Rhodes house in the morning, and the officer in charge told Peggy they were authorized to take whatever they needed.

"That's alright," Peggy said. "I have been a loyal Union woman all along, and I am willing to do whatever I can to preserve the Union and put an end to this war."

The soldiers impressed the plow horse from the upper field by simply removing his harness and dropping it on the ground. Then they took all four of Peggy's large fattening hogs—butchering two of them in the yard, loading the best cuts of meat onto their horses, and leaving the rest to rot. They killed four bleating sheep in much the same way. As they were getting ready to leave, the officer gave Peggy receipts for everything they had taken.

"If you keep these vouchers, the government will reimburse you after the war," he said.

As soon as the foragers left, Peggy, Johnny, and Mary scrambled to salvage every scrap of meat, fat, and skin from the discarded carcasses. They were not prepared to butcher, and the soldiers had done a shoddy job of it, so their efforts were tedious and difficult. They worked quickly until darkness stopped them.

On Tuesday, yet another fine day, a dozen or more soldiers took two horses from the pasture. One of the men, who was riding a lame horse, switched his saddle to Peggy's sorrel, mounted up, and led his own limping horse away by the reins. When another soldier tried to take the gray mare, Peggy begged to keep it and was shocked when he relented. She also begged for a small colt that she recognized as belonging to John Wenger.

"That young colt will be more trouble than it's worth to an army on the move. Please let me return it to its owner?" she pleaded.

"She's right," said the leader of the squad. "Let her have it. She's saving us a bullet."

Later that day, a foraging party of Ohio infantrymen came to the house and took twenty sheep, five young beef cattle, and four milk cows. Peggy ran after the soldiers as they drove the animals down the lane.

"Please let me keep the milk cows!" she shouted. "They're not intended for beef."

"We have strict orders to round up all the cattle we can find!" the sergeant hollered back at her. "The army is short on provisions, and hungry soldiers don't care much whether they're eating Holsteins or Herefords."

Peggy continued to press the point as she followed the men to the end of the lane and out onto the Dayton Road. Finally, the sergeant agreed to let her keep the smallest heifer.

It rained hard that night and into the next day, and there was no sign of foragers. It misted on the following morning, and when the clouds parted in the afternoon, Peggy saw that the sky appeared smoky to the south, where Sheridan's men had been setting fire to mills, barns, and haystacks for several days. As Sheridan's Third Division of Cavalry slowly burned its way north, its commander, General George Custer, moved his headquarters to Dayton, just two miles south of the Rhodes place.

On the first day of October, it rained all day and turned cold, and the inclement weather once again seemed to repel the federal foragers. But the next day was warm and dry, and another squad of cavalry came to the house and snatched Peggy's prized gray mare—the farm's last horse—from the front yard. They also helped themselves to saddles and bridles. The soldiers again gave Peggy receipts for what they took, but she was beginning to question the value of these vouchers. Later in the day, a much larger foraging party arrived with six four-horse wagons. The soldiers filled two of them with hay and wheat-in-the-straw and loaded another wagon with fifty bushels of clean wheat. Peggy and Mary watched helplessly from the porch as the soldiers emptied the barn.

While they were loading the wagons, one of the officers came to the house and ate dinner with the Rhodes family, a fine feast of salvaged mutton scraps, sweet potatoes, and fresh-baked bread. The officer thanked Peggy for the meal and gave her yet another receipt for the wheat and hay.

"I have a fine collection of these vouchers," she said, "but receipts won't feed my children come winter. I have been loyal to the Union all along, and now your General Sheridan has taken more food from us in the past week than all the Confederate foragers put together."

"It's only going to get worse," the officer confided, "but the general plans to take refugees north with him when he leaves the valley. He's offering to furnish wagons and teams to loyal Union families. You should go."

"We will not be forced from our home!" Peggy declared. "The Secesh hotheads threatened to run us out of the valley because my husband refused to vote for secession. And now the Union army is trying to starve us out, but we will not leave our home!"

"You should go," the officer repeated calmly. "In a few days, there will be nothing left for you here."

❖ ❖ ❖

On October 3, many Dunker and Mennonite families started loading their most essential belongings onto wagons and making their way to Harrisonburg to accept Sheridan's offer. Peggy had no intention of going north, but she strongly encouraged Johnny to tag along with the John Brunk family.

"As soon as these federal troops are gone, the conscription scouts will come looking for you," she reminded him. "You would fare much better working in Maryland than hiding under the house."

Johnny rejected the idea initially, but Peter and the other boys from his baptismal class were planning to go north, and the prospect of spending the fall and winter in a dark, cold cellar changed Johnny's thinking. At first light on October 5, he left the Rhodes farm carrying a haversack stuffed with provisions and a few silver coins, all the hard currency Peggy could spare. She hated to see Johnny go. She had raised him as one of her own, but she knew he would be safer in the North.

Peggy had not cried since Priscilla and Henry died, but she could not hold back the tears as she watched Johnny walk up through the white pine field. He turned and waved to her, and she waved back with all her might.

"He'll be alright with the Brunks," she kept telling herself, as he disappeared into the trees.

Johnny cut through the woods and walked briskly up the Rawley Road toward the Brunk place. Leaving the only home he had ever known filled him with fear and sadness, but he also was excited about going north to see some of the places and things he had only read about in Mr. Heatwole's mail-order books.

As Johnny approached the Brunk farm, he spotted Chris Brunk waiting for him at the end of the lane.

"Good morning! Glad to see you!" Johnny said, with as much enthusiasm as he could manage under the circumstances. "Where's the rest of your family? Ain't they goin' north."

"We were all planning to go, but last night the cavalry stole our entire rig—horse, harness, and wagon. So now it's just me. I figure I can make it to Yankeedom on foot."

The two boys walked up the hill to Weavers Church, where Peter Hartman, John Coffman, and two other teenage boys were waiting. Peter was almost eighteen and had been dodging the draft for nearly a year. Coffman, the eldest son of Bishop Coffman, was not quite sixteen, about the same age as the other two boys.

Soon after the six teenagers reached court square, they heard that Sheridan's chief engineer, Lieutenant John Meigs, had been shot and killed near Dayton. Meigs was a handsome young product of West Point, where he had graduated first in his class. He also was the son of Montgomery Meigs, quartermaster general for the entire Union army. More to the point, he was Sheridan's beloved aide-de-camp. The boys knew nothing about Meigs, or his special status, so they were shocked to learn that Sheridan had ordered Custer to burn everything within five miles of the spot where the young lieutenant had been killed.

"How far is that from Weavers Church?" Chris asked.

"I don't know exactly," Johnny replied, "but it's considerable less than five miles."

The boys also learned they would need to obtain passes before joining the wagon train, so they headed east from court square toward Sheridan's headquarters. Halfway up Red Hill, two of Sheridan's sentinels arrested them and took them to his camp in front of Abraham Byrd's house.

"Who do you have there?" Sheridan asked, as the guards ushered them into his tent.

"Six men who came into the line to go north."

❖   ❖   ❖

At age thirty-three, Sheridan was much younger than Johnny had imagined, but he was still the most savage-looking man the boys had ever seen. He was short overall but long and thick through the arms and torso with muscles that threatened to rip through his tight uniform. He had a full beard and a receding crop of dark hair plastered to his scalp. His ferocious eyes were set in a dog-shaped head, a physical quirk that gave him the menacing look of a bull terrier.

Sheridan motioned for the boys to sit down on camp chairs that surrounded a make-do desk.

While his adjutant wrote their passes, the general asked them several questions and listened intently to their answers.

"You are farm boys, I expect."

"Yessir."

"Then you are wise to go north because it is my intention to render farming quite difficult throughout this valley. Do you understand my purpose?"

"I think so," Johnny volunteered. "You want to leave nothing behind to supply the rebels."

"That's true as far as it goes," Sheridan replied, but the more important purpose is to put an end to this war by discouraging not only the rebel soldiers but also the Southern civilians. Those who rest at home in peace and plenty don't see the horrors of war. They encourage every able-bodied man to enlist in the Confederate army to replenish its ranks as death depletes them. It is another matter, however, when deprivation and suffering are brought to their own doors. Reducing civilians to poverty brings more prayers for peace more surely and more quickly than does the destruction of human life. The singular selfishness of mankind has revealed this truth in more than one great conflict.

"Where do you boys live? What part of this county?"

"We live near Weavers Church, about three miles to the west," Johnny replied.

"How far from the road between here and Dayton?"

"Not much more than two miles as the crow flies."

"No doubt you have heard that I ordered General Custer to burn all barns and houses in your area. Do you know why I gave such an order?"

"Revenge," Peter blurted. "The rebel soldiers killed one of your lieutenants."

"They were rebels, but they were *not* soldiers," Sheridan insisted, raising his voice and pounding his fist. "They were bushwhackers! And they didn't just *kill* one of my lieutenants, they *murdered* him. Lieutenant John Meigs was a good man, the finest officer under my command, a true soldier of Christ and country."

The boys did not know how to respond to Sheridan's suggestion that a "soldier of Christ" was helping to burn their families out of the valley, but they were too afraid to say anything, and Sheridan did not expect them to reply.

At that awkward moment, a sentinel entered the tent with two terrified men.

"Who've you got there?" Sheridan growled.

"Two men that we took out in the woods bushwhacking our soldiers. What do you want us to do with them?"

"Take them down and put chains on them from head to foot and show them no favors whatsoever."

The guards removed the prisoners from the tent, and Sheridan picked up where he left off.

"Two more bushwhackers," he scoffed. "The people of this valley are meek-faced citizens in the presence of any considerable body of Union troops, but as soon as they get the chance, they attack my men like savages. The murderers of Lieutenant Meigs might never be known, but I am determined to teach a lesson to the abettors of this foul deed."

"What about the innocent people?" Johnny ventured. "There are many folks who live near Dayton who have opposed secession and remained loyal to the Union."

"Aye, there are those who insist they have supported the Union all along, but their protests leave me cold," Sheridan said. "Since I came into this valley from Harper's Ferry up to Harrisonburg, every train, every small party, and every straggler has been bushwhacked, and many of the bushwhackers have protection papers from Union commanders who have been here before me.

"I do believe that many people in this valley are true blue, but I dare not take anyone's word for it. That's why I am giving people a chance to prove their loyalty by going north with me, and I'm glad you boys are smart enough to accept my offer. Do you have horses? Or will you be traveling on foot?"

"Uh ... our horses have been stolen," Peter replied.

"If any of my men have taken any of your horses and you can find them, you go and get them and take them along north," Sheridan said, with the hint of a smile. "But you must come back here and get passes for the horses if you expect to keep them for long."

Four of the boys found their families' horses in Sheridan's camp and brought them back to the general's tent. Soon after they left, a courier arrived with an urgent message from Lieutenant Colonel Thomas Wildes of the 116th Ohio Infantry. The courier insisted that he must give the message directly to the general. Sheridan's sentinels were not inclined to grant such a pretentious request, but the courier protested with sufficient volume for the ruckus to reach the general's ear.

"It's alright!" Sheridan shouted. "Let him in."

"I have an urgent message from Colonel Wildes," the persistent courier repeated, holding up a small envelope.

"If you know what it says, please save me the trouble," Sheridan replied, in a weary voice.

"It says that Colonel Wildes has delayed your order to burn Dayton. He is vouching for the strong character of the townspeople and begging you to reconsider."

Sheridan jumped up and snatched the envelope from the courier to see for himself. He read the note and cursed it. He read it again and cursed it again. He examined and cross-examined the courier. Then he paced back and forth in his tent, muttering to himself, as he weighed the merits of mercy against the value of vengeance.

Finally, he looked up at the anxious courier and said: "Tell your Colonel Wildes that he may keep his precious town, but the rest of my order stands."

CHAPTER 20

The Burning

*"We've come to burn your buildings.
You have fifteen minutes ..."*

While Wildes' 116th Ohio Infantry was saving Dayton, Custer's Fifth New York Cavalry was executing the rest of Sheridan's vengeful order on the morning of October 5. Some of the soldiers relished the chance to take revenge—even against civilians.

"Remember Chambersburg!" they shouted, as they frantically searched houses from attic to cellar before setting them on fire. They stole money, watches, clothes, and shoes while threatening to kill anyone who tried to stop them.

From the front porch, Peggy saw the southern sky turning reddish orange as flames from numerous fires illuminated a growing cloud of overarching smoke. Individual columns of smoke were coming closer and closer as the cavalry moved slowly north from Dayton, burning nearly everything in its path. By midmorning, the air was thick with the smell of smoke, and Peggy trembled at the faint sounds of destruction and despair that began echoing through the dale. All she could think of was her fireball nightmare. It was coming true, but the evil wasn't roaring down Mole Hill—as it had done in her dreams. It was slithering slowly up Cooks Creek.

Peggy tried not to cry as she watched a large plume of smoke ascend from the foot of Mole Hill near Doc's place. The elevation of the upper field blocked her view of what was fueling the fire.

"Maybe it's just the barn," she hoped.

It was bad enough to witness unattributed columns of smoke, but it was terrifying to see a cavalry squad dismount in Reuben Swope's front yard and set his barn on fire. They didn't bother to torch the house, but they certainly knew what the wind would do.

Mottie came out onto the porch carrying little Lydia, who could not stop crying. Mottie handed the inconsolable child to Peggy and asked the obvious question: "What on earth will we do if the Yankees burn our house and barn?"

"I don't believe it will come to that," Peggy lied, as she perched Lydia on her hip. "They might burn the barn, but I don't think the flames will jump across the creek. And I can't imagine that the Union army would leave loyal citizens starving *and* homeless."

But Peggy could not sustain her false bravado. Fear—the paralyzing variety—welled up inside her as the fiery destruction began to surround the Rhodes farm. And her fear spiked to panic when the incendiary squad rode into the front yard.

"We've come to burn your buildings," the sergeant said. "You have fifteen minutes to get your property out the house. Don't bother about the barn. Whatever's in the barn goes up with it."

In that moment, the full weight of the war came crashing down on Peggy. It was *her* war now. It no longer belonged to rebels and Yankees or politicians and soldiers. It was no longer about slavery or Southern independence or preserving the Union. It was about saving her children.

Peggy's silent prayer was frantic but efficient: "Dear Lord, thy will be done, but please don't take any more of my children."

Almost immediately, Peggy regained her courage. The time had come to reveal her most dangerous secret.

"I am not your enemy," she told the sergeant, her voice quivering only slightly. "I took the side of the Union from the start. I aided the Union cause by helping hundreds of refugees and deserters escape to the North. I did not believe in secession and neither did my husband. We adhered to the Union at all times."

"That's all well and good," the sergeant responded. "We have no quarrel with you, but we have orders to burn everything in this area, and that's exactly what we intend to do."

"I understand about the barn, but why must you burn my house?" Peggy demanded. "Have you no compassion for a widow with five children living and two in the grave?"

The sergeant turned abruptly in his saddle and looked her straight in the eye.

"What did you say?"

"I said, 'Have you no compassion for a widow with five children living and two in the grave?'"

"We do not burn the homes of widows, Mrs. Rhodes, but every woman whose husband marches with Early's army says she's a widow today."

"My husband refused to fight," Peggy countered. "He never even drilled with the rebels. He died this summer, and I have been a widow for nearly three months."

"Is your husband buried here on your place?"

"No. We laid him to rest in the cemetery on the other side of Fairview Hill," she said, pointing east toward Weavers Church. "It's the freshest grave in the yard, and there's a fine new marker with his name inscribed in stone, Henry H. Rhodes."

The sergeant sent his corporal over the hill to the cemetery to check on Peggy's story, but while he was gone, the soldiers continued to take things from the house and do whatever they could to trample Johnny's crops and ruin Mary's garden.

When the corporal returned, he said that he could not find a marker with the name Henry H. Rhodes.

"I found a tombstone with the name 'Henry Rodes' dated 1855," he said, "but there was nothing new about it."

Peggy's fear spiked again, and she stubbornly shoved it aside.

"That's my husband's father," she replied, "but I tell you there's a fine new marker for Henry H. Rhodes! I gave up two bushels of clean wheat for it just two months ago."

The corporal squirmed in his saddle before offering a possible explanation to the sergeant.

"Beg your pardon, sir, but I have seen some of the men using tombstones to make camp tables."

"Well … I suppose I've seen that, too," the sergeant admitted. "Did you see any fresh graves in this cemetery?"

"Yessir. There are two fresh graves side by side, one marked, one unmarked."

"Who is buried beside your husband, Mrs. Rhodes?" the sergeant asked.

"Priscilla! We buried my daughter, Priscilla, there in June."

The sergeant glanced at the corporal, who nodded in agreement.

"Let me get this straight," said the sergeant. "Your daughter died in June, and your husband died in July?"

"Yessir. It's been grief upon grief with tears overflowing. Please do not burn our home. I am begging you!"

The sergeant leaned down from his horse and addressed three-year-old Willy, who was clinging to his mother's long dress.

"Did your sister die, son?"

"Yeth."

"And what was her name?"

"Prithila. Mama said she had drophty."

"And did your daddy have dropsy, too?"

"No. He had c'thumption."

"Did he go away to the war?"

"No. Mama says he went to heaven."

"That's good enough for me," the sergeant said, as he sat up straight in his saddle. "We won't burn your house, Mrs. Rhodes, and we won't burn your barn. Corporal, tell the men to put everything back, right where they found it."

When the soldiers finished carrying Peggy's possessions back into the house, the sergeant blew a whistle, and they mounted their horses and headed north along the creek.

Overcome with relief, Peggy hugged Mottie and the children. Then she dropped to her knees and said a silent prayer of thanksgiving. She tried to stand up, but her strength was gone, so she rocked back onto her haunches and prayed out loud for her neighbors. When she opened her eyes, she saw a new column of smoke rising to the north as they burned Bishop Coffman's barn. Then two more large plumes ascended in the east.

"That can't be Betsy Weaver's place," Peggy agonized. "She's been a widow for seven years."

❖ ❖ ❖

On the following day, Custer's cavalry broke camp and again started moving north from Dayton. Despite Union assurances of protection, they burned Daniel Bowman's mill as they bid a fiery farewell to the outskirts of the tiny town. Then they torched nearly all the barns and mills they had missed on the previous day from Dayton to the Rawley Road.

Custer's incendiary squads again flowed around both sides of the Rhodes farm, making it an island of refuge in a river of fire. None of the conflagrations came within a quarter mile of Peggy's house and barn, reminding her of what Doc had said about living in "the perfect place."

Sympathetic soldiers ended up sparing most of the homes around Mole Hill, but the barns of western Rockingham burned all day and into the night, and the neighbors worried that the flames would spread from their barns to their houses. Some of them slept in Peggy's barn, but most of them spent the night out in the open with fires raging around them.

CHAPTER 21

The Wagon Train
"Do you remember Chambersburg?"

Johnny and his friends spent a miserable night in Harrisonburg praying for their families and wondering if they would ever see them again in this world. They managed to stay dry under some wagons as it started to sprinkle, but a wounded soldier in one of the wagons moaned and groaned all night, making it nearly impossible for them to sleep.

At the first sign of light, an ambulance arrived, and the boys scrambled to their feet to get out of the way. One of the orderlies asked Peter to help transfer the man from the wagon to the ambulance, but when Peter got a good look at the mutilated man, his stomach churned and his knees buckled. John Coffman quickly stepped in to take Peter's place.

Peter sat on the ground for a few minutes, holding his stomach, breathing deeply, and trying to forget what he had just seen. The other boys enjoyed a breakfast of pork scraps and fresh apples, but Peter could not eat.

Word soon came that the wagon train would be moving in a few minutes, so the boys tied their haversacks together to create three makeshift saddlebags. Just before sunrise, the long train began to go north, slowly at first, as it departed Harrisonburg on the Valley Turnpike.

The pike was a macadam road, mostly straight and considerably wide but filled with the pockmarks of war. The infantrymen went first—marching in six columns—followed closely by the artillery units. The commissary wagons came next, trailed by 400 refugee wagons traveling two abreast. Just behind the refugees, squads of soldiers drove large herds of confiscated cattle and sheep. They added to the herds along the way, shooting any animals that were contrary or otherwise difficult to drive.

As the train gradually achieved a plodding pace, the sun breached the horizon just south of Massanutten Peak in the east. The rain had stopped, and the northern sky was clear, but smoke lingered behind the train as Sheridan's cavalry divisions dragged one last harrow of destruction over the entire width of the valley.

Looking over their shoulders, the boys saw dozens of columns of smoke stretching from Little North Mountain in the west to Massanutten in the east. Johnny hated to see such destruction, but he was almost mesmerized by it. After glancing back many times, he finally resolved to keep his eyes fixed on the road ahead.

The boys did not stop for dinner—mostly because they were trying to stretch their provisions. Instead, they pressed forward as the wagon train picked up speed. They mostly stayed on the right shoulder of the road, yielding the paved portion of the pike to the wagons. Alternating between walking and riding Peter's horse, Johnny could hear the cattle lowing, the sheep bleating, and the cow bells clunking behind them. Hundreds of ragged refugees lined the wayside, and many of them joined the somber procession on foot.

"These people look half starved," Johnny observed.

"Yeah, well, maybe that's how we'll look in a few days," Peter replied.

The sky clouded over late in the afternoon, and a misty rain began to fall, which hastened the onset of twilight as the unseen sun slipped behind the western mountains. The boys plodded along in the dark until 10 p.m., when they finally stopped for the night between New Market and Mount Jackson. After eating a small supper, they were still hungry, but they were more thirsty than anything else because they had foolishly failed to take on water during the day. Peter heard there was a nice little pond up ahead, so he carried everyone's canteens there and back.

The water was cool and sweet, and it filled their bellies long enough for them to fall asleep, but the crisp morning breeze of October 7 forced them onto their feet before first light.

The sun came up, and the sky turned a brilliant blue. The mountains to the east seemed close enough to touch—green guardians of the valley with patches of red, yellow, and orange. But to the south, an enormous cloud of smoke hovered between the mountains, a grim reminder of the devastation that was driving them north. When the wagons started moving again, the boys—having learned their lesson from the previous day—were eager to top off their water supplies. But as they approached the pond where Peter had filled their canteens, they saw the remains of two mules decomposing in the stagnant water.

Johnny was the first one to notice them. "Hey Peter!" he teased. "You forgot to mention the two dead mules floating in your nice little pond!"

"It was dark and raining," Peter replied.

"Couldn't you *smell* those mules?"

"I guess the wind was blowing the other way. All I could smell was smoke."

The boys found plenty of mule-free water when they crossed the North Fork of the Shenandoah River one mile south of Mount

Jackson. They had to ford the river because McNeill's Rangers had burned the bridge to slow down Sheridan's retreat and turn his soldiers into better targets for bushwhackers.

As soon as they made it across, the infantrymen resumed foraging on both sides of the pike, stealing whatever they could carry and burning anything else that might give aid to the enemy. The boys were close enough to hear the crackling of combustion and the cursing of women who were furiously fighting the flames. As they entered Mount Jackson, they saw a distraught young mother weeping on the upper portico of her home.

One of the soldiers looked up at her and shouted the question that the boys had heard many times on the previous day: "Do you remember Chambersburg?"

In the afternoon, rifles began popping and snapping to the west, not far from the wagon train, as bushwhackers took long-range pot shots at the caravan. The boys ducked into the ditch on the right side of the road as bullets tore through the canvas covers of some nearby wagons. The infantrymen returned fire, and when the shooting stopped, they brought a man to the pike who had been struck by a bullet that entered his skull behind his ear and exited through his mouth. When a soldier ordered Peter to apply pressure to the gaping wound, his knees held up better this time, but his life-saving efforts were equally futile.

Beyond Edinburg, Sheridan's rear guard took over the task of burning along the pike, and the infantrymen focused on foraging. Obtaining food had become the top priority as hunger plagued soldiers, refugees, and livestock alike.

"There are 10,000 head of cattle and sheep right behind us, enough to feed everybody on this train for a month," Johnny marveled. "But if we stopped long enough to butcher, we would be the ones cut to pieces."

As the caravan approached Woodstock, the land along the pike became more rugged, along with the women who were left to defend it. The boys saw one such woman chasing soldiers away from her pigsty with a broom. She won her battle to preserve some pork for the winter, but the women of Woodstock proper were not as fortunate. When the Union cavalry torched the railroad depot, a stiff breeze carried the flames to some nearby homes. Sheridan's men attempted to douse these unintended fires, but the pursuing Confederates seized the opportunity to attack, and the Union soldiers ran to their horses and retreated down the pike.

The boys did not hear the gunshots from that skirmish because they were now several miles ahead of Sheridan's rear guard. As they prepared to spend the night at Cedar Creek, just north of Strasburg, the smell of smoke was beginning to dissipate. The creek provided plenty of water, and for the first time, the commissary wagons distributed rations to the refugees. It bothered the boys that most of the food they received had been stolen from the half-starved people along the pike, but Johnny was too hungry to refuse sustenance of any origin.

The weather was better that evening, so the Mennonite families gathered to sing hymns, including a song that had been written by a grandnephew of John Peter Muhlenberg, the famous preacher from Woodstock. During Sunday services in January 1776, on the eve of the war for independence, Muhlenberg descended from his pulpit and said: "In the language of the Holy Writ, there is a time for all things, a time to preach and a time to pray, but those times have gone away. Now is the time to fight." He removed his ministerial robe to reveal a military uniform and asked for volunteers to follow him into the war.

Johnny was unaware of Muhlenberg's famous call to arms—it was not a story that the Mennonites embraced—but he was well-acquainted with the popular hymn that was closely associated with the Muhlenberg name.

> I would not live always, I ask not to stay,
> where storm after storm rises dark o'er the way;
> The few cloudy mornings that dawn on us here,
> Enough for life's woes, full enough for its cheer.
>
> I would not live always thus fetter'd by sin;
> Temptation without, and corruption within;
> Where rapture of pardon is mingled with fears;
> The cup of thanksgiving with penitent tears.
>
> I would not live always; no—welcome the tomb—
> Since Jesus has lain there I'll enter its gloom;
> There sweet be my rest till he bid me arise,
> To hail him in triumph descending the skies.
>
> Who, who would live always, away from his God?
> Away from yon heaven, that blissful abode;
> Where rivers of pleasure flow o'er the bright plains,
> And noon-tide of glory eternally reigns.

As the Mennonites sang Muhlenberg's masterpiece in four-part harmony, several of the infantrymen who had crowded around to listen broke down in tears. The boys felt sorry for the sentimental soldiers, but their pity did not translate to trust. They remembered that Sheridan's adjutant had advised them to take turns guarding their horses at night if they expected to keep them.

❖ ❖ ❖

In the morning, specks of sleet stung Johnny's face as the refugees continued to move steadily north along the Valley Pike, but the commissary wagons and most of the infantrymen stayed behind on the south side of Cedar Creek. The burning and looting stopped there, not for pity's sake but because Union forces already had ruined everything from Cedar Creek to Winchester during a previous campaign.

As the boys passed through Winchester, the skies cleared, and the air remained cold. They could no longer smell smoke, but they could see some of the makeshift cemeteries that surrounded the town, and they could not help but notice the shallow graves on both sides of the pike. Here too, further destruction was unnecessary: Union forces already had torn down fences, burned crops, and sacrificed most of the livestock to the gods of political gain and military advantage. High grass was encroaching on the little villages, whose citizens were either running, hiding, or dying.

"I wonder if this is how things are back home?" Johnny pondered.

"I wouldn't doubt it." Peter replied. "But all we can do is pray that our families will be alright."

The boys stopped for the night about ten miles south of Martinsburg. The Mennonite families gathered again to sing hymns, but there weren't many soldiers around to enjoy the music. Even so, the boys still thought it would be prudent to keep an eye on the horses. Johnny took the first watch, and Peter spelled him at midnight.

"I think there's going to be a battle to the south," Peter predicted, as he claimed Johnny's seat beside the horses before the ground lost all its warmth. "The infantry and cavalry are both behind us now, and it don't take that many soldiers to herd cattle and sheep."

Peter was right. Beginning at daybreak, cannon blasts reverberated through the valley for nearly two hours. Initially, there was no way to know who had won the Battle of Tom's Brook, but noon came and went, and there was no sign of Union retreat, so the boys correctly assumed that Sheridan's rear guard had turned and struck a decisive blow against the Confederate cavalry.

For the rest of the day, the refugee wagons moved much more slowly, as the walkers and horses suffered from the cumulative effects of hunger and fatigue. The excitement of hot pursuit was long gone, which made the October air seem even colder.

By the time the boys reached Martinsburg, they were forty miles ahead of Sheridan's soldiers, so they no longer worried about their horses, but it was impossible to rest easy. Sheer exhaustion would lull them to sleep; then a sharp blast of arctic air would wake them up. Johnny suffered through this insomnious cycle more than a dozen times before morning dawned with a heavy frost. The cold hungry boys struggled to their feet and waited in line at the provost marshal's office to take the Union oath of allegiance.

Later in the day, as Johnny crossed the Potomac River on a ferry, the cold snap subsided, and a warm breeze transformed October 10 into a lovely day to be alive.

CHAPTER 22

Survival

"You sure did leave a lot of troubles behind on this side of the creek."

Back at the Rhodes farm, the early morning light of October 7 revealed a dense blanket of smoke surrounding Mole Hill. An indescribable odor filled the air—the smell of charred wood and smoldering hay mixed with the stench of dead chickens and decomposing pigs. It was the catastrophic culmination of Peggy's recurring nightmare.

From the second level of the barn, Peggy stared at Mole Hill, her eyes overflowing with tears that blurred an inspiring sight. Three Mennonite men emerged from the timberline, leading horses behind them and driving cattle before them. It was like watching the sons of Noah descending the sacred slopes of Ararat. They had been hiding in the woods on top of the hill with the livestock for eleven days and eleven nights, and now they were going home. Peggy wiped away her tears and resolved to cry no more. There was too much work to be done.

It was quite cold on those first two days of desolation, but Peggy's neighbors started sifting through the ashes, trying to salvage hinges, bolts, and nails—anything that might be useful. Mottie kept the younger children busy gathering walnuts. This was a high priority in October because squirrels and other small mammals would soon start hoarding them.

Custer's cavalry had failed to damage the orchard, so apples were plentiful. The Rhodes family ate the fresh fruit, and Mary started cutting and drying apples for the winter ahead. She also helped the younger children forage for whatever corn they could salvage, including some that would have been barely fit for fodder in better times. As with the apples, they consumed some of the corn and dried the rest.

There was almost no meat on the Rhodes farm, only the scraps from the carcasses that the Yankees had left behind and the milk cow Peggy had begged to keep. The soldiers had done a fair job of ruining the garden, but in their haste, they had overlooked some of the turnips and taters hiding underground. Mary hurried to harvest these root vegetables and store them in the cellar before the first hard frost.

Their situation was desperate, but Peggy planned ahead nonetheless. Johnny had sowed all of the winter wheat before Sheridan arrived, so there was hope for a respectable harvest. In the meantime, Brunk's secret granary under the steps still concealed a good supply of clean wheat, enough to give Peggy some financial flexibility. She immediately traded some of the wheat for a plow horse. It seemed risky to give up grain, which had become the coin of the Confederacy, but Peggy knew the price of horses would only go higher when it was time for spring plowing.

Many of the older men and women were barely surviving, and Sammy's sickly mother died on October 21. On the way home from the funeral at the Pike Church, Peggy visited Henry's grave to see if she could find his missing tombstone, but nothing remained except a shrinking mound of orange clay covered with weeds and crabgrass. Peggy picked up a clod of the clay, crushed it in her fist, and let the dirt slide through her fingers the way she had done at Henry's funeral just three months earlier.

She knelt between the modest headstones for Davy and Priscilla and prayed for wisdom, courage, and strength. Then she stood up and addressed the unmarked mound of clay as though Henry were still alive: "You sure did leave a lot of troubles behind on this side of the creek."

❖   ❖   ❖

By the end of October, Peggy was back in the refugee business, so she had more mouths to feed with her dwindling supplies. The final wave of Mennonite and Dunker refugees had gone north with Sheridan, but the underground was now assisting deserters from General Early's demoralized army, which had retreated to New Market.

Warm weather prevailed in the valley until after Lincoln's re-election in November, so Peggy's children went barefoot to conserve leather. They tolerated cold feet for one more month, but in early December, they had to don some semblance of shoes and stockings to guard against frostbite.

The lack of adequate footwear was also a big problem for the soldiers in Early's army, as they marched south through Harrisonburg in December on their way to winter quarters near Waynesboro. It snowed six inches overnight and into the next day, and another wave of deserters entered the underground. They were neither Mennonite nor Dunker; they were just exhausted men with frozen feet, empty bellies, and no more will to wage war.

Peggy washed their frostbitten feet with lukewarm water and wrapped them in strips of linen. She fed them, as best she could, and confined them to the cellar until the troop movements dissipated. She hoped that the marching and fighting was done for the winter, but on December 20, Custer's cavalry reappeared with 3,000 soldiers near Lacey Spring about nine miles northeast of Harrisonburg.

PEGGY'S WAR

A severe storm of freezing rain struck late that night, and General James Rosser's cavalry—no more than 700 men—attacked the Union encampment before dawn. They caught Custer's men completely off guard and chased them a short distance before turning back to avoid a head-to-head fight. This surprise attack provided a modicum of revenge for Custer's rout of Rosser at the Battle of Tom's Brook, and it reminded Peggy that the war was not over in Rockingham.

Sure enough, Sheridan's forces moved south through Harrisonburg in late February on their way to Staunton. Rosser's depleted cavalry tried to make a stand at Mount Crawford, but the Yankees crossed North River after a brief firefight. Then they easily defeated the remnants of Early's army at Waynesboro and sent the rebels fleeing across Afton Mountain in total disarray.

The *Register* downplayed this stampede to peace. Instead, the newspaper reported that the Confederate army was offering pardons to deserters who returned to their commands within twenty days. But most of the rebels who quit the war in March 1865 had no intentions of going back.

The first week of April brought fine weather for spreading manure and plowing for corn, but there were no men to work the Rhodes farm and still no word from Johnny.

On Friday, the *Register* reported that General Robert E. Lee had evacuated Richmond and Petersburg and was retreating westward with the Union army in hot pursuit. Lee surrendered at Appomattox on April 9, and rumors of peace reached Rockingham two days later. But, as it was with the murder of Elder Kline, Peggy refused to believe it until she read it in the *Register*.

She was overjoyed on April 14, when she saw L. J. running toward the house waving the newspaper high over his head.

"It's true!" he shouted, just as he had when he delivered the initial news of John Brown's raid. "It's true! General Lee surrendered! The war is over!"

Peggy snatched the *Register* from L. J., ripped it open, and read the editor's lamentations.

"We are sorry to announce that, for the present, at least, our means for perpetuating the unequal struggle we have so long carried on with the Federal Armies have become exhausted, and we have been obliged to yield to the force of uncontrollable circumstances. Our noble Army of Virginia, the pride, the joy, and the defense of our people, has been obliged, after all their toils, privations and heroic sufferings, to yield to the combined power of the Federal Armies. ... It was unavoidable, as our Army were out of provisions and ammunition."

By the time L. J. delivered this news, Confederate soldiers were streaming down the Valley Pike on their way home to the war-torn reaches of the lower Shenandoah. Technically, they were prisoners of war, but General Grant had paroled them at Appomattox.

Peggy was pleased to hear that many people in the valley seemed ready to accept Lincoln's offer for Virginia to return to the Union on favorable terms, but within a few days, Peggy heard the news that Lincoln had been assassinated. That's all she knew until the April 28 issue of the *Register* arrived and Mary read the story to the whole family.

"President Lincoln was assassinated at Ford's Theatre, in Washington City, on Friday night, the 14 of April, about half past 9 or 10 o'clock. He was seated in the box appropriated to his service, in company with Mrs. Lincoln, and Miss Harris, and a Major Rathbone. ... He was shot from behind, with a pistol, supposedly in the hand of one J. Wilkes Boothe, a moody, gloomy, unemployed theatrical performer."

"I pray this man Booth is not a Southerner," Peggy said. "If the South revels in the murder of Lincoln, the retribution and retaliation may never end."

"Just this once, I think the editor of the *Register* agrees with you," Mary replied. "He says, 'We hope and trust the more intelligent of the Northern people, when passion and excitement subside and reason asserts her sway over their minds, will be perfectly persuaded that the South had nothing in the world to do with Mr. Lincoln's death. ... Indeed, we might go farther and declare that if the present crusade against us goes on, the South has probably lost much by the event which has overwhelmed the Northern people with affliction. They say he was our best friend. Perhaps he was.'"

The end of the war brought a backlog of letters to the underground, including one addressed to Bishop Coffman from his son, John. Peggy had delivered two such letters in the past few months, but neither of them made any mention of Johnny. This latest letter, she hoped, would be different.

Peggy immediately carried the letter to the bishop, who scanned it quickly and read it out loud for the benefit of the impatient postmaster.

> Dear Father and Mother.
>
> Now that the war has ended, I have greater hope that this letter will reach your hands. I am currently working on Sam Zimmerman's farm near Shiremanstown, Pa., and he has been more than kind to me. Peter Hartman and Chris Brunk are working on farms nearby, but Johnny Bell and Abram Weaver

stayed in Maryland when we took the cars to Pennsylvania, so I don't know where they are living at present.

Last week me and Peter went with Henry Zimmerman to Harrisburg to see the body of President Lincoln at the statehouse. Thousands of people were there to mourn the loss. In the evening, we watched the procession convey his casket from the statehouse to the funeral train. They had six horses pulling the hearse. I did not know you could make horses walk so slow. They had five bands playing "O Come and Let Us Worship," and when the hearse got down to the depot, a photographer took a picture of the crowd.

I have hired on here for the summer, but if Brother Zimmerman will release me from that obligation, I might be home in time to help with the harvest.

With kindest remembrances to all, I remain as ever your son, John S. Coffman

One week later, a letter finally arrived from Johnny. His message was more succinct than Coffman's, but the gist was the same. Johnny was looking forward to a harvest homecoming while reflecting on the untimely death of the president.

"I was sorry to hear that Abe Lincoln was kilt," he wrote. "I reckon he *was* my neighbor after all. I wish Uncle Henry could hear me say such a thing, but I don't wish him back to this sinful world for even one day."

Peggy was overjoyed when Johnny finally came home in the middle of May. It was a little late for spreading manure and plowing for corn, but he was determined to do his best to catch up to the seasonal cycle.

In addition to working in the fields, several of the young men who returned from Maryland, Ohio, and Pennsylvania formed construction crews to rebuild barns. John Coffman and Chris Brunk started one such gang. People around Mole Hill called them the singing carpenters because they sang hymns and other inspirational songs both on the job and in the evenings.

Joyful noises were in short supply that summer in Rockingham County, but rain was plentiful, and some of the corn that was trampled to the ground by the hooves of Custer's cavalry sprouted miraculously well. Johnny's winter wheat did better than expected, and other nearby farms produced large crops of oats and rye with little cultivation.

There were no oxen to roast on top of Mole Hill, but among the Virginia Mennonites, prayers of praise and thanksgiving ascended everywhere in abundance. Peggy's war was far from over; she would lose yet another child in the years ahead, but she no longer attributed her trials and tribulations to the evils of Mole Hill.

Epilogue

Henry Brunk reunited with his wife, Susanna, and his daughter, Sarah, at Hagerstown, Maryland. After the burning of Chambersburg, they retreated to Illinois. And in 1873, they moved to the Kansas prairie, where Henry died of typhoid fever just a few days after they arrived.

Johnny Bell married Sarah Petry in 1866 and started a greenhouse near Harrisonburg. His marriage and business both failed, and the census of 1900 suggests that Johnny moved to Augusta County, where he found a second wife.

Peter Hartman married Fannie Weaver in 1867 and bought a small farm about one mile north of the Rhodes place. Several years later, he hired William Rhodes as a farm hand, and Will married Peter's daughter, Bettie, in 1891. They had three children, including the author's grandfather.

Mary Rhodes married Samuel M. Burkholder in 1872, and they probably moved to the tenant house in 1873. Mary and Sam raised five children on the farm.

Susanna "Suzy" Rhodes died of cancer in 1873 at age 18. She had been sick for three years.

Joseph Beery's body was found hanging in his barn in 1874. The *Register* reported his death as a suicide, but the coroner's report stated that he died of a gunshot wound.

Gabriel "Doc" Heatwole succumbed to dropsy in 1875 at age 85.

Elizabeth "Mottie" Rhodes died in 1880 at age 97. She was believed to be the oldest person in Rockingham County when she passed away. Her funeral was one of the last, if not the last, to be held in the old Weavers Church. The congregation built a new church in the following year.

Rebecca "Becky" Rhodes married Perry Shank in 1881. They moved into the tenant house on the Rhodes farm and had six children.

Lydia Rhodes married Israel Rohrer Jr. in 1886 and moved to his farm near Rushville, a small settlement southwest of Mole Hill. They raised eleven children.

Margaret "Peggy" Rhodes relinquished her dower rights to the family farm in 1885, when she married Michael Shank, the man who was hauled away to the Confederate army "in his shirt sleeves and dirty clothes."

Sam and Mary Rhodes Burkholder purchased the family farm from Mary's siblings in 1887 and built a new house on the other side of the creek. The farm remained in the Burkholder family for two more generations.

The white pine field became part of Belmont Estates, a suburban neighborhood populated by many Rhodes-Heatwole-Burkholder descendants. But some of the land east of Cooks Creek remains pasture, and some of the land west of the creek remains in cultivation. The barn still stands on its original limestone foundation.

Acknowledgements

This book would not have been possible without my wife, Kim Rhodes, who helped with everything from designing the front cover to proofing the endnotes. She also listened patiently, while I droned on endlessly about Peggy's nightmares and Henry's consumption and Doc's confinement and Sammy's escape and Brunk's disguise and Kline's demise and Johnny's salvation.

Kim was also one of my beta readers, as were my brothers, Gene and Elvin Rhodes, and my son, Eric Rhodes, who also provided patient technical expertise. Other beta readers included my longtime friend, Richard Blair, and my former Federal Reserve editor, David A. Price. Their honest input and gentle suggestions made this book much better. Special thanks, as well, go to Ray McAllister, who gave me timely advice on how to market this book.

Several institutions provided invaluable research support, most notably the Library of Virginia, the Eastern Mennonite University Archives, Rocktown History, Massanutten Regional Library, and the Mennonite Church USA Archives. Within these organizations, I am especially indebted to Simone Horst, the archivist at EMU, and Dave Grabarek, an archival assistant at the Library of Virginia.

At the Brethren & Mennonite Heritage Center in Harrisonburg, Executive Director Sam Funkhouser provided excellent input on Mennonite and Brethren singing; Board Member Paul Roth shared his extensive knowledge of Elder John Kline; and volunteer Ervie Glick helped convert key phrases into German. (Thomas Lubik of the Federal Reserve also assisted with linguistics.)

Distant cousins on the Burkholder side of the family treated me like a long-lost brother as I researched the book. Pete Burkholder guided me on tours of the old Rhodes-Burkholder farm, and Judi

Espinoza regaled me with Civil War stories she had heard as a child from her great-grandmother, Mary Rhodes Burkholder.

Local historians also contributed to this project, most notably Norman Wenger, Emmert Bittinger, and the late David Rodes, who produced a treasure trove of information called *Unionists and the Civil War Experience in the Shenandoah Valley*. Nancy Hess Carr, Evan Knappenberger, Patricia Turner Ritchie, and Elwood Yoder also gave me the benefit of their expertise. And we all stand on the shoulders of their predecessors: Harry A. Brunk, Daniel Hays, John L. Heatwole, Samuel Horst, Samuel F. Sanger, John Wayland, D. H. Zigler, and many more.

Finally, this book owes much to the genealogical genius of Brent Rodes and the ancestral annotations of the late Grace Showalter. Without them, I might have missed the Rhodes family connections that pulled this project together into one cohesive story. And I must mention the hospitality of George Judy, who welcomed me to "Judy's on the South Fork," a picturesque farmstead in Peru, West Virginia, and a long-lost depot on the underground railroad. Judy's great-great-grandparents sheltered my great-great-grandfathers on the rainy night of March 14, 1862.

These wonderful people deserve much of the credit and none of the blame for the content of this book. Any mistakes are entirely my own.

—*Karl Rhodes*
July 2023

Notes

PROLOGUE

6   The Rawley Pike took on this name after its promoters formed a toll road company in 1870, according to Wayland (1912), p. 224. Before that, the thoroughfare was simply called the road to Rawley Springs or the "Rawley Road." Today it is the old alignment of U.S. Highway 33 or "Old 33."

6   Descriptions of Minnich and his store come from Hess (1979), p. 147, and Suter and Grove (1986), p. 79.

6   The impression of Minnich as "brickety" comes from Hess (1976), p. 250, although she spells the word differently.

6   Regarding Minnich's controversial marriage to the bishop's daughter, see Coffman (1964), p. 77.

6   The name "Dale Enterprise" originated when Minnich opened his store and post office in 1872.

7   For descriptions of the property taken from the Rhodes farm during General Philip Sheridan's occupation of the Shenandoah Valley, see Rodes and Wenger (2005), pp. 692–713.

7   The description of Lizzie Minnich comes from the photograph on page 80 of Suter and Grove (1986).

8   For transcriptions of testimony supporting Peggy's claim, see Rodes and Wenger (2005), pp. 707–712. Her "foster son" is John H. Bell, a young man who had grown up on the Rhodes farm.

8   "Do you swear to tell the truth …" These are the words that Baldwin used to swear in witnesses, according to Rodes and Wenger (2005), p. 702.

8   The precise alternative wording (without swearing) is unknown, but Baldwin clearly gave Peggy the option of swearing or affirming that her testimony was true.

8   Baldwin's questions come from Rodes and Wenger (2005), pp. 903–904. Peggy's replies come from Rodes and Wenger (2005), pp. 702–703. Some questions and answers have been edited for clarity and brevity.

10   Baldwin's notation regarding Peggy's loyalty comes from Rodes and Wenger (2005), p. 712.

10   The reimbursement to Peggy includes the $519.25 allowed by the commission in 1875 plus $50 that the federal government had paid previously. See the summary chart of Rodes and Wenger (2005), p. 712.

PEGGY'S WAR

CHAPTER 1: MOLE HILL

11 Descriptions of the Rhodes homestead are based on the author's observations, oral history among Peggy's descendants, the Lake (1885) Atlas of Rockingham County, and the 1871 diary of John S. Coffman, who lived on the farm from 1869 through 1873. Little is known about the two houses on the farm except their approximate locations and sizes. The main house accommodated nine or ten people in 1864. The tenant house was adequate for a family of three, but not five, according to Coffman (1964), p. 78.

12 The physical description of Henry is based on assumed family resemblance to his son, William H. Rhodes.

12 The physical description of Mary is based on the Burkholder family photograph on page 101 of Hess (1979). As with Henry and William, the assumption is that Peggy looked like her daughter, who was probably in her late thirties when the Burkholder family photograph was taken.

13 "Mole Hill is evil." In the nineteenth century, Rockingham residents realized that Mole Hill was different from other hills. One explanation was that Mole Hill was evil or haunted. Other 19th century theories were not much better. Today, geologists believe Mole Hill is the remnant of a volcano.

13 Peggy left no record of her dreams, but another Mennonite woman, who was married to Peggy's first cousin, had a prophetic barn-burning dream in March 1862, according to Hildebrand (1996), pp. 5–6.

14 The census of 1850 places John Bell in the Rhodes household, and he lived with the family until October 1864, according to Rodes and Wenger (2005), p. 709. It is not known why Johnny was living apart from his mother, Sophia Getz Bell, who appears in other Rockingham County households in the censuses of 1850 and 1860.

15 Steiner (1903), p. 15, states that Heatwole taught night classes at a small schoolhouse (probably Walnut Grove) "for the benefit of the boys of the neighborhood."

15 *Mennonite Confession of Faith* is an abbreviated name for the *Confession of Faith of the Christians Known by the Name of Mennonites*, which was translated from German to English by Joseph Funk in 1837.

16 All dialogue and specific actions in chapter one are imaginary but plausible and reasonable. For example, we know that in the late 1850s, farmers in the Shenandoah Valley invariably spent much time spreading manure in April, but we don't know that Henry and Johnny were spreading manure on April 17, 1858. Unless otherwise noted, this approach applies to all chapters of this book.

16 Regarding the time-consuming task of loading and unloading manure, see Grove (2001), p. 7.

17 Henry's parents married in 1808, but the actual month and day are unknown, according to Rodes (2023).

17 The idea of a ball of fire rolling down Mole Hill comes from Hess (1979), p. 109. On the same page, Hess discusses longstanding myths that Mole Hill is evil or haunted.

CHAPTER 2: CONSUMPTION

18 Characterizations of work on the Rhodes farm in all chapters of this book are based on the 1871 diary of John S. Coffman.

19 Several sources, including Weaver (1932), pp. 302–303, and Hess (1979), pp. 112–113, refer to Gabriel Heatwole Sr. as a Thomsonian doctor, an herbal physician who followed the methods set forth in Samuel Thomson's *New Guide to Health*. Hess states that Doc began studying medicine around 1835, the year of the most recent edition of Thomson's guide, which is the primary source for this chapter.

19 Based on the date of birth on Priscilla Rhodes' tombstone in the Shank Cemetery, Peggy would have been pregnant in the fall of 1858.

21 Unless otherwise noted, genealogical connections throughout this book come from Brunk (1987) and Rodes (2023). Information from Brunk (1987) has been supplemented—and in some cases superseded—by tombstone inscriptions and first-hand accounts.

21 Descriptions of Doc and his enterprises come from Hess (1979), pp. 111–119, who quotes Heatwole (1882), p. 12, and other Heatwole family sources.

21 Joseph Heatwole first married Maria Rhodes, who died on March 6, 1852. Joseph then wed her younger sister, Lydia Rhodes, on September 6, 1852. Apparently, the requisite grieving period was exactly six months.

23 "He saw patients through a window that opened onto the porch." Hess (1979), p. 118.

23 Medical discussions in chapters two and three are based on Thomson (1835).

CHAPTER 3: DROPSY IN THE HEAD

29 Henry suffered from consumption (tuberculosis) for ten years, according to Hess (1979), p. 101.

30 Mottie's formal name was Elizabeth Good Rhodes. The nickname "Mottie" was noted by Brunk (1943) p. 2, quoting Peggy's daughter, Mary Rhodes Burkholder.

30 Descriptions of court day and the annual muster of 1859 are based on Hess (1976), pp. 243–244.

30 During World War I, German Street became Liberty Street. See Wayland (1949), p. 184.
30 "General Gilbert S. Meem reviewed …" Wayland (1949), p. 227.
30 Horst (1967), p. 27, put the prewar penalties at "50 cents or 75 cents," which Hartman (1937), p. 49, characterized as "not very heavy."
31 Symptoms of tuberculous meningitis come from Schoeman (2009), p. 826.
31 Susan's son, Jacob D. Weaver, died in 1852, soon after he turned two, according to Brunk (1987), p. 671. Jacob's cause of death is unknown.
32 Doc's contempt for the diagnosis of "dropsy in the head" is based on Thomson (1835), pp. 126–127. Doc's treatment of Davy is inspired by the same source.
32 Davy died on May 27, 1859, according to his tombstone in the Shank Cemetery. The Virginia Bureau of Vital Statistics lists the cause of death as "unknown," but given his long-term exposure to consumption, tuberculous meningitis (TBM) is quite plausible. Robert Whytt (1768) gives the classic account of TBM in his *Observations on the Dropsy in the Brain*. He equates "dropsy in the brain" with hydrocephalus, which is a common complication of TBM.
33 Swartz lived and worked on the nearby farm owned by Peggy's father, Abraham Heatwole, and her brother, Daniel Heatwole, according to the census of 1860.
34 Davy's wake is inspired by Coffman (1964), pp. 64–65.
35 The description of the church comes from Brunk (1943), p. 2, quoting L. J. Heatwole's centennial address of 1926, and from Brunk (1959), pp. 70–71.
35 This graveyard is currently called the Shank Cemetery or the Old Weavers Church Cemetery.
37 The church's floor plan and seating customs come from Brunk (1943) p. 2, and from Brunk (1959) p. 303, quoting Peggy's oldest daughter, Mary Rhodes Burkholder.
37 The names of preachers, deacons, deaconesses, and song leaders in 1860 come from Heatwole, Brunk, and Good (1910), pp. 6–10.
37 A photograph of a somewhat older Samuel Coffman appears in Rodes and Wenger (2005), p. 626.
38 In the 1871 diary of John S. Coffman, the April 23 entry notes that his father, Sam Coffman, based a sermon on Psalm 103 for the funeral of a small child.
39 According to their adjacent tombstones in the Shank Cemetery, Priscilla was born two days after Davy died.
40 David Rhodes' death notice appeared in the *Rockingham Register* on October 14, 1859, p. 2.

CHAPTER 4: RUMORS OF WAR

41 Henry may or may not have read the *Rockingham Register*, but Peggy's second husband, Michael Shank, certainly did. See Rodes and Wenger (2005), p. 537, testimony of Lydia Shank.

41 Grove (2001), p. 14, says young L. J. wore a straw hat made by his mother.

41 Fairview School House replaced Walnut Grove in 1859. See Rhodes (2018), pp. 1–2.

42 "There were 500 to 700 whites *and* blacks …" *Rockingham Register*, October 21, 1859, p. 2. This newspaper account, like many early reports of John Brown's raid, contains errors and exaggerations. Throughout this book, direct quotes from the *Rockingham Register* are verbatim.

43 Doc's explanation of nonresistance is paraphrased from Burkholder (1837), p. 312. The biblical reference is Matthew 5:44.

44 Doc's long list of militia fines appears in Wayland (1930), pp. 132–140.

44 The ox-roast story comes from Hess (1979), p. 109. Other accounts say that celebrants roasted a steer on top of Mole Hill.

44 The Mexican War reference is inspired by Wright (1931), p. 20.

44 "Virginia would be the battlefield …" This quote is borrowed from Rodes and Wenger (2012), p. 815, testimony of Daniel Bowman.

45 Hartman (1937), pp. 47–48, says, "The people were more excited about [John Brown's] raid than they were when the war really began. Children were afraid to go out of doors."

45 "A large majority of the villains were killed …" *Rockingham Register*, October 28, 1859, p. 2.

46 Letters to and from Governor Wise ran in the *Rockingham Register* on November 11, 1859, p. 2.

46 "We are liable to be attacked at any moment …" *Rockingham Register*, December 2, 1859, p. 2.

47 "Our Country—Our Soldiery—Our Townswomen." Ibid.

48 The origin of Mottie's nickname is pure speculation.

48 There is no direct evidence that Sammy worked on the Rhodes farm, but he clearly spent multiple nights there in the spring of 1862. See Rhodes (1864), pp. 11–12. It was not uncommon for Henry's nephews to work on the Rhodes farm, according to diary entries in Coffman (1871).

48 Sammy's age comes from Rhodes (1864), p. 1. Clues regarding his personality come from his entire journal.

48 The newspaper's endorsement of Douglas ran in the *Rockingham Register* on June 29, 1860, p. 2.

PEGGY'S WAR

48 "Black Republicans ..." The scornful term "Black Republicans" referred derisively to those Republicans who allegedly advocated abolition.
49 Governor Letcher's endorsement appeared in the *Rockingham Register* on September 7, 1860, p. 2.
49 D. M. Switzer's attempt at humor ran in the *Rockingham Register* on September 28, 1860, p. 2.
50 "It's Lincoln!" This exclamation is based on Coffman (1964), p. 24.

CHAPTER 5: SECESSION

51 "REVOLUTION IN THE SOUTH ..." *Rockingham Register*, November 16, 1860, p. 2.
51 Expressions of great loss at the death of Martin Burkholder are based on his obituary, which ran in the *Rockingham Register* on December 28, 1860. The final tribute was signed D**** H******, which probably stood for David Hartman.
52 "Federal troops had fled ..." This ominous news from Charleston ran in the *Rockingham Register* on January 4, 1861, p. 2.
52 The announcement of a state convention to consider secession appeared in the *Rockingham Register* on January 18, 1861, p. 2.
52 Several letters from convention candidates ran in the *Rockingham Register* on January 25, 1861, pp. 2–3.
52 "We are most happy to announce ..." This uncharacteristic spurt of optimism appeared in the *Rockingham Register* on January 25, 1861, p. 2.
53 The results of the election ran in the *Rockingham Register* on February 8, 1861, p. 2.
53 "I'm not talking about *preacher* Sam Coffman ..." See Rodes and Wenger (2005), p. 880, testimony of Christian Showalter.
53 The comment from John Tyler appeared in the *Rockingham Register* on February 15, 1861, p. 3.
54 "The Tunkers and Mennonites do not hold slaves ..." *Rockingham Register*, February 15, 1861, p. 2.
54 The term "Dunkers" often was meant to include Mennonites as well, according to Horst (1967), p. 9.
54 See Horst (1967), p. 16: "The stress of the Dunkers on immersion as the only rightful mode of baptism could not be accepted by the Mennonites."
54 Suzy joined the Mennonite Church in 1870, according to her obituary in the *Herald of Truth*, May 1873, vol. 10, no. 5, p. 87.
55 The letter from George Chrisman ran in the *Rockingham Register* on March 8, 1861, p. 1.

PEGGY'S WAR

55 The lopsided vote *against* secession was noted by Horst (1967), p. 23.
55 "OPENING OF CIVIL WAR!" *Rockingham Register*, April 19, 1861, p. 2.
56 Lincoln called for 75,000 militia men, but the *Register* incorrectly reported 70,000. On the following day, Secretary of War Simon Cameron sent a communiqué to governors specifying each state's quota.
56 See Hartman (1937), p. 48: "When Lincoln soon called for 75,000 men to whip the Southern states back into the Union and looked for Virginia to furnish her quota, Virginia rose up in rebellion."
56 "My granddaddy and Abraham Lincoln's great-granddaddy …" Lincoln's great-grandfather, John Lincoln, moved from Pennsylvania to Linville Creek in 1768. He died in 1788, four years after Henry's grandfather, Heinrich Roth, moved his family from Pennsylvania to the same area, according to Showalter (2000), p. 16.
57 The call for a new bishop appears on page 18 of Heatwole, Brunk, and Good (1910). The clarification on the use of slave labor is on page 20.
57 See Yoder (2015), p. 71, for similar wording used in a ministerial lot at Weavers Church in 1887.
57 Daniel S. Heatwole "pledged himself to unfalteringly stand with and by Bishop Coffman," according to Brunk (1959), p. 317.
57 "TO THE POLLS!" *Rockingham Register*, May 17, 1861, p. 2.
58 "We have heard that some of our peaceful …" Ibid.
58 Algernon Gray's alleged change of heart was reported by the *Register* on May 17, 1861, p. 2.
59 There is no direct evidence that anyone tried to influence Henry's vote, but conversations similar to this imaginary one are well-documented in all six volumes of Rodes and Wenger (2003–2012). Lineweaver was one of the few men near Weavers Church who was neither Mennonite nor Dunker. One of his sons, William T. Lineweaver, joined the Confederate army at age seventeen, but after the war, he married into the Wenger family and joined the Mennonite Church, according to his obituary in the *Gospel Herald*, June 22, 1933, vol. 26, no. 12, p. 255.
59 "Governor Letcher turned Lincoln down flat …" This quote is based on Lehman and Nolt (2007), p. 44.
59 Lineweaver's unified-front argument is paraphrased from Ayers (2003), p. 155, quoting Alexander H. H. Stuart, a prominent Unionist leader in Augusta County, who changed his position after Lincoln ordered Virginia to provide troops. Witnesses before the Southern Claims Commission quite often cite the unified-front argument as the reason why quite a few Mennonites and Dunkers voted *for* secession.

60   Peggy testified that Henry did not vote for secession and often spoke against it, according to Rodes and Wenger (2005), p. 703.

60   "Then you better change your mind ..." This quote is paraphrased from attorney G. K. Gilmer, who was summarizing the threatening rhetoric that preceded the referendum on secession. See Rodes and Wenger (2003), p. 70. For specific examples, see Rodes and Wenger (2005), p. 369, testimony of Henry Early; pp. 443–444, testimony of Daniel Bowman; p. 659, testimony of David Hartman; and p. 813, testimony of John Brunk.

61   "You're a damn Black Republican ..." This quote is inspired by Rodes and Wenger (2005), p. 839, testimony of Daniel J. Good.

61   "MAKE WAY FOR ROCKINGHAM!" *Rockingham Register*, May 24, 1861, p. 2.

61   The full name of Sammy's older brother was Henry L. Rhodes. To avoid confusion, this book refers to him as H. L.

61   For a summary of conditions at the polls, see Rodes and Wenger (2005), p. 18: "The fact that the vote was taken by voice rather than by written ballot magnified the fear and danger felt by loyalist voters."

61   The description of how members of the Mount Crawford Cavalry voted comes from Rodes and Wenger (2003), pp. 70–71, testimony of S. E. Chamberlin, a special agent of the Southern Claims Commission.

61   "According to the newspaper, *no one* voted against secession at Mount Crawford ..." See the *Rockingham Register*, May 24, 1861, p. 2, which provides a breakdown of voting by precinct.

62   The harassment of John Harrison at Mount Crawford is documented in Rodes and Wenger (2003), p. 76, p. 108, p. 158, p. 172, p. 184, and p. 400. These pages include testimony from Sammy's brother, Henry L. Rhodes.

62   "Reverend Perry preached 'em outta it ..." This quote is based on Rodes and Wenger (2005), p. 288, testimony of Rev. William S. Perry.

62   "They still arrested him ..." See Rodes and Wenger (2003), p. 400, testimony of congressman John T. Harris, who said he "advised taking him (Harrison) before a magistrate and requiring him to give security for his good behavior, which he did, and this appeased public sentiment, and he was discharged and sent home."

CHAPTER 6: CONSCRIPTION

63   See Heatwole (1905), p. 207: "A few of the younger brethren went into the army with the first volunteers."

64   Weaver (1932), pp. 302–303, notes that fourth-Sunday services at Weavers Church began at 10 a.m.

65 Timothy Funk was a son of Joseph Funk, who produced hymn books and provided musical instruction. Timothy led singing schools at Weavers Church on Saturdays. See Heatwole, Brunk, and Good (1910), p. 18.

65 The wording and tone of this message come from the "Notice to Conscripts" that appeared on the front page of the *Rockingham Register* on August 14, 1863. The content of this message is based on a letter dated June 24, 1861, from Lieutenant Colonel George Deas to General Joseph E. Johnston.

66 The Weavers Mennonite Church conscription story comes from accounts in Hartman (1937), p. 49, and in Coffman (1964), p. 26.

66 "The time of conflict for our people has arrived ..." The quotes from Bishop Coffman are based on Coffman (1964), p. 26.

67 "Even as many of his Mennonite neighbors ..." Hartman (1937), p. 49.

67 Hartman (1937), p. 50, states that a time was appointed on July 4 "for a delegation from the South and one from the North to get together to see if they could not come to an agreement."

67 Descriptions of the comet and its exploding debris come from Hartman (1937), p. 50, and from Funk (1900), p. 444, quoting the July 4, 1861, diary entry of Elder John Kline.

68 "Here's a letter addressed 'To the Tunkers, Mennonites, and others opposed to war.'" *Rockingham Register*, July 5, 1861, p. 2.

69 Michael Shank was the son of Jacob Shank, who ran a depot on the underground railroad near Weavers Church. See Rodes and Wenger (2005), pp. 530–537, for details of Michael Shank's unceremonious removal. (Many years after the war, Michael Shank married Peggy.)

69 "The scouts carried him off in his shirt sleeves ..." This quote comes from Rodes and Wenger (2005), p. 535, testimony of Daniel Bowman.

69 Regarding medical exemptions, see the *Rockingham Register*, July 12, 1861, p. 1. Also, see Rhodes (1864), p. 2.

70 "I guess you're not too sick to make babies ..." There is no evidence that conscription scouts insulted Henry, but they certainly harassed other Mennonite and Dunker men in western Rockingham. See Rodes and Wenger (2005).

71 Henry's fake hemorrhage is imaginary, but it illustrates the fact that Mennonites in Rockingham County at the time of the Civil War were not completely nonresistant.

CHAPTER 7: THE PERFECT PLACE

72 See Funk (1900), pp. 444–445, Kline's diary entry for July 21, 1861: "A report of negroes breaking out and committing fearful outrages flew as on the wings of the wind. Women were frightened and men dismayed. It was, however, soon discovered to be false."

72 "We'll all be dead by morning ..." Sammy's quote is borrowed from Morgan (c1942), p. 2.

72 "They were compelled, because of the horrid stench ..." *Rockingham Register*, August 2, 1861, p. 1.

73 "That's only once ..." Henry's optimistic quote comes from Rodes and Wenger (2005), p. 704, Peggy's testimony.

73 The fall furloughs are mentioned in Hartman (1937), p. 53, and in Heatwole (1905), p. 208.

73 Christian Good's no-shoot story comes from Hartman (1937), p. 51, and from L. J. Heatwole's letter to J. S. Hartzler dated December 11, 1918, and published in the *Mennonite Historical Bulletin* of June 1972. The story varies somewhat between these two sources.

74 Singing in the military camps comes from Heatwole (1905), p. 208, and from Lehman and Nolt (2007), p. 59.

75 Brunk, Hartman, Good, and Shank ran active depots on the underground railroad in the Weavers Church area, according to their testimony in Rodes and Wenger (2005). John Wenger also concealed refugees but did not claim to operate a depot.

75 Regarding Wenger's denomination, see Rodes and Wenger (2005), p. 787.

75 An apple butter pig is apple butter baked inside a sleeve of pie dough.

76 Descriptions of Kline come from Langhorne (1886) and Funk (1900).

76 Hess (1979), p. 112, says that Doc purchased Samuel Thomson's "home study course" around 1835, and Kline was so impressed he ordered one, too. "These two friends both became excellent herb doctors who frequently consulted one another on difficult cases." Heatwole (1995), p. 51, states that Doc and Kline "often went off on herb gathering expeditions together."

76 There is no doubt that Kline's extensive travels through the mountains would have provided invaluable contacts and intelligence for establishing and maintaining the underground railroad. There is no direct evidence that Kline was the mastermind of the underground in Rockingham County, but he would have been well-qualified for the job.

77 "It has become my considered opinion that Dunkers and Mennonites must work together ..." Based on Horst (1967), pp. 41–42 and 115, and on Rodes and Wenger (all six volumes), it seems clear that Mennonites and Dunkers worked well together to organize an underground railroad, but Funk (1900) makes no mention of such cooperation. It is possible that Funk intentionally excluded diary entries that documented Kline's direct involvement. Funk may have done this to avoid rekindling animosity against Dunkers and Mennonites. This theory also might explain why Funk destroyed Kline's diary after publishing selected excerpts in 1900.

PEGGY'S WAR

77 "Many of the brethren have already expressed to me their determination to flee …" Funk (1900) p. 446, Kline's diary entry for December 20, 1861.

77 "What I propose is an underground railroad …" Mennonites and Dunkers used the term "underground railroad" to describe their escape network, but there is little evidence that Mennonites and Dunkers used their network to help fugitive slaves. Colby (1928), pp. 584–585, says, "There was no regular Underground Railway [for fugitive slaves] among the Mennonites."

77 On August 10, 1861, Confederate forces won the Battle of Wilson's Creek in Missouri, according to the "Civil War Timeline" of the U.S. National Park Service.

78 "This here's the perfect place for hidin' draft dodgers and deserters." This quote is based on Rodes and Wenger (2005), p. 703, Peggy's testimony.

78 Brunk testified that he hid fugitives in the church and at his house. See Rodes and Wenger (2005), p. 812.

79 At some point during the war—perhaps even before the war—Peggy took charge of the Rhodes farm. The testimony in Rodes and Wenger (2005), pp. 702–712, always refers to Peggy acting alone. Henry is barely mentioned as "an invalid." The testimony of Bishop Sam Coffman certainly suggests, however, that Henry approved of Peggy's Unionist actions. "He was a sound Union man," Coffman said, "and was in perfect accord with the acts of the claimant (Peggy), so far as I could learn and judge."

80 "He was raccoon clever." Later in life, Swartz designed a "grasshopper gate" that could be opened and closed from a buggy or horse by pulling a rope or lever. See Swope Family History Committee (1971), p. 22.

84 Southern voters elected Jefferson Davis on November 6, 1861.

84 Regarding troop movement through Harrisonburg, see the *Rockingham Register*, December 6, 1861, p. 2. The four regiments were quite likely the First Georgia, the Third Arkansas, the Twenty-Third Virginia, and the Thirty-Seventh Virginia. They marched from Monterey to Manassas in December 1861, according to Taylor (1975), p. 37.

85 Weather conditions in this chapter—and in all subsequent chapters—come from the journals and diaries of Samuel Rhodes, Jedediah Hotchkiss, Jacob Hildebrand, Henry Saint John Rinker, and John Kline.

85 The surge in underground activity in the winter of 1862 is based on Hartman (1937), p. 53.

CHAPTER 8: SWORD OF THE SPIRIT

87 The reporting date of March 14 comes from Hildebrand (1996), pp. 4–5, diary entry for March 14, 1862. "Today I have to report in Staunton and from there to Winchester."

87 "It also struck my mind that maybe this was some trap ..." This quote comes from Rhodes (1864), p. 2.

88 "He's been drivin' teams for the rebels ..." This quote is based on Rodes and Wenger (2003), p. 273, testimony of Henry L. Rhodes.

88 "The Rhodes depot was overflowing with refugees ..." See Rodes and Wenger (2005), p. 703. Peggy testified that she hid "five or six together at a time and would stay sometimes several days waiting for the guides to take them through the mountains." The assumption is that all depots near Weavers Church would have been busy on the evening of March 13, 1862, as seventy-plus refugees were preparing to flee.

89 Several accounts place Brunk and Rodgers in this refugee group, but there is no direct evidence that they, or Peter Blosser, were at the Rhodes depot on March 13.

89 Regarding young Peter Hartman's role as a guide, see Rodes and Wenger (2005), p. 663.

89 See Sanger and Hays (1907), p. 109, quoting from an interview with Simeon Heatwole, one of Doc's sons. Heatwole stated that the group "started from Samuel Beery's near Crissman's and went through Hopkins Gap." Berry and Chrisman (slightly different spellings for both) appear near Hopkins Gap on the 1866 Map of Rockingham County by Hotchkiss.

90 The religious affiliations of the group come from Sanger and Hays (1907), p. 108, quoting Simeon Heatwole, and from Zigler (1914), p. 105, quoting a 1906 letter from David M. Miller.

90 Blosser (1888), p. 135, claims the group was "under the guidance of Brother Daniel Suters," and according to Emanuel Suter's testimony in Rodes and Wenger (2005), p. 829, Daniel Suter (Emanuel's father) was among the seventy-plus men. Daniel Suter's name, however, does not appear among the forty-five men who were recommended for exemptions in Richmond. One likely explanation for this omission is that Suter was too old for military duty and therefore did not need an exemption. Brunk (1959), p. 155, states that Joseph Heatwole, "was the leader of the apprehended group." This could be true, or Brunk may have assumed that Heatwole was the leader because he was riding at the front of the group when it was captured.

91 "They spilled out onto a wagon road ..." Given the timeline that emerges from first-hand accounts, the refugees traveled about thirty-five miles in roughly twenty hours to reach the farm where they spent the next night. This quick pace suggests that the seventy-plus men and thirty-plus horses took the most direct route possible using the best roads available after they crossed Little North Mountain.

91 Dovesville is now called Bergton.

PEGGY'S WAR

91 The road that leads to the top of the Shenandoah Mountain is now called Overly Hollow Road.

92 On the west side of the Shenandoah Mountain, the road is now called Peru Hollow Road, but the alignment of that road has shifted since 1862.

93 "Welcome to Judy's on the South Fork." See Sanger and Hays (1907), p. 109, quoting Simeon Heatwole. Please note that Kline's diary entries in Funk (1900) refer to "Judy's on the South Fork" and "Nimrod Judy's" interchangeably. This farm is currently run by George and David Judy, great-great-grandsons of Nimrod and Mary Ann Judy.

93 Sanger and Hays (1907), p. 61, note that Petersburg "at times was occupied by Union forces."

94 Adam Ketterman was one Kline's many friends in the mountains west of the Shenandoah. See Funk (1900), p. 400, Kline's diary entry for October 8, 1857. There is no evidence that Ketterman advised the refugees, but they probably walked right past his home.

94 Crossing the swollen river would have been dangerous on March 15, but Brunk's near-drowning experience is imaginary.

95 "You gotta take yer horses back over …" Sanger and Hays (1907), pp. 66 and 109, quoting the first-hand accounts of Joseph A. Miller and Simeon Heatwole, respectively.

95 "A clamorous undertaking that entertained the townsfolk …" Sanger and Hays (1907), p. 66, quoting Joseph Miller.

95 Stories of the group's capture vary somewhat. For first-hand accounts, see Sanger and Hays (1907), p. 109, quoting Simeon Heatwole, and Zigler (1914), pp. 104–105, quoting the 1906 letter from David Miller.

95 "Oh, brethren! Pray mightily unto God …" See Brunk (1959), p. 155.

96 "By my own word of honor, I have no right to bother you." This quote is inspired by Hartman (1937), pp. 55–56.

96 "Don't you dare feel sorry …" Sanger and Hays (1907), pp. 68 and 109, quoting the accounts of Joseph Miller and Simeon Heatwole, respectively.

96 "The damn Union rascals ought to be shot." This quote is based on Rodes and Wenger (2004), p. 329, testimony of John Geil.

96 The "disarming" story comes primarily from Sanger and Hays (1907), pp. 68 and 109, quoting the accounts of Joseph Miller and Simeon Heatwole, respectively.

96 "That is very good, you can keep that kind of sword." Ibid.

97 The group spent the night at John Bond's place on North Mill Creek, according to Sanger and Hays (1907), pp. 69 and 109–110, quoting the accounts of Joseph Miller and Simeon Heatwole, respectively.

97 See the summary of Bond's life in "Senate Concurrent Resolution 54," introduced on March 1, 2016, to the West Virginia Legislature.

97 "Many people in this part of the county remain loyal ..." This quote is based on Taylor (1975), p. 4. Pendleton County was predominately Southern in sentiment, but "a minority of citizens concentrated in the county's northwest corner remained loyal to the Union, banding together in military companies to protect their homes and farms from Confederate guerrillas and regulars." Also, see West Virginia Legislature (2016) regarding Bond's role in leading this Unionist home guard, which became known as "Swamp Dragons."

98 The story of Blosser's escape and return to the valley is based on Rodes and Wenger (2005), p. 598, quoting the second-hand account of Blosser's son, Samuel H. Blosser. The younger Blosser's journal is in the Eastern Mennonite University Archives.

CHAPTER 9: WHICH WAY IS WEST?

100 See Rhodes (1864), p. 2. Sammy identified his starting point as "Pleasant Run near J. B. Mill." Byerly's Mill appears on Pleasant Run on the 1866 Map of Rockingham County by Hotchkiss.

100 Unless otherwise noted, Sammy's travels in the western Rockingham mountains are based on his journal: Rhodes (1864), pp. 2–10.

100 Peter S. Heatwole was a grandson of Doc and the oldest son of Joseph Heatwole and his first wife, Maria Rhodes, who was Henry's deceased sister. At this point, Sammy's journal does not mention that Peter or H. L. are with him, but their presence becomes obvious on subsequent pages.

100 Henry L. Rhodes testified that his group was "one day behind the party of 70." Rodes and Wenger (2003), p. 273.

101 "Dry River Road." See Horst (1980), p. 285, note 14: "This road paralleled the Dry River, via Rawley Springs, deep into the mountains." Also, see the 1866 Map of Rockingham County by Hotchkiss.

101 "They arrived at the home of Henry May ..." See Rhodes (1864), p. 3. Sammy does not name the occupant of this house, but May lived at the head of Dry River and was later arrested for assisting deserters, according to the *Rockingham Register*, October 9, 1863, p. 2. Another reasonable assumption is that Henry May was John H. May, who testified before the Southern Claims Commission that his brother-in-law, Martin Beery, was in the group of seventy-plus. See Rodes and Wenger (2004), p. 367.

101 "A rugged path north to the Pendleton Road ..." See Rhodes (1864), p. 3. Sammy called this route the "Petersburg Road," but it was more likely the "Pendleton Road," which later became Little Dry River Road.

103 This pivotal moment of uncertainty is based on Rhodes (1864), p. 6.

103 "The rebels stopped for the night and took charge ..." See Sanger and Hays (1907), p. 69. Joseph Miller mentions these six or seven additional prisoners but provides no information about them.

104 The nighttime interrogation at Franklin is based on Sanger and Hays (1907), pp. 69 and 110, quoting Joseph Miller and Simeon Heatwole, respectively.

104 "Only to keep from fighting ..." This quote is paraphrased from Sanger and Hays (1907), p. 69. Joseph Miller did not identify any of the other five men who were questioned, but Brunk could have been one of them.

104 "Up North there's a law ..." This quote is inspired by Wright (1931), p. 124, who notes that President Abraham Lincoln and Secretary of War Edwin Stanton were both somewhat sympathetic toward conscientious objectors.

105 "I say you're nothin' but a bunch of horse thieves!" This quote is based on Sanger and Hays (1907), p. 110, quoting Simeon Heatwole: "There was an attempt made the next morning to frighten them that they might have an excuse, as was supposed, to capture their horses."

105 Regarding the night spent at Monterey, see Sanger and Hays (1907), p. 69, quoting Miller. Also, see Blosser (1886), obituary of Joseph Heatwole, regarding the role of the Churchville Cavalry. Blosser states that the seventy-plus men were captured by the Churchville Cavalry, but this seems to conflict with other accounts of the group being captured by "parolees." On March 25, 1862, the *Staunton Spectator* reported that the prisoners were "brought to this place ... under charge of some of the members of the Churchville Cavalry." One possible explanation is that the parolees captured the men and turned them over to the Churchville Cavalry at some point.

105 "One of the Dunkers just kept going ..." See Sanger and Hays (1907), pp. 81 and 110. The escapee was David Sanger, the oldest brother of S. F. Sanger, who was Hays' co-author.

105 "Gentlemen, I will trust to your honor tonight." This quote and the story of the foiled escape plan come from Sanger and Hays (1907), p. 70.

106 "The cavalry confined them to the courthouse and posted guards ..." Waddell (1888), p. 293, diary entry for March 19, 1862.

106 "We lost our horses, but at least we have plenty to eat." This quote is based on Sanger and Hays (1907), p. 70.

106 "Don't tell them that they have to go to Richmond tomorrow ..." Ibid.

106 Taking crackers with them onto the train. Ibid.

107 See Coulter (1950), p. 471: "Prisoners almost invariably asserted that the boxcars into which they were crowded were unclean cattle cars."

107 Trains at the time were capable of going about fifty miles per hour, according to the *Rockingham Register*, January 7, 1859, p. 1.

107 "Many of the boxcar brethren expected to die ..." Brunk (1959), p. 155.

108 The railroad from Staunton to Richmond passed through Rockfish Gap via the Blue Ridge Tunnel, which is not quite one mile long.

108 According to Sanger and Hays (1907), p. 70, the ride to Richmond lasted "all day and part of the night." This length of time suggests that the train made several stops.

108 "Broad is the Road that Leads to Death." There is no record of what hymns the prisoners sang, but these lyrics by Isaac Watts appear in both Mennonite and Dunker hymn books used at the time of the Civil War.

109 The train stations mentioned in this chapter were some of the larger ones between Staunton and Richmond, according to the *Twenty-Seventh Annual Report of the Virginia Central Railroad Company*, 1862, p. 35.

109 "They had to get away from Brock's Gap ..." Sammy's adventures in this section of chapter nine are based on Rhodes (1864), pp. 6–9.

CHAPTER 10: CASTLE THUNDER

112 "The larger group of refugees arrived in Richmond around midnight on March 20." This date is based on the *Staunton Spectator* of March 25, 1862.

112 See the 1864 Map of Richmond by Adams. Based on this map and on Joseph Miller's account, the group likely spent the night in the "machine shop" on the southwest corner of Cary Street and 17th Street.

112 "Gentlemen, this is the best we can do for you tonight." This quote comes from Joseph Miller's account in Sanger and Hays (1907), pp. 70–71.

113 "Indeed, this would not be an easy night." Ibid.

113 "Then the guards marched them two blocks east to Castle Thunder." Sanger and Hays (1907), p. 81. Other sources, such as Hartman (1937), have claimed that this group was held at nearby Libby Prison, but Horst (1967), pp. 52–53, asserts that far more evidence points to Castle Thunder.

113 "Looking down from a south-facing window ..." Sanger and Hays (1907), p. 110, quoting Simeon Heatwole. Vintage photographs of the building show barred windows on both the second and third floors, but the higher floor would have provided the view of the canal and river that Heatwole describes.

113 The keepers of Castle Thunder became notorious for abusing political prisoners, but the Mennonites and Dunkers apparently were treated better than inmates held there later in the war. See Coulter (1950), p. 89.

113 "He thought his life would soon be over ..." See the obituary for Gabriel D. Heatwole Jr. in the *Gospel Herald*, March 9, 1922, vol. 14, no. 49, p. 975.

114 "This was particularly painful for him ..." See Rodes and Wenger (2005), p. 958, medical exemption form for Gabriel D. Heatwole Jr.

114 See Sanger and Hays (1907), p. 71, quoting Joseph Miller, who did not specify which twelve men were selected.

114 "I am a habeas corpus commissioner ..." Neely (1999), pp. 81–85.

115 "Now I am going to ask you a number of questions ..." This quote is paraphrased from Sanger and Hays (1907), p. 71, quoting Joseph Miller, who also gave examples of the questions.

116 Muster fines increased dramatically as expectations of war escalated. See Heatwole (1905), p. 207.

116 "They mustered me into the 146th Virginia ..." Horst (1967), p. 30, quoting the *Compiled Service Records of Confederate Soldiers*.

117 "I was furloughed for five months ..." Ibid.

117 "Would you feed the *enemy* if he came to your home?" This question and answer are paraphrased from Sanger and Hays (1907), p. 71.

118 "This book explains our beliefs better than I can ..." See Burkholder (1837), pp. 295–313.

118 Sanger and Hays (1907), p. 111, mention Hopkins' visit. Gray's presence at Castle Thunder is assumed because of his persistent efforts to free the men.

119 "It won't be easy ..." Blosser (1888), p. 138, says the *Mennonite Confession of Faith* was "brought into court at Richmond by Algernon S. Gray."

119 "Tell your families that you are safe, for now, ..." This quote is based on Sanger and Hays (1907), p. 82. They note that "letters were allowed to pass in and out of prison."

119 "Benjamin Byerly, an influential Dunker from Rockingham, visited the prisoners ..." Sanger and Hays (1907), p. 111.

119 See Horst (1967), pp. 65–84, for examples of Kline's letters to Confederate officials.

119 "Some of the legislators suggested that the men could work as teamsters ..." Sanger and Hays (1907), p. 71.

120 For a summary of the exemption act, see Zigler (1914), pp. 101–102.

120 "On March 28, Baxter issued ..." See Horst (1967), p. 53. "Stonewall Brigade" was often used to refer to Jackson's entire army rather than the original regiments that famously fought under his command at Manassas.

121 "The fact that two parolees captured all of you boys without a fight ..." This quote comes from Sanger and Hays (1907), p. 73. It's not clear whether Gray's comment referred to passage of the Virginia exemption law in March or passage of the Confederate conscription law in October, but the sentiment is the same.

121 "Baxter sent another report to the war department on March 31." See "Report of S. S. Baxter," *Official Records*, Series II, vol. 3, p. 385, quoted on page 54 of Horst (1967).

PEGGY'S WAR

121 "All militia men will promptly report …" Jackson's order, dated March 31, 1862, was recorded in a notice signed by Lieutenant Colonel John R. Jones of the 33rd Regiment of Virginia Volunteers. This original document resides in the Eastern Mennonite University Archives.

CHAPTER 11: THE JURY ROOM

122 Horst (1967), p. 58, states that Doc and Kline were "being closely watched." Details of Doc's arrest are imaginary but plausible.

123 "Doc was surprised to see his son-in-law, Hugh Brunk …" Sanger and Hays (1907), p. 109.

124 "They took our gold …" *Staunton Spectator*, March 25, 1862, p. 1.

124 "We spent a day or two at Mount Jackson …" Sanger and Hays (1907), pp. 61–65, quoting the first-hand account of J. M. Cline.

124 "The guards pushed Elder Kline into the room." Funk (1900), p. 448, Kline's diary entry for April 5, 1862.

124 For a biographical sketch of Joseph Beery, see Wenger (1905), pp. 24–25.

124 "I voted against secession and made no apologies …" This quote is based on Rodes and Wenger (2003), p. 532, testimony of P. H. Showalter.

124 Doc Heatwole gave only a brief account of his imprisonment with Kline and Beery. See Rodes and Wenger (2005), p. 442: "We were taken as the head Union men."

124 "Men's hearts are failing them for fear." This quote is borrowed from Funk (1900), p. 440, Kline's diary entry for April 21, 1861.

125 "He's one of the few who voted against secession …" This quote is inspired by Rodes and Wenger (2005), p. 573, quoting S. E. Chamberlin, a special agent of the Southern Claims Commission.

125 The location of the jury room within the courthouse is based on Funk (1900), pp. 448 and 452, quoting Kline's diary entries for April 5 and 10, 1862, respectively. The description of the room is derived from the photograph of the courthouse that appears on page 230 of Hess (1976).

125 "Send up a dozen cakes …" This quote is based on Hess (1976), p. 244.

125 "On Sunday morning, Kline did what he could to lift the men's spirits." See Funk (1900), p. 448, quoting Kline's diary entry for April 6, 1862.

126 "The Lord into His Garden Comes." See Sanger and Hays (1907), p. 80. Sanger recalled his family singing this song on the night before his brother, David, left with the group of seventy-plus. See the *Brethren Hymnal* of 1901.

126 "We are in prison close confined." Hartman (1937), p. 57, says that this song was composed by the prisoners in Richmond, but Sanger and Hays (1907), p. 156, say the verses were written by the young men at Mount Jackson, and

the chorus was added by Kline at the Rockingham Courthouse. These four verses come from the arrangement given on pages 156–157 of Sanger and Hays (1907). The lyrics vary slightly from those that appear on pages 57–58 of Hartman (1937).

128 "Righteousness, Temperance, and the Judgment to Come." See Funk (1900), pp. 448–452, for a more complete version of Kline's sermon.

130 "When the guards allowed some Dunker men …" Funk (1900), p. 452, Kline's diary entry for April 7, 1862.

130 "These men are becoming sick." Sanger and Hays (1907), p. 64, quoting the account of J. M. Cline.

130 "The guards are not providing enough wood …" This quote is based on Sanger and Hays (1907), p. 129, quoting a biographical sketch of Kline written by Benjamin Funk.

130 "The rebel rags, however, were filled with nothing but enthusiasm for war." Funk (1900), p. 452, Kline's diary entries for April 8–9, 1862.

131 "They are so broken down by the sad state of the country …" This quote is based on Funk (1900), p. 452, Kline's diary entry for April 9, 1862.

131 "The friendly guard allowed them to have visitors again." See Funk (1900), p. 452, Kline's diary entry for April 10. The assumption is that these Dunkers were the same ones who had visited Kline on April 7.

131 "Your dear wife carries sunshine with her wherever she goes." Ibid.

131 "When it came time for Catherine to leave …" See Sanger and Hays (1907), p. 146, quoting from Hays' interview of Catherine Showalter.

131 "Confederate soldiers marching north …" Funk (1900), p. 452, Kline's diary entry for April 10, 1862. The assumption is that these soldiers were marching north to reinforce Jackson's army at Rude's Hill.

131 "An article that branded the prisoners …" See Zigler (1914), pp. 109–110: "On the 11th of April there appeared in the columns of the *Register* an article that displeased Elder Kline." This issue of the *Register* could not be found, but the gist of the letter can be inferred from Kline's response to it.

132 "I can see the bullet hole in the ceiling." Sanger and Hays (1907) describe this attack on pages 64–65, quoting the account of J. M. Cline, but Funk (1900) makes no mention of this remarkable incident. It is impossible to know whether Kline failed to record it or whether Funk chose not to include it, but no diary entries appear for April 11 and 12, the days when this attack most likely occurred.

CHAPTER 12: OATH OF ALLEGIANCE

135 "Kline preached another sermon …" Funk (1900), p. 452.

135 "More food arrived ..." See Sanger and Hays (1907), p. 143, who quote a letter from Rebecca Bowman. Also, see Zigler (1914), p. 112.

135 "The guards released John and Joseph Cline ..." Funk (1900), p. 453.

135 "It was Kline's turn to be sick." Ibid.

135 "Mr. Editor of the Register ..." The *Register* never published Kline's response, and Funk (1900) makes no mention of the letter, but a photocopy and transcription of the letter appear on pages 109–111 of Zigler (1914).

136 "Speak only in English or I will arrest you ..." This quote is based on Rodes and Wenger (2005), p. 444, testimony of Daniel Bowman.

137 The release of prisoners at Judge Smith's place is based on Zigler (1914), p. 108, quoting Daniel Miller. The assumption is that "the Judge Smith place" is Smithland, the mansion built by Daniel Smith, one of the first justices of Rockingham County.

137 The stop at Bethlehem Church comes from Zigler (1914), p. 109.

137 "The provost marshal authorized the guards to release the prisoners ..." See Rodes and Wenger (2005), p. 442, Doc's testimony: "We got released that time (underscore added) by the near approach of General Banks' army." The words "that time" are intriguing because they imply that Doc may have been arrested along with Kline and/or Beery on other occasions.

138 "I am an old man, and I do not want to die in prison." This quote is paraphrased from Rodes and Wenger (2003), p. 369. Given that Beery admitted taking the oath of allegiance "in order to effect my release," it seems likely that his captors would have required his fellow prisoners to take the oath as well. Another courthouse prisoner, George S. Wine, denied taking the oath of allegiance. See Rodes and Wenger (2007), p. 1023. Wine said, "I was compelled upon being released to swear that I would not during the war give aid and comfort to the United States." It is worth noting that Wine and the other younger prisoners were being held for dodging the draft, while Kline, Doc, and Beery were being held on the more serious charge of treason. Perhaps this distinction explains the conflict in testimony. The guards also may have singled out Beery because of his vote against secession.

138 The guards also released Kline on that day, but historians who have studied his life insist that he would not have sworn the oath of allegiance.

138 "The Mennonites and Dunkers of the valley ..." See Horst (1967), p. 62: "The death sentence [for desertion] was carried out sufficiently often to impress the public."

138 "We don't have much of that ..." Confederate currency was already losing value quickly in the spring of 1862. See Ashby (1914), p. 68.

139 "I have never seen people rise so generously to any cause." This quote is based on Hartman (1937), p. 59.

139 Brunk (1959), p. 158, names Emanuel Suter as the person appointed to carry the funds to Richmond to pay the fines for the Mennonite prisoners.

139 "He heard someone tapping on the bedroom window ..." See Rodes and Wenger (2005), p. 645, quoting the testimony of Daniel P. Good: "He made his escape and came back to my house, and gave a signal warning on my window." The assumption throughout this book is that this signal was the same for all depots and safe houses in Rockingham.

139 "Henry Brunk, and I got Charles Rodgers with me." See Rodes and Wenger (2005), p. 703. Peggy testified that Henry Brunk hid at the Rhodes depot "for nearly a year" and that "another man named Charles Rodgers, who was captured with the 70 and sent to Richmond, was put into the Rebel Army and he ran away and came and staid at our house several weeks." It seems likely that Brunk and Rodgers both deserted on April 18, as Jackson's army was retreating through Harrisonburg.

139 "Pap" is John Brunk, a cousin who helped raise Henry Brunk after his parents died, according to the journal of Samuel H. Brunk, which appears on pages 939–953 of Rodes and Wenger (2005).

140 Brunk's desertion comes from Erb (c1944), p. 19.

140 The names of the two Dunker emissaries to Richmond come from Zigler (1914), pp. 105 and 107.

140 "Two days ago, the Confederate Congress passed a conscription act ..." See *Public Laws of the Confederate States of America, Passed at the First Session of the First Congress; 1862*, edited by James M. Matthews. Chapter 31: "An Act to Further Provide for the Public Defense," April 16, 1862. Also see Horst (1967), p. 122, note 35. Horst speculates that the Richmond prisoners were released on April 14 (two days before the Confederate Congress passed this act), but that date seems highly unlikely in light of the 1906 letter from David Miller published in Zigler (1914). Based on Miller's timeline, a much more likely release date is April 21.

141 "General Johnston called out Virginia militia ..." This quote is based on a letter from Lieutenant Colonel George Deas to General Joseph E. Johnston, dated June 24, 1861.

141 The conversation between Baxter and Byerly is imaginary, but it does provide a plausible explanation for why the fines and affidavits were not immediately accepted. According to Sanger and Hays (1907), p. 72, Baxter attributed the delay to "the press of business," which was probably true in a general sense, but the conflict between the Virginia law and the Confederate law would have been obvious to Baxter.

141 For more information on the Rockingham Rebellion, see Chambers (1959), p. 483; Casler (1971), pp. 69–70 and 302–303; Also, see Hotchkiss (1973), pp. 17 and 21.

142 "The war department has decided …" This imaginary quote provides one possible explanation for why the prisoners were released despite the new Confederate conscription law. Another plausible explanation is simply delayed enforcement. See Zigler (1914), p. 113: "This (Confederate) act was passed April 16, 1862, and shortly after (underscore added) the return of the Brethren, it was being executed."

142 "Each prisoner must take an oath …" See Rodes and Wenger (2005), p. 454, testimony of Joseph Heatwole. "I took some oath to get my release. I think it was, not to engage in war against the Confederate States. I am sure it was not the oath of allegiance."

142 "Now you can all go home." This quote comes from Sanger and Hays (1907), p. 111, testimony of Simeon Heatwole.

142 "Arriving on April 23 …" This homecoming date—which differs by one week from the timeline proposed by Horst (1967)—comes from Zigler (1914), quoting the 1906 letter from David Miller. "We started about five weeks before April 17, 1862," the birthday of Miller's son. "I was gone six weeks, and when I got back, the boy was a week old."

CHAPTER 13: SAMMY'S ESCAPE

144 "By the time the prisoners returned from Richmond, Banks' army had taken control of Harrisonburg." Chambers (1959), p. 480, states that Banks sent his advance guard into Harrisonburg on April 22.

145 Unless otherwise noted, Sammy's adventures in chapter thirteen are based on Rhodes (1864), pp. 9–19.

145 Abraham D. Heatwole lived very close to Sammy's family. Abraham was a first cousin to Peggy, whose father's name was also Abraham Heatwole.

145 "H. L.'s gonna claim the religious exemption …" This quote is based on Rodes and Wenger (2003), p. 273.

146 "He arrived at Doc's house at noon …" Rhodes (1864), p. 12. Sammy's statement that Henry picked him up at Doc's place on May 1, 1862, is the only documentation of Henry leaving the Rhodes farm during the war.

147 A. J. Bowers was Andrew Jackson Bowers. He was ordained by the Reformed Church in 1875, according to the "Acts and Proceedings of the Synod of the Potomac of the Reformed Church in the United States Convened in Convention, Winchester, Va., October 1875," p. 13. Bowers' identity becomes clear in Sammy's letter home dated August 18, 1863.

147 "The federal troops had left …" Kellogg (1903), p. 55.

147 "Maybe we should just go back to Abram's house." See Rodes and Wenger (2003), p. 167, testimony of Abraham D. Heatwole, who lists "Samuel

Rodes" and "Jackson Bowers" among the men he hid. Bowers may or may not have helped Sammy dig the child's grave.

149 "They're probably looking for Union troops ..." Ashby's cavalry likely was scouting the western reaches of Rockingham for any sign that Frémont's army was crossing the Shenandoah Mountain. See Hotchkiss (1973), p. 44, diary entry for May 10, 1862.

150 Daniel Showalter's home appears on the Lake (1885) Atlas of Rockingham County near the top of page 34.

150 "They found Fifer at Trissels Mennonite Church ..." See Brunk (1959), pp. 240–243, especially the map on page 243, which shows both the Jacob Fifer place and the Daniel Showalter place. Sammy probably was referring to Fifer in his journal when he mentioned "Phifer."

150 "I think his pursuit of Banks was just a bluff." See Vandiver (1957), p. 225: "Ashby's advance toward Banks was in reality a screening move for the march of the main army."

150 "One of his neighbors directed the refugees to Elder Kline ..." Despite Sammy's spelling of "Cline," Horst (1980), p. 290, note 44, states that this helpful person was probably Elder John Kline.

151 "Hoover was an affable man in his mid-30s ..." For Emanuel Hoover's age and location, see Rodes and Wenger (2007), p. 788, and the Lake (1885) Atlas of Rockingham County.

151 "One of them was Bishop Coffman." See Rodes and Wenger (2005), p. 619. Coffman testified that he "went to Penna. in May 1862, because I had been threatened, stayed six weeks." Sammy's conversation with the bishop is imaginary, but it is highly likely that Coffman fled north with Bank's army along with other Mennonites who had gathered in New Market that day.

151 "I am exempt from the military ..." This quote is inspired by Coffman (undated), who states that the bishop "received his exemption from all military duty" from the 145th Regimental Court on June 26, 1861.

151 "I started preaching directly against conscription." On page 158, Brunk (1959) notes that Bishop Coffman took a firm stand "from the pulpit" against the April 1862 law.

151 Threats against Coffman are noted in Heatwole (1905), pp. 208–209, and in several other sources, but Coffman (undated) is the only source that mentions hanging. The most likely person to make a credible threat was Lieutenant Colonel John R. Jones.

152 Henry Saint John Rinker was a reverend in A. J.'s denomination and a staunch supporter of the Confederacy. He lived about twelve miles north of New Market on the Middle Road (Route 42). In his journal, Sammy refers to Rinker as "Revrant John Rinkerd ... a very rank Secesh."

PEGGY'S WAR

152 The description of Rinker's family comes from Rinker (1999), p. 2.

152 Andrew Jackson Bowers matriculated at Franklin and Marshall in 1859, according to Harbaugh and Heilser (1888), p. 333. The reason for his return to Virginia is unknown, but the outbreak of war seems like a reasonable assumption. In a letter dated August 18, 1863, Sammy notes that "A. J. Bowers is in Lancaster yet going to school." (Franklin and Marshall is in Lancaster, Pennsylvania.)

152 "Among the first things I learned …" According to Franklin and Marshall's website, Franklin College's founding mission was "to preserve our present republican system of government," and "to promote those improvements in the arts and sciences which alone render nations respectable, great and happy."

153 "I can do that easier in Ohio …" On page 14 of Rhodes (1864), Sammy says his original destination was Ohio.

CHAPTER 14: WAR ARRIVES

156 Grove (2001), p. 14, states that Confederate forces commandeered Weavers Church at some point. She offers no time frame and few details, but certainly Sammy saw a squad of Ashby's cavalry about two miles west of the church on May 6. According to Avirett (1867), pp. 179–180, ten companies of Ashby's cavalry went with Jackson to McDowell, while Ashby himself remained in Rockingham with his other charges.

156 For details of Jackson's exploits near McDowell, see Chambers (1959), pp. 504–508, and Hotchkiss (1973), pp. 38–45.

156 Hildebrand (1996), p. 12, places the 52nd Virginia Infantry two miles west of Harrisonburg on May 19.

156 Regarding the federal armies of Banks, Frémont, and Shields closing in on Jackson, see Casler (1971), p. 305.

157 "Deluge after deluge drenched the valley …" Chambers (1959), p. 565, and Vandiver (1957), p. 269.

157 "I believe these men are hungrier than us …" See Hess (1979), p. 129. "In the Mole Hill community, they (soldiers in Frémont's army) reportedly took food from Mrs. Rhodes' children." Also, see Coffman (undated). "Soldiers would arrive at mealtime and sit down and eat while they (Coffman family members) patiently waited."

157 See Rauch and Thomson (1906), p. 11, for the story behind the caps worn by Pennsylvania's Bucktail Brigade.

157 "Could I interest you in some fresh-baked bread?" See Rodes and Wenger (2005), p. 708, testimony of Samuel Coffman: "I have been told by union soldiers that she (Peggy) baked bread for them."

158 See Hess (1979), p. 129. Sergeant Hunt is an imaginary character, but Kane's Bucktails were near the Rhodes farm in early June.

158 According to Rodes (2023), Henry's parents (Henry Rodes Sr. and Elizabeth "Mottie" Good) were born in Lancaster County, Pennsylvania, in the 1780s.

159 "By feeding me, you think you're heaping hot coals on my head …" The biblical reference is Romans 12:20: "Therefore if thine enemy hunger, feed him; if he thirst, give him drink: for in so doing thou shalt heap coals of fire on his head."

160 The description of the skirmish at Dale Enterprise comes from Hess (1979), p. 129, and Grove (2001), pp. 14–15.

160 See Hess (1979), pp. 129–130: "Little children at the Rhodes' home just a mile away, hid under beds, others crouched in front of the fireplace for protection from volleys." It seems logical that the Bucktails were the soldiers who warned the Rhodes family because the Bucktails were said to be positioned on the same side of the swollen Cooks Creek.

160 Hess (1979), p. 129, puts this skirmish on June 5, one day before Kane's Bucktails killed Turner Ashby. A better bet is June 6. Chambers (1959), p. 566, states that Frémont's advance guard (which included Kane's Bucktails) did not reach Harrisonburg until midday on June 6. Likewise, Rauch and Thompson (1906), pp. 152–153, say that Kane's Bucktails arrived in Harrisonburg at 2 p.m. on June 6. One possible scenario is that *some* of Kane's Bucktails were guarding Frémont's western flank on June 6 when they encountered Confederate stragglers who were trying to return to the main body of Jackson's army. See Casler (1971), pp. 81–82, for a first-hand account of small squads of Confederate stragglers in western Rockingham at that time.

160 "Loading wounded Confederate soldiers …" Hess (1979), p. 130.

161 "We're gonna try to make it to John Wenger's house." This quote is based on Hess (1979), p. 130.

161 "On June 11, Rodgers left …" See Rodes and Wenger (2005), p. 703. Peggy testified that Rodgers left with Frémont's army, which departed from Harrisonburg on June 11–12, according to Chambers (1959), p. 588.

161 H. L. occasionally referred fugitives to the Rhodes depot, according to his testimony before the Southern Claims Commission, but there is no evidence that he did so immediately after the Battle of Cross Keys.

162 "If you carry a gun …" See Rodes and Wenger (2012), p. 583, quoting from the cross-examination of John W. Gaither, regarding John W. West hiding in the mountains to avoid conscription. Question: "Did he have his gun with him?" Answer: "No sir. If he had been caught with that, he would have been taken for a bush whacker."

164 According to oral tradition in the Hartman family (often attributed to Peter S. Hartman), Mennonites in Rockingham "hid guns in the cave on the hill behind Weavers Church." For the general location and description of this long-lost cave, see the *Rockingham Register*, February 15, 1901.

CHAPTER 15: INVISIBLE BRUNK

165 "We're holding more than 2,000 prisoners ..." *Rockingham Register,* June 20, 1862, p. 1. The *Register* reported that between 2,500 and 3,000 prisoners of war were being held in the enclosure surrounding the courthouse and clerk's office. The newspaper's estimate seems somewhat exaggerated.

165 Regarding the behavior of Confederate foragers, see Rodes and Wenger (2005), p. 704, Peggy's testimony: "We were not personally threatened, but the rebels would come to our place and treat us very roughly, and carry off our property because we were union people."

166 "Peggy always declined, but ..." Ibid. Also, see Heatwole (1905), p. 212.

166 "The foragers increasingly took food ..." See Sanger and Hays (1907), p. 83.

166 The meeting to discuss hiding valuables is imaginary, but Coffman's hiding places are mentioned in Coffman (undated) and in Heatwole (1911), p. 444.

167 "This here wall needs ..." This quote is inspired by Erb (c1944), p. 18.

167 "Just remove the closet door ..." See Heatwole (1998), p. 21. The account of hiding wheat in walls comes from the Stoneleigh House file at the Harrisonburg-Rockingham Historical Society (Rocktown History). A similar story of converting a closet into a secret granary appears in Morgan (c1942), p. 3.

168 Amos Shiflett and the peter monkey story are imaginary, but men called "peter monkeys" did search for niter dirt under houses in Rockingham County during the Civil War. See Hartman (1937), p. 60. The term "peter monkey" comes from Whisonant (2001), p. 41.

168 See Whisonant (2001), pp. 36–41, for a good overview of saltpeter production in Virginia during the Civil War.

171 "Brunk had left John Albert's bedside ..." See Erb (c1944), p. 21. Erb does not reveal the cause of death, but diphtheria was the most common fatal illness among children in Rockingham County during the war, according to Kline's diary and records from the Virginia Bureau of Vital Statistics.

171 Wenger's height comes from Lehman and Nolt (2007), p. 240.

172 Some accounts say Brunk attended the funeral "in disguise," but no source suggests what type of disguise he may have employed. The Dunker ruse is merely a guess.

172 "The scouts searched ..." See Erb (c1944), p. 21.

172 "As the mourners sang the last hymn ..." Ibid.
173 "He flailed away at the wheat ..." See Rinker (1999), p. 87: "Before the advent of threshing machines, small grain, such as wheat, oats, etc., was cut and stored in the barn. Then during the winter, the grain was flailed out by hand on the barn floor."
173 References to Brunk's willow-whip baskets are in Erb (c1944), p. 19.
173 The idea of refugees working covertly on Mennonite farms comes from Rodes and Wenger (2005), p. 469. Abram Swartz testified that "Coakley and Carrier shucked [corn] for him (John G. Heatwole) at night."
174 Ayray's inability to recognize Brunk comes from Heatwole (1948), pp. 3–4.

CHAPTER 16: POSTMASTER PEGGY

175 "Now she was concealing and trusting men she did not know." Rodes and Wenger (2005), p. 703. Peggy's testimony.
175 Peggy's postmaster duties come from Rodes and Wenger (2005), p. 704.
176 "Peggy asked Mottie to watch the children ..." Ibid.
176 This May 1863 letter could not be found, so the author reconstructed it based on a subsequent letter that Sammy wrote to his mother that referred to the May letter. It is likely that Sammy entrusted the May 1863 letter to Elder Kline, who moderated the annual meeting and likely brought the letter back to the valley in June. See Funk (1900), pp. 465–466. The wording of Sammy's May letter is unknown, but in the subsequent letter, he repeated portions of the earlier letter. The remainder of the May letter's reconstructed content is based on key events documented in Sammy's journal from May 12, 1862, through May 24, 1863. The final paragraph mimics the closing of Sammy's subsequent letter.
178 "Great, glorious, and overwhelming victory ..." *Rockingham Register*, July 10 and 17, 1863, p. 2.
179 Regarding Manassas Heatwole's desertion after Gettysburg, see Horst (1967), p. 31, from the *Compiled Service Records of Confederate Soldiers*. Also, see Heatwole's obituary in the *Herald of Truth*, December 15, 1890: "He suffered himself to be driven from place to place ... and from battle to battle, the last of which was the battle of Gettysburg."
179 "If there is such a thing as hell on earth ..." This quote is borrowed from Manassas Heatwole's description of an earlier battle, possibly the Battle of Manassas. See Coffman (1964), p. 28.
179 It is likely that Heatwole deserted when Imboden's wagon train arrived in Harrisonburg. See Imboden (1964) p. 7.
179 "General Imboden assumed command ..." Duncan (1996), p. 108.

179 Imboden's notice first appeared on page three of the August 7 issue of the *Register*. Then the newspaper moved it to the front page on August 14.

180 Regarding Kline's arrests, Funk adds only that he was "taken before the military authorities." Funk (1900), p. 467.

180 Governor Letcher's proposed expansion of the conscription age range was reported in the *New York Times* on September 12, 1863, p. 1.

181 As noted previously, the assumption is that Henry May was John H. May, who was married to Joseph Beery's niece, Anna, according to Wenger (1905), p. 49. May's testimony in Rodes and Wenger (2004), p. 367, shows he had at least some knowledge of refugee movements. He was probably the man who assisted Sammy and H. L. near the headwaters of Dry River on March 15, 1862.

181 "I'm not as worried about Kline." This quote is inspired by the report of Kline's death in the *Rockingham Register*. The newspaper said that he "was passing frequently by permission of our authorities within the Yankee lines to preach and hold other religious services."

181 Beery's "reckless" actions come from his testimony in Rodes and Wenger (2003), pp. 370–371.

181 "ARRESTED—Joseph and Solomon Beery …" *Rockingham Register*, October 9, 1863, p. 2.

182 "The war department released the Beerys …" See Rodes and Wenger (2003), p. 370. Beery testified that he spent four weeks in Castle Thunder after he was arrested in October 1863. He was released on bail, and the war ended before he was tried.

182 "On December 7, President Jefferson Davis proposed removing all conscription exemptions …" Wright (1931) p. 111.

182 "By the end of the year, the Confederate Congress had abolished …" Lehman and Nolt (2007), p. 67.

183 The conscription age range of seventeen to fifty comes from Wright (1931), p. 112.

184 "We have been informed …" *Rockingham Register*, March 4, 1864, p. 2.

184 "We have been assured …" *Rockingham Register*, March 11, 1864, p. 2.

184 One boy company was activated on April 3, 1864, according to Heatwole (2000), p. 13.

185 Given Henry's rapidly failing health, it is quite possible that Johnny was detailed to work on the Rhodes farm, but there is no direct evidence to support this assumption. In his testimony before the Southern Claims Commission, Johnny only stated that he remained on the Rhodes farm until October 1864.

PEGGY'S WAR

CHAPTER 17: SWAMP DRAGONS

186 After Brunk left the Rhodes depot, he hid at the David Hartman depot and the Jacob Shank depot, according to Rodes and Wenger (2005), p. 732, testimony of David Hartman.

186 "R. J. finally agreed to head for the mountains …" Unless otherwise noted, the events of this chapter are based on R. J. Heatwole's first-hand accounts in Heatwole (1948), pp. 2–4, and Heatwole (1911), p. 445. Also, see Erb (c1944) for information about Brunk's guardianship of R. J. and Susanna.

186 David Frank is sometimes mentioned among the group of seventy-plus as "David Funk." See Horst (1967), p. 31, and his corresponding note 15 on page 118.

187 "Earlier in the war, desertion had been somewhat tolerated …" Horst (1967), pp. 21–22, says that some soldiers deserted three or four times. Casler (1971) makes similar assertions.

187 See Ayers (2003), p. 359, regarding the increasingly severe consequences of desertion.

187 According to Heatwole (1948), p. 4, the group carried "letters to friends in the north," but there is no direct evidence that the letters went through the Rhodes depot. This assumption, however, seems quite plausible given that 1) Peggy was a postmaster for the underground; 2) Brunk knew Peggy well; and 3) the Rhodes depot was on the way between Weavers Church and Rawley Springs.

188 The $20 amount comes from Zigler (1914), p. 103, but it is not obvious whether the refugees paid with Confederate currency or federal greenbacks.

190 It is clear from Heatwole (1948), p. 4, that the pilots turned back and Brunk took charge soon after the group entered West Virginia, but the haggling over payment is imaginary.

194 R. J. Heatwole does not say when the three black men joined the group, but his first mention of them comes soon after the rich widow expressed concern that her slaves might run away with Brunk's group. Ibid.

CHAPTER 18: VALLEY OF THE SHADOW

199 "His forage masters ravaged several Mennonite farms …" Some claimants sought compensation from the Southern Claims Commission for property taken by Hunter's army near Weavers Church in June 1864, but Peggy did not attribute any of her losses to Hunter's foragers.

199 Pond (1959), p. 28, details Hunter's destruction at Staunton, quoting Colonel Edwin Lee's June 17 dispatch to Adjutant General Samuel Cooper.

199 Description of Hunter's burning at Lexington comes from Duncan (1998), pp. 223–227.

199 No one was ever convicted of Kline's murder, but suspicion was cast on rogue members of the Linville, Virginia, home guard. According to Jerviss (2019), p. 3, the shots probably were fired by "an unspecified number (most likely two or three) of Confederate irregulars."

199 "His Secesh neighbors suspected he was a Union spy …" Wayland (1957), p. 401. More specifically, a rebel soldier claimed that Kline was murdered "for traveling west carrying news and helping people to get out of the S. Confederacy," according to an anonymous letter published in the *Gospel Visitor*, August 1, 1864, vol. 14, no. 8, p. 228.

199 The story that appeared on June 24 in the *Rockingham Register* could not be found, but the *Gospel Visitor* reprinted it on August 1.

200 "Hunter's diversion to Lexington …" See Duncan (1998), p. 228, and Pond (1959), p. 31.

200 Duncan (1998), pp. 137–302, provides a good summary of Hunter's costly campaign of 1864.

201 "The foregoing pages were written by your son …" Sammy's letter and Peter S. Rhodes' letter appear in Rodes and Wenger (2003), pp. 702–704.

203 Sammy died on April 26, 1864, in Hagerstown, Maryland, according to Lehman and Nolt (2007), p. 71.

204 Peggy's imaginary offer would have been generous. Six months later, wealthy families in Staunton were able to hire servants for the year "only for grain and at very high rates, men bringing 100 bush. of corn or wheat." Hotchkiss (1973), p. 251, diary entry for January 2, 1865.

205 Priscilla's "more violent" symptoms of tuberculous meningitis (TBM) are based on Peterson (1976), p. 447, quoting from James Copland's 1859 *Dictionary of Practical Medicine*. According to the Virginia Bureau of Vital Statistics, Priscilla died of "brain fever," which was probably the same disease that killed Davy. (See notes for chapter three.) The role of the "town doctor" is imaginary.

206 "The preacher prayed for the destruction of his enemies …" This quote is based on Brunk (1937), pp. 7–8.

206 The assumption of very poor attendance at Priscilla's funeral is based on Heatwole (1905), p. 212.

207 "On July 1, there was another urgent call …" See Shank (1864), pp. 82–83, and Steiner (1903), p. 17. Also, see Ashby (1914), p. 260, and Grove (2001), p. 20. These sources put the new upper age limit at sixty. Confederate conscription laws never exceeded age fifty, but it is possible that General Imboden took it upon himself to raise the upper limit to sixty because he was desperate.

PEGGY'S WAR

207 Peggy's brother, David Heatwole, was later named administrator of Henry's estate. See Rodes and Wenger (2005), pp. 704–705. The assumption is that he also helped Henry write his will.

207 "All his property would go to …" Henry's will made all of the provisions listed here, according to Peggy, but he never signed it. Ibid.

207 "Saved on Independence Day …" See Coffman (1964), p. 36, quoting the diary of John S. Coffman: "Thirty years ago this Fourth of July I was baptized in Muddy Creek. ... Those baptized at the same time were Peter Hartman, Abram Weaver, John Bell, and others."

207 On page 702 of Rodes and Wenger (2005), Peggy testified that Henry's date of death was July 8, 1864, but his tombstone in the Shank Cemetery says July 9, 1864.

CHAPTER 19: SHERIDAN

209 "This will only make things worse." This quote is inspired by Gallagher (2006), p. xii.

209 Regarding growing opposition to the war in the North, see Stackpole (1992), pp. 81–83.

209 "Grant put General Philip Sheridan in charge …" Gallagher (2006), p. xiii.

209 "Nothing should be left to invite the enemy …" Stackpole (1992), p. 141, quoting Grant's orders to Sheridan.

209 The dangers of pride and "amusements indulged in by the young" are noted in Heatwole, Brunk, and Good (1910), p. 20.

210 "Nearly 250 Mennonites …" Landis (1864), p. 81, and Hildebrand (1996), p. 51.

210 The agricultural bounty of the valley in August 1864 is based on Heatwole (1998), p. 2.

210 "The faces of the soldiers …" Heatwole (1998), p. 21.

210 "Sheridan's vanguard swept into town …" Ibid.

210 "Dogs barked all night …" Hartman (1937), p. 64.

211 "They saw Union troops streaming toward them …" Ibid.

211 "One of Sheridan's quartermasters …" Wildes (1884), p. 189.

211 "Another company of soldiers commandeered the church …" Brunk (1959), p. 162, and Heatwole (1998), p. 110.

211 Descriptions of property taken from the Rhodes farm come from the testimony of Peggy, Johnny, Mary, and their close neighbor, Abraham Swartz. See Rodes and Wenger (2005), pp. 697–712.

211 "The soldiers impressed the plow horse …" Rodes and Wenger (2005), p. 710, Mary's testimony.

211 "The officer gave Peggy receipts ..." See Rodes and Wenger (2005), p. 705, Peggy's testimony.

212 "Peggy begged to keep it ..." See Rodes and Wenger (2005), p. 709, Johnny's testimony. Also, see Rodes and Wenger (2005), p. 788, testimony of John B. Wenger.

212 Abraham Swartz testified that these soldiers claimed to be from West Virginia, but other sources say that infantrymen foraging in the area were from the 116th Regiment of Ohio Infantry, which was attached to Custer's cavalry and camped just north of Dayton.

212 "Please let me keep the milk cows!" This quote is based on Rodes and Wenger (2005), p. 706, Peggy's testimony.

213 "Sheridan's men had been setting ..." See Lehman and Nolt (2007), p. 203, and Heatwole (1998), pp. 32–54.

213 "General George Custer, moved ..." Heatwole (1998), p. 56.

213 "Another squad of cavalry came to the house ..." Rodes and Wenger (2005), pp. 710–711, Mary's testimony.

213 Regarding the taking of saddles and bridles, see Rodes and Wenger (2005), p. 709, Johnny's testimony.

213 "Peggy and Mary watched helplessly ..." Rodes and Wenger (2005), pp. 706 and 711, testimony of Peggy and Mary, respectively.

213 "One of the officers came to the house ..." Rodes and Wenger (2005), p. 706, Peggy's testimony.

213 "The general plans to take refugees north ..." This quote is based on Wayland (1930), p. 194, and Hartman (1937), p. 65.

214 "At first light on October 5, he left the Rhodes farm ..." Rodes and Wenger (2005), p. 709, Johnny's testimony.

215 Brunk (1959), p. 165, names C. H. "Chris" Brunk as one of the six teenage boys who traveled together on Sheridan's wagon train. He also names Samuel Brunk, which seems unlikely given his father's testimony in Rodes and Wenger (2005), pp. 813–814.

215 "Last night the cavalry stole our entire rig ..." Ibid.

215 One of the other two boys was likely Peggy's nephew, Abraham D. Weaver. As previously noted, he was baptized on the same day as Johnny, Peter Hartman, and John Coffman. Also, see Hartman (1865): "I will let you know that J Bell A Weaver and I was were just redy to start in a half an hour [from Maryland to Ohio] when the man come that I hired too."

215 Meigs was "greatly loved by Sheridan." Wildes (1884), p. 190.

215 See Sheridan (1888), vol. 2, p. 52: "I ordered all the houses within an area of five miles to be burned." Some historians have stated that Sheridan issued this order on the morning of October 4, but Wildes (1884), p. 190, puts the

PEGGY'S WAR

time at 2 a.m. on October 5. This day-later timing matches Samuel H. Brunk's first-hand account in Rodes and Wenger (2005), p. 950.

216 See Hartman (1937), p. 66. The boys' encounter with Sheridan probably occurred near the home of Abraham Byrd, who had been the Confederate provost marshal. His limestone house on East Market Street was later called "Stoneleigh." See Wayland (1930), pp. 197–198.

216 "Who do you have there?" This quote comes from Hartman (1937), p. 66.

216 Description of Sheridan comes from Hartman (1937), p. 66, and the Mathew Brady photograph used to produce the engraving that appeared on the cover of *Harper's Weekly* on October 8, 1864. Also, see Gallagher (2006), p. 4.

216 "The general asked them several questions ..." See Hartman (1937), p. 66. The actual questions Sheridan asked and the answers the boys gave will probably never be known.

217 "Those who rest at home ..." This quote is paraphrased from Sheridan (1888), vol. 1, p. 488. There is no evidence that Sheridan tried to justify his actions during his conversation with the boys, but their exchange likely did take place on the morning of October 5, just a few hours after the general gave the order to burn everything within five miles of where Meigs died.

218 "Take them down and put chains on them ..." The exchange between Sheridan and the sentinel comes from Hartman (1937), p. 66.

218 "I am determined to teach a lesson to the abettors of this foul deed." This quote is paraphrased from Sheridan (1888), vol. 2, p. 52.

218 "Since I came into this valley ..." This quote is paraphrased from Kellogg (1903), p. 213, quoting Sheridan's letter to Grant dated October 7, 1864.

218 The exchange regarding horses is based on Hartman (1937), p. 66.

219 "Four of the boys found their families' horses ..." See Hartman (1937), p. 68.

219 "Colonel Wildes has delayed your order ..." This anecdote comes from Wildes (1884), pp. 189–191.

CHAPTER 20: THE BURNING

220 "They frantically searched houses from attic to cellar ..." This description of looting and burning comes from Shank (1864), pp. 82–83.

221 The Reuben Swope house, about 800 yards to the south, was clearly visible from the Rhodes place. For an account of its destruction, see Swope Family History Committee (1971), pp. 15–16.

221 "We've come to burn your buildings." This quote is based on Rodes and Wenger (2005), p. 705, Peggy's testimony.

222 "I took the side of the Union ..." This quote is paraphrased from Rodes and Wenger (2005), p. 703, Peggy's testimony.

222 "We have orders to burn everything …" This quote is based on Sheridan (1888), vol. 2, p. 52.

222 Regarding Sheridan's order against burning the homes of widows, see Heatwole (1998), pp. 100 and 130.

223 Henry's tombstone was stolen at some point, and it is plausible that some of Sheridan's soldiers used it as a tabletop. This practice was not uncommon during Sheridan's occupation of the valley. See "Buried Tombstone Uncovered," Harrisonburg *Daily News-Record*, September 3, 1982. Albert L. Zigler unearthed Henry's tombstone "while rebuilding the front porch of his mobile home off Va. 619 in the Fridleys Gap area," which is several miles northeast of Harrisonburg, not far from the route of Sheridan's wagon train.

224 "We will not burn your house, Mrs. Rhodes …" This quote is based on Rodes and Wenger (2005), p. 705, Peggy's testimony.

224 "The sergeant blew a whistle …" According to Heatwole (1998), p. 37, the leader of each burning party used a whistle to signal when it was time to go to the next farm. Morgan (c1942), p. 4, also mentions an officer blowing a whistle for this purpose.

224 "They burned Bishop Coffman's barn …" Coffman (1964), p. 55.

224 The Union cavalry did burn Betsy Weaver's home and outbuildings, according to Heatwole (1998), pp. 110–111, but the burning of her house may have been unintentional.

224 "They burned Daniel Bowman's mill …" Rodes and Wenger (2005), p. 351, affidavit of Annie Kerlin.

224 "Then they torched nearly all the barns …" See Grove (2001), p. 15, quoting L. J. Heatwole's first-hand account written in 1884. Also, see Brunk (2005), p. 950.

225 "Most of them spent the night out in the open with fires raging …" Grove (2001), p. 15, quoting L. J. Heatwole's 1884 account.

CHAPTER 21: THE WAGON TRAIN

226 "John Coffman quickly stepped in to take Peter's place." This anecdote comes from Hartman (1937), p. 67.

227 "The infantrymen went first …" Heatwole (1998), p. 130.

227 "Sheridan's cavalry divisions dragged one last harrow of destruction …" Heatwole (1998), p. 131.

227 "Hundreds of refugees lined the wayside …" Heatwole (1998), p. 211, quoting from Tomes (1948), pp. 492–493.

228 "The mountains to the east seemed close enough to touch …" Heatwole (1998), p. 202.

228 The story of six thirsty boys and two dead mules comes from Hartman (1937), p. 67.
229 "McNeill's Rangers had burned the bridge ..." See Landis (1864), p. 82. The assumption is that McNeill's Rangers, who were active in the valley at the time, were the most likely suspects.
229 "Do you remember Chambersburg?" This quote and the distressed-mother story come from Heatwole (1998), pp. 199–200.
229 "They brought a man to the pike ..." Hartman (1937), pp. 67–68.
229 "There are 10,000 head of cattle and sheep right behind us ..." This quote is inspired by Heatwole (2005), p. 34.
230 "The boys saw one such woman chasing soldiers ..." This anecdote comes from Suter (1959), pp. 42–43. It is plausible that the boys witnessed this event because they were traveling with or near the Suter family.
230 "Sheridan's men attempted to douse ..." Kidd (1969), p. 400.
230 The location of the boys' overnight stops between Harrisonburg and Martinsburg comes from Suter (1864), diary entries for October 6–10, 1864.
230 The dramatic account of Muhlenberg's revolutionary call to arms is based on Muhlenberg (1848), p. 53.
231 This version of "I Would Not Live Always" comes from the *Mennonite Hymnal* of 1875. There is no record of what hymns the refugees sang, but "I Would Not Live Always," was popular among valley singers at the time of the Civil War. According to Kieffer (1890), p. 72, the lyrics were written by John Peter Muhlenberg himself, but other sources attribute them to Muhlenberg's grandnephew, William Augustus Muhlenberg.
231 "Sheridan's adjutant had advised them ..." See Hartman (1937), p. 68. Also, see Suter (1864), diary entry for October 7, 1864.
232 "Most of the infantrymen stayed behind on the south side ..." See Sheridan (1888), vol. 2, p. 59.
232 "Union forces already had ruined ..." See Pond (1959), p. 136. Earlier in the campaign, as Sheridan retreated from Cedar Creek to Winchester, he ordered General Alfred Torbert to burn the barns and crops as they withdrew.
232 "Cannon blasts reverberated through the valley ..." See Sheridan (1888), vol. 2, pp. 57–58. This was the Battle of Tom's Brook.

CHAPTER 22: SURVIVAL

234 "The early morning light of October 7 revealed ..." Grove (2001), p. 15, quoting L. J. Heatwole's 1884 account.
234 "Three Mennonite men emerged ..." This anecdote is based on Heatwole (1998), p. 107.

234 "Peggy's neighbors started sifting ..." Heatwole (1998), p. 224.
235 "Apples were plentiful." Grove (2001), p. 9.
235 "Mary hurried to harvest these root vegetables ..." Ibid.
236 "Peggy's children went barefoot ..." Ashby (1914), p. 299.
236 "Another wave of deserters ..." See Hotchkiss (1973), p. 247, diary entry for December 9, 1864. Also, see Beringer et al. (1986), pp. 434–435.
237 The story of Rosser's surprise attack comes from Wayland (1957), pp. 393–394, and from Hotchkiss (1973), pp. 248–249.
237 "Rosser's depleted cavalry tried to make a stand ..." Pond (1959), p. 252, and Wayland (1957), p. 395.
237 "Rebels fleeing across Afton Mountain ..." See Hotchkiss (1973), pp. 259–260, diary entries for March 2–3, 1865.
237 "The Confederate army was offering pardons ..." *Rockingham Register*, March 24, 1865, p. 1.
237 "General Robert E. Lee had evacuated Richmond ..." *Rockingham Register*, April 7, 1865, p. 2.
238 "It was unavoidable, as our Army were out of provisions and ammunition." *Rockingham Register*, April 14, 1865, p. 2.
238 "People in the valley seemed ready to accept ..." Hotchkiss (1973), p. 267, diary entries for April 17–18, 1865.
238 "President Lincoln was assassinated ..." *Rockingham Register*, April 28, 1865, p. 2.
239 "They say he was our best friend ..." Ibid. Also, see Casler (1971), p. 284: "We were sorry, too, because we knew they would think that the South had something to do with it, and then we knew that it would have been better for the South if he had lived."
239 "Peggy immediately carried the letter to the bishop ..." See Rodes and Wenger (2005), p. 707. Bishop Coffman testified that he received letters from his son, John Coffman, via Peggy.
239 "Johnny Bell and Abram Weaver stayed in Maryland ..." See Rodes and Wenger (2005), p. 709, Johnny's testimony. Also, see Hartman (1865).
240 The letter from John Coffman is imaginary, but the content is based on his experiences in the North as documented in Hartman (1937), pp. 69–72, and in Coffman (1964), pp. 53–57.
241 "People around Mole Hill called them the singing carpenters ..." See Steiner (1903), pp. 19–20, and Coffman (1964), pp. 61–62.
241 "Other nearby farms produced large crops of oats and rye ..." Ashby (1914), p. 299.

EPILOGUE

242 "Henry Brunk reunited with his wife ..." Erb (c1944), pp. 25–29.

242 "Susanna "Suzy" Rhodes died of cancer in 1873 ..." See her obituary in the *Herald of Truth*, May 1873, vol. 10, no. 5, p. 87.

242 "The *Register* reported his death as a suicide ..." Bittinger (2009), p. 29.

242 Doc Heatwole's cause of death comes from the Virginia Bureau of Vital Statistics, R26-1875-3-20.

242 "Elizabeth 'Mottie' Rhodes, Henry's mother ..." Brunk (1959), pp. 303–304.

References

Adams, I. H. "1864 Map of the City of Richmond Virginia." Available from the Library of Congress.

Ashby, Thomas A. *The Valley Campaigns; Being the Reminiscences of a Non-Combatant While between the Lines in the Shenandoah Valley during the War of the States*. New York: Neale Publishing Company, 1914.

"Atlas of Rockingham County, Virginia." Published in Philadelphia by D. J. Lake & Company, 1885. Reprinted by the Harrisonburg-Rockingham Historical Society (Rocktown History) in 1982.

Avirett, James B. *The Memoirs of Turner Ashby and His Compeers*. Baltimore: Selby and Dulany, 1867.

Ayers, Edward L. *In the Presence of Mine Enemies: War in the Heart of America, 1859–1863*. New York: W. W. Norton, 2003.

Beringer, Richard E. et al. *Why the South Lost the Civil War*. Athens, Ga.: University of Georgia Press, 1986.

Bittinger, Emmert F. "Dissenters from the 'Southern Cause': Unionists in the Shenandoah Valley" in *Home Front to Front Line: The Civil War Era in the Shenandoah Valley*. Edited by Jonathan A. Noyalas and Nancy T. Sorrells. New Market, Va.: Shenandoah Valley Battlefields Foundation, 2009.

Blosser, Abraham. Obituary of Joseph Heatwole. *Watchful Pilgrim*, vol. 6, no. 4, September 15, 1886.

Blosser, Abraham. "The Trials and Afflictions of the Virginia Mennonites During the Late Civil War." *History of the Mennonites in America*. Edited by Daniel K. Cassel. Philadelphia, 1888, pp. 134–142.

Brunk, Harry A. *Life of Peter S. Hartman*. Harrisonburg, Va., 1937.

Brunk, Harry A. "Meetinghouses of the Weaver's Church." *Mennonite Historical Bulletin*, vol. 4, no. 2, pp. 1–3, June 1943.

Brunk, Harry A. *History of Mennonites in Virginia 1727–1900*, vol. 1. Staunton, Va.: McClure Printing Company, 1959.

Brunk, Harry A. *David Heatwole and His Descendants*. Harrisonburg, Va.: David Heatwole and His Descendants Publication Committee, 1987.

Brunk, Samuel. "A Short Story of the Life of Samuel Brunk." Published in *Rodes and Wenger* (2005), pp. 939–953.

Burkholder, Peter. "Reflections from Different Passages of the Holy Scriptures" in Joseph Funk's German-to-English translation of the *Confession of Faith of the Christians Known by the Name of Mennonites*. Winchester, Va.: 1837, pp. 265–405.

Casler, John O. *Four Years in the Stonewall Brigade*. Fourth edition reprinted in Dayton, Ohio: Morningside Bookshop, 1971.

Cassel, Daniel K. *History of the Mennonites in America*. Philadelphia, 1888.

Chambers, Lenoir. *Stonewall Jackson*, vol. 1. New York: William Morrow & Company, 1959.

Coffman, Barbara F. *His Name Was John: The Life Story of an Early Mennonite Leader*. Scottdale, Pa.: Herald Press, 1964.

Coffman, John S. Diary entries from 1871.

Coffman, Nellie. Biographical sketch of Samuel Coffman, Eastern Mennonite University Archives, undated.

Colby, Lydia. "From the Shenandoah Valley in Virginia to Henry County, Illinois." *Journal of the Illinois State Historical Society*, vol. 22, no. 4, pp. 584–591, January 1928.

Coulter, E. Merton. "The Confederate States of America, 1861–1865" in volume seven of *A History of the South*. Edited by Coulter and Wendell Holmes Stephenson. Baton Rouge, La.: Louisiana State University Press, 1950.

Duncan, Richard R. *Alexander Neil and the Last Shenandoah Valley Campaign*. Edited and annotated by Duncan. Shippensburg, Pa.: White Mane Publishing Company, 1996.

Duncan, Richard R. *Lee's Endangered Left: The Civil War in Western Virginia, Spring of 1864*. Baton Rouge, La.: Louisiana State University Press, 1998.

Erb, Ethel Estella (Cooprider). *Through Trial to Crown of Life: Story of Grandmother Heatwole Brunk Cooprider*. Hesston, Kan.: The Book and Bible Room, c1944.

Funk, Benjamin. *Life and Labors of Elder John Kline, the Martyr Missionary*. Excerpts from Kline's diary selected and edited by Funk. Elgin, Ill.: Brethren Publishing House, 1900.

Gallagher, Gary W. *The Shenandoah Valley Campaign of 1864*. Edited, introduced, and partly written by Gallagher. Chapel Hill, N.C.: University of North Carolina Press, 2006.

Grove, Grace. "L. J. Heatwole: A Granddaughter's View." Manuscript, 2001, Eastern Mennonite University Archives.

Harbaugh, Henry, and D. Y. Heilser. *The Fathers of the Reformed Church in Europe and America*, vol. 6. Reading, Pa.: Daniel Miller, 1888.

Hartman, Peter S. Letter to his sister, Sarah Wenger, March 18, 1865. Wenger Family Papers, Virginia Sesquicentennial of the American Civil War and the Albemarle and Charlottesville Local Sesquicentennial Committees.

Hartman, Peter S. "Reminiscences of the Civil War" in *Life of Peter S. Hartman* by Harry A. Brunk, Harrisonburg, Va.: Hartman Family, 1937.

Heatwole, David A. *A History of the Heatwole Family*. Dale Enterprise, Va., 1882.

Heatwole, John L. *Shenandoah Voices*. Berryville, Va.: Rockbridge Publishing, 1995.

Heatwole, John L. *The Burning: Sheridan's Devastation of the Shenandoah Valley*. Berryville, Va.: Rockbridge Publishing, 1998.

Heatwole, John L. *Chrisman's Boy Company*. Bridgewater, Va.: Mountain and Valley Publishing, 2000.

Heatwole, John L. "The Burning: The Valley Burned for 13 Days" in *1864: The Valley Aflame*. Staunton, Va.: Lot's Wife Publishing, 2005.

Heatwole, L. J. "Trials of the Virginia Mennonites During the Civil War" in *Mennonite Church History*. Edited by Jonas Smucker Hartzler and Daniel Kauffman. Scottdale, Pa.: Mennonite Book and Tract Society, 1905.

Heatwole, L. J. Letter to Jonas Smucker Hartzler, December 11, 1918. Published in the *Mennonite Historical Bulletin*, June 1972.

Heatwole, L. J., C. H. Brunk, and Christian Good. *A History of the Mennonite Conference of Virginia and Its Work*. Scottdale, Pa.: Mennonite Publishing House, 1910.

Heatwole, R. J. "Reminiscences of War Days." *Gospel Herald*, vol. 4, no. 28, October 12, 1911.

Heatwole, R. J. "A Civil War Story." Written in 1919 and published in the *Mennonite Historical Bulletin*, vol. 9, no. 1, pp. 3–4, January 1948.

Hess, Nancy Burkholder. *The Heartland: Rockingham County*. Harrisonburg, Va.: Rockingham County Extension Homemakers, 1976.

Hess, Nancy Burkholder. *By the Grace of God*. Harrisonburg, Va.: Hess Book Company, 1979.

Hildebrand, Jacob R. *A Mennonite Journal, 1862–1865: A Father's Account of the Civil War in the Shenandoah Valley*. Edited by John R. Hildebrand. Shippensburg, Pa.: White Mane Publishing, 1996.

Horst, Samuel. *Mennonites in the Confederacy: A Study in Civil War Pacifism*. Scottdale, Pa.: Herald Press, 1967.

Horst, Samuel. "The Journal of a Refugee." Journal of Samuel Rhodes transcribed and annotated by Horst. *Mennonite Quarterly Review*, vol. 54, pp. 280–304, October 1980.

Hotchkiss, Jedediah. "Map of Rockingham County." Created by Hotchkiss in 1866 and published by the United States Army in 1875.

Hotchkiss, Jedediah. *Make Me a Map of the Valley: The Civil War Journal of Stonewall Jackson's Topographer*. Edited by Archie P. McDonald. Dallas: Southern Methodist University Press, 1973.

Imboden, John D. "Civil War Unvarnished: General J. D. Imboden's Report after the Battle of Gettysburg." *Mennonite Research Journal*, vol. 1, no. 5, pp. 7–8, January 1964.

Jerviss, Aaron D. "'Living and Moving Amongst Us Again': John Kline and Civil War Martyrdom." *Brethren Life and Thought*, vol. 64, no. 1, pp. 1–14, spring/summer 2019.

Kellogg, Sanford C. *The Shenandoah Valley and Virginia, 1861–1865: A War Study*. New York: Neale Publishing Company, 1903.

Kidd, J. H. *Personal Recollections of a Cavalryman with Custer's Michigan Brigade in the Civil War*. Grand Rapids, Mich.: Black Letter Press, 1969.

Kieffer, Aldine S. "Reminiscences: Chapter XVII." *The Musical Million*, vol. 21, no. 5, pp. 72–73, May 1890.

Landis, D. H. Account of Sheridan's refugee wagon train, published in the *Herald of Truth*, vol. 1, no. 12, pp. 81–82, December 1864.

Langhorne, Orra. "A Story of War Time." *New England Magazine*, vol. 5, no. 26, December 1886.

Lehman, James O., and Steven M. Nolt. *Mennonites, Amish, and the American Civil War*. Baltimore: Johns Hopkins University Press, 2007.

Morgan, Edith Wenger. "Stories My Father Told Us." Unpublished manuscript (c1942). Eastern Mennonite University Archives.

Muhlenberg, Henry A. *The Life of Major-General Peter Muhlenberg of the Revolutionary Army*. Philadelphia: Carey and Hart, 1848.

Neely, Mark E. *Southern Rights: Political Prisoners and the Myth of Confederate Constitutionalism*. Charlottesville, Va.: University of Virginia Press, 1999.

Peterson, Audrey C. "Brain Fever in Nineteenth-Century Literature: Fact and Fiction." *Victorian Studies*, vol. 19, no. 4, pp. 445–464, June 1976.

Pond, George E. *The Shenandoah Valley in 1864*. New York: Jack Brussel, 1959. Originally published by Scribner in 1883.

Public Laws of the Confederate States of America, Passed at the First Session of the First Congress; 1862. Edited by James M. Matthews, April 16, 1862.

Rauch, William H., and O. R. Howard Thomson. *History of the Bucktails*. Philadelphia, 1906.

Rhodes, Edith Layman. *Dale Enterprise School*. Johnson City, Tenn.: Pacer Publishing, 2018.

Rhodes, Samuel A. *The Rebellion: The Cause of My Traveling Adventures to the North*, a personal journal most likely written in early 1864.

Rinker, Henry Saint John. *The Diary of Henry Saint John Rinker*. Edited by Daniel Warrick Burruss II and Sandra Helsley Yelton, Edinburg, Va.: Shenandoah County Library, 1999.

Rodes, Brent L. "Descendants of Anthony Roth." Ancestry.com, accessed on January 16, 2023.

Rodes, David S., and Norman R. Wenger. *Unionists and the Civil War Experience in the Shenandoah Valley,* volumes 1-6. Harrisonburg, Va.: Valley Research Associates and Brethren & Mennonite Heritage Center, 2003–2012.

Sanger, S. F., and D. Hays. *The Olive Branch of Peace and Good Will to Men*. Elgin, Ill.: Brethren Publishing House, 1907.

Schoeman, Johan F. "Tuberculous Meningitis" in *Tuberculosis: A Comprehensive Clinical Reference*. Edited by H. Simon Schaaf et al. Saunders Elsevier, 2009.

Shank, Michael. Account of Sheridan's raid and fleeing the valley. Published in the *Herald of Truth*, vol. 1, no. 12, pp. 82–83, December 1864.

Sheridan, Philip H. *Personal Memoirs of P. H. Sheridan*. New York: Charles L. Webster & Company, 1888.

Showalter, Grace I. "The Virginia Mennonite Rhodes Families." *Pennsylvania Mennonite Heritage*, April 2000.

Stackpole, Edward J. *Sheridan in the Shenandoah*, second edition. Harrisburg, Pa.: Stackpole Books, 1992.

Steiner, Menno S. *John S. Coffman: Mennonite Evangelist*. Spring Grove, Pa.: Mennonite Book and Tract Society, 1903.

Suter, Emanuel. Diary entries from October 1864. Eastern Mennonite University Archives.

Suter, Mary Eugenia. *Memories of Yesteryear: A History of the Suter Family*. Waynesboro, Va., 1959.

Suter, Mary Eugenia, and Grace Grove. *Keepers of the Spring: A History of Little North Mountain Sparkling Springs*. Harrisonburg, Va., 1986.

Swope Family History Committee. *History of the Swope Family and Descendants of Rockingham County, Virginia*. Verona, Va., 1971.

Taylor, John Craft. "Civil War in and About Pendleton County, (West) Virginia." Master's thesis in history. Pennsylvania State University, 1975.

Thomson, Samuel. *New Guide to Health; or Botanic Family Physician*. Boston: J. Q. Adams, 1835.

Tomes, Robert. *The Great Civil War: A History of the Late Rebellion*, vol. 3, New York: Virtue and Yorston, 1948.

Vandiver, Frank E. *Mighty Stonewall*. New York: McGraw-Hill, 1957.

Waddell, Joseph A. *Annals of Augusta County, Virginia 1726–1871*. Richmond, Va.: J. W. Randolph & English, 1888.

Wayland, John W. *History of Rockingham County*. Dayton, Va.: Ruebush-Elkins Company, 1912.

Wayland, John W. *Virginia Valley Records*. Strasburg, Va.: Shenandoah Publishing House, 1930.

Wayland, John W. *Men of Mark and Representative Citizens of Harrisonburg and Rockingham County, Virginia*. Compiled and edited by Wayland in 1943.

Wayland, John W. *Historic Harrisonburg*. Harrisonburg, Va.: C. J. Carrier and Company, 1949.

Wayland, John W. *Twenty-Five Chapters on the Shenandoah Valley*. Strasburg, Va.: Shenandoah Publishing House, 1957.

Weaver, H. D. "Weavers Mennonite Church, Near Harrisonburg, Virginia" *Christian Monitor*, October 1932.

Wenger, Joseph H. *History of the Descendants of Abraham Beery*. South English, Iowa, 1905.

Wenger, Joseph H. *Geil History*. Elgin, Ill., 1914.

Whisonant, Robert C. "Geology and History of Confederate Saltpeter Cave Operations in Western Virginia." *Virginia Minerals*, vol. 47, no. 4, November 2001.

Whytt, Robert. *Observations on the Dropsy in the Brain*, 1768.

Wildes, Thomas F. *Record of the 116th Regiment Ohio Infantry Volunteers in the War of the Rebellion*. Sandusky, Ohio, 1884.

Wright, Edward Needles. *Conscientious Objectors in the Civil War*. Philadelphia: University of Pennsylvania Press, 1931.

Yoder, Elwood E. *How Firm a Foundation: A History of Weavers Mennonite Church 1827-2015*. Harrisonburg, Va.: Weavers Mennonite Church, 2015.

Zigler, D. H. *History of the Brethren in Virginia*. Elgin, Ill.: Brethren Publishing House, 1914.

"Blessed are the peacemakers:
for they shall be called the children of God."
— *Matthew 5:9*